DEADLY ASSETS

DEADLY ASSETS

A BADGE OF HONOR NOVEL

BOOK XII

W.E.B. GRIFFIN

AND WILLIAM E. BUTTERWORTH IV

G. P. PUTNAM'S SONS
NEW YORK

PUTNAM

G. P. PUTNAM'S SONS
Publishers Since 1838
An imprint of Penguin Random House LLC
375 Hudson Street
New York, New York 10014

Copyright © 2015 by William E. Butterworth IV

Library of Congress Cataloging-in-Publication Data

Griffin, W.E.B.
Deadly assets / W.E.B. Griffin, William E. Butterworth IV.
p.   cm.—(Badge of honor ; Book 12)
ISBN 978-0-399-17117-8
1. Payne, Matt (Fictitious character)—Fiction.   2. Police—Pennsylvania—Philadelphia—Fiction.
3. Murder—Investigation—Fiction.   I. Butterworth, William E. (William Edmund), author.   II. Title.
PS3557.R489137D42   2015   2015019808
813'.54—dc23

Printed in the United States of America
1   3   5   7   9   10   8   6   4   2

I

Matt Payne impatiently squeezed past the small groups of passengers that had just gotten off the subway train cars of the Broad Street Line, and moved with purpose down the tiled concourse toward the exit.

The muscular twenty-seven-year-old was six feet tall and a solid one-seventy-five. His chiseled face had a two-day scrub of beard. Behind black sunglasses, dark circles hung under sleep-deprived eyes.

He wore a Philadelphia Eagles ball cap and a gray hooded sweatshirt with the red TEMPLE UNIVERSITY logotype. Concealed inside the waistband of his blue jeans, at the small of his back, was an Officer's Model Colt .45 ACP semiautomatic pistol. And in his back pocket, in a black leather bifold holder, were his badge and the Philadelphia Police Department–issued card identifying him as a sergeant of the Homicide Unit.

Taking the subway, which Payne had boarded at the City Hall station after paying the $2.25 fare, hadn't been his first—or his second—choice. But considering his options at the time, it had seemed the fastest.

And with leads in the killings all but dried up, he had no time to waste.

After exiting the concourse, he took the steps, two at a time, up to street level, then started across the deep gray slush of snow and melted ice that covered the sidewalk.

At the newsstand shack on the southeast corner of Erie and Broad, he quickly tugged a newspaper from a stack topped with a chunk of red brick, stuffing it beneath his left arm, then peeling from his money clip a pair of dollar bills. He handed the cash to the attendant—a heavily clothed elderly black man with leathery hands and a deeply wrinkled face and thin beard—and gestured for him to keep the change.

Payne turned and glanced around the busy intersection.

The storefronts were a blend of bars and fast-food chain restaurants, banks and pharmacies, barbershops and convenience stores. Payne thought that the facades of the aged buildings, as well as the streets and sidewalks, looked much like he felt—tired, worn out.

On Erie, halfway down the block, Payne saw the coffee shop he was looking for—tall stenciled lettering in black and red on its front window read THE DAILY GRIND—then grunted.

On the second floor, above the diner, was a small, locally owned bookstore that had signage advertising WE SHIP TO PRISONS. Directly across the street, a new billboard on a rooftop had in bold lettering REPORT CRIME TIPS! LEX TALIONIS PAYS CASH REWARDS UP TO $20,000—800-LEX-TALN, and, in a strip along the billboard's bottom, the wording MAKE A DIFFERENCE—BECOME A PHILADEL-PHIA POLICE OFFICER next to a photograph of the smiling faces of attractive young women and men attending the police academy.

Payne walked quickly to The Daily Grind.

As he pulled on the stainless steel handle of the diner's glass door, then started to step inside, he almost collided with a grim-faced heavyset Latina in her twenties carrying three waxed paper to-go coffee cups. He made a thin smile, stepped back, made a grand sweep with his free arm for her to pass through the doorway first, then went inside.

It was a small space, permeated by the smell of fried grease and coffee. The only seating was at a stainless steel countertop at the back that overlooked the open kitchen. Elsewhere, customers could stand at the nine round high-top tables and at the worn wooden counter that ran at chest height along the side walls and the front windows.

There were just two customers now, both older men who were seated at opposite ends of the back counter and busy with their meals. An enormous coal-black man in his forties, wearing a grease-stained white apron tied over jeans and a sweaty white T-shirt, stood stooped at the gas-fired grill, his large biceps bulging as he methodically worked a long-handled wire brush back and forth. Flames flared up with each pass.

The cook stopped, looked over his shoulder, saw Payne, called out, "Hey, man, he'll be right with you," then turned back to scrubbing the grill.

At the far right end of the counter, under a sign reading ORDER HERE/PAY HERE that hung from the ceiling tiles by dust-coated chains, was the cash register. And just beyond it was a faded emerald green wooden door with TOILET FOR PAYING CUST ONLY!! that appeared to have been handwritten in haste with a fat-tipped black ink permanent marker.

The bathroom door began to swing open, and a brown-skinned male in his late teens stepped out, drying his hands on a paper towel.

Daquan Williams was five-foot-eight, extremely thin, and, under a ball cap with THE DAILY GRIND in stenciled letters across its front, his shoulder-length wavy reddish-brown hair was tied back with a rubber band. He wore black jeans and a tan T-shirt that was emblazoned with a coarse drawing of the Liberty Bell, its crack exaggerated, and the wording PHILLY—NOBODY LIKES US & WE DON'T CARE.

The teenager made eye contact with Payne, nodded just perceptibly, then looked away as he went to the rack of coffeepots. He pulled a heavy china mug from a pyramid-shaped stack, filled it with coffee, then carried it to Payne, who now stood by a window in the front corner of the shop, opposite the door, watching the sidewalk traffic over the top edge of the newspaper as he casually flipped its pages.

The teenager placed the steaming mug on the wooden counter beside a wire rack containing packets of cream and sugar.

"Thanks, Daquan," Payne said, then yawned widely as he reached for the coffee. "I really need this."

He held out a five-dollar bill.

Daquan didn't take it. He nodded toward the enormous cook cleaning the grill.

"Boss man say you don't pay," he said, keeping his voice low so as not to be overheard.

"I appreciate that, but I like to pay my way."

Payne put the money on the counter, then sipped the coffee.

Daquan nodded. He took the bill.

Payne glanced at Daquan's left ear. What looked like a new diamond stud sparkled in the lobe. Payne considered mentioning it, but instead gently rattled the newspaper cover page.

"So," Payne said quietly, "what do you know on this hit?"

Daquan's eyes shifted to the front page of the newspaper, and his facial expression changed to one of frustration.

The photograph showed, behind yellow tape imprinted with POLICE LINE DO NOT CROSS, two members of the medical examiner's office standing at the rear of a white panel van. They were in the process of lifting through the van's back doors a gurney holding a full body bag. Splashed across the image was the headline: #360. ANOTHER MURDER, ANOTHER RECORD.

The teenager, head down, quickly turned on his heel and marched to the cash register. He punched in the coffee, made change, then carefully closed the cash drawer as he scanned the front door and windows. Then, from beneath the register, he pulled out the busboy cart and rolled it to the front of the diner.

"Your change," he said in a normal voice, holding the money out to Payne.

"That's your tip. Keep it."

"Thanks."

Daquan stuffed it in the front pocket of his jeans as he immediately turned his back to Payne. He busied himself clearing the small plates and cups from the nearest high-top table.

"What about the drive-by?" Payne pursued, again speaking quietly as he flipped pages.

"I really can't say," Daquan replied, almost in a whisper, without turning around.

"Can't?" Payne said. "Or won't?"

Daquan shrugged.

"Peeps talk, they get capped. That's what happened to Pookie. Law of the street. That's why I texted you now, after they came—"

"Who did it?"

"Capped Pookie?"

"Yeah."

"That's just it—I don't know," he said, then looked over his shoulder at Payne. "Matt, I didn't even know the dude. They're threatening me over something I don't know."

"Any guess who did do it?"

Daquan turned back to busing the table and shrugged again.

"I heard word that King Two-One-Five knows," he said.

Payne thought: *Tyrone Hooks knows—or ordered it done?*

He pulled his cell phone from the back pocket of his jeans, rapidly thumb-typed and sent a short text message, then tucked the phone back.

"When's the last time you saw your parole officer, Daquan?" he said, picking the newspaper back up.

"Few days ago."

"It go okay?"

"I guess."

"How's school coming?"

"Hard, man. Just real hard."

"One day at a time. You'll get that GED."

Daquan then pulled a hand towel and a spray bottle of cleaner from the cart and began wiping the tabletop.

Payne said, "Nice diamond stud. Is it real?"

Daquan stopped wiping.

"Uh-huh. S'posed to be, anyway," he said, made two more slow circles, and added, "Got my momma something nice for Christmas, and this earring, it was part of the deal."

"Really?"

Daquan grunted.

"Really," he said, then moved to the next table. "You know, I'm trying to get my life straight, staying away from the street. You think I like busing tables? Only gig I could find."

"I know. Remember?"

Daquan sighed.

"Yeah, of course I remember. You know I appreciate the help, man."

"Keep your nose clean, make it through the probation period, and we'll work on getting your record cleared. Have the charge expunged. Then we'll find you something else. Right now, this is good, honest work."

"I know."

"You should be proud. Your mother told me she is. Especially now, after Dante's death . . ."

At the mention of his cousin, Daquan looked over his shoulder at Payne.

Payne saw deep sadness in his eyes. They glistened, and it was obvious that he was fighting back tears.

"I can't get past that, Matt. We were real close, you know, going way back. Now he's gone, and I'm here." He looked down and rubbed his eyes. "But I'm really not here. I'm just a shell walking around."

Daquan lifted his head, looked at Payne—then his eyes immediately looked past Payne, out the window.

Payne saw the sadness in Daquan's face suddenly replaced with fear.

"Shit!" Daquan said. "They're back!"

He grabbed the busboy cart and started pushing it quickly to the back of the diner.

Just then, as Payne turned and looked out the window, the glass front door swung open.

Two teenaged black males wearing thick dark parkas marched in, the first one, tall and burly, raising a black semiautomatic pistol in his right fist.

Payne dropped the newspaper and quickly reached behind his back to pull his .45 out from under his sweatshirt.

Daquan shoved the busboy cart at the pair and then jumped behind the back counter as the tall, burly teenager fired three shots.

The sound of gunfire in the small diner was deafening.

Payne leveled his pistol at the shooter as he shouted, "Stop! Police! Don't move!"

The ringing in Payne's ears caused his words to sound odd.

The tall, burly teenager turned and tried to aim at Payne.

Payne instinctively responded by squeezing off two rounds in rapid succession.

The heavy 230-grain bullets of the specially loaded .45 ACP cartridges left the muzzle at a velocity of 1,300 feet per second, and almost instantly hit the shooter square in the chest. Upon impact and penetration, the copper-jacketed lead hollow points, as designed, mushroomed and then fragmented, the pieces ripping through the teen's upper torso.

The shooter staggered backward to the wall, dropping the gun when he struck the wooden counter there.

The second teenager, who had frozen in place at the firing of the first shots, immediately turned and bolted back out the glass door.

The shooter slid to the floor.

As Payne rushed for the door, he kicked the shooter's gun toward the back counter. The two customers there were lying on the floor in front of it. The one to the left was curled up in the corner with his back to Payne and, almost comically, shielding his head by holding a white plate over it. The one on the right was facedown and still. Blood soaked the back of his shirt.

The enormous cook, who had ducked below the counter, now peered wide-eyed over its top.

Payne shouted, "Call nine-one-one!" then threw open the door and ran out.

Daquan, blood on his right hand as he gripped his left upper arm, crawled out from beneath the cash register.

Daquan hesitated a moment before moving toward the shooter, who was motionless. He picked up the small-frame semiautomatic pistol from the floor.

The cook stood and shouted, "Daquan, don't!"

Daquan went out the door.

He turned right and took off down the sidewalk, following Payne.

The storefronts along Erie Avenue gave way to a decaying neighborhood of older row houses. Daquan Williams watched the teenager dart into traffic and dodge vehicles as he ran across Erie, headed in the direction of a series of three or four overgrown vacant lots where row houses had once stood.

He saw that Matt Payne, arms and legs pumping as he picked up speed, was beginning to close the distance between them.

"Police! Stop!" Payne yelled again.

The teenager made it to the first lot off Thirteenth Street, then disappeared into an overgrowth of bushes at the back of it.

Payne, moments later, reached the bushes, cautiously pushed aside limbs, swept the space with his pistol, and then entered.

Daquan started to cross Erie but heard a squeal of brakes and then a truck horn begin blaring. He slid to a stop, narrowly missing being hit by a delivery box truck. It roared past, its huge tires splashing his pants and shoes with road slush from a huge pothole. A car and a small pickup closely following the truck honked as they splashed past.

Daquan finally found a gap in traffic and made his way across.

He ran to the bushes, then went quickly into them, limbs wet with snow slapping at him. One knocked his cap off. The dim light made it hard to see. After a long moment, he came out the other side, to another open lot. He saw Payne, who had run across another street, just as he disappeared into another clump of overgrowth at the back of another vacant lot between row houses.

While Daquan ran across that street to follow, a dirty-brown four-door Ford Taurus pulled to the curb in front of the row house bordering the lot. Daquan dodged the sedan, running behind it, then started across the lot.

Ahead, from somewhere in the overgrowth, he heard Matt Payne once again shouting, "Stop! Police!"

This time, though, was different.

Almost immediately there came a rapid series of shots—the first three sounding not quite as loud as the final two.

Daquan heard nothing more as he reached the overgrowth and then, while trying to control his heavy breathing, entered it slowly. He raised the pistol and gripped it tightly with both hands.

More snow fell from limbs onto his soaked T-shirt and jeans. He shivered as he stepped carefully in the dim light, listening for sounds but hearing only his labored breath. He finally reached the far side.

He wiped snow from his eyes.

And then his stomach dropped.

Oh, shit!

Matt Payne was lying facedown in the snow.

The teenager, ten feet farther into the vacant lot, was making a blood-streaked path in the snow as he tried to crawl away.

Then he stopped moving.

"Matt!" Daquan called as he ran to him.

Payne turned his head and, clearly in pain, looked up at Daquan.

"Call nine-one-one," he said. "Say 'officer down . . . police officer shot.'"

Daquan, now kneeling, saw the blood on the snow beneath Payne.

His mind raced. He looked at the street ahead.

There ain't time to wait for help.

I've gotta get him to it. . . .

"Hang on, Matt."

Daquan then bolted back through the overgrowth of bushes.

As he came out the far side, he saw the driver of the Ford sedan, a heavyset black woman in her late fifties, leaning over the open trunk, looking over her shoulder as she rushed to remove bulging white plastic grocery bags.

He ran toward her and loudly called, "Hey! I need your car . . ."

The woman, the heavy bags swinging from her hands, turned and saw Daquan quickly approaching.

Then she saw that he was holding a pistol.

She dropped the bags, then went to her knees, quivering as she covered her gray hair with her hands.

"Please . . . take whatever you want . . . take it all . . . just don't hurt me . . ."

Daquan saw that a ring of keys had fallen to the ground with the bags.

"It's an emergency!" he said, reaching down and grabbing the keys.

Tires squealed as he made a hard right at the first corner, going over the curb and onto the sidewalk, then did it again making another right at the next intersection. He sped along the block, braking hard to look for Payne down one vacant lot, then accelerating again until braking at the next lot.

He finally found the one with Payne and the teenager—Payne was trying to sit upright; the teen had not moved—and skidded to a stop at the curb.

Daquan considered driving across the lot to reach Payne faster, but was afraid the car would become stuck.

He threw the gearshift into park and left the engine running and the driver's door open as he ran toward Payne.

He saw that Payne was holding his left hand over the large

blood-soaked area of his gray sweatshirt. And, as Daquan approached closer, he saw Payne, with great effort, raise his head to look toward him—while pointing his .45 in Daquan's direction.

"Don't shoot, Matt! It's me!"

"Daquan," Payne said weakly, then after a moment lowered his pistol and moved to get up on one knee.

Daquan squatted beside him. Payne wrapped his right arm around Daquan's neck, and slowly they stood.

"This way," Daquan said, leaning Payne into him and starting to walk.

The first couple of steps were awkward, more stumbles than solid footing, but then suddenly, with a grunt, Payne found his legs.

They managed a rhythm and were almost back to the car when Daquan noticed a young black male in a wheelchair rolling out onto the porch of a row house across the street.

"Yo! What the fuck!" the male shouted, coming down a ramp to the sidewalk. "What'd you shoot my man Ray-Ray for?"

Daquan said nothing but kept an eye on him as they reached the car and he opened the back door. He helped Payne slide onto the backseat, slammed the door shut, then ran and got behind the wheel.

"Yo!" the male shouted again.

As Daquan pulled on the gearshift, he could hear the male still shouting and then saw in the rearview mirror that he had started wheeling up the street toward the car.

And then he saw something else.

"Damn!" Daquan said aloud.

He ducked just before the windows on the left side of the car shattered in a hail of bullets.

And then he realized there was a sudden burning sensation in his back and shoulder.

He floored the accelerator pedal.

Daquan knew that Temple University Hospital was only blocks down Broad Street from Erie Avenue. He walked past it every day going to and from his job at the diner. It wasn't uncommon for him to have to wait at the curb while an ambulance, siren wailing and horn blaring, weaved through traffic, headed to the emergency room entrance on Ontario Street.

Driving to the ER would take no time. But Daquan suddenly was feeling light-headed. Just steering in a straight line was quickly becoming a challenge.

He decided it would be easier to stay away from Broad Street and its busy traffic.

He approached Erie Avenue, braked, and laid on the horn as he glanced in both directions, then stepped heavily on the gas pedal again.

His vision was getting blurry, and he fought to keep focused. He heard horns blaring as he crossed Erie and prayed whoever it was could avoid hitting them.

By the time the sedan approached Ontario, Daquan realized that things were beginning to happen in slow motion. He made the turn, carefully, but again ran up over the curb, then bumped a parked car, sideswiping it before yanking the steering wheel. The car moved to the center of the street.

Now he could make out the hospital ahead and, after a block, saw the sign for the emergency room, an arrow indicating it was straight ahead.

Then he saw an ambulance, lights flashing, that was parked in one of the bays beside a four-foot-high sign that read EMER-GENCY ROOM DROP-OFF ONLY.

Daquan reached the bays, and began to turn into the first open one.

His head then became very light—and he felt himself slowly slumping over.

The car careened onto the sidewalk, struck a refuse container, and finally rammed a concrete pillar before coming to a stop.

Daquan struggled to raise his head.

Through blurry eyes, he saw beyond the shattered car window that the doors on the ambulance had swung open.

Two people in uniforms leaped out and began running toward the car.

Daquan heard the ignition switch turn and the engine go quiet, then felt a warm hand on him and heard a female voice.

"Weak," she said, "but there's a pulse."

"No pulse on this guy," a male voice from the backseat said. "I'm taking him in . . ."

Then Daquan blacked out.

TWO DAYS EARLIER . . .

[TWO]
JFK Plaza
Fifteenth and Arch Streets, Philadelphia
Saturday, December 15, 9:55 A.M.

The moment she caught a glimpse in the distance of the iconic steel sculpture towering above the park's granite fountain—the pop-art twelve-foot-tall bright red letters stacked like so many children's blocks to spell LOVE—Lauren Childs knew that she absolutely had to be photographed in front of it.

All morning the nineteen-year-old had taken shots with the camera on her cell phone, and then uploaded her favorites to Facebook for her friends to see. She knew that this photograph would be the best yet.

She didn't know it would be her last alive.

Lauren Childs and her boyfriend, Tony Gambacorta, had come down from Reading, about sixty miles north of Philly. They'd met there in September, as sophomores at Albright College, and began dating almost immediately. Tony, tall and olive-skinned with dark good looks, had been taken by the outgoing personality of the petite fair-skinned blonde with the pixie face. Lauren was open to almost any adventure, and the day trip to Philadelphia had been her idea.

"I want to soak up the holiday magic of the city," she had told him.

After some window-shopping along Walnut Street in Center City—what the city's tourism advertisements touted as "the Fifth Avenue of Philadelphia"—they had walked to JFK Plaza, commonly called LOVE Park, which covered an entire tree-filled block across the street from City Hall.

A festive holiday crowd packed its German-themed Christmas Village, which was patterned on Nuremberg's sixteenth-century Christkindlesmarkt. Rows of Alpine-influenced wooden huts offered traditional German food and drink and holiday wares, and there were live performances by string quartets and dancers in authentic period outfits.

Tony had bought Lauren a genuine Bavarian felt hat, dark green with a brown feather in the hatband, which she now wore at a rakish angle while sipping a warm cup of *Glühwein*, red wine spiced with clove, cinnamon, and orange. He wasn't sure if it was the alcohol or the weather—it had snowed heavily the previous night and looked like it might again—that caused her high cheeks and perky nose to glow with a cute rose hue.

Lauren, looking more closely at the area surrounding the sculpture, realized that her idea was far from an original one. There clearly was a line of at least twenty people waiting for a turn before the artwork and the lit Christmas tree behind it. The line wound around the circular granite fountain behind the piece. But she didn't mind.

She pointed at it.

"What?" he said.

"I want a photo of us in front of that, Tony," she announced, tilting her head back to look up at him, her bright eyes beaming beneath the brim of green felt.

Over a tight long-sleeved black top she wore a sleeveless white goose-down jacket. Tony, in brown corduroy pants, flannel shirt, and a fur-collared black leather bomber jacket, had on a floppy red-and-white Santa hat.

"Of course you do," he said, and smiled at her. "You want a photo with everything."

"Let's go, then!"

She grabbed his hand and led the way, weaving through gaps in the heavy crowd. As they went, Tony caught the smell of meat grilling, then looked around and saw a trail of smoke drifting up from a wooden hut. Its signage read BRATWURST MIT SAUERKRAUT. He suddenly felt hungry.

They reached the back of the line for the sculpture. After a moment, Lauren realized that it was moving faster than she'd expected. And then she saw why, and smiled: The people in line were helping each other. When someone was ready to pose in front of the artwork, they would hand their camera to the person in line behind them, who then stepped up to take their picture. Then that person would take their turn, and the next in line would take that person's photo.

Not ten minutes later, Lauren and Tony were kissing in front of the LOVE artwork and the forty-something woman who'd joined the line immediately after them was snapping their picture with Lauren's cell phone.

Lauren retrieved her phone and thanked the woman. Then, inspecting the images and smiling from ear to ear, she and Tony moved away from the sculpture. After a few steps, Lauren stopped beside the fountain.

"Hold this, babe," she said, handing him her cup. "This shot is amazing. I want to post it!"

As her fingers flew across her cell phone, she said aloud what she was typing: "At LOVE with my Love in the City of Brotherly Love! Love, love, love this place!"

She looked at him and smiled.

"I'm so happy," she added.

He leaned over and kissed her rosy cheek.

"And I'm happy you're happy," he said, then added: "How about hungry? Those brats back there smelled great."

"Sure. I can always eat," she said, taking back her *Glühwein* and grasping his hand. "Lead on."

Lauren sipped her wine as Tony worked a path through the thick crowd. It was tight, and he repeatedly smiled politely and said, "Excuse us," as they brushed past. At one point, he found a gap. He took it, and a moment later bumped shoulders hard with someone he passed. He didn't see who it was, but he certainly heard it was a male when the guy muttered, *"Asshole!"*

Still, Tony replied, "Sorry," and kept moving—until a split-second later he heard Lauren make a terrible moan and felt her grip loosen. She suddenly stopped.

Tony glanced back and said, "You okay?"

At first Tony thought that Lauren had spilled the cup of red wine on herself. But then he saw that the stain on her white jacket was a bright red—and that it was spreading quickly.

She had a look of pain and confusion in her eyes. She slipped down to the granite.

"Lauren!" Tony said.

A woman screamed and backed away as he dropped to his knees and held Lauren. The crowd formed a circle around them.

"Please," Tony yelled, looking up over his shoulder, "someone call an ambulance!"

Not a minute later, the crowd parted as a uniformed Philadelphia police officer came running up.

"Hang on, Lauren," Tony said, stroking her head as she just gazed back. Her face had turned pallid, the rosy color on her cheeks and nose gone.

The officer got down on one knee. "I radioed for paramedics. Be here any moment. What happened?"

"I— I don't know," Tony said, a tear slipping down his cheek. "We were just walking, then . . . this." He waved his hand helplessly at the blood-soaked jacket.

"What's her name?" the officer said, placing his ear close to her nose and mouth.

Tony heard her make a gurgling sound.

"Lauren," he said.

"Lauren, can you hear me?" the officer said, then raised his voice: "Help is coming! Hold on! Talk to me, Lauren!"

There was no immediate response.

But then a trickle of blood escaped the corner of her mouth and her nostrils. Her eyes became glazed.

The officer put his right index and middle fingertips to the side of her neck for a long moment.

"Oh, *shit*," the officer said softly.

Tony jerked his head to look at him.

The officer met his eyes, then looked at Lauren, and slowly shook his head. "I'm really sorry . . ." he said, then automatically crossed himself, touching his right fingers to his forehead, his chest, and then his left and right shoulders.

There were gasps from the crowd.

Tony struggled to breathe. Tears now flowed down both cheeks.

"But . . . but . . ." he said, then cried out, "Lauren!"

Slowly rocking her, he buried his face in her neck and began sobbing.

[THREE]
Franklin Square
Sixth and Race Streets, Philadelphia
Saturday, December 15, 10:20 A.M.

Not a half hour later and a dozen blocks away, Melanie Baker, an attractive thirty-two-year-old brunette, had just helped her daughter, Abigail, climb off the seat of a fiberglass replica of a giant bald eagle in flight on the Liberty Carousel.

"Santa now! I want to see Santa!" the six-year-old said, pointing across the snow-covered park to the big white tent nearby. It had a huge sign reading NORTH POLE and a pair of twenty-foot-tall striped candy canes marking the entrance. Elves in green outfits seemed everywhere, most handing out real candy canes to the children.

Melanie looked over her shoulder, scanning the heavy crowd. She glanced at her cell phone and saw that her husband had just sent a text: "Almost there."

Having forgotten his wallet, he had run a dozen blocks to retrieve it from their apartment in the Northern Liberties section, just north of Center City.

Melanie adjusted the fleece stocking cap, a white one dotted with little green Christmas trees, over Abigail's sandy blond hair as she looked in her eyes. "You want to wait for Daddy?"

Abigail shook her head. "Santa now? Please?" She pronounced it *peas*.

Melanie glanced at the big white tent and thought, *Well, they probably have heaters in there.*

"Okay, Abby, okay," she said, smiling. "Daddy can catch up. Let's go see Santa."

Melanie walked Abigail over to where they had left their stroller with those of the other visitors. She slipped her handbag over the right handle and, holding Abigail's hand, pushed the stroller through the gate in the low black iron fence that surrounded the carousel. Then they went onto the brick walkway and joined the crowd of families headed to the white tent.

Franklin Square, dating back to 1682, was one of the five original public spaces that William Penn designed when laying out the city. It had gone through rough periods over the years—the worst most recently in the 1960s, when it was a squalid area all but abandoned to the homeless for years on end.

But now the park—which legend held was where in 1752 Ben Franklin had flown the kite dangling a key in a storm and captured electricity from lightning (others said he flew it from the spire of Christ Church a few blocks away)—had again become a family-friendly spot. It featured the city's only miniature golf course, the carousel, and playgrounds, and, now for the holidays, a child-pleasing Christmas light show that flowed out from the ten-foot-tall kite "flying" above the water fountain and the big white North Pole tent for visits and photographs with Santa Claus.

Abigail was now anxiously pulling her mother toward the tent. They passed the path that led to the miniature golf course; it was roped off, and a sign read CLOSED FOR MAINTENANCE. A loud-speaker on top of a pole on the corner filled the air with the Philly Pops orchestra performing "Santa Claus Is Coming to Town." Standing under the speaker, a green-costumed elf—Melanie noticed he was a young teenager with a bad case of acne—handed out candy canes.

The teenaged boy handed one to Abigail, who said, "Thank you!" then looked up at her mother, grinning as she waved it like a trophy.

"Almost to Santa!" Abigail said, and tugged again on her mother's hand.

"Almost," Melanie said, then heard her phone going off. It was the ring tone of Sinatra singing "Fly Me to the Moon" that she recently had linked to her husband's cell phone number.

"Let's go faster, Mommy!"

"Hang on, Abby, it's Daddy calling," Melanie said, steering the stroller off the crowded brick walkway.

They stopped short of where a great big man with light brown skin sat hunched over on one of the park's wooden benches. He wore jeans and a black hooded sweatshirt, and was sweating and clearly trying to catch his breath.

As Melanie quickly reached with her free hand into her purse to dig out the phone, the sudden motion made the stroller tip backward. It gained momentum, then slammed to the ground, causing the purse to spill most of its contents, including the phone, which had stopped ringing. The stroller handle also knocked the candy cane from Abigail's hand, crushing it.

"Damn it!" Melanie blurted, then let go of Abigail's hand and bent over to pick up everything. The phone began ringing again and she grabbed it first, and answered it: "Hey, meet us at the North Pole tent."

She listened as she refilled her purse, then said, "I'll ask her, but she really wants to see Santa," then turned around to Abigail.

"Ab—"

A deep chill shot through Melanie.

Abigail wasn't standing there.

"Abby!" she called out, standing up and frantically looking around.

Melanie then looked over at the white tent, and walked quickly toward it, scanning the crowd as she went.

Nothing.

She stopped.

"Abby!"

Where could she have gone?

Sick to her stomach, Melanie suddenly felt on the edge of throwing up.

Stay calm!

She inhaled deeply, then slowly let it out as she looked back to where the stroller lay on the ground. Then she looked farther back—and in the crowd caught a glimpse of a white-and-green cap.

Oh, thank God!

Abigail was walking toward the teenager in the elf costume.

"Abby!" Melanie yelled, running after her.

Abigail kept walking. Melanie thought that the Christmas music blaring from the loudspeaker caused her not to be heard.

Melanie then noticed that the big man who'd been on the wooden bench was also walking toward the teenager in the elf costume, who now was bent over his candy bag.

Then Melanie couldn't believe her eyes—the big man suddenly reached down and took Abigail by the hand, pulling her around the pole that roped off the path to the miniature golf course.

"No!" Melanie yelled from deep down.

And then in the next instant, Abigail disappeared around the corner.

Melanie screamed, "Help! He grabbed my daughter!"

As people in the crowd began to comprehend what Melanie was saying, a path opened for her, some horrified parents pulling their children into their arms and holding them tight.

The teenager in the elf costume saw Melanie running and yelling. Then he realized that she was looking at him, and pointing past him.

Melanie again screamed, "He grabbed my daughter!"

The teenager looked around the corner, then bolted down the path after them.

A minute later Melanie rounded the corner where the teenager had been standing. The huge loudspeaker began playing "I'll Be Home for Christmas."

Melanie's lungs burned. She had been running down the empty path for what she thought felt like forever. Her mind raced—*What will happen to Abby? What if I never see her again?*—and then she told herself to think positive thoughts.

I'll find her. I have *to find her.*

She came to a sharp curve—and wondered if she was hallucinating.

"Oh my God!" she said, and felt herself running faster than she thought possible.

Abigail, alone, had suddenly appeared around the curve and was walking toward her.

"Come to me, Abby!" Melanie cried, her arms outstretched.

It wasn't until Melanie held Abigail tightly that she noticed there was blood—it had smeared off the back of Abigail's winter coat. Melanie frantically pulled off the coat and checked her daughter for wounds. She found none.

Melanie then heard the heavy footfalls of someone running up behind her.

She quickly turned to look.

Two Philadelphia policemen were coming down the path.

[FOUR]
3001 Powelton Avenue, Philadelphia
Saturday, December 15, 10:22 A.M.

"Tim, I asked that there not be any more talk about any death threats," Emily O'Brien said, crouching and pouring water from a plastic pitcher into the Christmas tree stand.

She looked over her shoulder. Her husband leaned against the door frame to the kitchen. He wore a faded navy cotton bathrobe, under which a white T-shirt was visible, and he had his bare feet stuffed into fleece-lined slippers.

"Okay, Tim? Please? Nothing came of the others, and I don't want that awful feeling of being afraid again. Especially during the holidays."

Emily, an attractive redhead with pale, freckled skin, stood and crossed the room to him. Getting up on tiptoes, she tenderly kissed her husband of twenty months.

At six-foot-three and two hundred thirty pounds, Tim O'Brien was beefy but soft, a teddy bear of a guy whose idea of a workout was pounding down a couple—or more—pints of Penn Pale Ale after an intense day of researching and writing investigative news stories. Now, having just awoken after a late night out, the reporter's big hands were wrapped around a steaming mug of black coffee that he cradled to his chest.

"This should be a happy time," Emily went on, smiling as she met his dark eyes.

Tim nodded.

"Em, I'm simply repeating what I was told at the office. Just be careful. You should always—not just now because of the threat—be conscious of your surroundings when you're out. Don't be distracted by your phone, texting, talking, whatever. The security guys at work call it—"

"*Situational awareness,*" she interrupted. "I know. I remember from the last two threats after your stories ran."

He grunted, then leaned down and, dropping a hand to her lower back and pulling her in against him, kissed her deeply. After he let her loose, she smiled and squeezed past him, heading into the kitchen with the empty plastic pitcher. He admired her beautiful figure—wondering when it would start showing signs of her pregnancy—then quickly took two steps after her and swatted her swaying buttocks.

She jumped and squealed, then looked back over her shoulder. "You're bad," she said.

"I do love you, Em. Just want you safe."

She blushed, then playfully wagged an index finger at him. "But I love you more!"

Tim O'Brien smiled and gently shook his head. Then he took a sip of coffee and for a long moment seriously considered grabbing Emily by the hand and tugging her back to what he figured was probably still a warm bed.

Then he felt a different call of nature, an urgent one.

He glanced at the front door of the eighty-year-old row house that was in the University City section of Philly, just across the Schuylkill River from Center City. The upper third of the wooden door, like those of the other ten homes on their side of the block, framed a glass pane. When they'd moved in—they'd been renting since their senior year, hers at Drexel and his at Penn, both institutions a short walk away—Emily had hung beige lace over the window for some semblance of privacy.

Now, through a gap in the lace, Tim could see a wall of steady snowflakes. He felt a draft as an icy wind whistled in through the door frame. His eyes went lower and he saw, more importantly, that the door's new heavy-duty dead bolt still was locked.

Tim quickly turned and headed for the half-bath off the hallway.

The tiny room was chilly. Pulling the door shut with his left hand, he flipped the wall switches for the light and exhaust vent with his right elbow. The single bulb in the fixture over the mirror flickered on, then glowed steadily as the old exhaust fan rattled to life in the high ceiling.

Maneuvering his big frame in the cramped space, he hurriedly put the coffee cup on the floor, grabbed the copy of *Philly* magazine off the cracked porcelain lid of the water tank, adjusted his bathrobe accordingly—then grimaced as he settled onto what felt like a frozen plastic seat.

A few minutes later, as Emily washed and dried plates and glasses and returned them to the cupboard, she thought she heard the sound of knocking. She eased the last dish onto the stack on the shelf with a light *clank*, then turned her head to listen. Almost immediately there came the sound of rapping on the wooden front door.

"Tim, babe?" she called out over her shoulder. "Can you get that?"

When he didn't answer, she sighed and walked out of the kitchen. She glanced around the living room, found it empty, then heard the unmistakable rumbling of the bathroom vent fan.

He could be in there for days, she thought, then, as knuckles rapped loudly on the glass pane, quickly turned to look at the front door.

Wiping her hands on a kitchen towel as she walked toward the door, she could make out through the window, silhouetted against the snowfall, the dark forms of two Hispanic-looking men standing on the covered porch. They wore identical uniforms, faded navy blue, that Emily thought looked vaguely familiar. Coming closer, she then saw the company logotype on the breast pocket of one man's jacket—a cartoon cockroach on its back, legs stiff in the air, bulging Ping-Pong ball–like eyes with black Xs, and the words PETE'S PEST CONTROL.

Did Tim call for the bug guy?

When she pulled back on the beige lace window cover, the larger, heavyset man who had been knocking on the door noticed. He then held up a clipboard and pointed to what looked like a standard order form on it. Emily had a moment to make out, under another representation of the cartoon cockroach, a hand-written "3001 Powelton Ave, U-City" but little more before he pulled it back. The other man had what looked like an equipment bag hanging from his shoulder, his right hand inside it.

He must have, she thought, reaching for the latch of the dead bolt, *either him or the landlord . . .*

Tim jerked his head when he thought he heard a muffled scream. A moment later, he definitely heard and felt a *thump* reverberate on the hardwood flooring and then heavy footfalls moving quickly through the house.

What in the hell . . . ? he thought, dropping the magazine and quickly getting off the can.

Then he clearly heard Emily cry out in pain. And then glass breaking and another *thump*.

"Emily!" he called as he reached for the doorknob.

The bathroom door exploded inward, a dirty tan leather boot splintering the wood. Tim saw that the toe of the scuffed boot was coated in blood. The boot kicked again at the door, holding it wide open.

Filling the doorway was a heavyset Hispanic male in a blue uniform. His face had a hard, determined look—and his right hand held a black, long-bladed weapon. The blade also was wet with blood.

A machete . . . ?

The blade flashed as the man swung it up, then quickly down, striking Tim.

Tim did not immediately notice any pain. But there was an odd smell, almost a metallic one, and a strange warm moistness on his torso. He looked down at his open robe—and saw his T-shirt was slit, a bloody gash along the center of his big belly and a tangle of what looked like bluish-white tubing bulging out from the gash.

Then he heard the man make a deep primal grunt, saw the blade flash again—and for a split second felt something strike hard at the side of his neck.

And then Tim felt . . . absolutely nothing.

[ONE]
Office of the Mayor, City Hall Room 215
1 Penn Square, Philadelphia
Saturday, December 15, 12:36 P.M.

"The bastard killed one of Santa's elves, Mr. Mayor!" James Finley said, his usually controlled voice now practically a shriek. The frail-looking forty-year-old—he was five-foot-two and maybe a hundred pounds—was head of the Philadelphia Convention and Visitors Office. "'Murderer Savagely Slits Throat of Santa's Elf!'

That's how the media will play this. And there's no way we can put a happy face on that!"

From behind his massive wooden desk, Mayor Jerome H. Carlucci, who was fifty-nine, looked at Chief Executive Adviser Edward Stein, Esquire—a slender, dark-haired thirty-year-old who was writing notes on one of his ubiquitous legal pads while leaning against the door frame that led to his office—and then looked to the couch at First Deputy Police Commissioner Dennis V. Coughlin, fifty-one, who met Carlucci's eyes and raised his bushy gray eyebrows in a gesture that the mayor read as *What can I say? There is no way to put a happy face on that.*

The close relationship between Jerry Carlucci and Denny Coughlin—they looked as if they could have been brothers, or at least cousins, both tall, heavyset, large-boned, ruddy-faced— went back decades to when Carlucci and Coughlin had been hotshot young cops being groomed for bright futures. Carlucci often boasted that before being elected mayor he'd held every position on the Philly PD except that of policewoman.

Stein and Finley were recent additions to the Office of the Mayor. Neither had been there quite a month.

Finley was pacing in front of the large flat-screen television that was on the wall of the mayor's elegant but cluttered office. Tuned to Channel 1009, which was *Philly News Now* around-the-clock coverage on the KeyCom cable system, the muted television showed a live camera shot of Franklin Park.

Behind the intense, goateed, middle-aged African-American reporter speaking into the camera lens was a yellow POLICE LINE DO NOT CROSS tape strung across a snow-crusted brick walkway. A uniformed policeman was holding the tape up as two men wear-

ing medical examiner office jackets wheeled under it a gurney carrying what clearly was a full body bag. A small crowd of bystanders
watched from the far side of the yellow tape.

Finley, pointing at the screen with his cell phone, went on: "I
don't know how badly this is going to play out, but it's already
absolutely disastrous. God only knows what that monster was
going to do to that little girl. A kidnapped child—now that's a PR
nightmare. A horror story that would have media legs forever. And
if she were found dead . . . ?"

The image then switched to a live shot of JFK Plaza. Another
reporter, this one a large-bosomed blonde in her late twenties,
made a solemn face as she spoke into her microphone and gestured
toward more yellow crime scene tape in the background.

"And this!" Finley said, pointing to the television again. "Right
across the damn street"—he dramatically jabbed his free hand's
index finger in the direction of the park—"a beautiful young
woman's life tragically cut short . . ." He stopped when he realized
the word he'd used. "Tragically *ended*, I should say."

Finley held his cell phone at shoulder level, waving it as he
went on: "Both of the stories are being spread all over social media
with the key phrase 'Stop Killadelphia.' I can't repeat the disgusting things people are saying about us. Especially after what that
poor girl had just posted—'My Love in the City of Brotherly Love'
with a beautiful romantic picture—before being murdered in
broad daylight! For christsake, it's *Christmas*! What is wrong with
these people?"

Mayor Carlucci, looking at the city's new public relations head,
thought, *Finley's not suggesting there's a better time for murdering
someone?*

But I guess he does have a point.

He can be a real pain in the ass, but Stein swears he's clever as hell and apparently good at what he does.

Not that that matters to the families of the dead kids.

The mayor then wondered how much of Finley's dramatics could be attributed to genuine emotion—his hysterical fits already bordered on legendary—or be blamed on alcohol, or both. Finley had announced that he had been enjoying brunch with friends just blocks away in his Washington Square West neighborhood, with plans to walk the shops along Walnut Street for Christmas gifts afterward, when the news broke.

"Our new tourism campaign, well, this is just going to kill it." Finley paused again. "Oh, damn it, I'm so upset I cannot think or speak properly. And it's my job to use the proper words." He gestured at the television once more. "This is going to *scare off* countless people. Look at this crime scene tape next to one of our most popular tourist attractions. Who wants to celebrate where someone's been murdered? Or become the next murder victim? This insanity keeps getting worse."

The room was quiet for a long moment.

"He is right, Mr. Mayor," Ed Stein said, looking up from his legal pad and tapping it with his pen. He wore a well-cut conservative gray two-piece suit with a white dress shirt and a striped blue necktie. "It is worse. For starters, we're now at three hundred sixty-two killings for the year. Four more than last year's total, and it would appear racing for an all-time record."

Carlucci met his eyes. Stein, who had proved to be both exceptionally sharp and a voice of reason, was starting to grow on him. But the mayor damn sure did not always like what Stein had to say.

Stein picked up on that and shrugged, adding: "It's why I'm here. It's why we're all here."

[TWO]

While Edward Stein and James Finley were officially listed as being executives on the City of Philadelphia's payroll, they fell under a unique provision of the law. The mayor, at his discretion, was permitted to have as many staff members as he deemed necessary for the good of the city—as long as the total of their salaries and pension liabilities did not exceed that of his office's budget for personnel. To that end, Stein and Finley were each receiving a city payroll check once a year in the amount of $1.

Their real income, not including bonuses and stock options, was in the middle six figures—as appropriate for their level as senior vice presidents of a major corporation—and was paid by Richard Saunders Holdings, which had its headquarters at North Third and Arch Streets in Old City.

Thus, the reality of it was that they were on loan to the city by local businessman Francis Franklin Fuller V.

The forty-five-year-old Fuller traced his family lineage to Benjamin Franklin. He enthusiastically embraced everything that was Franklinite, starting with "Richard Saunders," the pen name Franklin used in writing *Poor Richard's Almanack*. Fuller even physically resembled his ancestor. He was short and stout and had a bit of a bulging belly. Tiny round reading glasses accented his bulbous nose and round face.

Fuller had been born into wealth, and had built that into a far larger personal fortune, one in excess of two billion dollars. Under his main company, Richard Saunders Holdings, he owned outright or had majority interest in KeyCargo Import-Exports (the largest user of the Port of Philadelphia docks and warehousing facilities), KeyProperties (luxury high-rise office and residential buildings), and the crown jewel, KeyCom, a Fortune 500 nationwide telecommunications corporation.

His Old City headquarters also housed a nonprofit organization that he funded. A devout believer in the Bible's "an eye for an eye, a tooth for a tooth," Fuller chose the name Lex Talionis, which came from the Latin phrase for "Law of Talion" and essentially translated as "an eye for an eye."

Tragedy had struck Fuller's family five years earlier. His wife and young daughter, after making wrong turns and driving their Mercedes-Benz convertible into North Philadelphia West, had become collateral damage, killed in a hail of buckshot from the crossfire of a drive-by shooting. The gunmen were never caught.

A frustrated Fuller responded by setting up Lex Talionis and endowing it with an initial five million dollars. Every Friday— "Payday Friday," Fuller came to call it—he ran advertisements in local media and all his KeyCom cable channels: "Lex Talionis will reward twenty thousand dollars cash to any individual who provides information that leads to the arrest, conviction, and/or removal from free society of a criminal guilty of murder or attempted murder, rape or other sexually deviant crime, or illicit drug distribution in the City of Philadelphia. Tipsters are provided a unique code to keep them anonymous. Lex Talionis works with the Philadelphia Police Department and courts to protect the identities of those providing the information, ensuring their anonymity."

Carlucci had not liked it—in large part because it had been almost immediately effective, and thus embarrassed the leader of the East Coast's second-largest city. At any given time, Philly had approximately fifty thousand criminals "in the wind"—robbers, rapists, junkies, and other offenders who'd jumped bail by ignoring their court date. They then became wanted on outstanding warrants. While some had fled the city, many remained. And when Fuller put a bounty on their heads, the fugitives—either dead or bound and gagged in some makeshift manner—were being dropped at the doorstep of Lex Talionis, and the rewards were promptly being paid.

It wasn't that Carlucci didn't want the criminals behind bars—or, in the case of known killers, in a grave. What the longtime law enforcement professional didn't like was that the cash reward caused civilians to take the law into their own hands.

Carlucci had to use his iron fist—declaring that anyone who did not include the police department in apprehending the criminals would themselves be arrested and prosecuted, and then did so—while at the same time carefully bringing Lex Talionis more or less under the purview of the police department.

Shortly thereafter, Fuller, uninvited, had appeared at Carlucci's office.

You arrogant sonofabitch! Carlucci thought as he watched Fuller push past the mayor's secretary and then wave her off. *The last thing I want to do is make nice with you.*

"No interruptions, please," Fuller said to the secretary as he closed the office door behind him.

He turned and looked at Carlucci.

"Jerry, I have two words for you."

Carlucci was on his feet and coming out from behind his desk with his right hand outstretched.

"Frank, to what do I owe the pleasure of this surprise?"

"Hold the bullshit," Fuller said, sticking his hand up, palm out. "I've got a busy day."

Fuller then gestured with the same hand for Carlucci to take his seat. Fuller settled onto the couch.

"This is my office, Frank," Carlucci said, coldly furious.

"Please," Fuller replied evenly, and gestured again.

Carlucci made an angry face, then found his chair while impatiently gesturing back *Let's have it* with his hand. "Okay. Two words."

"Detroit and reelection."

Carlucci cocked his head. "What the hell does that mean? I don't know much, nor give a good goddamn, about Detroit politics."

"Well, as Benjamin Franklin said . . ." He paused. "I'm sure you recall that I am a descendant of the wise patriot. He said, 'When the well's dry, we know the worth of the water.' And we all would be wise to learn from Detroit's dry well."

"I'm not sure I follow you, Frank. Not sure I want to."

Fuller nodded, then explained, "Being a product of this great city, it pains me that Philadelphia has such genuinely grave problems. There is the very real chance that it is on that proverbial slippery slope to becoming the next Detroit."

Carlucci grunted. "You mean bankrupt? That's not going to happen."

"That's what I would expect a politician, particularly one in your position, to say. That's what they all said about Detroit. No one believed, or certainly wanted to believe, that that city would go broke. After all, it was home to the giants of the automobile manufacturers, including General Motors Corporation. Remember what they said about that powerful global corporation? 'As goes GM, so goes the nation.' And then what? Boom to bust, that's what. It went bankrupt. And then the city went bankrupt."

Carlucci grunted again. "We're not Detroit. We have thriving universities and leading hospitals and more."

"Again, spoken like a politician, but as great as our 'Eds and Meds' are—and they are indeed first class—they cannot sustain the entire city. Philadelphia, as you know, in addition to being *the birthplace* of this great nation, was known as the Workshop of the World. We made everything for everyone, locomotives to warships, textiles to firearms. Today, that's all gone, leaving vast lots and deserted crumbling buildings in once-thriving neighborhoods like Kensington and Frankford and empty docks at the Navy Yard."

He let that sink in, then went on, his voice rising: "Our city—third poorest in the country—has a great many challenges that can no longer be ignored, Jerry. We cannot afford to go bankrupt. I will not let it. I have too much invested in this city, both emotionally and certainly financially. It is our moral obligation to leave, as our ancestors did, the city better than we found it. Which brings me to reelection."

"The primaries are more than a year out—"

"I am well aware of that," Fuller interrupted. "Allow me, please, to finish. I'm also aware that there already are plenty of people planning on gunning for you, if you will forgive my choice of words. And they have ample ammunition. Crime being of course a significant issue with our citizens. I would suggest it is the main issue. The murder rate would be worse were it not for our excellent hospitals—specifically trauma surgeons performing miracles. It's a war zone out there, Jerry! And I speak from personal experience"—he suddenly dropped his head forward to rub his eyes, and then cleared his throat, and almost in a mumble added— "as you know."

Carlucci felt his own throat catch.

I cannot imagine what emotional hell he must've gone through— clearly is still going through—losing his wife and child that way.

No amount of wealth can replace that.

"Frank, you know you have my sincere—"

Fuller again held up his hand, palm out. After a moment, he raised his head and looked again at Carlucci.

"You'll please excuse me for that," he said, then went on: "Another significant issue is the wretched failure of our city schools. The buildings arc run-down, those students who actually graduate high school are ill-equipped for the real world, and more than a few disgraceful teachers and principals, to make themselves look better and thus teaching all the wrong lessons, are going to jail for correcting test answers in that cheating scandal.

"And then there is the matter of city finances—or lack thereof. The budget shortfalls are across the board, pensions are unfunded to the tune of some five billion dollars, and both property and wage taxes have repeatedly risen and are now at record levels. We're selling any assets we can to try to keep afloat. What happens next when all those are gone?" He paused, caught his breath, then said, "Jerry, this city is falling apart—literally—as it does not even have sufficient funds to demolish all the dangerous structures before they simply collapse on their own."

Fuller saw that Carlucci had a weary look. And that he was nodding.

"Welcome to my world, Frank," Carlucci said, not pleasantly.

"I understand that I am telling you nothing new. But that does not change the fact that these issues are grave. My companies, as you would expect, constantly study demographics. We have to know all about our customers, both current ones and potential ones. What we have found is disturbing, from the perspective of both the future of my companies and the future of this city. And that is: The majority of those in the current generation of eighteen- to thirty-five-year-olds, citing concern with issues I've just listed, say they won't raise their families in Philadelphia. They are graduating college, sticking around a few years before or after getting married—then moving where taxes and crime are lower and schools are better. This has been going on for years, and it's accelerating. We—you and me and everyone else in this city—need those families and the taxes they pay. Or—"

"Or we go broke," Carlucci interrupted. "I get it."

"I must say that I do believe in your style of leadership, Frank. An iron fist properly wielded is effective. But I have come to better appreciate that there are nuances to politics, to getting—and then most importantly, keeping—the support of corporations. Corporations that will create jobs that will keep those families here, and in so doing build a healthier city and generate more tax revenue that in turn will better provide for our citizens."

"So, what are you saying specifically?"

"What I'm saying, Jerry, is that I believe with my help you can accomplish that, presuming (a) you do what I say and (b) we get you reelected."

"'Do what I say,'" Carlucci quickly parroted, trying not to lose his temper.

"For the good of the city," Fuller said, his tone matter-of-fact and unapologetic. "It's your choice. If you're not open to (a), then I have a number of candidates who are."

Carlucci met his eyes.

That's damn sure not a veiled threat.

I should tell you to go straight to hell.

But . . . that would not be productive. I don't need you as an enemy.

Carlucci said: "There's no guarantee these others can get elected."

Fuller shrugged.

"I will grant you that. But I can guarantee that whoever I back will win the primary election, with great odds of winning it all." He paused to let that sink in, then finished: "And I can guarantee that those who fail to win their second term as mayor, as history has proven, never find themselves going on to win higher office in Harrisburg or Washington."

Carlucci looked off in the distance. He had not risen to police commissioner and then mayor by being easily intimidated. He was from South Philly and enjoyed a good fight. But long ago he also had learned to be pragmatic.

I may not like the message worth a damn, but I can appreciate its frank delivery.

His candidate, no matter if the guy won or lost in the general election, would leave me out of office.

Forget not being a lame duck—politically I'd be a dead duck.

On the other hand, if I have his backing for mayor, then I probably could bank on it for governor.

What the hell. One step at a time.

I only have to put up with him until my victory speech on election night.

"I'm listening," Carlucci said, after a moment.

Fuller nodded.

"Good," he said. "Here's what I'm going to do. I have a fine young man, another product of our city, who graduated at the top of his class at Penn Law. I like to hire our hometown people, and he is an outstanding example of why. I lured him—Edward Stein is his name—away from Mawson, Payne, Stockton, McAdoo, and Lester."

Carlucci's eyebrows rose. He was well-acquainted with what was arguably Philadelphia's most prestigious law firm, particularly founding partner Brewster Cortland Payne II.

"I imagine Brew Payne was not happy with that," Carlucci said.

"Perhaps. But as his firm represents a great deal of my business, you might say it's all in the family. Much like Stein working for you. Presently, Stein is one of my senior vice presidents. He will be your executive counsel, or whatever you wish to call him, and will provide counsel to you. He will also report to me."

Carlucci watched as Fuller then stood, nodded once, and, without another word, walked out of the office.

[THREE]

Chief Executive Adviser Ed Stein tapped his pen on his legal pad again.

"The media coverage from those murders will have a direct impact on revenues," he said.

James Finley added: "Do I have to remind you, Mr. Mayor, that this city will implode without the revenue from tourism? Kiss some four billion—or potentially more—dollars good-bye. That's how much the thirty-five million leisure visitors spent last year in Philly, generating for the city almost five hundred million—a half-billion—in tax revenue. And that's not counting convention business. It's long been on the decline, and the fewer people who come for business translates into fewer who will return with their families."

"I would not characterize it as imploding," Stein offered, earning him a glare from Finley. "But it certainly is the tip of the financial iceberg, and that has to improve or else Center City's shiny towers, high-end retail spaces, and hotels and restaurants could slowly empty and eventually falter. If people see Philly as a place of crumbling buildings and slain tourists—which is today's reality—they will take their money elsewhere." He paused, and then added, "When was the last time you heard someone say, 'Hey, how about we take the family for a vacation in Detroit!'?"

First Deputy Police Commissioner Coughlin chuckled, and immediately felt Finley staring at him. He looked at Stein.

"Sorry. I take your point."

Stein went on: "When the tourists don't show, everyone suffers. Especially now. For many businesses, how well holiday sales go makes or breaks them for the year. And no sales means no sales tax. It's lose-lose."

"Something is going to have to be done about stopping these murders!" Finley said. "Something different that works. And now. It's only ten days until Christmas . . ."

"Listen," Carlucci said, "I like to think I know a thing or two about police work—"

"I know, I know," Finley interrupted, his tone clearly one of frustration. "You've 'held every job but meter maid'—"

"Every job but *policewoman*," Carlucci snapped, and was immediately sorry he'd lost his temper.

Did that bastard just goad me into that?

"Let me be clear," Finley said. "I do not need this job. I took it because I love this city. And because you asked me. That is, Ed asked me to work with him."

Carlucci looked at him.

And you—maybe both of you—will report back to Frank Fuller what you perceive to be my failures.

"Look," Carlucci went on evenly, "I take great pride in my time on the force. And, as mayor, I continue to take great pride in seeing that our laws are enforced, our people protected."

"Then what do you plan to do?" Finley said. "Two families are about to visit the morgue and have to identify their dead teenage son and daughter. And that animal put a young mother through hell by kidnapping her child!"

"We're as disgusted by this as you are, James," Carlucci said.

"The first thing we're doing is putting more uniforms on the street, beginning with a surge in Center City."

He looked at Coughlin, who nodded.

"Including all of the Mounted Patrol Unit," Coughlin added.

"'Mounted Patrol'?" Finley repeated.

"Officers on horseback," Coughlin said. "Very effective, both from the vantage point of being higher and seeing more ground and from the ability to cover a lot of that ground quickly. There's also a PR aspect—the public really likes seeing the horses, and are more prone to interact with the officers, take pictures, that sort of thing."

Stein nodded thoughtfully.

Carlucci then turned and looked between Finley and Stein as he went on: "But know that even if we put a uniform on every street corner, there simply is no definitive way to protect against a thug hell-bent on killing. Take, for example, John Kennedy and Ronald Reagan. Both were surrounded by layers of Secret Service agents actively looking for a possible attack, yet determined men still got to them. So, even if we'd had a uniform dive in front of the girl, there's no guarantee it would've saved her from being stabbed."

"Murders are up and our case clearance rates are down," Coughlin put in, "because things are different now. Back in the day, most victims knew their killers, and it was only a matter of time—usually within the first forty-eight hours—before we connected those dots, caught the doer, and gave the district attorney's office a solid case to put them away."

"But . . . ?" Finley said, crossing his arms.

"Today, though, random stranger-on-stranger crime—murders,

robberies, purse snatchings, carjackings—it's everywhere. Drug dealers kill one another battling for turf—something that might explain what happened again just yesterday in Kensington. And these murders this morning could have been, say, some gang's rite of initiation. Anything's possible. We will know more from our investigations." He paused, then added, "But understand that budget shortfalls have hit us hard, too. We're stretched thin. Our department is down significantly from our onetime strength of eight thousand. I've had to cancel two police academy sessions. And I won't get into our outdated gear, et cetera. If it weren't for federal grants for equipment and things like the FOP getting local supporters to donate body armor, we'd be in trouble."

"The Fraternal Order of Police is having to do that?" Finley said, then, with a look of frustration, slowly shook his head as he looked down at his shoes.

Behind Finley, on the television, the attractive female reporter had turned from looking into the camera and was reaching up with her microphone, putting it before a nicely tanned male in his mid-twenties who looked as if he'd just stepped out of a Brooks Brothers advertisement.

The caption at the bottom of the screen read HOMICIDE SGT. MATTHEW PAYNE ON PARK MURDERS: "WE WILL NOT REST UNTIL WE FIND WHO COMMITTED THESE ATROCITIES."

Jesus, Coughlin thought, *don't let Finley see Matty or he'll really get his shorts in a knot.*

Then he glanced at the mayor, who had a slight grin as he looked at the TV, and guessed he was having similar thoughts.

But Jerry's probably smirking because he's hoping that it gets under Finley's skin.

Then Coughlin looked back toward Finley, and on the television saw the caption had changed to A POLICE SOURCE REPORTS THAT SGT. PAYNE WAS CLEARED LAST WEEK BY INTERNAL AFFAIRS IN NOVEMBER'S SHOOT-OUT ON CASINO BOARDWALK THAT LEFT 3 DEAD.

Finley looked up and saw that everyone was looking behind him.

He turned to the television just as the caption changed to SGT. PAYNE IS ALSO KNOWN AS THE WYATT EARP OF THE MAIN LINE.

"Damn it!" Finley said. "And now him!"

"What?" Carlucci said, now stone-faced, purposefully having lost the grin. "Payne gets his man. It's what you said you wanted."

Finley's head jerked. He met the mayor's eyes.

Here it comes, Coughlin thought.

Finley, he's playing you like a fine instrument . . .

"What I *want*," James Finley snapped, "is for there to be fewer killings so he will have fewer bastards to go after—and fewer chances for him to get in shoot-outs that wind up sensationalized in the media with that Wild West tagline!"

"When that nickname first made headlines," Carlucci said, somewhat sharply, "the reporter meant it as a compliment. Marshal Earp was considered the most effective lawman of his time. Matt comes from a family of good cops. His father was killed by a robber months before Matt was born. And it reflects well on the department to have in its ranks officers from the Main Line, especially one who's smarter than hell. He graduated from the University of Pennsylvania summa cum laude and, not surprisingly, scored the highest in the department on the sergeant's exam." Carlucci glanced at Coughlin, then looked at Finley. "And, because Matt also comes from money, he doesn't need his job, either. In a sense the same as you, James—with one difference."

"And what is that?"

"He's time and again put his life on the line to save people in this city," Carlucci said.

Finley stared for a long moment at Carlucci, then looked at Stein.

"Ed? What do you say?"

Stein looked between Finley and Carlucci.

"I agree the media sensationalizes the O.K. Corral thing. If, however, you mean about Matt? You won't be thrilled, James, but I say I like him. And that's not because I used to work for his father's firm." He paused, then in a lighter tone added, "Or because it would appear that we frequent the same clothier . . ."

Finley snorted.

Stein shrugged. "I'm with the mayor. I think Matt's a great cop doing a great job that most people do not understand and would never do once they learned what it takes to protect our society from the barbarians. He does not go to work looking to shoot someone. He's a deadly asset, and without such deadly assets, crime soars."

I suddenly like you even more, Stein, Carlucci thought.

"Well, that is putting a happy face on it," Finley said sharply. "Because that's damn sure what happens. Over and over. He's been in—what?—three shootings that resulted in deaths in just as many months? And that's just recently."

"And every one has been found to be righteous. It's a dirty job, but someone's got to do it," Carlucci said, his tone smug. After a moment, he added, "What I'd like to do is find out who the hell's the source in the department that's leaking the names of cops."

"What do you mean?" Finley said.

Carlucci looked at Coughlin.

"In an Officer-Involved Shooting," Coughlin offered, "we don't release the officer's name until after the incident has been thoroughly investigated, and only release it then if the officer is found to have erred."

"Why not before?"

"Because," Carlucci picked up, "if the officer is cleared and then his name gets released, he'll get dragged through the mud that is the news media, and then could become targeted—simply for doing his job correctly. A shooting that is determined to be righteous is exactly that."

Carlucci exchanged glances with Coughlin, then looked quickly at the television. "Now what the hell are they doing?"

All eyes turned to see a small group of African-American men marching into view behind the reporter interviewing Payne. They were wearing black cape-like flowing garments over white shirts, some with clerical collars. They carried four-by-six-foot homemade signs atop what looked like wooden broomsticks.

The first, with rows of photographs of dead men, read PASTORS FOR PEACE NOW! The one behind it had NO MORE MURDERS! and the numbers 360 and 361 crossed out and 362 written next to them. The last one read STOP KILLADELPHIA! All had across the bottom: WORD OF BROTHERLY LOVE MINISTRY.

"Well," Finley said, "I didn't want to mention the good Reverend Josiah Cross, but I wondered when he and his flock would get involved. That last sign would indicate to me that they're the ones fanning the flames on the Internet."

Another sign then appeared right behind Payne. It had an enlarged photograph of Payne that had run widely in the media a few months earlier. It showed him lit by camera flash in a darkened parking lot. He was wearing a dinner jacket and holding his Colt Officer's Model .45 ACP pistol—and standing over an armed

robber he had just shot. Above that image were the words PUBLIC
ENEMY #1.

"*That,*" Carlucci said angrily, almost spitting out the words, "is
what I mean by targeting a police officer cleared of any wrongdo-
ing whatsoever."

"Not to mention another PR fire for me to put out," Finley said
sarcastically, and then in a more excited tone added, "You don't
think Payne will shoot them?"

Finley then sighed.

"What the hell else could happen today?"

[FOUR]
Lucky Stars Casino & Entertainment
North Beach Street, Philadelphia
Saturday, December 15, 12:55 P.M.

You ain't going to be smiling in a minute, Tyrone Hooks thought as
he returned the doorman's automatic greeting with a curt nod
and entered the casino through a revolving door. *And smile all you
want, but I know you really checking me out. On those cameras, too.*

Overhead, closed-circuit surveillance cameras were clearly visible, as well as the countless black bubbles in the high ceiling tiles
that concealed additional recording devices. They were all completely capable, Hooks had heard when he'd joined a group taking
the casino's free introductory tour, of capturing every move of anyone in the casino.

But the last thing the rail-thin five-foot-ten twenty-five-year-old was worried about was being recorded. If anything, the security cameras would show him nowhere near the crime when it went down.

He paused a moment to stomp the snow from his new high-top gray leather athletic shoes, then he slipped off his heavy winter coat and hung it over his right arm, taking care so that the wad of twenties and hundreds didn't fall out of the coat's inside pocket. Underneath he had on a black short-sleeved T-shirt covered by a baggy orange and blue Philadelphia 76ers jersey.

He made a grand gesture of checking the time on his wristwatch. The new eighteen-karat yellow-gold Rolex President hung loosely, and he had to rotate it in order to see its hands showing it was five minutes before one. The watch was heavy and enormous, and against his skinny black wrist looked even larger, almost counterfeit. But it was genuine. A month earlier, Hooks had paid for it in part with his winnings from the blackjack tables.

The cash for the vast majority of the total price—$8,999 before tax, to be exact—had come, however, from the street. His crews pushed plastic baggies of crack, smack, and pot on street corners in the shadows near the Market-Frankford Line El, particularly along a sad stretch of the ironically named Hope Street, no more than a mile from the casino.

Hooks thought the Rolex's high cost had been worth every penny, because when he flashed the watch—and the cash and told everyone at the tables that he was an upcoming rap music artist, "King 215"—no one tried kicking the rapper to the curb of the Lucky Stars parking lot.

They ain't throwing my ghetto ass out, he thought as he walked toward the main floor. *That'd be bad for business when I rap about it.*

Lucky Stars was the newer of two casinos on the Delaware River—in the section of Philly known as Fishtown, which was enjoying a surge of gentrification—and, according to tax payments made to the Commonwealth of Pennsylvania, already had surpassed the other as the most profitable. (Harrisburg collected about $1.5 billion a year from casinos across the Keystone State, then redistributed it, a portion of which returned to the City of Philadelphia.)

Lucky Stars' brand-new five-story complex, with restaurants and bars and large performance theaters, featured a hundred gaming tables and twenty-five times as many slot machines. The cavernous high-ceiling area that Tyrone now approached held rows of slots as far as the eye could see, their lights flashing and bells clanging as people pulled—and pulled and pulled—on the one-armed bandits. The area reeked of stale cocktails and cigarette smoke—twenty-five percent of a gaming floor, by state law, had to be set aside for tobacco users—and of the floral-scented carpet-cleaning chemical that failed to mask the sharp smells.

While the casino had helpful signage—it indicated, for example, that gaming tables and restaurants and more could be found on upper floors, reached via multiple elevators and escalators—Tyrone Hooks had cased the place enough times to find his way around with his eyes closed. He knew that on the right side of the first floor was one bank of cashier cages. And that beyond those cages was the entrance to the miniature mall of a dozen luxury retail stores hawking to lucky winners—and anyone who hadn't lost all their money, including next month's rent—everything from expensive electronics to designer clothing to jewelry.

Tyrone also knew that while the cashier cages were well-protected, he had learned that the retail stores appeared anything but.

As he turned and headed for the mall, he surveyed the rows and rows of slots. They looked to be not quite half full, making it a slow Saturday afternoon. For his purposes, he figured a busier crowd would have been better—more people caused more confusion and chaos.

After passing the cashier cages, he approached, then entered, the retail mall. It was an open-air design, brightly lit with white marble flooring and columns and undulating walls of clear, thick glass panels that separated the individual stores. Averaging about twenty by thirty feet, each retail space was compact in size but had the appearance of being bigger because of all the clear walls.

Tyrone Hooks saw that the first store to the left, Medusa's Secret Closet, had well-formed female mannequins in its front windows, ones made of glass, wearing undergarments that were mere ribbons of material. He caught himself staring at the display before realizing he'd walked past his destination, the first store on the right, Winner's Precious Jewels.

He quickly turned back toward the store, then entered. There were only two customers—husband and wife, he guessed—and they were looking at the glass display cases on the left side of the store. Behind the case was the manager, a chubby, balding, middle-aged man in a shiny black two-piece suit. When he saw Hooks, he excused himself to the couple, then turned away and moved quickly toward the entrance.

"Good to see you again, sir," the manager greeted Hooks, then gestured toward the gold Rolex that he'd sold him. "That certainly is a beautiful timepiece. Excellent choice. You're still enjoying it, I trust."

"Uh-huh," Tyrone Hooks said, briefly making eye contact.

"Splendid! And what can I show you today?"

"Just looking."

"Well, you're in luck. We recently replenished our holiday inventory. It's even larger than before, so we have more than the usual number of interesting pieces that would complement your President nicely."

"Comp— What?"

"Complement. Look nice together . . ."

Hooks thought, *Yeah, I'm going to get plenty here to look good.*

". . . We could create, for example, a very nice heavy gold chain with a customized 'King 215' hanging from it."

Hooks smiled that the manager remembered his artist name, which Hooks had based in part on Philadelphia's telephone area code, and nodded.

"Maybe. If I get lucky again. Just looking right now."

The manager made a thin smile. "Lucky indeed. Well, we'd be more than happy to accommodate you. Just let us know if there's anything that interests you."

Who's "us" and "we"? You the only one here.

Tyrone nodded again, then stepped past the smiling salesman, slowly scanning the merchandise on display in the brightly lit glass cases. He stopped for a closer look at a display on the far right.

These weren't here last time. They changed out stuff.

But what he said is no lie! They got way more necklaces and rings than last time! Look at all them diamonds!

The two other customers on the opposite side of the room left the store as he started toward them.

Tyrone saw that the display cases in the middle held the flashy but inexpensive merchandise—the man-made cubic zirconia that sparkled like diamonds, for example, that the manager had first shown him the day he bought the Rolex, before learning that Tyrone had real cash burning a hole in his pocket.

Then he reached the far left cases.

And more watches!

Shit! A whole line of Presidents!

He looked for a long moment, then walked back toward the entrance, glanced over his shoulder at the salesman, and said, "Later."

"Good luck at the tables! I'll be here until five, or after that if you wish."

Tyrone Hooks nodded as he left.

After entering the casino floor, and nearly knocking over a short, old white-haired woman who was waddling into the mall, he glanced at his watch. He then looked back at the jewelry store and pulled out his cell phone. He thumbed a text message—"1 dude rocks right clocks left skip junk in middle"—and hit SEND.

He went to one of the cashier cages and pulled the wad of cash from his pocket. In it was a plastic Lucky Stars Rewards debit card, and he gave it and ten twenty-dollar bills to the cashier. She added the two hundred dollars to his card's account, then handed back the card.

He then went to the escalators that led to the second level of the casino. As he rode up, he looked out the wall of windows and saw, through a heavy snowfall, the enormous outline of a cargo ship making its way against the current of the Delaware, headed toward the Philadelphia Port Authority docks. On its deck, intermodal containers were stacked twenty high, looking like so many multicolored toy boxes. His cousin who worked at the docks had heard that a lot of meth and coke got smuggled in them, and Tyrone wondered what-all else could be inside. Then he scanned to the left and saw a large swarm of teenagers—at least fifty— moving quickly through the slush of the casino's huge parking lot.

Right on time, he thought as he looked at his cell phone screen. The cracked Liberty Bell icon labeled ROCKIN215, which was the social network name he'd created on the *Philly News Now* website, showed that there were seventy new instant messages under "lucky stars hookup," and more by the second.

He sent the text message "rock it" then looked back across the casino floor and, after a minute, picked out one, two, then three and four black males, all more or less dressed alike in black jeans, high-top boots, and heavy coats. They moved at a quick pace— coming from different directions and converging on the entrance to the miniature mall.

Tyrone knew they had obviously received his group text. He also knew that, concealed under their coats, two of them had short-handled ten-pound sledgehammers and the other two had black nylon bags. And, while he didn't know it for sure, he would quickly wager against any casino odds that all were packing pistols.

That bet I know I win, he thought.

He turned to take the next escalator up to the third floor just as the first of the teenagers entered the revolving doors.

Mrs. Gladys Schnabel, a somewhat pudgy grandmother with curly, blue-tinged white hair, a deeply wrinkled pale face, and large round eyeglasses that hung from her neck by a chain of tiny fake pearls, stood at a chromed clothing rack at the back of Medusa's Secret Closet. She was holding up a red velvet hanger emblazoned with the logotype FLEUR OF ENGLAND. Dangling from the hanger was a light tan silk satin undergarment set that consisted of an impossibly thin plunge bra and an even tinier thong panty.

Mrs. Schnabel seemed to be staring at the ensemble in stark disbelief.

She had arrived at the casino that morning with her daughter, forty-five-year-old Anna Cottrell, and her twenty-six-year-old granddaughter, Marie Cottrell. The two elder women had come down from Durham, a picturesque village that was a two-hour drive north. Marie lived in Philly. It was Mrs. Schnabel's seventieth birthday, and having a "girls' celebration" in the big city had been Anna's idea. A little gambling fun, some shopping, a nice meal and a show, then back to the peace and tranquillity of the rolling hills of northern Bucks County.

"You have an eye for quality—that set is one of our best sellers," the saleswoman, an olive-skinned brunette, said as she approached. She looked to be in her mid-thirties, and wore a tight black dress that accentuated her athletic body. Her small golden badge read SAMANTHA. "It's our finest silk, in the color that is called 'nude.'"

Mrs. Schnabel's skeptical gray eyes went from Samantha to the hanger, where she tugged the hidden price tag into view.

"My goodness!" she blurted. "How times have changed. I'm going to have to get really lucky at those one-arm bandits. Two hundred dollars?"

Samantha reached out and softly stroked the fabric of the bra. "But just feel this luxurious silk! And note that the ring and slides are of eighteen-karat gold."

The look on Mrs. Schnabel's face suggested that she was neither impressed nor sold.

But she then said, with obvious pride, "Well, even *if* I were to be so lucky today, it would be a gift for my wonderful granddaughter. Marie and my daughter are off powdering their noses. It's our girls' day—we're celebrating my birthday."

She looked past her, to the entrance, then put on her eyeglasses.

"Here comes my beautiful granddaughter now."

"Well then, let me wish you happy birthday!" Samantha said, smiling. Then she looked toward the entrance and saw an attractive bright-faced brunette about her age approaching. Then Samantha's eyes darted beyond Marie—and became suddenly huge.

"Oh no!" she said.

"What?" Mrs. Schnabel said, and then her head swiveled when she noticed that there suddenly was a loud commotion, the sound getting louder by the second.

The source was in the casino, coming from near the revolving front doors. She focused in that direction and saw that a huge pack of young kids, mostly teenagers, was flooding in through both revolving doors. They were laughing, shouting, whistling— and knocking over chairs and pushing people out of their way as they went.

"What hoodlums!" Mrs. Gladys Schnabel said, her voice almost a hiss.

"A flash mob," Samantha said.

"A what?" Mrs. Schnabel said, not taking her eyes off the crowd.

"Bored teens get together, cause trouble, then scatter," Samantha said. "They call it a flash mob."

"No fooling? We don't have those up in Bucks County."

They watched as terrified patrons fled the mob's path. At least those patrons who could. One older man, struggling with a walker made of aluminum tubing, rushed to move to the side but slipped and was knocked to his knees.

Security guards, and then a couple of uniformed policemen from the nearby Twenty-sixth District, gave chase. They tackled a pair of kids, then a third, at the back of the pack. But they were vastly outnumbered—and it was clear that they would remain unable to contain the rampage until backup help arrived.

There simply were too many kids to stop.

Mrs. Schnabel stood still, stunned by the sight as the mass pushed toward the retail mall. She made eye contact with one kid, then another, and suddenly became fearful that they not only could but likely would rush into the mall.

And why not? That other hoodlum almost knocked me over when I came here!

There then came from nearby the ear-shattering sound of heavy glass breaking. And then more glass breaking.

Mrs. Gladys Schnabel snapped her head to look.

"Robbers?" she whispered, not sure she believed her squinting eyes.

Working in pairs, young men in dark clothing had what looked like huge hammers, bigger than any she'd seen, and were smashing through the glass tops of display cases at opposite ends of the jewelry store. After two of the robbers cleared away the broken glass, their partners, wearing black gloves, quickly pulled jewelry and watches from the cases and stuffed it all in black sacks.

The store manager stood frozen, his hands covering his bald head.

"Grammy, get down!" Marie said, rushing up to her grand-mother.

Then one of the robbers ran out of the jewelry store. He carried one of the stuffed sacks into the main casino and was swallowed by the marauding mass.

Then a second robber followed, and he also blended into the mob, and then a third.

They heard shouting from the jewelry store, and turned in time to see the chubby, balding store manager, who must have decided he had a chance against just one man, reach for the stuffed black bag that hung from the last robber's shoulder.

As the manager yanked on the strap of the bag, the robber spun, pulled something from under his shirt, and then, off balance, pointed it in the direction of the manager's chest.

A gun! Mrs. Schnabel thought just as Marie rapidly tugged on her arm.

And then there came a series of loud shots—*Pop-Pop-Pop! Pop-Pop!*

As one of the glass mannequins shattered, Mrs. Schnabel saw the chubby bald man let loose of the bag strap. He crumpled to the marble floor as the robber, bag still on his shoulder, ran out of the mall.

She then felt Marie's grip ease and watched helplessly as her granddaughter collapsed at her feet.

And then she suddenly felt light-headed. Everything became a blur. She closed her eyes.

Samantha turned back to look at Mrs. Schnabel just as the elderly woman went limp, her knees buckling. She hit the floor first with her left shoulder, then rolled onto her chest, crushing her big round eyeglasses that had fallen from her face on impact. Her cheek came to rest on the bra and panties where a crimson pool of blood from her granddaughter had begun to form.

"Someone please help!" Samantha cried, kneeling beside them and starting to tremble.

Her plea was lost in the screams of patrons running out the emergency exit doors and in the blaring of alarms.

Samantha looked out through the glass walls and saw that the mass of teenagers in the flash mob, no longer laughing, were racing back through the casino, then out the doors.

Samantha then saw, closer to the mall, a middle-aged woman forcing her way past the fleeing mob. The woman ran into the mall, then into the store, then looked in Samantha's direction.

"Oh my God!" she wailed. "Mama! Marie! Oh my God!"

On the third floor of the casino, Tyrone Hooks was seated at one of the cocktail bars. He had ordered a beer, put his cell phone on the bar—he saw that the ROCKIN215 instant messages numbered more than two hundred—then swiped his Lucky Stars Rewards debit card in the video game machine embedded in the bar and began playing poker.

After a moment, the bartender slid a glass of draft before him and said, "Let me know if I can get you anything else, Mr. King."

Hooks again pulled the cash wad from his coat pocket and took from it his Lucky Stars debit card. He pushed the card across the bar.

"Close me out. Gotta go after this one."

III

[ONE]
Police Administration Building
Eighth and Race Streets
Saturday, December 15, 2:01 P.M.

Homicide Sergeant Matthew M. Payne, standing with a cell phone to his ear, listened to Homicide Detective Dick McCrory's update while looking out from the third-floor hallway windows of police headquarters.

The half-century-old complex, commonly referred to as the Roundhouse, was built of precast concrete and consisted of a connected pair of four-story circular buildings. Interior walls were also curved, including those of the elevators. The imposing design of the exterior, some said, resembled a massive pair of handcuffs.

Payne raised to his lips a coffee mug that had STOLEN FROM THE DESK OF HOMICIDE SGT M. M. PAYNE in gold lettering, and took a sip. He had had the cheap mugs custom-imprinted—there was a representation of his badge in addition to the wording—after his regular heavy china mugs had repeatedly wound up in the possession of parties unknown.

He had expected that the personalized ones would bring the disappearances to an end. They had had, in fact, the opposite effect—the one he now held was the last of the original dozen—

the unique mugs having become trophies of a sort around head-quarters.

There was a faint chanting coming from below, and he looked down.

At least fifty protesters marched up and down the steps past the mottled bronze statue—"A Friend," its plaque read—of a uniformed Philadelphia policeman holding a small child on his left hip in front of the Roundhouse.

Two uniformed officers of the Mounted Patrol Unit were across Race Street, standing by in support of the half-dozen uniforms of the Civil Affairs Unit who were on foot and creating a safety zone for the protesters, in effect defending their First Amendment rights of assembly and freedom of speech.

Payne watched as a young woman with a little girl—the latter licking a candy cane; they had just left Franklin Park—walked up to the officers on horseback. The woman then spoke to the closer of the two, and after he smiled and nodded, she lifted the toddler onto her shoulders so the girl could pet the horse's rich brown mane. The young woman then held out her camera and snapped a photograph of them, with the smiling officer looming in the background.

"Dick, you're right," Payne said into the phone, "if you don't try, you don't get. Maybe we'll get lucky if the CI is really onto something. Go find this guy he says wants to talk and bring him in. Lord knows no one else is talking about who took out Dante."

He paused, listened, then said, "Okay, and have Kennedy do his dramatic routine when you're slapping on cuffs, so all those watching from wherever they're hiding don't miss it."

He listened again a moment, chuckled and replied, "Yeah, right.

Nice try. If all else fails, I am not going to 'just shoot the knuckle-head,' as much as he might deserve it," then broke off the call.

The use of confidential informants was strictly regulated by Police Department Directive 15. First and foremost among its rules was that there had to exist an absolute professional relationship between an officer and a CI.

The CIs were paid for tips that, it was hoped, led to arrests. Money was also made available to them for street purchases of, for example, drugs and firearms—and even of, say, the renting of a row house needed for an undercover operation. Because these funds over time could run into the tens of thousands of dollars, procedures had to be followed to ensure that the police officers kept a distinct arm's length from the informants.

There's more than the usual BS going on with this, Payne thought, taking another sip of coffee.

Why wouldn't McCrory's CI just tell them what the other guy knew about the drive-by?

And why does this guy say he needs to see me?

He slipped the phone into his pants pocket. His Colt Officer's Model .45 ACP, snapped into a black leather shoulder holster, hung under his left bicep, and his shield—Badge Number 471, which had been his father's—was midway down his striped neck-tie, hanging in its black leather holder from a chromed bead chain looped around the button-down collar of his stiffly starched white shirt.

The Colt did not technically meet Philadelphia Police Depart-ment regulations. When Payne had begun carrying the semiauto-matic, during a stint with Special Operations, .38 caliber revolvers were still the department-issued sidearm. Payne disliked wheel guns in general and .38s in particular. He argued that the smaller caliber did not have the stopping power of a .45 bullet and that the Officer's Model carried more of the powerful rounds and could be reloaded more quickly.

Because of the nature of Special Operations cases—especially its undercover work; Payne made the point that the blued steel .38 caliber revolver screamed "Cop!"—the department had made an allowance for him.

After Payne left SO, if anyone asked about the .45, he waved the allowance at them, arguing that his Colt had been grandfathered. That particularly annoyed those who—wrongly—believed it was another case of his connections getting him preferential treatment.

But what really annoyed them even more was that Payne had then appeared vindicated in his assessment of the underpowered .38 when the department was given approval by the city council to issue Glock 9-millimeter semiautomatics as the standard sidearm. Officers who passed muster on the department's shooting range with a .40 caliber Glock were given the option of carrying one—if the officers paid for the optional weapon with their own funds.

The magazines of the Glocks held three times as many rounds as the revolvers they replaced, and put the police officers on more or less equal footing with the bad guys, who (a) were not subject to the whims of the city hall politicians who had been against replacing the .38s and thus (b) had long been packing the more powerful semiautos.

Once again Payne had bent the rules to his needs—and once again had not only gotten away with it, but proved that he thought ahead of the conventional curve.

Payne wasn't sure which pissed off his detractors more. But

he really didn't give a damn. He was right. And he knew it. And he wasn't going to risk his life because of some outdated bureaucratic rule.

The CI said that his guy likes that "Wyatt Earp shoots dudes"? Payne thought. *That it gives me "street cred"?*

He shook his head.

My bet: the bastard's blowing smoke.

But it's a lead. Maybe another to nowhere. But for now a lead.

Be wary of wrestling with a pig, Matty ol' boy. You can get very dirty—and the pig likes it.

It was Payne's opinion that confidential informants were a pain in the ass and, with rare exceptions, tended to be more trouble than they were worth.

But, reluctantly, he also considered them a necessary evil.

They knew the streets and they knew what the players were up to . . . and sometimes they even told the damn truth. Not the whole truth and nothing but the truth so help them God. The bastards were dirty themselves—the threat of doing time often was the leverage used to get them to act as CIs—and always working an angle, one beyond getting cash payments and other considerations.

Payne knew that some off-the-books information was better than nothing. Because nothing was all that most witnesses wanted to give cops. Getting them to answer any questions—truthfully or not—was next to impossible.

The reason for that wasn't just that the citizens didn't have enough faith in the police; it was more that if they talked to cops they feared retaliation from the neighborhood thugs. They knew there really was no way that the cops could protect them from that, and thus it was safer just to keep their mouths shut and not risk being accused of dropping a dime on anyone.

Unfortunately, they really don't trust cops.

And the reality is the best we can do is deter crime. Because, unless we somehow develop some lead, nabbing a bad guy before he actually commits a crime is practically impossible.

We nab him before he does his next one.

Or next ones, plural.

If we nab him and if the charges stick . . . CIs or not.

The faint chanting from the sidewalk directly below seemed to be getting louder. He took a sip of coffee as he looked down again.

The chants sounded like "Stop Killadelphia! No more murder, no more pain!" And if one were to only hear their chanting, it made perfect sense to believe that that indeed was their message.

The message, however, took on a distinctly different tone when one saw some of the dozen signs that the protesters pumped over their heads. While there were posters painted STOP KILLADELPHIA!, others read NO MORE MURDER! NO MORE PAYNE! and had, so that their message was made unequivocally clear, the enlarged image of Homicide Sergeant Matthew Payne standing over the dead robber.

Payne drained his coffee cup.

Not exactly fine poetry, he thought, disgusted, *but it does get your point across.*

Worthless point that it is.

I could disappear right now, and the murders would continue.

Just as they have forever.

So screw you!

He looked up and out, to north of the Roundhouse. Directly

across Race Street, he could see most of Franklin Park and, a mile or so beyond it and the Vine Street Expressway, the gleaming glass five-story tower of the Lucky Stars casino on the bank of the Delaware River.

Three innocent people killed, and a fourth who may not make it.

All in just a few hours.

And all in high-profile places that everyone expects to be safe.

He looked back to Franklin Park. He could easily make out the long lines outside the white tent that was the North Pole. And nearby, just north of the fountain at the center of the park, he saw the links of green plastic turf that made up the miniature golf course. A small section of it was marked off with yellow police tape, beside which two Philly PD squad cars were parked, light bars and wig-wags flashing, on either side of a Crime Scene Unit van.

Payne was a little surprised at the vast number of people—couples holding hands, families pushing strollers, the green-costumed elves passing out candy—who remained at the park. It was a heavy crowd, one that he knew was keeping the dozen or so plainclothes officers circulating among them, busy looking to see if the suspect returned to the scene—or if anyone else looked intent on committing a crime.

Payne then decided that the crowd remained strong because the part of the miniature golf course with all the ongoing crime scene activity was not visible from the rest of the park.

Out of sight, out of mind.

And surely no one's running around ruining everyone's day by dwelling on what happened.

The show must go on!

But that quickly could change when news of the murders spreads . . .

Payne felt a presence behind him—an enormous one—and then heard the familiar deep mellifluous voice.

"Were this not a situation to take very seriously, Matthew, I would say that congratulations are in order."

Payne turned as Lieutenant Jason Washington stepped beside him and glanced down at the protesters. The superbly tailored forty-three-year-old was very big—six-foot-three, two-twenty-five—and very black. He also was very well respected, considered to be one of the top homicide detectives up and down the East Coast. He took no offense to those—including Payne—who referred to him as the Black Buddha.

"A Buddha is an enlightened individual who is indeed venerated," Washington said, "and there certainly is no denying this skin tone."

In the chain of command, Payne, who months earlier had been promoted to the rank of sergeant and then became a supervisor in Homicide, reported to Washington, one of a handful of Homicide lieutenants who answered to the unit's commander, Captain Henry Quaire, a stocky balding forty-four-year-old. Quaire was under Chief Inspector of Detectives Matthew Lowenstein—a barrel-chested fifty-five-year-old with a quick temper and a reputation for strictly going by the book—whose boss was First Deputy Police Commissioner Dennis Coughlin.

Personally, however, Payne had another connection with Coughlin, a closer one that went back more than twenty-seven years—to months before Payne had been born.

Denny Coughlin had been the one to break the news to Matt's pregnant mother that Sergeant John F.X. Moffitt—her husband and Coughlin's best friend since they were rookie cops right out of the academy—had been shot dead trying to stop a robber. Cough-lin subsequently became Matty's godfather, and Payne was known to address him, when appropriate, as "Uncle Denny."

"Congratulations?" Payne said. "For what, Jason?"

Washington made a sweeping motion with his huge hand to-ward the protesters.

"It would appear that you are the poster boy—quite literally—of all that is wrong with our beloved city."

Payne grunted. "Hell, you know that game," he said. "Some-one's got to be the scapegoat. No sense wasting time actually trying to fix the real social issues that contribute to bad guys committing crime. Just complain about cops until another crisis makes head-lines. Rinse and repeat."

"As I just inferred, you being personally targeted is not to be taken lightly, Matthew. Denny Coughlin said that Mayor Car-lucci declared that when any member of the department is tar-geted, the entire department is considered targeted, and he won't stand for it."

"I can't speak for the entire department, but I know I'm getting love notes from my usual fans," Payne said as he pulled out his cel-lular telephone, tapped its screen, then held it up for Washington to read. "This is the 'Stop Killadelphia' conversation on Philly-NewsNow-dot-com."

"'Fire and jail the killer cop Payne,'" Washington read aloud.

"Now look at the one that follows it, from the person calling himself Justice of the Piece. The one using the picture of a revolver as their avatar."

Washington read: "'Forget firing him! Fire at him! Cap the cop! If we're dying, Payne's dying.'"

"Not my first death threat," Payne said, "but at least it's one that's a little more clever than the others."

Washington read farther down, then looked from the phone to Payne.

"I would hesitate using the word *clever*, Matthew, but I will grant that it rises above the crudeness of these other illiterate messages. Regardless, they all anger me."

Payne shrugged. "You know that people get brave online when they can hide behind their keyboard, Jason."

"True. Let's just hope that's all it is, nothing more than tough rhetoric fueled by Reverend Cross," Washington said. "Denny also said he was impressed with your remarkable restraint when Cross attempted to ambush you during the television interview at the LOVE Park scene."

Payne's mind flashed back to the moment he caught a glimpse of the tall, skinny, bearded forty-year-old African-American in his black cloak and white clerical collar, approaching the camera crew.

"Fortunately," Payne said, "I saw him coming out of the corner of my eye and figured what he probably was up to."

"The posters being your first clue?" Washington said drily.

Payne grinned.

"I admit I can be more than a bit slow, Jason, but I eventually figure things out."

Washington chuckled.

"I damn sure didn't want a confrontation," Payne went on, "at least not one caught on camera. I leaned in close to the microphone so I'd be heard over the chanting, and said, 'Excuse me. I have a job to do. And I would suggest that someone trying to create a cause célèbre on the spot where a young woman has just been brutally murdered is disrespectful at best, and damned disgusting at worst.'"

Washington raised an eyebrow.

"That sound bite should make headlines," he said. "Especially when they edit out all but the last part, and begin with '. . . I would suggest.' Between the two of us, good for you. But I caution you to be careful. As you know, he was just elevated to chairman of CPOC."

"So?"

"So you well could be the trophy he wants to make a name for himself."

Pronounced *See-Pock*, the acronym stood for Citizens Police Oversight Committee. The five people on the self-governed entity were appointed to staggered terms by each of the city council members serving on the council's Committee for Public Safety. Current members were a female African-American pro bono publico criminal defense lawyer, a white Roman Catholic bishop, a Temple University professor of sociology who was a female of Puerto Rican heritage, a male civil engineer whose parents had emigrated to Philly from India, and its longest-serving appointee, whose five-year term would expire within the next ten months, the Reverend Josiah Cross.

CPOC had come into existence a quarter-century earlier, in the aftermath of the city's race riots. The then mayor had thrown it out as a bone, hoping to appease, if not silence, community activists. They complained that the police department's Internal Affairs Unit was nothing more than the cops policing themselves—read:

paying lip service to allegations of misconduct, and doing next to nothing about said misconduct—and demanded an independent board.

Over the years, the members of CPOC, charged with only a mandate of reviewing and advising the mayor and city council on matters pertaining to police department policy, rarely accomplished anything beyond creating self-serving headlines. Which many observers said wasn't exactly a surprise, as it was very much in line with the accomplishments of the city council members themselves, ones who (a) knew they were appointing them to a position that in essence was political patronage, and who (b) quietly expected a portion of the CPOC member's annual $80,000 salary to find its way into the patron's reelection war chest.

"I appreciate what you're saying, Jason," Payne said. "He's a grandstanding troublemaker. And I'm not going to let anyone from CPOC bother me. Every damn member comes with some ax to grind. Starting with that fraud who says he 'found' religion in the slam."

Washington chuckled deeply.

"Discretion being the better part of valor, Matthew, I probably should not tell you this, but I heard that the new head of the city's public relations department—"

"That tiny guy who's working for Ed Stein? Whatshisname? Finley?"

Washington nodded. "That's right, I forgot you met him shortly after Ed was tapped as the mayor's new adviser and brought him for a tour here. James Finley. As I was saying, I shouldn't tell you that Finley was said to have, at least at first, appeared quite excited by the tension of the moment. But then he announced to the mayor that he was terribly afraid you actually were about to shoot Cross right there on live television."

Payne grinned.

"The thought crossed my mind. He deserved it for any number of reasons. But then I realized there's probably a line of people ahead of me really wanting to whack Skinny Lenny, beginning with his old drug-running pal he ripped off."

Washington knew the story. The grittier details had been circulated by Cross's detractors shortly after his appointment to CPOC.

[TWO]

A decade earlier—listed in police records as "MUGGS, Leonard Robert, Also Known As 'Skinny Lenny'"—the Reverend Josiah Cross had completed a year and a day in the slam. His offenses included assault and forgery of a financial instrument—while hopped up on crack cocaine, he'd beaten an elderly neighbor with a baseball bat, then cashed the old man's welfare check. Cross had, as he put it, "suffered an unfortunate incarceration for a simple misunderstanding at a difficult point in life, and I've paid my dues for it," then returned to society penniless but on a mission and with a new identity.

Having arranged for a money order in the amount of thirty-five dollars to be sent to Utopian World Ministries of Cleveland,

Ohio, he had received at the jail by return mail a certificate, suitable for framing, signifying that Leonard R. Muggs was licensed as an ordained minister of the Utopian World Order.

Certificate in hand, he headed straight back to the old rundown neighborhood where his mother still lived—the area known as Strawberry Mansion for its most prominent residence, though the place no longer was a shining landmark—and slept on the threadbare couch in her row house when he wasn't out looking up his old contacts.

Within days he had convinced, if not coerced, one Smitty Jones—the not very bright but very tightly wound thirty-year-old who was his onetime street-corner business partner—to front him a kilogram of marijuana on credit.

Cross moved the product, and with that cash then rented, for next to nothing, an empty building in the neighborhood that most recently had been City Best Chinese Eggroll for three years, before the owners tired of the regular robberies and fled.

The edifice had a mock pagoda facade, with a distinctive red-tiled roofline that curled out and upward, and a faded crimson red front door, on which he had painted in gold WORD OF BROTHERLY LOVE MINISTRY, REV. J. CROSS PASTOR and, above that, a big crucifix.

When Smitty showed up at the door and said that he wanted payment for the dope, Josiah announced that it had been "the work of a higher power" for the money to go to the new church. Josiah suggested that it might be possible Smitty would be repaid somewhat later, but then again he could make no promises.

"I have been redeemed," Cross explained, somewhat piously, "and am now a man of the cloth. It's out of my hands, brother."

Smitty wasn't buying it.

"That's bullshit, bro! I'm gonna snuff your sorry skinny ass out if I don't get my money back now!"

But about the time he finished making that threat he was staring at the black muzzle of the Reverend Josiah Cross's Beretta Cheetah .380 caliber semiautomatic, which Cross had instantly produced from somewhere beneath his black robe.

Smitty didn't think the tiny pistol could do much damage—he knew guys got hit all the time with a 9, which was bigger than a .380 and what most everyone else packed, and even those bigger bullets just went right through them and the ER doctors stitched them up and sent them home the same night—but he figured Skinny Lenny just might get lucky and hit some important part on him.

Wordlessly, hands above his head, Smitty slowly walked backward to the faded crimson front door.

Five years later—with a growing congregation that had come to include, after he put them on the church payroll as deacons, both Smitty Jones and the elderly man who "miraculously" had forgiven the old Skinny Lenny for assaulting and robbing him—Cross had preached himself into a position in the community that, courtesy of City Councilman (At Large) H. Rapp Badde Jr., was considered worthy of an appointment to the CPOC.

Matt Payne looked at Jason Washington and said, "It's no wonder that Badde bought his old neighborhood buddy. They're cut from the same corrupt cloth. I won't go into Badde's—the list is too long—but the quote Reverend unquote Cross's hypocritical behavior is nothing short of an outrage. As you well know, there are honest to God nuns and monks and others serving in those hard-hit neighborhoods. They're the real deal, actually doing God's work. They're not making a mockery of it all for personal gain like Cross, starting with his shilling for Badde from the pulpit and essentially turning that bogus church into a campaign office."

"You are aware that Cross got on camera after your interview . . ."

"Yeah, I saw him as I was leaving."

". . . and when the reporter asked if he felt what he was doing in a place where a young woman had just been murdered was 'disrespectful' or 'disgusting,' he dodged the query by stating instead that he felt that three hundred and sixty-two murders was 'disgusting' and that 'a trigger-happy cop contributing to the bloodshed of citizens in the city was despicable.'"

Payne grunted. "I guess he'd rather have those murderers still running the streets."

"It is anyone's guess what his genuine motives are . . ."

"Beyond personal gain, you mean," Payne put in.

". . . but he then announced that he would be leading a protest rally at his church this afternoon at five. The interview was then drowned out with the chants of 'No more murder, no more Payne.'"

"Five o'clock?" Payne said, then touched the glass face of his cell phone.

From its speakerphone, a sultry, surprisingly real-sounding female voice practically purred, *"What can I do for you, Marshal?"*

Payne saw Washington's eyebrows go up, and that he shook his head and grinned.

Payne spoke into the phone: "New calendar entry with alarm: Protest today seventeen hundred hours."

"Protest December fifteenth at five P.M.," the sexy, artificially generated voice confirmed. *"Calendar alarm set thirty minutes prior."*

"Thank you," Payne said, looking up at Washington.

"My pleasure, Marshal."

"If I did not know better, Matthew . . ."

"What?" Payne said mock-innocently. "Technology is our friend." He looked at the phone a second, then added, "But I should probably change that voice before Amanda hears it. The mechanical robot tone that reads the NOAA weather radio alerts might be safer." He then mimicked the disjointed droning computer-generated voice: "To-day's. Wea-ther. Fore-cast . . ."

Washington chuckled. "On that side note, how is your bride-to-be?"

Payne raised an eyebrow.

"She called, said she wasn't exactly thrilled to see me on TV being called Public Enemy Number One. She would be down there marching and chanting with a sign, too, if she thought it would hasten my finding other work."

Dr. Amanda Law—whose father, Charlie Law, was friends with Washington, dating back to their time together in Northeast Detectives—had made it clear she was not thrilled with the prospect of spending every day, as she had while growing up, wondering if someone she loved would leave in the morning—and not come home alive. That her father took retirement only after taking a bullet to the knee served to strengthen her resolve.

"It's certainly a reasonable fear," Washington said, "one my bride, who in decades hasn't gotten over it, is at least less vocal about after all these years."

He paused, then added, "But . . . I still see it in her eyes. Special indeed are the strong ladies who tolerate the toll this occupation takes on their relationships."

Payne nodded thoughtfully.

"What I meant a moment ago," Washington went on, "was, and apropos of that side note: If I didn't know better, I would take it that you intend on attending Cross's rally. That does not seem to be a wise idea for 'Public Enemy Number One.'"

Payne shrugged. "I'll have to think about it. Tell me no, and I won't go. We'll certainly have enough eyes in the crowd—"

Just then his phone vibrated, and he glanced at its screen. Then he looked back at Washington.

"Okay, that's a heads-up that the casino security camera imagery is finally all in the war room. Will be ready to review in ten. Want to take a look?"

Washington glanced at his wristwatch. "If I can squeeze it in. Speaking of Finley, you are aware that he visibly cringed during his tour of the Roundhouse when he heard you call the Executive Command Center the 'war room.'"

The ECC, the department's enormous and enormously expensive nerve center, was outfitted with highly secure communications equipment able to link up local, state, federal, and international law enforcement agencies, as well as integrate satellite, Internet, radio, television, and citywide fixed and mobile surveillance cameras. It was next to the police commissioner's office, down the hall from where they now stood.

Payne, his face showing he was unrepentant, shrugged, then added, "Tony's still working the scene at the casino."

"Tony" was Detective Anthony Harris, a slight, wiry, starting-to-bald thirty-six-year-old. He had fifteen years on the job, and longer in Homicide than Payne's entire four years on the force. On the surface, it would reasonably follow that Harris would harbor a bitter resentment that someone younger and far less experienced— it was no secret that plenty among the rank and file complained that Payne was "a rich kid with connections playing cop"—could be his immediate superior, as well as over other veteran Homicide detectives.

But that simply wasn't the case. Harris had worked with Payne before the promotion. He appreciated that, while Payne may have earned the position by making the top score on the sergeant's exam, he really had earned Harris's respect with his intellect and his genuine willingness to learn from those with more time on the job.

"Tony was on the Wheel?" Washington said. "It was my understanding that he finally had a weekend off."

Payne nodded. "I think he has set a new department record for overtime. For once, he did plan to take the weekend off. But you know him. When he heard Charley Ogden had it, and what the case entailed, he volunteered to take it off Ogden's hands."

The Wheel wasn't actually a wheel, but a roster of Homicide Unit detectives on duty. Whichever detective was at the top of the roster had the job to "man the desk," which included answering incoming calls. When a job came in, the detective at the top of the Wheel took the case. Then he tapped the detective who was "next up on the Wheel"—the next name on the roster—and he or she then came to man the desk.

With as many homicides as the city suffered, the system did not spare anyone from juggling multiple cases, both new ones and older unsolved cases, including decade-old cold cases. But it came close to taking what otherwise would be an overwhelming work-load and distributing it in a more or less equitable manner.

Payne went on: "It's not like we don't have enough cases to go around. Ogden already was working two recent ones on top of his others. And I've got McCrory out with Kennedy on yesterday's drive-by shooting in Kensington that killed the twenty-year-old Dante Holmes. Hank Nasuti has the LOVE Park murder of Lauren Childs. Lucke is running the Jimmy Sanchez job." He paused when Washington shook his head slightly, then said, "The murdered fifteen-year-old elf?"—Washington nodded, and then he went on—"And of course Tony owns the casino case, with the jewelry store manager, Malcolm Cairns, dead at the scene, and the victim who's looking like she may not survive, Marie Cottrell."

"The Northern Liberties young lady, not the grandmother?"

"Right. She's twenty-six, and recently moved to NoLibs. The grandmother, apparently after seeing her go down, fainted. While paramedics transported the granddaughter to the ER at Hahnemann, an EMT treated the grandmother at the scene for a cut from flying glass. Her fainting was attributed to medication she's taking"—he paused, then, with genuine disgust in his voice, added—"coupled no doubt with watching her granddaughter damn near dying at her feet. Happy holidays, huh . . . ?"

Washington looked at him a long moment, nodded slightly, then said: "About Lauren Childs. One of the things I wanted to tell you was I just got off the telephone with Dr. Mitchell. We were discussing another case, and he brought up her name."

Howard Mitchell, M.D., a balding, rumpled fifty-year-old, usually found in a well-worn two-piece suit, had served nearly a decade as the Philadelphia medical examiner.

"Yeah? We've already got autopsy results? I hadn't heard."

"Unofficial and incomplete results. He has not finished the autopsy on her. But she and the Sanchez boy came in at almost the same time. Dr. Mitchell, no surprise, stated that the cause of the boy's death was obvious. But he said he was curious about hers, and made time for a preliminary look. He went in and examined the damage and said it was clear why she bled out so quickly."

"Hit an artery?"

"That and worse. The knife was thrust in just beneath the rib cage"—he poked his finger upward at the bottom edge of the pocket on his shirt—"the sharp blade nicking the left lung before piercing the apex of the heart and then cutting the aorta. Dr. Mitchell said the doer twisted the blade so violently that it went through the walls of the heart, practically slicing it in two."

Payne grunted. "Thus explaining why she just instantly collapsed. And the great deal of blood. Jesus."

"It happened quickly. Similar to when you get a deep cut and don't immediately feel pain, which explains why she did not scream. He said that it had to have been a thin, long-bladed, almost surgically sharp instrument, one at least six inches in length."

"Like one used for cleaning fish?"

Washington nodded. "A fillet knife was the example he gave."

Payne took a sip of coffee.

After a moment he said, "And a fillet knife"—he drew his left pointer finger across his throat—"would do a damn effective job."

"Or similar tool."

Payne looked at him and thought, *Translation of which is: a gentle reminder not to lock on one possibility.*

He said, "Understood."

"But it is an angle to work until a better one presents itself. Keep turning over the stone under the stone."

Payne nodded, then looked out the windows.

"Certainly not at a loss for fish markets where he could work. Off the top of my head there's Golden and John Yi's in Reading Terminal Market, Darigo's in the Italian Market, there's an Asian one"—he pointed across the expressway—"right there on Spring Garden, which is in line with the direction the kidnapper was taking the little girl. And of course there's Fishtown, but that's more or less a misnomer these days. I'm not sure you could find a single shad for sale there, let alone a fully stocked fish market."

"There is also the distinct possibility that the doer simply could be an avid angler."

"Yeah, and/or just one sick sonofabitch," Payne said, then looked at Washington and added, "I wonder how he carried a long blade like that without anyone seeing it?"

"Perhaps in a sheath of some design up his sleeve?" Washington said, then demonstrated by putting his right fist to the cuff of his left sleeve and pulling out an imaginary blade. "Or in the upper of a boot."

Payne slowly nodded in thought.

"Possible, I suppose," he said, "if more than a little impractical. Could've just held it with the blade hidden by his arm close to his body."

"Would be more easily used that way," Washington said, paused, then added: "Anything more—anything at all—on identifying the doer in the Childs case?"

Payne shook his head.

"Only what little we had before. That the boyfriend, Tony

Gambacorta—who Nasuti just interviewed at length—never saw him, only felt the strong hit as they passed in the crowd, and decided he had to be a big guy, and that the guy called him an asshole when they hit. It all happened so fast, though, no one really knew that she'd been stabbed—as you said, she didn't scream—only that she'd collapsed and began bleeding heavily. Everyone was looking at her. By the time they figured out that she'd probably been stabbed, the doer was gone, and any solid witnesses—if there in fact were any at all who'd seen him and/or had a clue what just happened—had dispersed."

"And still no video from park surveillance cameras?"

"None capturing images near that exact spot. And the ones farther out aren't giving us anything useful."

Washington, nodding, looked at him in deep thought.

"There is imagery from Franklin Park," Payne went on, "and Melanie Baker, the mother of the little girl who was grabbed, gave a solid description of the doer, including the tattoo on his neck." He paused, tapped on the screen of his phone, then held it up to show Washington. "Here's the clearest shot we have of him. This and another were just minutes ago sent out in a Wanted flyer. Because both victims were killed with sharp blades and so close together in time and location, it has to be the same doer. Doc Mitchell should be able to find evidence that links the wounds to the same weapon."

"A weapon that, for all we know, could well be in the muck at the bottom of the Delaware River by now," Washington said, turning to the phone.

He studied the image. It showed the large man walking alone among the holiday crowd. He was heavyset, with a puffy round light brown face framed by a ragged mop of dreadlocks that drooped down to his shoulders.

"His eyes are empty, just dark holes staring out," Washington said. "Vacuous and cold, devoid of life. Even as he's about to commit a heinous act."

"These thugs have no respect for life. No way it's his first murder."

Payne then flipped to the other image, a barely in focus close-up of the suspect's face and neck framed by the sweatshirt hood.

"Check out those tats," Payne said. "The picture's not sharp but you can see that he inked an inverted heart on his cheek under his left eye, and an inverted peace symbol under his right eye, and 'Family' written in gothic lettering across the front of his neck, which Melanie Baker didn't miss seeing."

"An upside-down heart?"

Payne nodded. "A bright red one, about the size of a cherry, outlined in black."

Washington thought about that, then said, "The peace symbol is meant to be a dove's claw within a circle, so when inverted it stands for death. And the inverted heart stands for hate or for no love."

"And that 'Family' inked across his throat. A gangbanger embracing his fellow thugs as family. Touching, huh?" He tapped his chest. "Warms the ol' heart . . . or cuts it like a knife."

"Someone will recognize this miscreant, especially those body markings."

Payne raised his eyebrows. "Yeah, but as we know, the trick will be getting that someone to admit recognizing him."

He then turned to the window and pointed to Franklin Park.

"We were able to follow his tracks back to where he entered the park there at Race, and using images from our surveillance cameras outside the Roundhouse, we know he came this way down Race. Now we've got guys going store to store looking for more camera footage and possible witnesses that could help us backtrack his path. Maybe—hell, forget maybe, my gut says doubtless—all the way back to LOVE Park."

Washington nodded, then held up his index finger in a *Hold one* gesture. He reached inside his suit jacket and produced a vibrating cell phone with its screen glowing. He checked the caller ID and then answered the phone: "Jason Washington . . ." then, glancing at Payne, said, "Yes, sir, he's aware of the death threats," and after a moment added, "Will do. Okay, on my way."

Washington looked at Payne as he broke off the call.

"That was our boss, as I anticipated, so I'll have to pass on seeing the casino images for now. And I'm to tell you: 'Captain Quaire says not to let down your guard—take the death threats seriously.' That comes from me, too."

Payne met his eyes. "Got it."

Washington's big hand squeezed Payne's shoulder.

"Be careful. And let me know if anything interesting comes up, Matthew."

Payne glanced down at the protesters. "Like if I get whacked?"

Washington saw that he was smirking.

"I said interesting. Not expected."

[THREE]
Office of the Chief Executive Adviser to the Mayor
City Hall, 1 Penn Square, Philadelphia
Saturday, December 15, 2:06 P.M.

"Ed, we have to shut this Cross down now," James Finley said. "It's not just that it's the bad news of the murders. What he's doing—and I hate to agree with Carlucci because, if he heard me, it would encourage him to go on TV, which itself would be a PR disaster—is possibly, if not probably, incendiary."

Finley and Ed Stein had just left the mayor's office next door, Finley having taken care to shut the door between the offices before walking over to Stein and beginning to make his points.

Stein stood behind his large antique desk, tossing his legal pad on it and then pulling up the screen of his notebook computer and typing in his password.

"This day is off the charts," Finley went on. "Now we have another shooting at the casino? It's one thing to have to deal with those numbers. But Cross can very easily push this thing over the edge by equating cop shootings with actual criminal acts. It's all about perception."

"I understand. And agree."

Stein's eyes fell back to the computer screen. He typed some more, then said, "Here it is," then picked up the receiver of the desk telephone and punched in a phone number.

He impatiently rocked his head back and forth while listening to the rings, then stopped and in an officious tone said into the phone, "Yes, this is Edward Stein at City Hall. I'm the assistant to Mayor Carlucci. It is urgent that I speak with Reverend Cross."

He listened for a moment as he met Finley's eyes.

"That's correct," Stein went on. "Mayor Carlucci has asked me to reach out to Reverend Cross and— What's that?"

Finley mouthed, *What?*

"He's unavailable?" Stein said.

Finley mouthed, *Bullshit!*

Stein said, "Can you . . . I'm sorry. I did not get your name"— he listened for a very long moment—"okay, Deacon DiAndre Pringle of the Word of Brotherly Love Ministry, as I said, my name is Edward Stein and I'm calling on behalf of Mayor of Philadelphia Jerome Carlucci. Can you get me to Reverend Cross's assistant? . . . Oh, you are his assistant. I see. Deacon Pringle, would it be possible to get the reverend's mobile number? . . . I'm sorry. Did I hear you say he doesn't have one?"

Finley made a sour face and shook his head.

Judging by Stein's expression, he was having difficulty not losing his patience.

"Yes," he then said slowly, almost condescendingly, into the receiver, "I am aware of the rally planned at your 'house of worship.' That is one of the reasons Reverend Cross and I must speak as soon as possible." He glanced at his wristwatch. "Within the next hour . . . yes, you do that, please. This is urgent."

Stein held his arm out stiffly and started to slam the receiver into its base. Finley put his hand down to intercept it.

Stein then gently replaced the receiver and looked at Finley.

"Now what?" Finley said.

Stein reached across the desk and picked up a remote control. He aimed it at the television on the wall, thumbed the power and mute buttons, and a moment later *Philly News Now* came on-screen. It showed a dozen police vehicles parked with emergency lights flashing at the entrance to the Lucky Stars Casino. After a moment, the text in the ticker box across the bottom of the screen read . . . A NORTHERN LIBERTIES WOMAN, 26, SHOT WHILE CELE-BRATING HER GRANDMOTHER'S BIRTHDAY, REMAINS IN CRITICAL CONDITION FOLLOWING A CASINO JEWELRY STORE ROBBERY THAT LEFT THE STORE MANAGER, 45, DEAD FROM GUNSHOTS . . .

"Oh my God!" Finley said, glancing at Stein, then looking back at the television. "I can just see the headlines! 'Granddaughter Blown Away While Grandma Blows Out Birthday Candles.'"

The ticker then read . . . REV. CROSS, CHAIRMAN OF THE CITIZENS POLICE OVERSIGHT COMMITTEE, SAID THAT COUNCILMAN BADDE AND OTHER LEADERS WILL JOIN HIM TO ADDRESS ALL OF TODAY'S MURDERS AT 5 P.M. DURING A RALLY AT WORD OF BROTHERLY LOVE COMMUNITY CENTER IN STRAWBERRY MANSION . . .

"Surely Badde did not agree to that," Finley said.

"Whether he did or not, it puts him in an awkward position. If he does appear, it could look like he's calling cops killers. If he doesn't, he's turning his back on his base and the crime they're suffering."

Stein's eyebrows then shot up, and he quickly turned to his notebook computer, his fingers flying across its keyboard.

"That's it!" he blurted a minute later, glancing up from the computer screen to Finley. "Why am I not surprised?"

"What's it? What're you looking at?"

"The City Hall website page on CPOC members. Badde

'proudly appointed' the bastard to CPOC. I figured there had to be a connection."

"And . . . ?"

"And what thy crooked pol hath given the reverend, thy crooked pol can taketh away. Or at least convince him to stop calling cops killers."

Finley gestured *Continue* with his hand.

"The members of the city council's Public Safety Committee," Stein explained, "each get to appoint someone to a term on CPOC. The job pays eighty grand a year."

"What! *Eighty thousand dollars?* For doing nothing? No wonder this city is about to be broke! What was it that the great Iron Lady said? 'Patronage would seem all well and good—until you run out of someone else's money.' This is depressing. Beyond all else, you and I have to fight this culture of corruption, too? Try putting a happy face on that!"

Ed Stein grinned. He liked Finley, and especially admired his solid, fiscally responsible viewpoints. The fact that Finley voiced them was hardly surprising—Finley after all was a Master of Business Administration graduate of Penn's prestigious Wharton School—but what usually caught people off-guard was the flamboyant manner with which he expressed them.

Stein said, "What Maggie Thatcher said was: 'The problem with *socialism* is that eventually you run out of other people's money' . . ."

"Whatever. Close enough."

". . . But, yeah, agreed. Your point's painfully valid."

He looked back at his laptop.

"Damn. Cross is in his last year on CPOC. Which explains

why he's now chairman. It always goes to the member who's in their fifth year."

"You know," Finley said, "final year or not, it still would be very embarrassing to lose midterm such a prestigious position. It could adversely affect possible future income, including other patronage positions."

"Yeah, that and the eighty grand right now. The trick is first getting Badde to agree to put pressure on Cross, then for Cross to back off. If Cross doesn't, the challenge becomes getting Badde to force Cross's resignation. I don't think Badde actually has the power to relieve him."

Stein picked up the receiver, flipped through a phone directory of City Hall offices, found the number, and then started to punch it in. Then he said, "Damn it! I forgot it's Saturday!" He put the receiver down and looked at Finley. "Badde's not going to be in his office."

"I hear he's hardly ever in City Hall," Finley said as he dug his cell phone from the pocket of his bright green sweater, "no matter which day it is."

Finley tapped on its screen, then put the phone to his ear.

"Constantine? James Finley. How are you? . . . And a Merry Christmas to you! Listen, I need a fast favor. Can you please share with me our dear friend Rapp Badde's cell number?" Finley paused, then laughed loudly, and after a moment went on, "Yes, that was both terribly unintentional and possibly prescient. And, for the record, you know I don't embrace the 'dear friend' part, either. Anyway, I seem to have lost his *cell phone* number, if I ever had it."

Finley reached across the desk, grabbed a pen, flipped to a

blank page on Stein's legal pad, and then jotted "Rapp Badde cell" and a ten-digit number. Stein noted that he'd done it so swiftly and in a perfect penmanship that could only be described as elegant.

"Thank you," Finley said. "See you soon, Con."

"Con"? Stein thought.

He said, "May I ask who's Constantine?"

"Constantine Christofi," Finley said, gently tucking his phone back in his sweater pocket. "He's in your line of work—a lawyer—but in commercial property development and marketing. He's truly a dear old friend."

"How is it that he had—and you knew he had—Badde's cell . . . *cellular* number?" Stein then chuckled. "Although I wouldn't mind if it actually was a prison cell number."

"That snake in the grass is rather adept at pissing people off, isn't he? A classic example of an equal opportunity offender."

"I'm not in any way trying to excuse him," Stein said, "but he does come about it honestly, for lack of a better word. The entire city council is pretty much that way. Rapp's simply had a head start at perfecting it having learned from his father."

City Councilman (At Large) H. Rapp Badde Jr. was the thirty-two-year-old son of Horatio R. Badde Sr., a onetime South Philly barber who had also served on the city council before being elected mayor of the City of Philadelphia.

The younger Badde, who saw himself moving up in political office in a similar manner, could be at turns arrogant and charismatic. He carried on the elder's tradition of an above-reproach attitude, including the fevered application of deny-and-spin when confronted with anything that might appear unseemly.

Learning that skill at the master's feet had come in handy months earlier, when the bow-tied politician had been spotted on the tiny island of Bermuda. The fact that the usually publicity-happy Rapp Badde had been there attending a conference on—of all things in such a place—urban renewal hadn't been his biggest problem. What had set his deny-and-spin into high gear had been the photographs of him that had been leaked to the local media back home. Apparently someone had recognized Badde and snapped a series of images of him on the beach in a compromising position with his gorgeous twenty-five-year-old executive assistant.

That proved to be a bit much to swallow for even Philadelphia's tough-skinned taxpayers—not to mention Badde's wife of seven years. There was outrage. At least at first.

Like his father, Rapp Badde managed once again to deflect his detractors.

"To answer your question, Ed, I met with Constantine last week following a PEGI meeting."

Stein nodded. Finley had pronounced the acronym *Peggy*; it stood for Philadelphia Economic Gentrification Initiative.

"Aha," Stein said, "and like the Public Safety Committee, Badde also serves on the Housing and Urban Development Committee."

"Not only on it. The city council president appointed him as its chairman. HUD's PEGI is his baby—remember, that was his excuse for going with that hot young assistant of his, Janelle Harper, on a 'fact-finding mission' to the conference in Bermuda."

Stein chuckled. "Where he and said assistant were photographed rolling on the beach wearing little more than grins. Taxpayer-paid assistant, I might add. She gets a hundred and eighty grand, almost twice his council salary. And you have to give him credit for avoiding any divorce papers being served when he came back."

Finley snorted.

"Well, don't give him too much credit. Word on the street about that is the wife, Wanda, booted him out of their very nice house while she considers her options. I think she's a lawyer, too."

"Then she should know that divorce court judges in Pennsylvania," Stein said, "like those in many other states, don't want to hear the word *infidelity*—or even 'alienation of affection.'"

"Oh, really?"

"They've decided that if cheating on a spouse were the basis for finding fault and awarding assets, the courts would be clogged far worse than they are now. The judges send the warring parties to arbitration with instructions not to think about coming near the courthouse until they've reached a signed settlement."

"Huh. Well, I'm sure, like a lot of wives, she has some other dirt on him. Or can dig it up, which would fall under 'considers her options.'"

"That would be interesting."

"Yeah, as is the fact," Finley went on, "that PEGI is at least knee-deep, if not up to its neck, in the Volks Haus and Diamond Development projects."

Again Stein nodded thoughtfully. He knew that the city, which was to say the Philadelphia Economic Gentrification Initiative, had demolished multiple blocks of housing in the upper end of the Northern Liberties neighborhood. The demolition was to make way for a giant multiple sports stadium—a project of Diamond

Development—and it had forced residents from their decrepit row houses and taken ownership of the properties using the strong-armed provisions of Eminent Domain.

To temper the blow to those who were displaced—as well as to keep other of Badde's constituents happy—PEGI promised to offer low-rent housing in its new Volks Haus. The "People's House" would be built in the Fairmount area, only a few miles west of their old neighborhood.

Stein said, "Weren't there dead bodies discovered inside when the wrecking crew tore down those last row houses?"

"Yeah, maybe two, three men? They were holdouts remonstrating about being forced to leave after their landlords had to sell to PEGI. I think that they're part of this year's three hundred sixty-something total count."

"Then they were murdered?"

"If I recall correctly, the police could not find what had killed them—except maybe that twenty-ton wrecking ball that the first resident became snagged on. The deaths were ruled as suspicious."

"Strange."

Finley raised his eyebrows and nodded.

"Much like PEGI itself, Ed. Or I should say Badde. I haven't quite figured out the whole thing. Not that I really have time to do that. But something about it isn't kosher. The more I'm around that, the more uncomfortable I get. Still, I'm committed to working with Constantine on the future marketing of the Diamond Development stadium. And he's the one stuck working with Badde."

"And so he has his cell phone number."

Finley put his fingertips on the legal pad and spun it so that what he had written on it was right-side up to Stein.

"And now you do. This could well be a case of 'Be careful what you wish for, because you damn sure may get it.'"

Stein met Finley's eyes.

"Dumb question, James?"

"There are no dumb questions."

"How come you're doing this?"

"What do you mean?"

"I thought in Carlucci's office that I was about to lose you."

"That I'd quit? So quickly?"

"Yeah."

"You know me better than that."

"'In for a penny, in for a pound,' as Ben Franklin said when—"

"When quote he was our distinguished ambassador to England before the Revolution unquote," Finley finished. "At least that's what our fearless leader Francis Fuller keeps telling us."

Finley snorted again, and then in a serious tone went on: "Philly is the fifth-largest city in the United States, second on the East Coast, for which we're sometimes called New York City's sixth borough. We have one and a half million residents, yet more than twenty-five percent of them live in poverty. Our unemployment rate averages eleven percent—and in places like Kensington it spikes to fifty percent. That's got to change. Center City and a handful of neighborhoods are more or less going great. But cities rise and fall as a whole, and for Philly to truly thrive, the whole has to be healthy. As long as I'm on the job, I'll give all I've got and more for that to happen."

Stein nodded.

"My apology for misreading that."

"None necessary. I do believe what I said."

"Which part?"

"That I love this city, Ed. Correction: love the *possibility* of this city. Right now, I absolutely loathe the ugliness. But I have hope, for now at least, that we might fix that."

He pointed at his writing on the legal pad.

"Dial."

Stein grunted as he picked up the telephone receiver and began punching in the number.

"This damn well better work," he said.

[FOUR]
East Somerset and Jasper Streets, Philadelphia
Saturday, December 15, 2:15 P.M.

"We really shouldn't do this, man," Dan Moss said, staring out the car window as they drove through the area known as Kensington. "You know how many people get shot around here? I saw it on the news."

The pudgy seventeen-year-old Moss had shaggy dark hair and a round face with an angry red pimple on the bridge of his nose that looked as if it could burst at any moment. He turned in the front passenger seat of the five-year-old silver Volkswagen Jetta and looked at the driver.

Billy Chester, a wiry eighteen-year-old, had a bony face with birdlike eyes and a narrow nose, and kept his short strawberry blond hair spiked. He had met Dan Moss in a computer code writing class when they were high school freshmen.

Both now were wearing faded blue jeans and sneakers. Billy

had on a gray fleece winter jacket while Dan wore his Upper Marion Area High School sweatshirt, a navy blue hoodie with gold stenciled lettering on the chest: PROPERTY OF UMA VIKINGS ATHLETIC DEPT.

"Aw, c'mon and chill out," Billy said, his tone frustrated. "The girls said they wanted some weed. You going to tell them we couldn't score any?"

Dan couldn't believe how calm Billy was acting. The Kensington neighborhood looked like a war zone. They were a long way from the clean streets and tidy lawns of their homes in the suburb of King of Prussia. Too far from Dan's comfort zone. He thought the fifteen miles might as well have been fifteen thousand.

They had driven down expressways, the Schuylkill to Vine Street to the Delaware, along the way passing the impressive glass-skinned skyscrapers and other expensive real estate that made up Center City. Ten minutes later, just north of Center City, Billy had exited the Delaware Expressway at Westmoreland, then taken that to Frankford Avenue and made a left. Then, at Somerset, he'd hung a right and announced in a confident voice that it was only a few more blocks.

"Man, we just keep getting into worse and worse streets," Dan said.

The overcast sky, a dark blanket of thick clouds, added to the gloom.

He yanked the navy blue hood over his head while sliding lower in his seat and staring out the bottom edge of the window at a pair of burned-out row houses.

"I've never seen so many boarded-up places," Dan went on, almost in a whisper. "I heard on the news they're called zombie houses, 'cause they look like only zombies could live in 'em." Then he turned and looked at Billy, and in a louder voice said, "Why don't we just go get some beer, maybe even a bottle of Jack. We can hang out near the state store, and when one of those illegal migrants comes out, we'll pay him to go back in and get us a bottle."

Billy looked over and saw that Dan was highly anxious, his legs moving rapidly up and down as he looked out the window.

Billy laughed. "Dude, we can always do that. Don't worry. This is an adventure . . ."

An adventure? Dan thought.

". . . I've done this same thing four, five times. Seriously. It looks worse than it is. These guys just want to make a buck."

After a long moment, Dan said, "So, how's it work?"

"Just like the drive-through window at a fast-food place."

"What? You shitting me?"

Billy shook his head.

"You pull up to the corner," he explained, "and crack a window. Dude is working the corner. He comes up and you give him your order. Then he takes the money and signals a guy who's sitting on the stoop at the end of the block. Then you drive down to the other guy, who then is coming back from wherever they stash the weed. He comes up to the window, passes you the stuff, then you drive off. Fast food, fast weed. And I'm gonna super-size our order, so we can sell one zip to pay for ours."

"It's that easy?"

Billy nodded.

"Yep. That easy. We'll be out of here and back home in no time. Hell, we can even swing by the state store if you want."

They made a right turn, onto Jasper Street. There were two black men standing on the corner, each looking in different directions, scanning the street, then turning and talking with the other. Dan couldn't tell for sure but the skinnier of the two did not look much older than he and Billy. They wore dark jeans, high-top boots, and heavy winter coats over cotton hoodie sweatshirts, one black and one gray. The skinny one had the gray hood covering his head. The big guy had his shaved head exposed. Both had their hands in the belly pockets, stretching them.

As Billy drove toward the corner, the skinny one nudged the big guy with his elbow, gestured with his head toward the approaching car, then started down the sidewalk.

Billy rolled to a stop at the curb, then let down his window halfway.

The big guy leaned toward the window, then brought out his left hand, his fingers gripping the top of the open window.

Bet that other hand's got a gun, Billy thought.

The big guy's scalp and forehead glistened. His face was coarse, the skin pitted. His eyes were bloodshot, cloudy, dull. They darted from Billy to Dan then to the backseat then back to them.

"What up, bro?" Billy said.

The big guy glared at him. "I ain't your homey. What you want?"

"I was here last month. You remember?"

"No," the big guy said, shaking his head. Then he let out a big laugh. "All you white boys from the 'burbs look the same!"

When he laughed, Dan saw that the guy's teeth looked like

they were rotting. In his mind, photographs from a school text-book popped up.

Meth mouth, he thought, remembering that the caustic chemicals used in the making of methamphetamine literally disintegrated enamel, reducing teeth to black stubs.

The guy suddenly jerked his head to look over his shoulder. Then he looked back, first staring at Billy then at Dan.

"Who's this guy?"

Dan's stomach knotted.

He's looking at me really weird. I don't like it.

"My buddy," Billy said. "He's all right."

The guy turned back to Billy.

"How I know he ain't Five-Oh?" He narrowed his eyes. "Hell, how I know *you* ain't working for the man? Or trying to rip me off."

"Look. I just want some more weed."

The big guy looked at Billy a long moment. Then he jerked his head to look over his shoulder again as he said, "You want wet? I got wet." He looked back at Billy. "Good shit. Fuck your head right up."

"What's wet?" Dan said.

Billy quickly motioned at Dan with his right hand as a signal for him to shut up.

"No wet," Billy said. "Just plain weed."

The big shaved glistening head nodded. "Okay. How much?"

"Two zips. You got that?"

"Uh-huh."

"What're you getting for it? Same as before?"

"A zip be a buck-fifty." He said it *buck-fitty.*

"One-fifty for an ounce. Right?"

"What the fuck I just say?" He made a loud grunt, as if he were disgusted or impatient or both. He suddenly grinned. "Yeah. Unless you wanna pay more."

A regular comedian, this guy, Billy thought as he reached down for his worn fabric wallet in his lap. He tugged at the Velcro closure, making a ripping sound as it opened, then pulled out four fifties and five twenties. He folded the stack of bills twice and slid it to the top edge of the window.

"That's three hundred."

"Better be."

Billy knew it'd be counted before he reached the delivery point. He'd be damn stupid if he tried shorting the big guy. He'd just keep Billy's money. That, and maybe worse.

The wad of cash disappeared in the big guy's left fist, which he then stuffed in the belly pocket of his sweatshirt as he straightened up and stepped back from the car. His left hand then came out of the pocket with a tiny walkie-talkie.

He looked down at the far end of the street. Billy and Dan looked there, too, as they heard the guy say into the walkie-talkie, "Two green Zs."

They saw the skinny guy down on the corner lowering his left hand from his ear, then motioning to a young kid who was sitting on the crooked dirty concrete stoop of a row house. The kid, who looked maybe ten, then got up and disappeared behind a chain-link fence gate.

"All right, Little Man down there will fix you up," the big guy said, then turned and went back to his corner.

Billy put the car in gear. It slowly began to move.

After a moment, Dan shook his head.

"Damn! You see how much he was sweating?" he said, nervously glancing back at him. "Like it was the middle of summer!"

"And paranoid. That's why I shut you up. That's the wet."

"The sweat?"

"The *wet*—it's weed, or sometimes just a cigarette, that's been laced with PCP. That angel dust makes them sweat, yeah, but it really makes them crazy."

"Huh," Dan said, then in a mocking tone added, "'Good shit. Fuck your head right up.' Yeah, right. That's why they call that crap hallucinogens."

The car, its tires crunching on the snow, pulled to a stop at the end of the block. Billy put the gear shift in park.

The man on the corner stood staring at them.

"Is he going to get the dope or what?"

"No. He's the lookout. Watching for cops. And he makes sure no one messes with the kid and the stash."

How does he know all this? Dan thought.

He really must come here a lot.

The kid then reappeared from behind the fence. He carried something wrapped in a white plastic grocery bag.

"So, the kid hands over the dope? What's up with that?"

Billy shrugged. "I guess they think the cops won't bust a kid."

The boy reached the car and went to slip the bag through the open window.

"Thanks, man," Billy said, taking the bag and stuffing it in his coat pocket.

He then noticed the skinny guy on the corner was fast approaching.

"Oh, shit!" Billy blurted.

"What?" Dan said, looking. Then, "Oh, shit!"

Dan was staring at the muzzle of the black revolver pointing through the gap of the open window.

"Don't you fucking make a move!" the skinny guy said. "Get outta the car! *Now!*"

Billy turned off the engine. He started to pull out the key from the ignition.

"Leave the key!"

Billy yanked back his hand. Then he and Dan slowly opened their doors and got out, taking careful steps on the snow.

The guy gestured with the pistol at them and nodded toward the boy.

"Get on the sidewalk. Give him your phones and wallets."

When Dan came around the car, the little kid laughed and pointed at Billy. Dan looked. The crotch of Billy's jeans was wet.

Damn! He pissed himself.

The kid took their wallets and phones.

The skinny guy said, "Somerset El's two blocks that way. You be in Center City in fifteen minutes."

"What?" Billy said, incredulous. "Take the train?"

"Get the hell outta here! And listen. You call the cops? I come and find your ass. I got your address on your IDs. You don't want me in your hood."

"Snitches get stitches! End up in ditches!" the kid blurted, almost as if rehearsed, then disappeared with their phones and wallets back behind the chain-link fencing.

Dan started to back away slowly.

Billy, looking terrified, stood frozen. He stared at the guy.

"Billy," Dan said, and when there was no reply, he shouted: "Come on, Billy! Let's go!"

The skinny guy waved the gun at Billy and said, "What you looking at? You hear what I said?"

Then Dan couldn't believe his eyes.

It all happened at once, and in slow motion—the loud *Bang-Bang-Bang!*, the bright flashes of fire from the muzzle of the weapon, and then Billy grabbing at his chest and staggering back and finally falling and then not moving.

And then the blood flowing, running from his neck and open mouth, and saturating his shirt and fleece jacket.

Dan took one step toward Billy—then saw the guy swing the gun, its muzzle still smoking, and aim it in his direction.

Dan rapidly shuffled his feet to back away, slipped and hit the sidewalk, then finally got traction just as the guy fired a round at him. Dan crawled around the corner, onto Hart Lane, then got to his feet. He took off down the sidewalk as he heard two more shots going off behind him—the bullets ricocheting off the street not fifty feet away.

After running two blocks down Hart Lane, Dan stopped. He breathed heavily, the cold air making his lungs burn. He looked back. No one followed.

He put his hands on his knees, leaned forward, and shook his head, trying to clear it.

Damn it! He killed Billy! What the hell?

He crossed his arms over his stomach and dipped his head. He then lunged forward, trying to reach a patch of dirt off the sidewalk. He didn't make it. There then came a deep guttural sound as he threw up, the vomitus splattering against the base of a flight of concrete steps, some of it splashing back on his shoes and jeans.

When the spasms stopped, he spit on the sidewalk and wiped his mouth with his sleeve.

Now what? I can't go back.

I can't call for help. He's got my phone.

And if I did, he's got our wallets. My license has my damn address. He knows where I live . . .

The foul acidic odor floated up to him, burning his nostrils and triggering his gag reflex. He fought it back, turning his head and quickly breathing in fresh air. His brain felt as if it were spinning.

Dan glared back down the street as he wiped his mouth with the back of his hand. He looked in the other direction and saw two rough-looking males across the street glaring at him. He jerked his head at the sound of a car that turned onto Hart, then rattled toward him. Frozen, he just stared blankly as a battered Ford sedan with darkened windows rolled past.

I've gotta get the fuck out of here.

And, his lungs still burning, he took off running.

The slick high-gloss tan brick and bright blue painted steel of the Southeastern Pennsylvania Transportation Authority train station stood out on the street, its modern design sharply contrasting with the neighborhood's dilapidated hundred-year-old gray stone storefronts and the dirty broken sidewalks.

The elevated station on the SEPTA Market Frankford Line

had been built over the five-way intersection of Kensington Avenue and Somerset Street.

There were four young males standing by the entrance, and Dan carefully kept his distance as he moved past them. He then ran up the steps, taking them two at a time, catching the distinct foul odor of urine as he went.

When he reached the level with the turnstiles, a line of them directly ahead, he picked up his pace.

What happens if I get caught jumping?

Screw that! I need a cop to catch me—and get me the hell out of here.

He tried to time his run so he would easily hop over the first turnstile.

He jumped, clearing most of it, but then his ankle caught the stainless steel arm—and the momentum slammed him down to the concrete.

He sat up, stunned, his shoulder burning from the impact, but nothing seemed broken. A couple of people looked at him but said nothing.

He pushed himself to his feet and ran for the train.

When he got to the platform level, he saw that the doors of the railcars were closing.

No!

He headed for the closest door—but it shut just before he reached it.

His stomach sank.

Watching the train leave the station, he stood feeling helpless, thinking he was going to cry at any moment.

Then he noticed that the train was headed eastbound, and saw the signage stating that it was going north, toward Frankford Allegheny.

That would've been a mistake, going deeper into this hellhole . . .

He then saw other signage for the train that ran south then west through Center City out to Sixty-ninth Street. And then he heard the deep rumble of a southbound train approaching.

As it entered the station, there came the ear-piercing metallic squeal of brakes. The train stopped, and he stood in front of a door. It seemed to take forever to open—but then all the doors swooshed open, and Dan, squeezing past two people who were exiting, quickly stepped inside. He found a corner seat, then looked back to the platform.

Two of the males he had just passed down at the entrance were rushing to board.

His stomach dropped.

Are they chasing me?

He tried to figure out what he would do—*Maybe wait till the last second and then jump off right before the doors close?*—but then the pair darted aboard the adjacent railcar.

Dan put his head in his hands, looked at the floor, and let out a long sigh.

The railcar was almost half-full. He scanned the other passengers. With the exception of an older man who was deep asleep in the back—*The guy looks passed-out drunk*—Dan was the only pale-skinned passenger. Still, no one seemed to be paying him any attention.

He realized that he was again holding his arms over his stomach, and that his stomach was in an enormous knot, and that he was gently rocking himself.

What am I gonna do? He killed Billy . . .

Fuck him! I can just say we got jacked.

Cops find the car, they find that fucker, he goes to jail.

Then he can't get me.

But what do I say when they ask why we were in that part of town?

"Just buying some dope" won't fly.

Dan felt a chill go up and down his entire body.

Hell, I don't know.

Oh man . . . I told Billy we should've just got a damn bottle of Jack.

IV

[ONE]
The Roundhouse
Eighth and Race Streets, Philadelphia
Saturday, December 15, 2:21 P.M.

Matt Payne approached the double wooden doors to the Executive Command Center. As he reached for the handle, the right door suddenly began to swing open toward him. He could hear the murmur of voices coming from inside. He hesitated a moment, waiting for whoever was going to come out the doorway. When no one did, he raised an eyebrow, then entered.

Payne glanced up at the door frame and nodded when he saw that there was an electromechanical arm, newly installed, connecting it to the top of the door. Then he noticed beside the door a new button that activated the arm.

Inside, his eyes automatically went to the focal point of the big room: the ten-foot-high wall of twenty-seven flat-screen televisions. There were three banks of nine sixty-inch high-definition LCD panels, and on the screen in the lower left-hand corner of the first bank he saw an image of himself. It had been captured on camera only moments earlier, as he stood before the double doors. It then showed the door swinging open and him entering the ECC.

Payne looked back across the room that held a dozen detectives, most sitting at the two massive T-shaped conference tables. They talked on telephones, worked at notebook computers, studied images on the wall of screens. Corporal Kerry Rapier, who was sitting behind a control panel just beyond the farthest table, made a casual salute in his direction.

The ECC—along with the Forensic Sciences, Information Systems, and Communications divisions—was run by the Philadelphia Police Department's Science & Technology branch. And the ECC's master technician was also its youngest tech, Rapier. The twenty-five-year-old electronics wizard had an impossibly small frame and soft features that caused many, upon first meeting him, to wonder not only if he had passed the department's minimum physical standards and really was a cop, but if he might also be skipping out of his sophomore year of high school. After they witnessed his skillful work, however, no one questioned him again.

The command center—originally funded almost entirely by federal monies in order to help protect politicians attending their party's national convention in Philly—had been designed to serve as the nerve center during a crisis. It took in a staggering amount of raw information—some argued an overwhelming amount at times—from highly secure intelligence sources to open intel sources and everything in between.

The dark gray conference tables could accommodate more than fifty people, with seating along the walls for another forty-plus support staff, who assimilated the information, then analyzed and acted on it. An auxiliary communications center, a facility built minutes from the Roundhouse with federal funds provided by the Department of Homeland Security, had been added to handle additional law enforcement personnel.

As Payne walked over to Rapier, he looked at the images cycling on the televisions. Two of the screen banks showed live video feeds from closed-circuit cameras around the city, and also news broadcasts from local and national channels and those from the Internet. The third bank of screens was filled with images of the morning's crime scenes at LOVE and Franklin parks and at the casino, and the recordings from surveillance cameras.

"Hey, Marshal," Rapier said, gesturing to the screen that showed a protester pumping a poster over her head. "Someone needs to call your buddy the reverend."

Payne crossed his arms over his chest.

"Okay, Kerry, I'll bite. Why?"

"He needs to update your sign. Got a report of another. Which would now make number three hundred sixty-three—"

"The granddaughter from the casino?" Payne interrupted. "Damn! Does Tony know yet?"

"No. I mean, no, it's not her. It's a guy."

Payne shook his head. "Small surprise. Where?"

"About a half hour ago in Kensington," Rapier said, "just a few blocks from the Somerset El."

Rapier then tapped on the glass monitor of the control panel. The top left screen on the third bank showed a blue shirt stepping off a sidewalk in front of two decrepit row houses with their windows boarded over. He was stringing yellow crime scene tape from the porch railing of one row house to a telephone pole across the street. The lower edge of the image included the white hood of a vehicle that had red and blue lights pulsing off it, making it obvious the video was being taken by a squad car's dash camera. There was a line of text at the top of the frame detailing the date, time, and GPS location of the imagery.

"Looks like drugs," Rapier added.

"A drug deal in Kensington! No!" Payne said, somewhat loudly and dripping with sarcasm, causing a few people to look up at him momentarily, grin, and turn back to their work. "Next you'll further surprise me by saying it's payback for Dante Holmes getting capped yesterday, that this dead guy's a teen—"

"A teenaged white male named Billy Chester," Rapier finished. "And it's probably not retaliation to settle scores. His buddy Dan Moss, also a teenaged white male, got collared getting off the El in Chinatown by a transit cop—they'd seen Moss on SEPTA surveillance cameras jumping the turnstile at Somerset."

"And?"

"And the transit cop said Moss—after the kid stopped hugging him and crying—reported he and Chester had gotten lost, wound up in Kensington, and then got carjacked. Said after they were robbed, Chester apparently took at least three large-caliber rounds to the chest and neck."

Payne looked at him a moment.

"A white teen? That's curious."

"You mean unusual?" Rapier asked, but they both knew it was a statement of fact.

[TWO]

A week earlier, Homicide Sergeant Matt Payne had been approached with a proposition—"cornered," he had claimed, but no one took the statement seriously. It was a hard argument to swallow considering (a) the person approaching had been in a motorized wheelchair and (b) who that person was.

The fact of the matter was that Payne would have done anything for Andy Radcliffe, a nineteen-year-old who was working an internship with the police department.

Andy had a kind, round face with gentle coal-black eyes and a full head of dark hair clipped tight to his scalp. He generally wore neatly ironed jeans and an oversized white cotton dress shirt with a somewhat worn navy blazer.

He was a sophomore—a double major studying criminal justice and computer science—at La Salle University, in North Philly, not far from where he lived with his mother and little brother.

Three years earlier, returning home with take-out dinner for the family, he had been robbed on the street by teenaged thugs. Not content with what little cash he had, they then stabbed him in the back. The knife had struck his spinal cord, leaving him paralyzed from the waist down.

Even before the robbery, Andy's life had been anything but an easy one. Yet he still managed to keep a positive attitude after the attack, overcoming as best he could the obstacles that came with the paralysis.

Payne had found himself immediately impressed when he had met Radcliffe in the Executive Command Center, and even more when he'd heard his story.

Andy politely had brushed off Payne's praise.

"What was I going to do? Not keep helping Momma and my little brother? Or, worse, become a burden to them? Momma taught me discipline, to work hard and never give up. Like my father."

Andy explained that Luke Radcliffe had worked as a crane operator at the Port of Philadelphia for fifteen years—until he found himself suffering severe shortness of breath. Doctors diagnosed him with pulmonary fibrosis.

Andy had just turned ten.

Luke Radcliffe, as he bravely fought the advancing disease, was put on a lung transplant list. But the scars quickly covered more and more of the lung tissue, and, just a week after being rushed to the hospital and hooked up to an artificial respirator, he succumbed to severe infections.

The medical bills had been unbelievably expensive, and the cash from the modest life insurance policy Luke had taken out through the port had not lasted long. The family struggled to make ends meet, even as Andy's mother took on extra work.

Andy, desperate to help, finally got a job at a grocery store. It was all the then-twelve-year-old could find. He worked part-time as a shelf-stocker and bag boy after school and on Saturdays. He would have worked Sundays, but his mother cautioned him to keep holy the Sabbath, and to take time to be with family. Later, the answer had been the same when he offered to go to full-time— his mother again thanked him, but adamantly refused to let him miss any school.

It had been because of the robbery, and his meeting the cop who worked his case, that Radcliffe found himself at La Salle studying criminology.

Detective Will Parkman was a former marine who Radcliffe said really wasn't the hard-ass that people presumed. He described him as "an M&M, hard on the outside, soft on the inside. His buddies call him 'Pretty Boy' Parkman because . . . well, he's the first to say he's not." Parkman had told him about a La Salle scholarship, helped him apply for it, and then later helped him apply for the police internship.

Rapier told Payne that Radcliffe really knew his way around computers. And Payne found he had the makings for a thorough investigator, which Andy had proved when he dug up a detail in a file that connected two critically important dots in Payne's Halloween Homicides case.

Andy was diligent, worked long hours, and never sought preferential treatment. Thus, when Payne had looked up from his desk in the Homicide Unit and seen Radcliffe, hand on the armrest joystick that controlled his wheelchair's direction and speed, fluidly rolling toward him, his next words had come as somewhat of a surprise.

"I have a favor to ask," Andy said, "and I understand if the answer's no."

"No," Payne said immediately, intending it as a joke.

"Yes, sir. Understood."

Radcliffe bobbed his head once, thumbed the joystick to the right, and, after his wheelchair pivoted, began rolling out of the cubicle.

The look on Radcliffe's face made Payne feel as if he had just kicked a litter of puppies off a cliff.

"Wait!" Payne said. "What is it, Andy?"

It was a moment before Radcliffe brought his wheelchair to a stop and spun back around.

Radcliffe said: "At La Salle there's a class—Criminal Justice 350: Violence in Society—that I'm taking. I got it okayed to bring the others in my class on a tour of the department . . ."

"Sounds like a great idea."

". . . if I got a sponsor . . ."

"Upon further consideration, sounds like a really bad idea."

Radcliffe stared at him, then finished, ". . . and it'd be great if you could do just the Homicide part. Detective Parkman's already agreed to be the sponsor."

"What? Pretty Boy? You asked him first? Why do I suddenly feel like the last kid picked for a team on the playground?"

Payne tried to feign a hurt look. When he saw it wasn't working, he smiled.

"All right. Sure, Andy. When?"

The next night in the Homicide Unit, Sergeant Matthew M. Payne, wearing gray woolen slacks, navy blazer, and a striped necktie, stood before twenty-five criminal justice students from La Salle University.

It was a fairly varied group, despite being made up mostly of males. All were nicely dressed, a few of the males even in coat and tie. While it was impossible to pinpoint their exact ethnic lineage, a dozen in the group, including of course Andy Radcliffe, clearly were African-American, with the remainder being a mix of backgrounds well representative of Philadelphia. Payne recognized signs of Irish and English heritage as well as those of Italian, Spanish, Asian, and Hispanic descent.

What a great bunch of kids, Payne thought.

"I've been asked to describe the makeup of crime here in Philly, with an emphasis on homicides," Payne said. "But I'd like to ask you a question first: How many of you have had friends or family who've been victims of crime?"

All but four in the group raised their hands.

"And how many of you personally have been victims?"

A moment later, six hands remained raised.

Payne nodded, motioned for them to put down their hands, then said, "I'm sorry to see that, but I have to say I'm not surprised. You guys are what age—nineteen, twenty?"

They nodded.

"Okay, tell me: What's generally considered the largest cause of death for people your age?"

"Car crashes," a tall, thoughtful-looking black male said.

"Correct. For those age fifteen to twenty-five, cars are by far the worst. That is, pretty much everywhere but Philadelphia. Anyone want to venture a guess what it is here?"

The group was silent, then a male voice in the back said, "Murder?"

Payne nodded solemnly. "Unfortunately, yes. Homicides are the top killer for that age group in Philly."

There was a murmur, then the same voice in the back, his tone now incredulous, said, "But why?"

"That's a very good question. One I wish we had an answer for—then I wouldn't have to work so hard."

That triggered polite laughter.

Then, toward the front, a light-brown-skinned female with short dark hair raised her hand to shoulder level and said: "Thanks to the media, it's not exactly a secret that you're known to get into shoot-outs. Weren't you just cleared in that shoot-out on the casino boardwalk?"

Payne thought that she probably was Puerto Rican.

He smiled.

"You don't beat around the bush, do you?" he said. "You're going to make a great cop."

There were chuckles.

"No offense intended, Sergeant Payne," she said. "I'm just curious about deadly force—that is, Officer-Involved Shootings—how the process works?"

Payne nodded.

She doesn't look like she's trying to corner me, he thought.

But she knows the proper terminology. Better be careful, Matty . . .

"Fair question, for which I have a fair answer. Let me say, first of all, Honor, Integrity, Service—that's our police department's motto. I believe devoutly in it. I took my oath to protect the city, protect its residents, and uphold the law and the United States Constitution. To do that, you have to embrace honor and integrity and service."

He saw nodding in the crowd.

"An Officer-Involved Shooting, or OIS," he went on, "is when a police officer, either on duty or off, discharges his or her firearm, either intentionally or accidentally. Each year, among our seven thousand–plus officers, there's an average of fifty Officer-Involved Shootings, with about ten of those resulting in the officer killing the bad guy. It's important to note that every OIS death in the last decade has been found to be righteous."

"Righteous?" a male, who looked, and sounded, like he was of Polish stock, asked.

Payne remembered him as one of the six whose hands remained up when he asked if anyone had been a crime victim.

"Justifiable," Payne said. "Proper."

"Then the bastard had it coming!" the male blurted.

"Kuba!" the olive-skinned female next to him said.

"If you'll forgive my French, sir," Kuba added, smiling.

Payne forced back a grin.

"Everyone makes choices, and some are fatal ones," he said. "Okay, so fifty Officer-Involved Shootings is a very low number considering (a) that there're every day about ten thousand calls to nine-one-one asking for police assistance and (b) that the bad guys are quick to wave weapons when police arrive on the scene."

"That's what happened to me," Kuba said. "The bastard . . . sorry . . . the bad guy robbed me at gunpoint when I was waiting for a SEPTA bus in West Philly."

"You didn't get hurt?" Payne said.

"No, sir," Kuba said, shaking his head. He glanced at Andy Radcliffe and added, "Luckily."

Andy acknowledged that with a nod.

"You were lucky," Payne said, paused for a moment, then went on: "All right, so after an OIS, the case gets sent to the district attorney's office to determine that the shooting was within the framework of Pennsylvania state law. There's also a police department investigation, one separate from the DA's and conducted by the Use of Force Review Board following the DA's decision. The Use of Force Review Board is made up of department heavy hitters—the deputy commissioners from Patrol Operations, Office of Professional Responsibility, Organizational Services, and Major Investigations. They determine whether or not department procedures and policies were followed and if there should be disciplinary charges, or maybe training, or even changing department policies."

"What about CPOC?" a male who looked to be of Asian descent said.

Payne looked at him, nodded, then addressed the group: "Everyone familiar with the Citizens Police Oversight Committee? It's exactly as its name suggests. Made up of five citizens appointed to represent all citizens, CPOC offers valuable suggestions to the police department, generally through the city council. Its members, who are not sworn officers or prosecutors, are not able to make professional investigations of an OIS, or for that matter any other official activity in the department."

After a moment, the dark-haired woman raised her hand again.

"So," she said, "you're saying that's ten bad guys killed by an officer each year in Philly? When the overall murder rate averages one a day? I don't mean any offense by this, either, but it's remarkable you haven't shot more than you have, Sergeant Payne."

Payne looked at her a moment, then noticed everyone's eyes on him.

Here it comes, Matty ol' boy—that sounds uncomfortably close to the impossible-to-answer question of: "So, sir, have you stopped beating your wife?"

"Yes! I mean, no! I mean . . ."

He avoided answering by digging into his coat pocket. He produced some folded sheets of paper, flipped to the second one, and handed it to Andy Radcliffe.

"This is the most recent Philadelphia Murder/Shooting Analysis," Payne announced. "Andy, how about you read the intro, and I'll then get into the numbers."

Andy looked at the sheet, then cleared his throat, and began: "'The FBI Uniform Crime Reporting Program establishes all guidelines and procedures for the submission of crime data to the State Police UCR. Murders are counted at the time Homicide investigators determine that, after investigation, there in fact has been an intentional killing of a human being by another. Clearances of murders occur when at least one person suspected of committing the murder is taken into police custody for prosecution. Clearance rates are determined by taking the total number of murder clearances for the year and dividing that number into the number of murders counted for that same period. Clearance rates are currently averaging fifty percent.'"

He looked up at Payne, who then looked at the group.

"Any questions about that?" Payne said.

He saw heads shaking; there were no verbal responses.

"Okay, let's talk about who's involved in these homicides," he then said. "Of those murdered, nearly ninety percent are male, sixty percent of that aged eighteen to thirty-four, seventy-five percent if you look at eighteen to forty-four. And of all those killed, seventy-five percent are African-American.

"The department's Twenty-second District—North Philly, Broad Street to the Schuylkill River, headquartered at Seventeenth and Montgomery—gets the dubious honor of handling the most murders citywide, one in ten. But the Twenty-fourth and -fifth and the Twelfth and Thirty-fifth and -ninth are right behind it."

Andy Radcliff said, "That's pretty much anywhere but Center City."

"That's correct. But Center City certainly isn't immune. Now, seventy-five-point-eight percent of homicides happen outside. No day is really any better or worse than another, although Saturday, Sunday, and Monday nights edge highest."

"Why not Friday?" a voice called out.

Payne shrugged.

"There's really not a lot of difference. Friday rates eleven percent versus sixteen percent for each Saturday, Sunday, Monday. A third of those murders clock in—or clock out, as the case may be—between twenty-hundred and twenty-four-hundred hours. About one in four are murdered after that, twenty-four-hundred to oh-four-hundred."

"Midnight, the witching hour," Andy Radcliffe said. "Small wonder the Homicide guys on the Last Out shift are the busiest."

"And why they don't get much sleep," Payne said, "considering they chase the leads night and day until they catch them or the trail goes cold. As for when the fewest murders occur, it's the period from oh-eight-hundred to twelve-hundred."

"Late morning. They must be sleeping in then," a female who looked to have Irish traits said.

There were chuckles in the group.

"That," Kuba said in a stage whisper, "or getting cozy with their bitches."

That triggered loud laughter.

Payne shook his head, but he grinned and then went on: "Almost half are categorized as the result of an argument. A distant second, around ten to twelve percent, are listed as 'Drugs' and about the same number are marked 'Unknown.'"

"Wouldn't there be a lot of crossover there?" the tall, thoughtful black male said. "I mean, a lot of those arguments have to be drug-related."

Payne nodded. "No doubt. There could've been drugs involved earlier, then a later argument triggered the killing. Fighting over territory is a prime example." He paused, then went on: "And 'triggered' is somewhat appropriate, as the cause of death by far is gunshots. More than eighty percent. Knives come in at just shy of ten percent. After that it's blunt force trauma and strangling. Anyone want to take a stab, so to speak, at when those numbers change dramatically?"

He glanced around the group, then his eyes fell on Andy Radcliffe.

"I've already read the report . . ." Andy said.

"Then you won't be taking a stab."

Andy nodded. "Okay, when it's domestic murder cases. Knife and gun use are essentially equal."

"Right. There were just over a hundred domestic-related murders over the last five years, and a knife or other sharp blade—scissors, say, or a cardboard box cutter—was used as often as a firearm. Interestingly, the numbers of male and female victims of domestic murders were also about equal."

"Equal?" Kuba parroted, his tone incredulous. "You said the other homicide figures showed some eighty percent of the victims were male. And here women committed half of the killings?"

"'Heaven has no rage like love to hatred turned,'" Payne recited, making dramatic stage-actor sweeps with his arms, "'Nor hell a fury like a woman scorned.' From Act Three, Scene Eight of ol' Billy Congreve's seventeenth-century play *The Mourning Bride.*"

"How do you remember stuff like that so quick and easy?" Andy Radcliffe said, smiling.

"Andy, I figure if that was written some three hundred years ago, and it still makes sense, there must be something to it," Payne said. "You might wish to write this down: One should strive to remember all things relevant that could see one's . . . posterior . . . kicked. Including, as this particular stat bears out, a furious wife, girlfriend . . ."

"Or girlfriends," Kuba said. "Lots of baby mamas out there getting angry when their man wanders off with another baby mama."

There were chuckles.

"Okay," Payne said, "let's wind this up. Eight out of ten murder victims had at least one prior arrest. Twenty percent, amazingly, had at least eleven priors, the vast majority being robbery, followed by murder."

"*Eleven?* Robbers and murderers let back out on the street?" the Puerto Rican female said. "Thank you very much, court system."

"And those are just the victims?" Kuba said. "Maybe we should thank the shooters for taking them out."

"Yeah," the female next to him said. "Who are they?"

"Curiously, pretty much the same demographic, just more so," Payne said. "Males at ninety-three percent. Eighty-three percent black, seventeen white. Half are age eighteen to twenty-four— which is where the Survive to See Twenty-five saying comes from, meaning you've beat the odds—or seventy-five percent if you go to age eighteen to thirty-four. And more than ninety percent had prior arrests. Of the total, a third had one to three priors, and a quarter had eleven or more.

"And as far as which guns are used, nine-millimeter is by far the round of choice, with .40 cal and .45 cal being used about half as often. A bit more than one in three wind up shooting multiple shots, hitting multiple parts of the victim's body. But, following that, curiously, one in four take only a head shot."

"Nice," Kuba said, his tone disgusted. "Probably taking their nine and squeezing off the head shot point-blank after making them get on their knees."

"Execution style is not at all uncommon," Payne said. "It sends a message."

Kuba grunted.

The group was quiet a long moment.

"So, Sergeant Payne," the tall, thoughtful black male said, "using all that real data, is it safe to paint this picture of the typical murderer and victim? That they're mostly black males between eighteen and thirty-four years of age with at least one prior arrest for robbery and that the crime is committed somewhere between Saturday at eight P.M. and Sunday at four A.M. with multiple shots from a nine-millimeter pistol?"

"Well put. Unfortunately, that is the case—the homicide numbers don't lie," Payne said, then glanced at Andy. "And we haven't even touched on the numbers of attempted murder of innocent people."

Kuba whistled lightly as he shook his head.

"I was damn lucky I only got robbed," he said.

[THREE]

"But here's the kicker on this Kensington carjacking," Kerry Rapier said, pointing toward the image of the crime scene on the ECC wall.

Payne looked at it and said, "You mean as in: Where's Waldo?"

Rapier snorted.

"Exactly. The uniform who was first at the scene reported an enormous amount of blood on the sidewalk. But no body. And no shell casings—"

"No spent rounds? Then the doer used a revolver," Payne said.

"That, or the shooter actually stuck around and cleaned the scene of all his spent rounds."

"Yeah, right. Possible. But it'd be a miracle."

"Police Radio broadcasted a Flash info with the description of the car—a late-model VW Jetta—but dollars to doughnuts it's probably already across the river in Jersey or Delaware. Or about to be."

"Maybe Waldo's not dead. Maybe he's wounded and in hiding. With wounds to the chest and throat, there'd damn sure be a blood trail."

Rapier shook his head. "More like a blood river. According to Moss, his buddy Waldo—*Billy Chester*—was killed. When Moss broke down talking to the transit cop, he said that right before he had to run for his life, it was clear that his buddy was dead."

Payne reached toward the conference table, grabbed one of the telephones, and punched in a number.

"It's Sergeant Payne," he said after a moment. "Who was on the Wheel when this carjacking case in Kensington came in?" His eyebrows went up as he listened, then he said, "And where's the kid, this Dan Moss, who reported it?" Then, after another moment, added, "Okay, thanks," and replaced the receiver in its cradle.

He looked at Rapier and said, "This should be good. Chuck Whaley is on his way to the scene. He couldn't find his ass with both hands even if he were spotted one cheek. And the Moss kid is in Homicide. He gave Whaley his statement and is now waiting for one of his parents to show up."

Payne looked up at the wall of televisions. Under the one with the Kensington crime scene, two screens showed surveillance camera imagery of the Lucky Stars Casino just before and during the robbery. Each had date and time stamps and camera identification text in the corner. Another screen showed a social media page on the Internet that had a cracked Liberty Bell icon next to ROCKIN215 and the title LUCKY STARS HOOKUP. The page, top to bottom, had line after line of instant messages.

Payne nodded toward it.

"What's with the 'hookup'?" he said.

Rapier pointed to a screen that showed the flash mob of teenagers coming through the casino's revolving doors.

"When Detective Krowczyk—"

"Who?" Payne interrupted.

Rapier nodded in the direction of a tall, lanky white male, maybe thirty years old, who was hunched over a notebook computer at the far end of Conference Table One.

Payne thought Krowczyk had to be at least six-foot-four but weighed maybe only one-sixty on a good day. He wore blue jeans, black sneakers, and a white, wrinkled knit polo shirt. A brown leather jacket hung on his seatback. He stared intently at the computer, the glow of the screen reflecting off his round frameless eyeglasses and illuminating his long pale face. There were cans of diet soda on either side of the computer and, behind it, a torn-open package of crème-filled Tastykake Dreamies.

"Danny Krowczyk's a SIGINT analyst recently assigned to our Digital Forensic Sciences Unit," Rapier said, using the abbreviation for Signals Intelligence. "This morning he had his software scanning the postings on social media, trying to find possible leads on anybody planning activity we should interdict, or at least keep an eye on, when he came across the alert calling for the flash mob at the casino. It flared up fast, otherwise we might have had a chance to shut it down before it reached the casino."

"And now we have all the instant message traffic?"

"Yeah. It's open source material. Anybody can find it if they want and they know where to look. But it's what's in the messages that can tell us what's important. I'm putting Andy Radcliffe on tracking who's behind the screen names of what appear to be the higher value messages. He's got a group of geeks—"

"Said the pot calling the kettle black," Payne interrupted, smiling.

"—who're really good at drilling down and linking traffic that otherwise would appear unconnected. They're in Andy's advanced coding classes at La Salle—and in touch with others in the coding world—and talk a language I don't understand. Anyway, bottom line, many screen names are going to come up bogus, of course, but if his guys can get enough legit ones, or even link to bogus ones, they can digitally map out who was involved, maybe even whoever set it up."

Payne nodded thoughtfully. "It's likely a long shot, but maybe they'll turn up a connection between the flash mob and the doers of the jewelry store robbery. That flash mob could very well have been a diversionary tactic for the theft."

"Maybe. Or some other event that may link back to it. People post all kinds of incriminating things. Some of it just blows your mind. Like the gangs that self-promote and taunt other gangs . . ."

"'Internet banging,'" Payne put in, nodding.

"Right. It's like they forget there's a whole world watching. And that's before we get warrants to monitor and search their accounts and devices."

"It is amazing."

"Anyway, Krowczyk is also now doing a really huge search of other open source intel to see if anyone's talking about suddenly having fancy jewelry and watches—or trying to sell it—like those that were stolen."

Payne watched each of the screens for a long moment, then his eyes drifted to the center bank of screens where the top middle one was set to *Philly News Now.*

The news reader at the desk, a serious-looking forty-something with her brunette hair in a pageboy cut, was wrapping up a report on the arrest of a ring of Mexican nationals caught pushing black tar heroin in Strawberry Mansion. The ticker of red text across the bottom read . . . *BREAKING NEWS: PHILLY POLICE ON SCENE OF CAR-JACKING THAT SOURCES REPORT LEFT 1 DEAD IN KENSINGTON . . . STAY TUNED FOR A LIVE REPORT . . .*

Then the broadcast faded to black and on came an advertisement. It showed delicate ballerinas in Tchaikovsky's *The Nutcracker* prancing *en pointe* at the Kimmel Center for the Performing Arts, and announced tickets remained available at the Center City venue.

Nice juxtaposition.

"The City of Brotherly Love: Home to drug cartels, junkies, carjackings, murders—and sugarplum fairies!"

Good luck selling all those tickets.

Payne looked back to the squad car dash camera image of the Kensington scene. The uniform, securing the scene, stood with arms crossed inside the yellow crime scene tape. Just beyond the tape, a dark-skinned man who looked to be about forty was pulling a video camera and tripod from the trunk of a Chevy compact. The sedan had the logotype of *Philly News Now* on its front door. The man set up the tripod a few feet outside the yellow tape, attached the camera to it, and then waved with a big black microphone in an effort to get the officer to come over to him. The blue shirt declined with a slow shaking of his head. The reporter raised his eyebrows, shrugged, then turned to the camera.

Payne, out of the corner of his eye, noticed that the wooden door to the ECC was opening. His eye dropped to the screen in the first bank where he'd seen himself enter the room, and saw no one at the opening door. Then, a moment later, Andy Radcliffe maneuvered his wheelchair into view.

"Aha," Payne said, "so that's really what the mechanical door opener is for."

"Andy wasn't too happy," Rapier said. "He thought he was getting special treatment. But I told him it was the law, that we'd finally got it installed."

"He did not hit any button on the wall. And I didn't see you buzz him in."

"That's because I also put a sensor in his wheelchair. Don't tell him, but that's not required by law."

Payne smiled. "Right."

When Radcliffe approached, Payne turned and looked toward him.

What the hell?

Andy had a shiny bruise on his left cheek, his lower lip had been busted, and there were scratches on his hands. Black tape wrapped the wheelchair's left armrest, securing it and covering its torn fabric.

"What the hell happened to you?" Payne said.

Andy shrugged.

"Last night one of my wheels got caught in a busted sidewalk. I took a tumble."

"That was more than some tumble," Payne said. "You look like you bounced down three flights of stairs. Where did it happen?"

Andy hesitated a moment, seemed to avoid eye contact, then said, "Near my house. You know how bad those streets are busted up, especially in winter."

"Did you see a doctor?" Rapier put in. "Are you in pain?"

"Nah," Andy said, glancing briefly at him. "My mom fixed me up pretty good. Just a little sore in places."

"Anything we can do?" Payne said.

He looked past Payne toward the wall of flat-screen monitors. Payne thought that Andy appeared embarrassed by all the attention.

"No, thanks," Andy said, shaking his head. "I'm fine, Sergeant Payne. Just want to get to work."

Payne studied him.

"Sergeant Payne"? he thought. Not "Marshal"?

Something's not right. He must really have smacked the hell out of his head.

Andy pointed to the right bank of monitors.

"That's Tyrone Hooks at the casino. What's up with that?"

Payne was about to ask how Andy knew of Hooks, but felt his cell phone vibrate multiple times.

He pulled it from his pants pocket and saw there were four new text messages. They were all from Mickey O'Hara.

Payne enjoyed a close friendship with Michael J. O'Hara that had begun years back when Payne was a rookie cop.

A wiry thirty-seven-year-old with an unruly head of curly red hair, O'Hara was an unusual journalist, and not only because he had won a Pulitzer prize for a series of front-page above-the-fold articles that uncovered deep corruption in the Department of Human Services, specifically the Children and Youth Division.

The Irishman had a genuine respect for the police—it was said he knew more Philly cops than did the police commissioner himself, always correctly spelling their names in what they considered his fair and factual reporting—and in turn had earned their respect, which had resulted in him being allowed inside the Thin Blue Line.

When Payne had been involved in his first shoot-out, and a ricocheted bullet grazed his forehead right before he returned fire,

it had been O'Hara who photographed the bloodied Payne standing with his .45 over the dead shooter, a career criminal. That
image, along with O'Hara's article extolling the Triumph of Good
Over Evil in the City of Brotherly Love, appeared the next day on
the front page of *The Philadelphia Bulletin* under the headline:
OFFICER M. M. PAYNE, 23, THE WYATT EARP OF THE MAIN LINE.

Payne scanned the texts—then slowly read them a second time.

At first he wondered why there were four, and not just one. But
then thought that Mickey might be being overly cautious about
having the complete message self-contained. Which only added to
the mystery and urgency.

And why didn't he call?

Maybe he had only enough signal to send a text?

Or maybe he didn't trust himself to speak?

Or . . . ?

He looked at them again.

The first text read: "Matty, this is seriously bad shit." The second said: "One of my reporters was just brutally murdered." Next:
"Meet me at 3001 Powelton Ave." And finally: "I need you to
come ALONE."

[FOUR]
4400 North Seventeenth Street, Philadelphia
Saturday, December 15, 2:31 P.M.

"Jesus, Hal, what a lousy place to die," Homicide Detective Richard C. McCrory said as he steered the unmarked four-door—a dirty-gray eight-year-old Chevy Malibu—off Wingohocking Street onto Seventeenth. "For that matter, what a lousy place to live, if you can call it that. We're in what now? Nicetown?"

Dick McCrory, who'd just turned thirty-nine, had been with the department eighteen years, six of those in Homicide. He'd grown up in Boston—his thick brogue over the years getting somewhat beaten into the Philadelphia dialect—and had joined the department right after slipping an engagement ring on the finger of Mary-Margaret, the nice Irish girl he'd met six months earlier at a South Philly wedding. McCrory had close-cropped dark hair that was graying at the temples, was of medium build, his lean body fit, the defined, toned muscles clear evidence that he still worked out regularly.

Thirty-six-year-old Homicide Detective Harold W. Kennedy Sr., an enormous African-American (six-two, two-eighty) whose beefy frame dwarfed the front passenger seat, grunted as he looked out his tinted window.

This section, on the northwestern side of Philly, was little more than block after block of dilapidated two- and three-story row houses with an occasional corner market. Its broken, uneven sidewalks were nearly covered in trash, some stuffed into torn black plastic bags but a great deal of it strewn along the entire block and on the empty lots cleared of crumbled houses.

"Yeah," Kennedy said, "Nicetown-Tioga. But they oughta rename it Dumpville. Doesn't anyone have a damn trash can—and the basic decency to use it?"

"I'd think it's safe to say they don't have much of anything."

"Well, they sure got garbage. And plenty of it. Living large in ol' Filthadelphia." He paused and made a sniffing sound. "What is . . . *ugh* . . . it smells like a sewer line break?"

Then he pointed across the street in the direction of a dead-weed-choked lot, the snow dotted with discarded car tires. In front of it, by a storm drain at the curb, was a faded yellow plastic ten-gallon bucket on its side.

"Will you look at that! Don't tell me they're also dumping their crap down that drain . . ."

McCrory looked at the bucket, then scanned the row houses. Only one had any lights visibly burning.

"Okay, then I won't tell you," McCrory said drily. "But you should know, Detective, that if there's no power in a place, there's usually no running water, either. You can probably do the math from there."

After a long moment Kennedy said, "It's just un-fucking-believable."

They rolled farther down the block. Then the right tires of the unmarked sedan—it had been impounded after a drug bust, then confiscated in a forfeiture and released to the police department's motor pool—scrubbed the curb and bumped over it.

McCrory pulled to a stop in front of a burned-out, redbrick row house. Old dirty white vinyl siding sagged from the eaves. Entire panels were missing elsewhere on the facade. Windows, behind bent black metal burglar bars, were boarded over. Where the front door had once been, there now was a sheet of weathered plywood hanging at an angle from strap hinges and secured with a rusty chain and padlock. It had the crude rendering of a rodent—little more than a spray-painted black blob with huge whiskers and a long tail—with a large X painted over it. Written beneath it was NO RATS!!!

"You sure this is the place, Dick? Looks locked up pretty good."

"It's what Pookie texted," McCrory said, then pointed down the block. "If not, we must be getting close. Wonder if they did that for him."

Kennedy looked through the falling snow, then nodded. The two stop signs, on opposite corners, had been tagged with graffiti—silver spray paint that spelled SNITCHIN under the reflective lettering.

"Stop snitches? No rats? And you really think you can get one of these knuckleheads to talk, huh?"

He sighed as he pressed the wiper stalk to clear snow from the windshield.

"Hell, I dunno. Pookie said this guy knows who the doer is. What I do know is if you don't try, you don't get squat and . . ."

He stopped when an unkempt dark-skinned man came out of the house that was to the left of the burned-out red one. He had on a filthy faded black hoodie sweatshirt and dirty blue jeans with the cuffs stuffed into dull black leather lace-up boots. The sweatshirt's hood was pulled tight over his head, leaving little more than his thick black-framed eyeglasses and whiskers visible. He rubbed his bare hands together incessantly.

Without turning his head, he glanced at the car. Then he sauntered past, headed toward the corner at Wingohocking.

"Bingo," McCrory said. "Short black male, medium complexion. Coke-bottle glasses and a scraggly beard. That's our guy. The kid looks not even twenty."

"You see those eyes?" Kennedy asked.

McCrory watched the kid through the rearview mirror. "Uh-huh."

"He's damn sure hopped up on something."

"Uh-huh. Can't really walk a straight line."

"What's he doing?"

"Looking up and down the street. And now looking at us. And . . . and now he's coming back this way."

"And probably packing."

"Does a bear shit in the woods?"

Kennedy grunted. He gestured across the street. "Or, more appropriately, a junkie in a bucket?"

Both men pulled their department-issued Glocks from their hip holsters. They were sitting on their seat belts, which were buckled beneath them to allow for them to exit the vehicle more quickly, despite the canned message regularly broadcast over police radio to "always wear your seat belt—the life you save could be your own."

McCrory, who wore black leather gloves, placed his 9-millimeter semiautomatic on his lap under a New England Patriots knit cap; Kennedy crossed his arms, concealing his under his massive left bicep as he held on to it.

"Okay. He's crossing the street and coming at us," McCrory said.

McCrory bumped his window down a quarter of the way. An icy draft crept into the car. He kept a wary eye on the kid's hands.

The kid approached the open window. The wind carried his body odor.

Ugh. Reeks of weed, McCrory thought, *and no bath in who the hell knows how long.*

The kid leaned in closer, his dilated, bloodshot eyes darting between the men as his fingers wrapped over the top of the window. McCrory saw bruises and scabs on the top of his hands, the telltale pockmarks of needle tracks along the veins.

The kid mumbled, "What the fuck you doin' here, man?"

McCrory slowly leaned back, pressing against his seat, and thought, *Oh, man! That breath's foul . . .*

"Pookie said you had something for us," McCrory said.

"Pookie?"

"Yeah, Pookie. Said he'd texted you that we were coming because you said you had something for us."

He thought for a minute, then said, "Pookie, he's all right. What you want? Oxys? Xannys?"

"No. Pookie said you wanted to talk."

"Talk? About what?"

"Dante Holmes."

The kid's eyelids drooped, and he stuck a thumb and index finger behind his glasses and rubbed them. Then he said, "Dante? He from around here?"

McCrory grimaced, then sighed.

Need to try a different approach, he thought.

"How much for Oxys?" McCrory said.

"Forty a pill," the kid said, his blurry eyes surveying Kennedy.

"No T-bone?" McCrory said.

The junkie's eyes then tried to lock on McCrory's.

"I got T-bone. Got a pocketful. Nickel- and dime-bumps. How many you want?"

McCrory didn't respond.

"Look, man," the junkie said, looking back over one shoulder, then the other, "I don't wanna get my ass capped 'cause of you hangin' here!"

Jesus, Mary, Joseph, and all the fookin saints, McCrory thought.

And I don't want to touch this junkie, let alone have him stink up the backseat worse than it is.

But here goes . . .

"Don't worry, we're professionals," McCrory said, and heard Kennedy's deep chuckle.

McCrory, right hand on his Glock, pulled on the door latch with his left, then leaned hard with all his weight into the door panel. The door flew open, knocking the junkie off balance. He toppled backward on his heels, landing flat on the snow.

Guns up, McCrory and Kennedy were out of the vehicle about the time he hit the ground. Kennedy, scanning up and down the street, covered McCrory as McCrory put the muzzle of his pistol to the junkie's forehead, then grabbed his right wrist and spun him facedown. Putting a knee in the small of his back, he effortlessly handcuffed the right wrist, then the left.

Limp as a rag doll.

At least the smack and whatever else he's on is good for something.

McCrory then looked toward Kennedy, and saw that the Patriots knit cap had fallen to the sidewalk and now was by his feet.

"Hey, don't step on that!"

Kennedy shook his head as he slipped his Glock back in its black leather hip holster.

"That thing alone could get us shot at out here," Kennedy said, pulling on blue latex gloves. "Only thing worse might be a Dallas Cowboys one."

"Cowboys suck!" the junkie said.

"See?" Kennedy told McCrory, then said to the kid, "You got bigger problems than football right now."

"You got a name?" McCrory said, as he began patting him down.

He yawned. "Name? Why you need a name?"

McCrory showed him his badge.

"Now give me your name."

"Aw, shit, man." He sighed, and after a moment said, "I, uh, I go by Jamal . . ."

Right.

"You got a real name, Jamal?"

He looked over each shoulder, up and down the street, then said, "All right. It's Michael."

"What about a last name?"

"Hayward."

"Gimme your date of birth."

Michael Hayward, aka "Jamal," did. And Kennedy, who was watching every move and listening closely, then sent the information in an encrypted text on his phone back to the Homicide Unit.

"This Dante Holmes," McCrory then said, "he got capped in a drive-by last night over in Kensington. What do you know about it?"

Hayward sighed, then again looked up and down the street.

"I don't know nothing 'bout nothing."

McCrory heard Kennedy quietly reading him the reply to the text: "Five priors, two for public intoxication and three for pot, personal possession, less than thirty grams. No outstanding warrants."

McCrory rolled him onto his back and continued frisking him. At the belly pocket of the sweatshirt, he felt a familiar heavy object beneath the fabric. He carefully reached inside the pocket and came out with forty-five dollars in rumpled fives and tens, and a dozen postage-stamp-sized zip-top bags. A few of the clear glassine packets held a single pill each. The rest of the small bags contained various amounts of a brown powder and had a black drawing of a T-bone steak rubber-stamped on them.

McCrory then yanked up the bottom edge of Hayward's dirty sweatshirt.

"Well, look at what we have here," Kennedy said, squatting as he reached down with his gloved hand and pulled a black-framed .40 caliber Smith & Wesson semiautomatic from Hayward's waistband.

"Congratulations, Jamal," McCrory said. "Possession of a firearm just added an automatic mandatory five years to whatever other lucky sentence the judge hands down."

Hayward seemed unfazed by that.

McCrory looked at Kennedy.

"Don't forget what Matt Payne said about your little show."

Kennedy nodded, then stood.

Pointing the muzzle at the ground, he racked back the slide and smoothly engaged the lever that locked it open. In the process, a live round had ejected, and he caught it in midair. Then, using only his gloved index finger and thumb, he held the pistol high over his head for the benefit of anyone who might be watching. He looked up, studying it as he turned it back and forth. Then he brought it down and depressed the release for the magazine with his right thumb. The mag fell from the pistol grip into his left palm.

The magazine felt unusually light, and when he glanced at it he was surprised that it was empty.

Kennedy produced from his pocket a gallon-sized clear polymer bag and dropped the single bullet and the empty magazine into it. The heavy-duty bag was leak-proof and puncture-resistant, with one side imprinted EVIDENCE in large letters and, below that, lines to note such details as date evidence collected, case number, collector's information, chain of custody, et cetera.

"Only one round, Jamal?" Kennedy said.

Hayward shrugged.

"All I got left," he said.

McCrory and Kennedy exchanged glances.

Then Kennedy ran a plastic zip-tie through the barrel as a visual aid that the bore was empty. He slipped the weapon, its slide still locked back in the open position, into the evidence bag, sealed the adhesive closure, handed the bag to McCrory, then finished the pat-down.

McCrory looked at the lone .40 caliber round in the bag and noticed that the full metal jacket of the bullet had been scored, two cuts in the copper forming a crude *X* across the tip.

He looked back at Jamal and thought: *That drive-by scene had .40 cal and 9 mil casings all over the place.*

He says he doesn't know Dante Holmes. But there could be a damn good reason for saying that, and for knowing who's responsi-

ble for whacking Dante—because he damn well could've done it himself.

Small wonder he didn't show any response to the extra five years for weapon possession—a murder rap is bad enough.

And that prick Pookie, who clearly lied about Jamal wanting to talk, just sold him down the river.

Or . . . not.

If this is one of the weapons that was used in the shooting, ballistics oughta be able to make the match.

But that won't establish who pulled the trigger.

These guns get bought and sold and traded over and over—especially after a crime.

He squatted beside Jamal.

Hell, Pookie or someone else may have set this bastard up just by giving him the gun.

Only thing we know for sure: Jamal's a junkie, and high as a kite, and figuring out the truth is going to be a bitch.

"You're under arrest," McCrory said loudly, and pulled a playing card–sized paper and a ballpoint pen from his shirt pocket.

He held the card so that Jamal could see it.

"'You have the right to remain silent . . .'" McCrory began, reading from the card despite being able to recite every word of the Miranda Rights from memory.

When McCrory finished not thirty seconds later, he turned Hayward and put his knee in his back, unlocked the right handcuff, and waved the card and pen in front of his face.

"Sign this," McCrory said.

"I ain't signing nothing."

"Just sign the damn card."

"Why?"

"It acknowledges that I read you your Miranda Rights. That's all. But it's okay, I guess you enjoy lying in this nasty snow. Figure anyone's dumped one of those piss buckets on it lately?"

After a moment Michael Hayward sighed, grabbed the pen, then scribbled some semblance of his name across the card.

Kennedy knelt beside Hayward as McCrory clicked the right handcuff back on Hayward's wrist.

"Jesus, you stink," Kennedy said, grabbing Hayward's left bicep. He looked at McCrory, who had grabbed his other arm. "On two . . . a one and a . . ."

They yanked Hayward from the ground and marched him to the back door of the Chevy.

McCrory, scanning the neighborhood as he slipped his pistol into its holster, then squatted and retrieved his knit cap from the sidewalk.

Kennedy watched him carefully brush snow from it, then hold it close to his nose and gently sniff.

Kennedy laughed loudly.

McCrory met his eyes as he tugged the cap on his head, smirked, and said, "Fuck you, partner."

V

[ONE]
Owen Roberts International Airport
George Town, Grand Cayman Islands
Saturday, December 15, 2:35 P.M.

A smiling H. Rapp Badde Jr.—wearing sunglasses of Italian design, a white silk shirt, tan linen shorts, and brown leather sandals—had just stepped down to the sunbaked tarmac from the glistening white Gulfstream IV jet aircraft when he heard his Go To Hell cell phone start ringing.

He grimaced as he pulled it from an outer pocket of his leather backpack.

Badde carried two cell phones, one a smartphone that had what he considered his general use number and the other a more basic folding phone with his closely held private number. The latter he shared with only his small circle of legal and political advisers, and so when it rang, it was not unusual that something was about to go to hell.

He looked up at the doorway to the aircraft. A curvy twenty-five-year-old woman with silky light brown skin was stepping through it. Five-foot-six and wearing a low-cut white linen sundress, Janelle Harper was Badde's executive assistant.

From the beginning, many had suspected that there was far

more to his relationship with the young lawyer than strictly city business. And so it had come as little surprise when at least a dozen salacious photographs of them in Bermuda wound up splashed all over the local news.

Now Badde, his wife having banned him from their home, was cohabitating with Jan Harper in the luxury two-bedroom condominium in which he'd originally set her up. And as convenient as that certainly had seemed at first, both quietly found that spending so much time together—working and traveling and now living— was putting a strain on their relationship.

Badde looked at the telephone. The caller ID read PHILA MAYOR'S OFFICE.

What the hell? Carlucci?

Why would that Wop be calling me—and on a Saturday?

And why should I answer?

As Jan approached, he held up the ringing device and said, "It's Carlucci."

"Then answer it."

"You sure? Why?"

She shrugged. "Then don't."

He made a look of disapproval as he flipped open the phone and put it to his ear.

"Rapp Badde," he said, affecting a bored tone.

"Councilman, this is Edward Stein calling. How are you?"

Oh, I'm just peachy keen, Badde thought.

And you're not Carlucci.

Who the hell are you and how did you get this number?

"What can I do for you?" Badde said. "I'm rather busy, what with the constant demands of my office. I'm sure you understand."

Badde felt himself beginning to sweat in the bright tropical sun, and stepped into the shade of the aircraft.

"I do understand," Stein said. "Councilman, we haven't met. Do you know who I am?"

Edward Stein, he said?

Sounds familiar. But then Carlucci's probably got at least fifty on his staff.

Thank God for caller ID . . .

"Of course," Badde said. "Carlucci's office. What can I do for you?"

"We have a serious problem. And by 'we,' I mean you."

What the hell?

"What do you mean I have a serious problem?" Badde said, a sharp edge to his tone. "Does Carlucci know about this?"

"As you know, I'm the mayor's new chief executive adviser. I am specifically authorized to speak for him."

Badde was quiet a moment, then said, "What sort of problem?"

"It's about Josiah Cross."

"And what about the good reverend?" Badde said, his tone defensive. "He's an outstanding pillar of the community."

There was a pause, and then Stein, his voice incredulous, said, "Have you not seen the news?"

Oh, hell—now what happened? Badde thought, looking as Janelle Harper stepped into the shade. She was making a stern face while rapidly tapping on the screen of her cellular phone.

"I saw the news first thing this morning," Badde said. "Since then, as I said, I've been busy with other demands."

"Then you're telling me that you're unaware of today's murders . . ."

That's it? Just more murders?

Unless it's a real bad one, they barely even make the news anymore.

". . . and that Reverend Cross and his followers are calling the police killers? In particular, that they have declared highly decorated Homicide Sergeant Payne as 'Public Enemy Number One'?"

Badde thought: *What is that all about? That would definitely make the news.*

He did not respond.

"Hello?" Stein said.

"I'm here. Look—"

"What about Cross," Stein went on, "recklessly telling a TV reporter that Sergeant Payne is 'a trigger-happy cop' and that his 'contributing to the bloodshed of citizens in the city was despicable'?" He paused, then added, "Would you say that's what one expects to hear from 'an outstanding pillar of the community'?"

"Look," Badde said, "I hadn't heard that. But I don't see how it could be my problem. Correct me if I'm wrong, but the last I heard, it's your boss, the mayor, who hires the police commissioner, who reports directly to him."

"Actually, the city managing director does the hiring, with the mayor's approval."

"Same difference. That makes Payne the mayor's problem."

"But we're not talking about Sergeant Payne," Stein said, hearing his voice rise. He paused, collected himself, and added, "Who, incidentally, Mayor Carlucci doesn't consider a problem. It's Reverend Cross."

"And?"

"And you're on the Public Safety Committee—"

"Yes," Badde interrupted, "but I'm not a senior member. I have much greater responsibilities on other committees, which, actually, are what I'm dealing with today. So, can we get to the point of this?"

". . . and you're telling me that you haven't heard that Reverend Cross, whom you appointed to CPOC, is leading marches protesting Philadelphia's murder rate—"

"What's wrong with that?" Badde interrupted again.

"Are you serious? I have to spell it out?"

Stein waited for a response, and when none came, went on: "What's wrong is that the chairman of CPOC is declaring that the police his committee oversees are killers! And if that wasn't outrageous enough, apparently you have agreed to speak at his rally this afternoon to build support of that!"

What rally?

I didn't agree to nothing.

"As a rule, I do try to support my constituents and colleagues," Badde said, looking out across the airfield and at the Caribbean Sea beyond the palm trees in the distance. "But even if I wanted to attend this rally, today just wouldn't be possible. There must have been some confusion with one of my office assistants."

Stein was silent a long moment.

"Councilman Badde," he said, in a measured tone, "I just left an urgent message asking for Cross to call me as soon as possible, preferably before this rally. I have, unfortunately, absolutely no faith that that's going to happen. Which is why I've called you. It is critical that this situation be contained before it gets out of hand. Can I count on you, as a responsible elected official, to arrange for that call to happen? Even better, can you set it up for the three of us to meet today?"

Even if I could, Badde thought, *why would I?*

It sure doesn't hurt me when Carlucci looks incompetent.

Especially if his campaign promise of Law and Order crashes and burns.

"First of all," Badde said, "I'm out of town, so meeting today won't work. And, second, as much as I'd like, I just don't know how I'd help otherwise."

There was another long silence, during which Badde thought that he overheard someone in the background speaking to Stein.

Stein finally said: "I cannot tell you how genuinely disappointed I am to hear you say that. I was just thinking, however, that perhaps Councilman Lane could suggest some ways. One that comes immediately to mind: Cross repudiates the scurrilous message of the police being killers and then resigns from CPOC."

Willie Lane? Is that supposed to be a threat? Badde thought, and suddenly felt a chill despite the tropical heat.

And there's no way Lenny's gonna give up his CPOC gig.

"Resign?" Badde said. "Really?"

"That of course would be what I consider the best-case scenario. But it doesn't have to go that far. What he absolutely has to do is stop with the direct attacks on the police department. If he fails to do so, I'll see that he's removed for cause from CPOC. And his removal will not reflect well on the council member who appointed him."

Badde was quiet a long moment. He looked at Janelle Harper. She was holding up her phone and pointing anxiously at it.

Damn it! Badde thought.

I don't need this attention with everything else I've got going.

I need to think of something. Fast . . .

"Mr. Stein?" Badde said.

"I'm here."

"I think this might actually be Josiah calling," Badde lied. "Can I put you on hold a second?"

"Certainly. Go ahead."

"If somehow we lose our connection, I'll call right back," Badde said, then flipped the phone closed, breaking off the call.

H. Rapp Badde Jr. and William G. Lane had more than a little in common, beginning with the fact that both their fathers had been city council members, then served back-to-back terms as mayor of the City of Philadelphia.

When the senior Lane had left office—after midway through his term having been named as one of the top five worst big-city mayors in a *U.S. News & World Report* magazine cover story—the senior Badde won election to his seat. While a distinguished news-weekly publication later had not labeled Badde among the nation's worst mayors, his failure to improve on his predecessor's contemptible record had many saying that Badde certainly had, at least in one unfortunate sense, lived up to the family name.

It was no secret that both sons aspired to become mayor, and, like their fathers, had taken the first step of being elected to the city council. And that, also like their fathers' rivalry, they kept a wary eye on the other.

Philadelphia had seventeen total city council members, ten of whom were elected to represent their respective districts, and the remaining seven, to promote a balanced racial representation, were elected to "at large" seats.

As the first order of business upon beginning their term,

the seventeen members voted who among them would serve as the city council president. Among other duties, the council president selected who would serve on which of the council committees—more importantly, who got appointed chair of each committee.

As there were far more committees than council members, the members were appointed to as many as ten committees each. Juggling the demands of multiple committees—which covered all city business, from oversight of the international airport and the ship docks on down to ensuring the filling of potholes and the collecting of refuse—was an exhausting, if somewhat impossible, task.

Thus, there existed a mutually agreed upon, though unspoken, compromise—each member concentrated the vast majority of his or her energy on the committee that he or she chaired.

They would of course show due diligence. They sat in on meetings of all the various committees, sometimes even asking a pertinent question or two. In the end, though, the members usually followed the lead of the committee chair, whose expertise on the given subject they said was to be commended.

"Usually followed" because, occasionally, there was—there naturally had to be—dissent. It came in the form of "no" votes—after, perhaps, some calculated political theater, the raising of voices during debate, say, or even the leaking of embarrassing memos to the media. It all was accepted as the cost of doing business—unless, however, the "no" votes were too many and caused the chair of the committee not to accomplish what he or she felt necessary.

And that inevitably would lead those who had voted "no" to suffer a similar fate in the committee of which they were chair.

It was then possible that bigger and bigger waves of childish tit-for-tat "no" votes could roll through many other committees, threatening to bring city business to a halt.

Well before that happened, it was the responsibility of the city council president to step in, first attempting to get the various factions to make amends, then, failing that, going so far as reassigning members to different committees.

Including, if necessary, an adult variant of the parental disciplinary tools of "time-out" and "grounding"—the removal of the committee chairs themselves.

William G. Lang had been voted by his peers as the city council president, and in that capacity Lang, quickly collecting political favors, had awarded the chairmanship of the City of Philadelphia Housing and Urban Development Committee to the city councilman (at large) who had requested it, one H. Rapp Badde Jr.

"Rapp, this is not good," Jan Harper said, waving her cell phone in front of his face. "I've gotten a bunch of e-mails asking for confirmation if you're going to appear at"—she paused, and then read from the screen—"'the rally where Reverend Josiah Cross will talk about today's murders and his calling Philly cop Matt Payne 'bloodthirsty' and 'Public Enemy Number One.'"

"I know. That's why this"—he held up his Go To Hell phone, mocking her—"was Carlucci's new adviser calling."

"Don't you be a smart-ass with me, Rapp," she said, narrowing her eyes and slightly cocking her head. "This ain't gonna be my cross to bear, if you get my point. When the hell did you say you were going to participate in something like that? What were you thinking?"

"I wasn't."

"That's right. You certainly weren't thinking."

"No, I mean I wasn't planning I'd be at that, or any other, damn rally. I've got too much other stuff going on. I just now heard about it from this new guy Stein. And I need to call him back quick. What he said was . . ."

When Badde finished repeating the conversation, Jan shook her head.

"How do you get involved with all these jackasses like Cross?" she said, her tone disgusted. "Okay, here's what you're going to do, first call back Stein and then . . ."

Two minutes later, Badde was back on his Go To Hell phone, and the moment Stein answered, he announced: "Okay, Monday afternoon is Feed Philly Day. I'll be back for that, and we can meet then."

Stein did not immediately reply.

"I'm sorry," Stein then said. "You said Monday afternoon is *what?*"

"It's our annual Feed Philly Day. We park a delivery truck full of frozen turkeys in front of the Word of Brotherly Love, and pass them out to the citizens. And we—are you aware that there are people who don't even have a stove or oven, and many more who may have one but can't afford the power to use them?—we will serve a thousand holiday dinners at the fellowship hall. Do you know what a difference that makes in the lives of our citizens, especially during the holidays?" He cleared his throat, then self-righteously added, "That's how one who truly cares is supposed to reach out and make a difference in the community, something beyond the usual constituent services."

Stein was quiet a moment.

"All right," Stein finally said, "I'll be there. But today is Saturday. What about today's rally? I'm not at all suggesting the rally should not take place. It is certainly the mayor's position that there are too many murders, and that if Reverend Cross can help address that—and address it constructively—everyone will be better off." He paused, then in a stronger tone went on, "But the mayor will absolutely not tolerate the targeting of the police department and its officers. This demonizing is destructive. And besides being ethically wrong, it's also factually incorrect. As chairman of CPOC, Cross must know how few homicides are actually committed by police each year and that—at least in the last ten years— all have been cleared as justified." He paused again, then added, "Since you're on the Public Safety Committee, you should know how many."

There was a long moment's silence, and when Badde realized that he was expected to answer, he said, "Well, not off the top of my head, but I'm sure you can tell me. As I said, I'm deeply involved with other city committees and can't be expected to remember all the minutiae from every one."

He'd pronounced minutiae "minn-you-tee-uh," and now could be heard softly uttering, "Huh? It's 'min-eww-sha'? Oh." Then in a louder voice said into the phone: "Such *minutiae* from every one."

"Only nine all this year," Stein said, and then blurted, "And that's hardly *trivial* information. So you need to rein in your goddamn man. And now."

"What I can do," Badde said after a moment, "is call and attempt to persuade Reverend Cross to focus on the wider topic, and not the department."

"Fine. You do that. And have him return my call right after you do. Now, I'm going to touch base with Councilman Lane, whom I know is very concerned about today's events."

From the far side of the airplane, Badde heard a vehicle approaching. When he looked to the nose of the jet, a shiny gold Jeep Wrangler with oversized tires rolled into view, then stopped near the tip of the wing.

"I'll make the call," Badde said into the phone, "and get back to you."

Badde listened, heard nothing, then realized that Stein had hung up.

Jan, he saw, was surveying the Jeep. The sport utility vehicle had had its doors removed and there was no top, only a foam-padded roll-bar above the seats. Neat lettering along both sides of the hood read QUEENS CLUB, A ROYAL YELLOWROSE RESORT.

He also quickly noted that the driver, in her late twenties, was stunning.

She had a rich chestnut tan, and her short blond hair had been pulled back into a tight ponytail that bounced with the vehicle. She wore what appeared to be a nautical-themed uniform that consisted of tight navy shorts and a sheer white short-sleeved captain's shirt (each epaulet had gold stars pinned to it) that fit very snugly over her ample bosom. Badde looked—and looked—but could not see any suggestion of a suntan line.

She hopped out and waved as she walked toward them.

"Welcome to paradise!" she said. "Mr. Santos has been expecting you. I'm to take you to Queens Club."

Jan Harper had somewhat expected to hear an English accent. She knew the Caymans were, after all, a British territory, and the woman looked as if she'd be equally at home in, say, London's trendy Notting Hill. What came out of the woman's mouth, however, made Jan think she sounded Russian.

At least, she's Eastern European something.

But she could pass, on looks alone if she kept her mouth shut, for a Main Line wife at the Merion Golf Club.

Or one at Rittenhouse Square.

I guess that's why she does look so familiar.

Jan studied her.

Wait. That's it—the bar in Vista Fiume!

But you'd think I would've remembered that accent, especially because of Yuri.

The new five-star "River View" took up half of the entire thirty-seventh floor of Two Liberty Place, the city's third tallest tower that was midway—a few blocks—between Rittenhouse Square and City Hall. The fashionable restaurant and its enormous lounge featured panoramic views of the city and its iconic rivers, the Schuylkill and Delaware. It, and its moneyed international clientele, had set the new standard for late nightlife in Philly.

Janelle knew it was owned by a company controlled by the international investor Yuri Tikhonov, in large part because he also held, through shell companies, forty-nine percent of Diamond Development, which was in partnership with the Philadelphia Economic Gentrification Initiative.

Tikhonov—a wealthy forty-eight-year-old Russian rumored to have high connections in Moscow from his time in the intelligence agency Sluzhba Vneshney Razvedki—had struck fear in

Badde in early November at Vista Fiume when he very quietly announced, stone-faced, that "friends" had taken care of three people who were holding up the final demolition for their PEGI-sponsored project.

Badde, incredulous, asked how. Tikhonov, his tone matter-of-fact, replied that it had been done by injecting them with succinyl-choline, a muscle relaxant with a short half-life that could stop the heart and become undetectable after an hour.

Badde, not knowing what to believe at the time, now knew one thing for certain about the dead men—the cause of their deaths, from the start listed as "unknown," remained unsolved.

And that—having initially wondered why Tikhonov would share such a damning admission—in turn had caused Badde, with bile suddenly rising in his throat, to decide that the Russian's purpose had been coldly calculated.

Tikhonov was quietly suggesting that such "friends" could visit Badde, and anyone else, if they displeased the former spy. And, as with the three holdouts, there would never be any way to link Tikhonov to the act.

"I think we've met?" Jan asked, but she made it sound more of a statement.

"Yes, of course. I'm Illana," she said, offering her hand. "A month or so ago? At Vista Fiume. It's nice to see both of you again."

"Well," Jan said, shaking her hand, "I should say it's a small world. But I guess it's really not in certain circles."

Illana smiled. "I recognized you, too."

Jan glanced at the Jeep, and Illana followed her eyes.

"I'm sorry," Jan said, looking back at Illana, "but I forgot what you told us it is that you do."

"Of course," Illana said. "I am what I like to call a hospitality ambassador. Our company provides consulting services and more to world-class properties." She glanced at the Jeep, then added, "There's usually a driver, but Mr. Santos asked that I personally meet your flight."

"Properties like Vista Fiume?" Jan said, somewhat suspiciously.

"Yes," Illana said, not showing that she had picked up on the inflection. "And also to Yellowrose resorts, such as Queens Club, and various other fine properties." She turned to Rapp Badde. "I understand from Mr. Santos that we will soon provide the same to new properties in your Philadelphia."

"That's what I've been told," Badde said, nodding. He looked at Jan, and added, "That's what I was telling you we worked out when I met Santos in Dallas."

Jan looked at him, raised her eyebrows, then turned to Illana.

"I'm not exactly clear on what it is you provide," Jan said, her tone making it a question.

"In simple terms, everything except the building," Illana said. "We handle branding, marketing, staffing. I mostly consult on staffing. It is critical that guests receive the finest experience, and I, as well as others, travel from property to property to ensure that the highest of standards are kept. After I helped to staff and then open Vista Fiume, I was sent here. And after this tour, I expect to be back in Philadelphia to check on its progress and also work on the new hotel."

"Well," Rapp said, automatically flashing his politician's smile, "that new hotel is why we are here to see Mr. Santos."

Badde paused, and thought, *Which could all go down the tubes if Willie Lane—or anyone else—starts sniffing around PEGI. This deal takes it all to another level.*

"But first I need to make one quick call. Only take a moment."

"To who now? Can't it wait?" Jan said, and looked to Illana. "How far is the hotel?"

"It is perhaps ten minutes."

"Rapp," Jan said, turning back toward Badde—but he had already moved into the shadow of the aircraft and was almost yelling into his smartphone.

"Where's Len— I mean, where's Josiah?" Badde demanded. "Put him on the phone. *Now.*"

[TWO]
Molly's Olde Ale House
Chestnut Street, University City, Philadelphia
Saturday, December 15, 2:40 P.M.

"Okay, keep knocking on the neighbors' doors for statements— someone had to see or hear something—and let me know when the medical examiner releases the scene," Homicide Sergeant Matthew Payne said into his cellular phone as he watched Michael J. O'Hara throw back a shot glass—his third—brimming with eighteen-year-old Bushmills Irish whisky. "I'm a few blocks away, almost to the ME's office, actually."

The medical examiner's office was next to the Hospital of the University of Pennsylvania.

Payne and O'Hara were seated at the far end of the long wooden bar. Payne had his back against the wall. He looked at O'Hara, and beyond him, glancing around the half-full room of mostly college students watching sports on the overhead flat-screen TVs and—when it opened, bringing in a blast of cold air—at the front door.

"I'm repeating myself, I know, but the murder simply is barbaric beyond belief," O'Hara said, shaking his head, then extended his arm and held the empty glass above his head to get the bartender's attention. "Another Bushmills."

The bartender glanced at Payne. Payne shook his head.

Payne looked at the two empty shot glasses before him— O'Hara had ordered them two each to start when they first sat down—and hoped Mickey wouldn't override him and have the bartender bring them both another.

Then O'Hara, frustrated, practically slung the empty across the wooden bar. It slid into his two other empty shot glasses, making a loud clink that caused a couple of people down the bar to turn and look.

The bartender, who apparently had witnessed worse behavior, did not seem to care.

"Here ya go, pal," the bartender said, placing it before O'Hara, then collecting the empties and walking away.

"Tim was a really good guy, Matty, fearless and honest as the day is long," O'Hara said as he held up the glass, and stared at it a long moment.

Then he tossed back the shot.

"Maybe too fearless," Payne said.

O'Hara's tired eyes darted at him.

Not quite an hour earlier, Payne had pulled up to the U-City address O'Hara had texted him.

O'Hara was pacing on the sidewalk, following the path that he had packed in the snow halfway up the block. He wore a heavy black woolen coat over faded blue jeans and a brown checkered flannel shirt. His black loafers had a crust of snow.

Mickey barely acknowledged Matt as he parked the car and got out.

O'Hara, his head down, shoulders slumped, and with his hands stuffed in his overcoat pockets, didn't speak. His face showed a mix of intense concentration and a certain sadness. He motioned with a nod for Matt to follow him to the house.

Just shy of the concrete steps, O'Hara stepped around a yellow-stained melted spot in the snow on the sidewalk.

"That's mine," he said, his voice a monotone.

Payne looked at it.

Mickey threw up.

And, judging by the direction of his shoe prints, after he'd left the house.

He's seen a lot over the years. Not much bothers him.

But it can and does happen to all of us.

He followed O'Hara up the three concrete steps—and immediately saw bloody tracks across the worn paint of the wooden porch. They had an aggressive waffle pattern, suggesting they had been made by heavy boots, for either work or hiking, and they led out from the front door. He could see that the wooden front door was open about three inches, with no evidence of any forced entry.

O'Hara, stepping carefully around the bloody prints, stopped at the door.

He looked back at Payne.

"This is how I found it."

There was a glass pane in the upper third of the door. A beige lace curtain, knocked from its mount, hung at a crooked angle. As Payne stepped closer, he got a larger view of the interior beyond the lace.

"Jesus," Payne said softly.

He felt his stomach knot, and understood how O'Hara had succumbed to the nausea.

"Yeah. Jesus."

Payne looked at O'Hara.

"You went in, Mick?"

O'Hara nodded.

"I know it's a crime scene," he said. "But, yeah, the second I saw Emily there I had to. The door was unlocked. When I got closer to her, it was clear she had been long . . . gone . . . and then I turned and saw Tim's body. They both already had livor mortis—that is, from whatever blood they had left."

Payne knew, courtesy of Doc Mitchell's impromptu lectures during postmortem examinations, that when blood stopped circulating in the human body, gravity took over. The blood settled, and the skin color changed. Even through the window, he could see the distinct pooling pattern on her body, the lower flesh much darker than the light purple of the upper skin. He further knew that rigor mortis, the stiffening of the muscles, occurred about three hours after death, and took place before the heavy pooling.

Payne pulled out his cellular phone.

O'Hara put up his hand, palm out. Payne raised his eyebrows at the gesture for him to stop, and said, "What?"

"Before you call in the medical examiner, I want to ask a favor, Matty."

Payne met his eyes.

"Sure, Mick. Name it."

"You work this case personally. Own it."

Payne slowly nodded. "Okay. Sure. Want to tell me why? I know he worked for you, but . . ."

O'Hara narrowed his eyes, said, "Because you get it," then motioned with his head for Matt to follow.

They stood in a small utility room off the kitchen at the back of the house. It had a dented stackable clothes washer and dryer in one corner. The rest of the space had been fashioned into a home office. Wooden boards for shelving had been mounted to the wall above an old wooden door that served as the desk. The shelving sagged under the weight of books and papers and a computer printer. A folding metal chair lay collapsed under the desk.

Payne stared at the notebook computer on the desk—and the severed head thereon.

Tim O'Brien's dull, lifeless eyes gazed back in his general direction.

The scene did not surprise Payne.

After passing the badly bludgeoned body of Emily O'Brien, and Payne taking photographs with his cell phone camera, they had approached Tim's body, the legs and feet of which stuck outside the kicked-in door of the hallway half-bath while the upper torso lay inside. There was an enormous pool of blood. Overhead, the exhaust fan rattled. The bulb in the half-bath was still on, too, casting a harsh light over the body that not only had been crudely eviscerated but also decapitated.

O'Hara and Payne had followed the blood trail to the kitchen, then into the utility room turned home office.

"Remind you of El Gato, Mickey?"

O'Hara nodded.

Months earlier, Sergeant James O. Byrth of the Texas Rangers had come to Philadelphia hunting a twenty-one-year-old thug from Dallas who was trafficking drugs and teenaged Latinas from Central America to Texas and finally on to Philly. Juan Delgado—called El Gato for his jungle cat–like fierceness—befriended the young, vulnerable girls, then preyed on them, forcing them into prostitution, feeding them drugs and forcing them to have sex with a dozen johns in as many hours as the means to pay for their being smuggled into the United States.

When one fourteen-year-old ran away in Philly, Delgado became enraged. He beat her young female companion to death, cut off her head, and dumped the body in the Schuylkill River. He then went to the laundromat in North Philly where the fourteen-year-old girl had found work with other illegal immigrants, and slid the severed head across the floor.

The Mexican national who quietly ran the laundry business, and had witnessed Delgado's act, became a confidential informant. He helped Byrth and Payne track down Delgado to a dilapidated row house in Frankford, and then, with Byrth as witness to what he declared was an act of self-defense, ended Delgado's reign of terror with shots from a .45.

Payne, who'd been in the next room when the two rounds were fired, quietly wondered if the confidential informant's motive had been revenge. But while Payne could not prove it was not self-defense, there was ample evidence of Delgado's brutal crimes—including El Gato and his crew having kidnapped Amanda Law, throwing her inside a minivan in front of Temple University Hospital and holding her hostage at the Frankford row house.

No one had any doubt whatsoever that El Gato finally had used up at least nine lives and that the bastard deserved to die.

And now Payne understood what Mickey meant when he had said, "Because you get it"—Matt had personally experienced the evil.

When he saw O'Brien's butchered torso and then the severed head, he had flashbacks to when he'd been at the medical examiner's office for the autopsy of the young girl's body pulled from the Schuylkill and again when the confidential informant had showed him her head that he'd hidden in a bag in his basement deep freeze after it had been thrown in the laundromat.

"Like El Gato," Mickey O'Hara said, "only worse. Delgado was a deluded wannabe thinking he could operate his small crew in the shadows, outside of the cartels. These bastards are the real deal. And they have no problem killing anyone in their way—not just little girls. In Mexico alone, a hundred journalists have been killed over the last decade, another twenty gone missing—and not a single one solved. If their bodies are found, they show clear evidence of torture. Mexico is the fourth most dangerous nation in the world for journalists, after Syria, Somalia, and Pakistan."

He turned and met Payne's eyes.

"And now it's here. This is beyond intimidation. This is retaliation, Matty."

[THREE]

The tall bartender approached Payne and O'Hara. He carried an almost empty bottle of Irish whisky, and held it up to them.

"Looks like you've killed one, gents."

Mickey looked at the bartender, then at Matt—and suddenly burst into laughter.

Payne chuckled, and shook his head.

The bartender made a quizzical look.

"What?" he said.

"Bad reaction for a bad day," Payne said. "Good people were murdered this morning just blocks from here."

The bartender shook his head, his expression now one of disgust.

"What's wrong with this world today, huh?" he said.

"Give him one, too," O'Hara said, waving his index finger between both their shot glasses. "After what I'm about to show him, he's going to need it."

The bartender raised his eyebrows, then filled the two glasses, drained the bottle into a third, said, "They're on me. My condolences," and turned away.

O'Hara pulled out his cell phone and brought up a photograph on it.

He held it up for Payne to see.

The image was of the severed head of a bearded brown-skinned male on the keyboard of a notebook computer. The difference between that head and Tim O'Brien's was that it had a handwritten note stuck to the dried blood: *Editors of Obrien: This source no*

longer wishes to talk for your stories. Tomas was warned to stop. Now
you are. No more articles. Period. CDNA.

Payne shook his head and turned to O'Hara.

"CDNA?"

"Cartel del Nuevo Acuña."

"The New Acuña Cartel? Have you talked with Byrth about it?"
O'Hara nodded.

"I did. O'Brien did. Tomas certainly did. Jim put him in touch
with the Texas Rangers there. CDNA is a relatively small organization that's based just across the border from Del Rio, Texas. Its
plaza, which is what they call their smuggling routes, skirts the big
plaza at Nuevo Laredo, which is twenty miles downstream and
controlled by the Gulf Cartel."

O'Hara picked up his shot glass and held it up before him.

"To Tomas."

Payne did the same, then they banged the glasses on the wooden
bar, then downed the Irish whisky.

"Tomas? Who was he?" Payne then said, feeling the warmth of
the alcohol again reach from his throat to his belly.

"A stringer we hired to work with Tim O'Brien," O'Hara explained. "Tomas Rodriguez, thirty-five, married, one child, a boy,
and one on the way.

"Tomas needed work. About six months ago, he was having
lunch, sitting at a sidewalk *mercado* in Acuña, when an elderly
man, uninvited, took the seat across from him. The man put a
copy of that day's *Acuña Noticias* on the table and drummed his
fingers on the cover story. It was about four male bodies that had
been found in a *narco fosa*, their hands and feet bound and a single
bullet hole in their heads. The story bore Tomas's byline."

"A *narco fosa*?"

"It's what they call a cartel shallow grave. Just like mob ones in the good ol' guinea gangster days—whack 'em, maybe cut 'em up, maybe not, then bury them in a basement, an unmarked hole in a field, somewhere.

"The man said he'd been ordered to relay a simple message: *'No mas.'* He said that meant no more coverage of the shallow graves, no more coverage of drugs and humans moving through the plaza near Acuña and across the Rio Grande, no more mention of CDNA. *No mas.*

"Then the elderly man stood and left."

"And Tomas didn't stop," Payne said, unnecessarily.

O'Hara shook his head.

"Tomas, despite knowing full damn well that journalists are being targeted all over Mexico, did not think much of the old man's message. He was a newsman, he said, and he reported news. But the next day, after he published a piece on a stash house near where the dead from the shallow grave had last been seen alive, Tomas had been in his newspaper office—it's a two-room masonry building on the southern edge of town—when the roar of a motorcycle rattled his window. That was immediately followed by the sound of gunfire. He ducked under his desk. When the shooting seemed to be over, he peered out the window and saw that his Volkswagen had been shot up, its windows shattered, the two left tires flat."

"Jesus," Payne said.

O'Hara nodded, then went on: "That night he put his wife and their young son on a bus and sent them to stay with relatives in Texas, outside San Antonio.

"He remained in Mexico but backed off on the cartel articles.

Then, probably for pure intimidation purposes, they firebombed his newspaper office one night. Now he could not publish the newspaper. No matter. He wasn't intimidated. He went underground and started publishing about the drug war on the Internet, in a daily blog in addition to social media, writing under *La Verdad*—'The Truth.' When the cartel found out, they offered a bounty to anyone who gave them the name of who was behind *La Verdad*—or anyone in that person's family."

O'Hara pulled up another image on his cell phone. It showed a bloodied, shirtless male body hanging from a rope tied to a bridge overpass. A dirty white bedsheet with hand-painted lettering was draped over the bridge. It was in Spanish. Payne saw that it was signed "CDNA."

"Someone gave up one of Tomas's photographers," O'Hara said, "and, judging by the wounds, the cartel tortured him, most likely trying to get information on Tomas. Then they killed him. Hung him over an Acuña highway as an example. The *narco mantra* reads 'This will happen to all who write lies about us on the Internet. You will pay. Signed CDNA.' Tomas took off for San Antonio."

"And they killed him there," Payne said. "Just like O'Brien."

"Just like O'Brien," O'Hara repeated, "*and* his wife. Emily just learned she was pregnant."

"My God!" Payne blurted. His mind then immediately went to Amanda, who they recently had learned was with child.

"And the bastards knew she was pregnant," O'Hara went on. "They put on the Internet a photograph of Tomas's head on the computer with another note that read 'The sins of the father shall be visited upon the son.'"

"That's some damn message."

"If they weren't sending a message, Matty, he'd just wind up in a *narco fosa*. Hell, they hacked up Tim."

They were lost in their thoughts for a long moment.

O'Hara then said: "While reporting news is not a perfect craft—never will be—I would suggest that it is getting worse as fewer people are willing to pay for publications that produce long-form journalism—the hard-hitting, in-depth pieces. That's a damn necessary craft needed to protect this thing we call a free society. Corruption is a cancer wherever it feeds. And there no longer are real checks and balances in government."

"No argument," Payne said, nodding. "Seems that no matter which political party's in charge, the politicians essentially take turns enriching themselves and their supporters. Not that that's anything new. Remember what Mencken said about that a hundred years ago?"

O'Hara made a wistful smile.

"You mean good ol' HL, the Sage of Baltimore? My hero scribe? Every one of his social commentaries, alongside those of Samuel Clemens, should be etched in stone. I will take a wild guess that the one to which you refer is: 'Every election is a sort of advance auction sale of stolen goods.'"

"And yet," Payne said, "it's just accepted. To this day. Meanwhile, too much of what passes for today's so-called investigative journalism is some perky TV reporter, her ponytail poking out of an Action News ball cap, waving a failed health department inspection at a restaurant manager and demanding to know if he's cleared out all the cockroaches. No one puts the time into life-changing stories like your Follow the Money series. Tim seemed to be trying, which I suspect is in large measure your influence, including that solid piece he did on the Commish's grandson."

O'Hara met Payne's eyes. "And now his heroin stories that he connected to the guys who set up Garvey."

John A. Garvey—a thirty-six-year-old architect who was married to the granddaughter of retired police commissioner Joseph Gallagher—had been arrested at Philadelphia International Airport with two kilograms of cocaine hidden in his luggage. During a routine sweep of luggage coming off a flight from the U.S. Virgin Islands, Molly the chocolate Labrador retriever alerted on Garvey's bag. When he retrieved it at the baggage claim carousel, he was approached by a blue-uniformed officer from the department's Airport Unit, and Garvey immediately confessed. He explained that in Saint Thomas he'd been blackmailed to be a courier, that they threatened to kill his wife and kids if he did not transport the drugs.

"Every other news outlet," O'Hara said, "ran with the screaming headline: 'Former Police Commissioner's Relative Busted for Smuggling Cocaine.' That by itself was a cheap shot, because Gallagher had been one helluva top cop. But Tim wanted to know more. So, I approved the request to send him to the Virgin Islands to investigate the blackmailing angle. It's what led him first to the story of Colombian coke being routed through the USVI to here and then to yesterday's story about the ring of Mexican nationals pushing black tar heroin in Kensington and Strawberry Mansion. That one apparently was the one story too many."

"They're moving record amounts of smack," Payne said. "Especially now that prescription painkillers on the street are so expensive. Four hits of heroin cost the same forty bucks that a single Percocet or Xanax pill costs."

O'Hara nodded and added: "And if we hadn't reported on the coke and heroin connection—if we'd been more like all the other media, and just wrote up Garvey's arrest, and not dug deeper—then Tim and his wonderful wife would probably still be alive."

Payne shook his head.

After a moment he said, "How did you know to go to his house today? Couldn't be coincidence . . ."

"It wasn't. He e-mailed me."

"He what?"

"I got an e-mail this morning that said 'If you're reading this, either I screwed up the reset button—or I'm probably dead.' He'd set up a time-delayed e-mail. He wrote in it that it was insurance against losing the material in the event they acted on the death threats."

"A what? A time-delayed e-mail?"

"It's rather simple, actually. It's a remote e-mail server. He addressed an e-mail to me, attached the article with the sources and background material to it, and then, instead of clicking on SEND, he set a time and date for when he wanted the e-mail sent, anywhere from, say, a day in the future to a year in the future. Initially, O'Brien's were set to be sent after a five-day period, unless he reset the schedule, which he could do from any computer or even his smartphone by simply clicking an icon he'd set up. So, if something happened to him—he went missing or got whacked—out went the e-mail. If he didn't get kidnapped or whatever, then he'd click the icon, or go back into the e-mail, maybe update the file, and then the clock was reset for another five days."

"But this didn't happen five days ago."

"Anytime there was a heightened threat, usually coinciding with the publishing of his articles, the schedule got moved up. In this case, it was one day. He was probably about to reset the delay for another twenty-four hours."

"You said the schedule could be set up to a year in advance?"

"Or longer. Five days, five months, five years, doesn't matter."

Payne was quiet a moment, then said, "What do you think are the chances there's more coming from some remote server?"

O'Hara nodded.

"The e-mail this morning came with his first draft of the next piece he was working on attached. Another along the lines of Follow the Money. It's good stuff. And I'm betting that there's more."

[FOUR]
North Twenty-ninth and West Arizona Streets
Strawberry Mansion, Philadelphia
Saturday, December 15, 2:40 P.M.

The 2900 block of West Arizona, a single-lane one-way street of cracked asphalt, was lined mostly, except where there were empty lots, with two-story redbrick row houses. The majority of the hundred-year-old homes were inhabited and efforts were made to keep them more or less neat and tidy, despite being in various states of disrepair.

A few, however, with their windows and doors boarded over, were clearly deserted and deteriorating, well on their way to collapsing and creating another gap of an empty lot. (One entire side of the 3000 block was completely barren.)

At the corner where Arizona intersected with two-lane Twenty-ninth Street, two adjoining properties had been converted from residences to a single business space. Their brick fronts had been modified to create the elaborate facade of a pagoda. While the enormous plate-glass window had block lettering in gold paint that boldly stated the property now served as the ministry of the Word of Brotherly Love, the Reverend Josiah Cross presiding, if one looked closely, and in just the right lighting, one could read on the glass a faint CITY BEST CHINESE EGGROLL—WE NEVER CLOSE.

A block up Twenty-ninth, other corner row houses also had been converted to storefronts. One was a check-cashing business, its banners advertising a 99-cent-only fee for each cash withdrawal from its automated teller machines and, in Spanish, a low-cost wiring service for sending money internationally. Next door to it was a bodega, the market's windows containing more signs in both English and Spanish pushing cigarettes to fresh produce to pre-paid Visa debit cards.

Twenty-ninth, being a wider thoroughfare, provided for parallel parking along the curbs on either side of the street. There were various vehicles parked in spaces up and down Twenty-ninth, but almost directly across the street from the Word of Brotherly Love sat a rusty 1980 Chevrolet panel van. It once had been the property of the Philadelphia Electric Company, the PECO logotype on its sides long faded but still recognizable.

When Detective Harvey Simpson of the Philadelphia Police Department had parked the panel van in the spot not quite three hours earlier, there had been no activity at the Word of Brotherly Love.

Within the last hour, however, Simpson—a ten-year veteran cop who was thirty-two years old, of average build with a very dark complexion, and had grown up just ten miles away, across the Schuylkill River in West Philly—had witnessed more and more happening, beginning with a late-model Ford minivan dropping off a half-dozen young men at the corner, then speeding off.

Digital video cameras mounted in hidden ports on the van's roof rack captured live feeds. One camera angle was now focused on the front of the church, another looked down Arizona, and two others covered both directions of Twenty-ninth. The images, in addition to being viewed and recorded with notebook computers in the back of the van, could be sent on demand back to the Executive Command Center at the Roundhouse.

The two computers sat on metal shelving that had been welded to the bare ribs of the van body. Beside the computers Simpson had placed his stainless steel thermos of coffee and, wrapped in white wax paper, the second half of a rare roast beef hoagie that he'd started right after his arrival and getting the surveillance equipment set up.

The tallest of the dropped-off young men—Simpson estimated he had to be six-five—had gone directly to the crimson red door of the ministry and unlocked it, opened it, and anxiously motioned for the others to follow him inside.

Watching the new activity, Simpson thought: *Should probably test the feed with the Roundhouse.*

He clicked on a link on the notebook computer. A small window popped up on the computer screen. It showed Corporal Kerry Rapier in the ECC as his voice came across Simpson's headset: "Hey, Harv."

"Hey, Kerry. Finally got some activity. Figured now was a good time to make sure there's no burps in the system."

"Good idea," Rapier said, and Simpson saw his eyes turn to

look past the computer screen to the wall of flat-screen monitors as he said, "I'm looking at four males in their late twenties, maybe early thirties, three black, the fourth Hispanic, all wearing dark hoodies and jeans, coming out of the church's red door with some sort of big heavy black boxes. And . . . on the other cameras showing nothing except what looks like normal street traffic."

"That's all I've got. Looks like we're good to go then, Kerry."

"What are those guys doing?"

"I'm guessing probably not setting up for a FOP fund-raiser—"

Rapier made a raspberry sound, then said, "Ping me if it gets interesting."

Simpson chuckled at his own humor as Rapier and the pop-up window disappeared from the screen.

Simpson then watched the four males carry, with some difficulty, the black-painted four-foot-square plywood cubes, two men per cube, and put them on the snow-covered sidewalk under the ornate curved corner of the pagoda's roofline. They went back inside and reappeared with two more cubes and then, on a third trip, carried out a lectern and two massive loudspeakers.

They lined up the cubes, creating a sixteen-foot-long stage, on top of which they centered the lectern. The massive loudspeakers then went on either side of the lectern.

Simpson scanned the images captured by the other cameras and realized that with the stage set up in such a manner, there would be ample room for the crowds to fill up and down the streets.

Easily hundreds, Simpson thought, *maybe even thousands.*

Whoever was onstage speaking would have a clear view of everyone in all directions.

And the PECO van's cameras would have a perfect angle on everyone.

As the four men began running wires to the stage and the speakers, a rented yellow six-wheeled box truck rolled into view of the camera. It turned off Twenty-ninth onto Arizona, briefly going the wrong way on the one-way street before rolling up onto the sidewalk and parking in front of the former row house next door that had the sign reading FELLOWSHIP HALL over its double wooden doors.

The driver, a wiry young black male who walked with a spring in his step, hopped out, exchanged words with the four assembling the stage, then went back to the box truck and rolled up its door. Simpson, due to the angle, could see only a few feet inside the box, and there was nothing in view.

The driver then climbed up into the box and pulled out what looked at first to Simpson like a roll of a thin white sheet of linoleum flooring, and maneuvered it to the lip of the box's roof and then slid it completely on top. Then he smoothly hopped to the sidewalk—Simpson half expected him to slip on the snow but he didn't—and went to the nose of the truck. He then effortlessly climbed from the bumper to the hood, then to the roof of the cab, and finally to the roof of the box. There he unrolled the thin white sheet down the side of the box.

"Aha!" Simpson said, seeing that it was actually a vinyl fabric sign.

It read *Word of Brotherly Love Ministry 5th Annual Feed Philly Day Dec. 17th 4 p.m.–Midnight. Proudly Sponsored by Phila City Councilman H. Rapp Badde Jr. YOUR Voice in City Hall.*

"Four to midnight?" Simpson said aloud to himself. "Timed to make the five, six, and eleven o'clock news. Go f'ing figure."

Simpson, sipping from the stainless steel cap of his thermos, then watched the male slide down to the cab and hood and to the sidewalk, then walk to the double wooden doors of the Fellowship Hall. He called back to the four men assembling the stage, then went inside the hall.

After a few minutes, the Hispanic male walked from the stage over to the box truck. He hopped inside and began sliding big cardboard boxes to the outer edge. He popped open the flaps to one, reached in, and came out with a white T-shirt. He held it up to his torso to show the others. Simpson saw that its silkscreened block lettering screamed STOP KILLADELPHIA! on the front and back, the STOP in bright red ink, the KILLADELPHIA in black.

The Hispanic male pulled out more shirts from the box and tossed them to the others as they walked up. Everyone slipped one on over their hooded sweatshirts.

Then the Hispanic male began sliding five-by-three-foot posters to the outer edge, and when he handed them down, Simpson could see the front of them. They were enlarged images of murder victims, posters similar to those used in the Center City demonstrations at JFK Park and the Roundhouse.

The first showed Lauren Childs. She was in the photograph that she had posted online that morning, the one taken at the LOVE artwork with Tony Gambacorta. Her boyfriend had been inelegantly cropped from the frame—his arm, around her neck, was all of him that remained visible—and a white circle with MURDER VICTIM #362 in red text was positioned over where his head would have been. Along the bottom of the poster was her name, followed by "19 Years Young."

On the second poster was Jimmy Sanchez, his serious face

pockmarked with acne. He was wearing not a green elf costume but, instead, a shirt and tie and blazer. He sat staring at a chessboard, his right hand hovering over a white rook. Under his image was "Jaime A. Sanchez, 15 Years Young." The white circle in the upper corner had MURDER VICTIM #363.

The next poster showed a grinning black male with MURDER VICTIM #360 in the white circle. At the bottom was "Dante Holmes, 20 Years Young."

These were carried to the stage and leaned against its front.

When Simpson saw the next poster getting moved to the back of the truck, he muttered, "I'll be damned."

The poster was an enlargement of a digital image originally taken by police department closed-circuit cameras and then picked up by the media.

The image showed one of the PPD Aviation Unit's Bell 206 L-4 helicopters hovering over the Ben Franklin Bridge, the eighty-year-old steel suspension bridge that spanned the Delaware River. Traffic was stopped around wrecked vehicles, and everywhere were ambulances and fire trucks and police cruisers.

And standing in the middle of the mayhem—in front of a sheet that covered a human form—was Matt Payne.

He wore gray trousers, a pale blue starched shirt with a red-striped tie, navy blazer, and shiny black loafers. The slacks had been soiled and the shoes scuffed during the chase. He had his Colt .45 in hand, and was giving the helicopter a thumbs-up gesture.

Bright red lettering at the top of the poster read SGT. MATTHEW PAYNE, and PUBLIC ENEMY #1 was along the bottom.

Simpson clicked on the ECC button.

"Yeah, Harv," Kerry Rapier's voice came over Simpson's headset. "Saw it on the monitor here. I've sent word up the chain of command."

"Payne didn't shoot that guy, if I remember right."

"You're right. That guy—something Jones . . . *Kenny* Jones— had just fled the scene of a shooting. He stole a minivan, and Matt pursued him in an unmarked Crown Vic. Jones managed to get on the bridge going the wrong way—into seven lanes of oncoming traffic. Payne caught up in the Police Interceptor and executed a textbook PIT maneuver, bumping the minivan so that Jones spun out and hit the zipper barrier."

"Who knows how many lives he saved doing that. But you get no points for that, huh?"

"No kidding. And then Jones ditched the minivan and made a run for it—with Payne on foot in hot pursuit. It was anyone's guess what the hell the guy would do next—probably carjack someone headed toward Camden—but then he blindly ran into the path of a bus."

"At least there's not a poster of Jones."

"I wouldn't speak too soon, Harv."

Simpson grunted as the screen then showed the men placing another poster at the back of the van, this one of a pudgy, balding, middle-aged white male wearing a coat and tie.

"Who is Cairns?" Simpson said, reading the poster.

"The casino jewelry store manager shot this morning. Guess he wasn't 'young' enough."

"Huh?" Simpson said, then added, "Oh."

He saw that, while the poster had listed the name, Malcolm Cairns, and the white circle with a red MURDER VICTIM #361, there was no age mentioned. It was clear, however, he was long past his twenties and thirties.

The next three males shown on the posters were labeled as murder victims 350, 351, 352. Ricardo Ramírez was a chunky twenty-seven-year-old Puerto Rican, Héctor Ramírez a swarthy forty-year-old Cuban, and Dmitri Gurnov a tall, wiry, thirty-year-old Russian with sunken eyes and a three-day growth of beard.

"Aren't those guys from Payne's shoot-out last month on the casino boardwalk, Kerry?"

"Yeah, but it was the Russian who whacked the Cuban Ramírez, and maybe five minutes later Ricky Ramírez killed Gurnov. Then when Ricky Ramírez started shooting at Jim Byrth—"

"That Texas Ranger who was up here?"

"Yeah, that's him. Ramírez shot at Byrth and then took shots at the helo that came on station and was lighting up the scene. When Matt ordered Ramírez to drop the weapon, the bad guy made the mistake of getting in a shoot-out with the good ol' Wyatt Earp of the Main Line. That poster attests to the fact that it didn't turn out too good for Ramírez."

"Why the hell do they get included in this? Because Payne took out one? An active shooter who'd just killed a guy? That's pure horseshit."

"Well, technically they all are homicides and made the list. But I take your point."

The next poster was of an attractive, petite nineteen-year-old Puerto Rican. Krystal Angel Gonzalez was listed as MURDER VICTIM #348.

Rapier said: "And there's the poor girl who made the mistake of getting involved with Ricky Ramírez."

"That's the girl who was killed in the home invasion in Old City last month, right?"

"Yeah. Tragic story. Spent most of her life in and out of foster homes, then got conned by Ramírez. All the details haven't come out, but what we do know is that Ramírez was running drugs and hookers out of a dive bar in Kensington. He made the Gonzalez girl think she was his girlfriend, then tried to pimp her out, and beat her when she wouldn't do it."

Simpson grunted again. "Same old story. You're right—tragic."

"Same story but with a twist. After he began beating her, she got her hands on his books—contacts, schedules, everything—"

"And passed them to the woman who ran the foster home," Simpson finished. "I heard that. And the woman went into hiding when she found the girl killed in her fancy house, the place set afire with Molotov cocktails."

"And the woman who went into hiding used the books as leverage to get to Ricky Ramírez and the Russian, who owned the dive bar."

"Nice guys. And now all dead guys. Sergeant Payne should get credit for all three."

They watched as the final posters were being put up—with Payne's Public Enemy #1 poster being affixed to the front of the lectern.

"Those bastards," Rapier said. "Harv, if you knew Matt, you'd know he'd rather not get credit for even one. It's why this all stinks. Anyway, I'll check back in a bit."

"I'll be here with bells on," Simpson said, reaching for the thermos.

Five minutes later, Simpson watched over the lip of his stainless steel cup as a new shiny black Lincoln Navigator came flying up

Twenty-ninth and then, tires screeching, pulled up onto the sidewalk behind the rental box truck. The driver of the SUV slipped a paperboard sign on the dash that had a facsimile of a crucifix and the wording CLERGY—ON OFFICIAL BUSINESS.

Simpson saw the SUV's right rear door swing open. Out stepped Josiah Cross. The tall, skinny, bearded forty-year-old African-American wore a black cloak with a white clerical collar.

Bingo, Simpson thought.

He zoomed in for a close-up as Cross, dodging traffic, then walked out into the middle of Twenty-ninth Street. Cross put hands on his hips as he looked up at the banner on the yellow rental truck, then surveyed the stage and its posters, and nodded appreciatively.

He turned to start walking back toward the sidewalk—and almost stepped right in front of a car.

As the driver stood on the horn, and then the accelerator, Cross quickly stepped backward out of the path of the roaring car. Then, before he could catch himself, Cross pumped his right arm above his head, his fist in a ball, middle finger extended.

Simpson let out a loud laugh that filled the van.

Cross composed himself, then turned and made it to the sidewalk without further incident.

He went to the stage, hopped on it, and then surveyed the view from there. This time he raised both hands above his head, all fingers extended, turning right and then left, addressing an imaginary crowd. He then, apparently satisfied, nodded and lowered his arms, then hopped down from the stage.

As he walked purposefully toward the open red front door, a short, heavyset black male came out with a cordless phone handset and extended it toward Cross. He wore black jeans and a long-sleeved yellow T-shirt on the front of which was what at first glance looked like the logotype of the Warner Brothers movie studio.

But it wasn't.

Nice, Simpson thought.

"WarnaBrotha."

Keeping the no-snitching real in the hood.

How many of these murders can be directly connected to that bullshit? Nobody talking about who the doers are?

He watched Cross take the phone and follow the male back inside.

Simpson shook his head as he reached down and poured another cup of coffee.

VI

[ONE]
Word of Brotherly Love Ministry
Strawberry Mansion, Philadelphia
Saturday, December 15, 3:01 P.M.

"Hold on for a minute, Rapp," the Reverend Josiah Cross said into the cordless telephone handset, then motioned with it to get the attention of the heavyset male wearing the yellow *WarnaBrotha* T-shirt. "Deacon DiAndre, come back here!"

Hearing his name, twenty-five-year-old DiAndre Pringle, who was five-foot-four and one-sixty and had big brown eyes that seemed to slowly scan his surroundings and take in everything, looked up from his tablet computer, nodded acknowledgment, then walked toward Cross as his big eyes dropped back to the device and he rapidly typed on its glass screen.

The large main room, featuring gold-and-black-patterned wallpaper and red-painted trim, was filled with more than two hundred brown folding metal chairs. They formed two dozen rows arranged at an angle and separated in the middle by a wide aisle that went from the red front door to almost the far wall. There, a crucifix crafted of rough-hewn timber hung on the wall above a vacant area that an hour before had held the black wooden cubes and the lectern and speakers that now were outside on the sidewalk.

A series of more black cubes were arranged to one side, stacked to form two tiers, with five brown folding chairs lined up on each level to accommodate members of the choir. On the wallpaper just above the highest chairs, the outlines of lettering that had been pried off spelled out a faded BUFFET.

Pringle approached Cross, who stood beside a flight of wooden steps that led to the upper two floors. Two young men carried cardboard boxes down them, then went to the front door and out it.

"What up with the numbers, DiAndre?" Cross said.

Pringle held up the tablet computer for Cross to see, then tapped the glass screen and pointed to it.

"I just sent out another call to action to a new group in Frankford that's got about three hundred people," Pringle said. "But look here, Rev. There's five thousand two hundred and forty-one—and still climbing pretty quick—thumbs-up Liberty Bells for the Stop

Killadelphia Rally. If we get half that many people to show up, just that'll be some crowd."

"What's this call to action thing you said?"

"When I go on *Philly News Now*—you know, its social media site?—I can reach all kinds of people around the city. Who these people are and how many of them are in whatever group depends on what their interests are."

"Like that star one for my ministry here, right?"

"Right. Our *asterisk–Word of Brotherly Love* has almost a thousand followers. That ain't a bad number, 'cause their interest is this church and this neighborhood."

"What do you mean by that?" Cross snapped.

"Nothing bad, Rev. I mean it's just a limited group. You want some crazy serious numbers? Try being the Pope."

Cross narrowed his eyes and looked ready to snap again.

That wasn't lost on Pringle, who tried to recover with: "The good news is that almost all of your followers gave a thumbs-up to the rally. I'd bet it's a pretty good chance that they will be here."

"And you've got one of these star things for the turkey day, right?"

Pringle tapped the glass of the tablet computer.

"Here's *asterisk–Feed Philly Day*," Pringle said.

"Three thousand thumbs-up bells?" Cross said, then wondered aloud, "Jesus, are we gonna have enough food?"

Pringle shrugged. "Don't know about that. Need to find out, 'cause all of these here followers checked the box that they were coming for the meal. Who knows how many others are just going to show up? And there were more than a thousand boxes checked for a frozen turkey."

"Jesus!" Cross muttered.

"Ain't saying 'Jesus' a sacrilege, Rev?"

"Look, son," Cross snapped, then faintly heard his name being called repeatedly and realized it was coming from the cordless telephone handset he'd forgotten he still held.

"Keep getting more people for the rally," Cross ordered Pringle while pointing to the tablet computer, then put the handset to his ear.

Cross watched Pringle disappear up the steps to the second floor as he said, "Sorry about that, Rapp. Look, I'm glad you called. You gotta get me that check today."

"What check, Lenny?" H. Rapp Badde said.

"For the frozen turkey guy. I've got a lot of hungry folks saying they're coming. We may have to order extra birds. But he said he's still waiting for his money, up front. And said he's got other buyers if we don't come through."

"He's bluffing. He's probably still pissed you bounced that last check," Badde said, then added, "I thought you had the rental truck?"

"What about it?"

"What's in it?"

"What's *on* it is the banner saying turkey day is Monday. And saying it's sponsored by you."

"But what's in the truck? No turkeys?"

"I told you we get them Monday. If you get me that check. You really don't think I'd leave a truck full of frozen turkeys out there, do you? They'd be stolen in no time. Hell, the truck, too. We parked it here for the rally, so the news cameras can show it in the background. Right now it's got posters and boxes of T-shirts for the rally."

There was a moment's pause before Badde then said, "Look, Lenny, about that rally. I didn't call about the turkeys. What the hell is this about you calling that cop Payne a murderer?"

"What? You called about that? Well, I did. Because he did. He is."

"Jesus! You can't do that."

"He's Public Enemy Number One, Rapp," Cross said, his tone self-righteous.

"Lenny, damn it! Don't do it again! It's not helping the situation."

"Situation? What situation?"

"You're on CPOC and now its chairman—"

"And I'm done with using that position to make a change. Now I'm using the ministry—"

"But you're linked to CPOC."

"Rapp, how long has CPOC been around?" Cross didn't wait for a reply. "Fifteen, twenty years? A long damn time. And what's it ever done? Not one damn thing, that's what. Every member on CPOC is frustrated. I'm just the only one speaking up."

"Why, Lenny?"

"Because there's pretty much been a murder a day forever. It was Killadelphia then, and it's Killadelphia now. And it's mostly brothers. You get what I'm saying?"

Badde sighed. "I'm hearing you."

"So, I don't know why the hell you're pissed off about this. The rally is really getting to the people. You should check out the following we're getting on the *Philly News Now* link—"

"I've seen it. Trust me . . ."

"Over five thousand viewers have given it one of those bell thumb things. That means there'll be a big crowd at the rally." He paused. "It would look good if you showed up, made an appearance. Sure you can't make it?"

"Not if you keep calling the cops killers, I can't!"

"Whatever. Your choice."

"I'll be there for the turkey day. But, for now, listen to me, Lenny. I can't make this plain enough. You are putting a lot at risk here, starting with your CPOC position."

Cross was quiet a moment, then said, "You didn't just say that. You really mean that? Wait. You want to know what? I really don't care, Rapp. It's my last year anyway."

Badde blurted: "I meant what I said. You're going too far, and there's gonna be a price to pay. I've got Carlucci's new guy breathing down my neck because of this, because I got you on CPOC and now you're trashing the cops."

"Got Carlucci's attention? Really?" Cross said. "Then I'm onto something."

"You're onto something, all right. Out on your ass, Lenny!"

"Look, Rapp, I told you I don't care—"

"No, you goddamn look, Lenny! This is not just about you! What you're doing is putting me in a really bad light that I cannot afford. Got it?"

Cross grunted. "Is that what this is about? Putting you in a light? You've got your name on those construction signs all over town. You and ol' Willie Lane. Showing folks what all you're doing for them, just like your daddies done back in the day. But you know what, Rapp? They got put in office, and then we put you all in office, 'cause you promised things would get better."

"And they have . . ."

"Maybe better for you, Rapp! But there's still that killing a day, and no one seems to care. There's still good people who can't sit on their own porch 'cause they're afraid of crime, afraid of the gang-banging punks running the streets. I'm looking at a bunch of posters of folks—"

"Look, Lenny," Badde interrupted, his tone frustrated, "we can talk about all this when I get there. Right here, right now, I really need you to back off. Can you give me your word that you'll do that?"

"So you're saying that we just stop? Just let the killings go on and on?"

"No, Lenny. I'm saying just dial it down a few notches. Go after the goddamn murders, reach out to our people . . ."

Your votes, you mean, Cross thought.

". . . but just don't go after the police. Okay? It's important for you and for me."

Cross, silent and in thought, stared across the room for a long moment.

"And one more thing," Badde said. "You have to call Carlucci's guy. Just let him know you're not giving up on all the murders in Philly—that's your right—but you'll leave the police out."

Cross was silent for another long moment.

"Lenny . . . ?"

"When do I get that check for the turkeys?"

[TWO]
Torresdale Avenue and Kinsey Street
Frankford, Philadelphia
Saturday, December 15, 3:12 P.M.

The silver late-model Volkswagen Jetta slowed as it passed an automobile salvage yard, then braked hard and turned off the street. It nosed up to the faded orange overhead steel door of a freestanding two-story masonry building. Stenciled on the door in three-foot-high black letters was DO NOT BLOCK DOOR!!! TOW AWAY ZONE!!! To the right of the overhead door there was a steel man door, in the same faded orange, and stenciled in smaller black lettering was MARIANO'S COLLISION CENTER. FREE ESTIMATES.

The driver of the VW, a chunky five-foot-four twenty-year-old Puerto Rican with a black stocking cap pulled low on his head, anxiously hit the horn three times as his dark eyes scanned down the street. He took a long draw on his cigarette, then exhaled audibly.

Torresdale was lined with small businesses, most of which were involved in some fashion with the automotive trade. On one side of Mariano's was a three-dollar drive-through car wash, now closed due to the snow, and on the other side was Worldwide Quality Imports.

The larger of two used-car lots on the block, Worldwide had an eight-foot-tall chain-link fence topped with coils of razor wire. Strung from light poles above that were ribbons of faded multicolored plastic banners imprinted with SALE. The painted wooden sign on the fence read WE FINANCE. EVERYONE IS APPROVED. GOOD CREDIT. BAD CREDIT. BANKRUPTCY. REPOS. NO PROBLEM! YOUR JOB IS YOUR CREDIT! 215-555-2020. The lot itself was packed with about thirty late-model vehicles. Another half-dozen older models, with neon stickers on their windshields announcing LOW MILES! CLEAN! LIKE NEW!, were parked on the sidewalk and in public parking spaces at the curb. Two of them—a Nissan Ultima sedan and a compact Toyota SUV—the driver recognized as ones he had delivered a couple of weeks earlier.

The driver saw the steel man door crack open about six inches, then immediately swing shut. A moment later he could hear the sound of the overhead door clunking as it began opening.

Then the driver, remembering what he had meant to do minutes earlier, quickly glanced around the dashboard area. He reached for the glove box, yanked it open, and began rifling through it. He pulled out a handful of paper napkins and drinking straws wrapped in plastic sleeves from a fast-food chain, tossed them on the floorboard, then found a black vinyl folder that contained the owner's manual for the vehicle. He threw that back in, slammed the glove box shut, then opened the ashtray.

Here we go! he thought, glancing up to check on the opening door.

The ashtray held a mix of papers—gas pump and other store receipts crammed in with a wad of one- and five-dollar bills—and a small pile of coins. He stuck his fingers in, clawed at the mass, then managed to grab all but a few coins and stuff it in his pants pocket.

He looked again at the opening door. It was now about a third of the way up, and the snow was beginning to blow inside the garage. A brown hand then poked out and began motioning in a rapid fashion for the Volkswagen to pull inside.

The driver eased the car forward, stopped as the top of the VW's windshield neared the bottom lip of the steel door, then when clear pulled completely inside. The overhead steel door then began to close.

The interior was harshly lit in a gray-white of industrial mercury vapor lamps. There were seven or eight wrecked cars on either side of the workshop, all in various states of repair. At the back of the garage was a nearly new white Volkswagen Passat that had been badly rear-ended and, next to it, a red Honda Accord with no wheels sitting up on blocks, its damaged front end cut free from the rest of the vehicle.

The driver of the Jetta could now see the rest of the hand that had waved him inside—a Hispanic male who looked to be in his twenties, of average height but very thin, his faded blue overalls hanging loosely on him. It clearly was cold inside the shop; the driver could see moisture when the Hispanic male exhaled. His hand now motioned for the driver to stop.

After putting the Volkswagen in park and killing the motor, the driver stepped out just as an older man, wiping his hands with a dirty red shop towel, stepped out from a doorway by the big roll-up door. Above the doorway was painted OFFICE.

The older man, olive-skinned and rotund and balding, wore faded blue overalls that had paint splatters. The patch over his shirt's left breast pocket read MARIANO'S COLLISION CENTER; the one over his right read GABBY.

He approached the Volkswagen, not saying anything to the

driver as he circled the car, inspecting it. When he had made a full circle, he took a long moment studying the stickers on the inside of the front windshield on the driver's side. One was a red parking pass with six numbers under the letters "UMA HS."

"What's the story, Ruben?" Gabriel Mariano said to the driver.

"I need to get a thousand for it," Ruben Mora said, glancing at the silver Volkswagen while trying not to appear nervous. He dropped his cigarette butt to the grimy concrete floor and ground it with his toe. "You'll get five times that from it."

"What's the story?" Mariano repeated. "Where'd you get it? Any papers?"

Mora turned to him, and in a jerky motion pulled out a disposable butane lighter and lit another cigarette.

"That matter?" Mora said. "It's gonna be parted out anyway."

He leaned back against a steel worktable that held paint-splattered gallon cans—one was marked TOLUENE; the other, with a few dirty shop towels on top, had a paper label reading ACETONE—and exhaled a cloud of smoke through his nostrils.

"You told me what you needed," Mora said, "and I put the word out."

Mariano looked past him, to the back of the shop, then at him.

"I said Volkswagen Passat, Ruben, not Jetta. And do me a favor and don't be smoking around those cans."

Mora glanced at the worktable, shrugged, and took two steps away from it.

"This one's a cherry, not an hour old," Mora said, then, almost as an afterthought, nodded toward the bumper and added, "I stuck new plates on it just to be safe."

Mariano looked at the license plate, and immediately saw a

problem—the New Jersey plate was screwed on top of another license plate.

Damned lazy kid. He didn't ditch the old ones. Just left them on it.

If I picked up on that, a cop sure would.

He glanced up at the rear window. The bumper sticker on it read MARION VIKINGS FOOTBALL.

And what's a Jersey plate doing on a car with a high school sticker from a Philly suburb? Another thing that'd scream to the cops, "Pull me over!"

Stupid bastard.

Couldn't steal a local plate? Not like they're not everywhere . . .

Mariano sighed and shook his head. He walked to the driver's door and, using the shop towel, opened it and leaned inside.

"Got low miles," Mora said. "Under fifty thou."

"I've told you, low miles don't mean shit for parts. A fender's a fender."

Mariano looked over his shoulder. "I'm thinking five hundred."

"Come on, man. I need the grand."

"That's too rich for me. I'll go six, maybe six-five."

Mora frowned, then glanced across the garage as he considered the counteroffer. He took a pull on his cigarette, then said, "Okay. Seven."

Mariano ignored that as he reached down and pulled the release handle for the hood and pushed the button for the trunk. They each opened with a *Click!* He then went to the front of the car and, again using the red shop towel, raised the hood. He made a cursory inspection of the engine bay, grunted, slammed the hood, then went to the rear of the vehicle.

"It got a full-sized spare or one of those small donut ones?" Mariano said as he reached for the trunk lid.

"I dunno. I didn't—"

"What the hell!" Mariano suddenly exclaimed from behind the partially raised trunk lid.

He quickly slammed it shut and stared at Mora.

"What?" Mora said, looking at the now furious face of Mariano. "I can get you a tire—"

"You stupid fucking shit," Mariano said, failing to keep his composure while rapidly wiping his hands with the shop towel. He then nervously wiped where he had lifted the trunk lid. "Someone pay you to bring this here to dump on me?"

"Dump what?"

Mariano walked up to Mora and poked him in the chest.

"Get the hell outta here!" Mariano yelled, his face flushed bright red. "And you listen to me real good, don't you ever come back! Ever!"

Mariano started walking quickly back toward the office. He pointed at the Hispanic worker, then at the overhead steel door.

"You! Get that damn door opened back up now!" he shouted, then looked at Mora and added, "You were never here, you got it?" then went into the office, slamming the door behind him.

Mora quickly went to the driver's door and hit the trunk lid release that was on the door panel. He heard the latch click open again, then went and threw up the trunk lid.

"Holy shit!" he said softly, then slammed the trunk shut. "That bastard!"

He felt his heart start racing. He looked around. No one was nearby. The Hispanic male, his back to him, was standing by the overhead door and pressing the control button as the door clunked upward.

Mora started for the driver's door, passing the worktable with the metal cans and small pile of dirty shop towels. He quickly grabbed them and then tossed them on the floorboard of the front passenger seat, then hopped in and began backing out of the garage.

In his shop office, Gabriel Mariano stood with his hands on his hips while looking at the closed door to the garage.

I could kill that little shit for pulling that stunt, he thought.

You know what? Screw him!

Mariano pulled open a desk drawer, reached in, and produced one of the three old cellular telephones that he had inside. He held down the phone's on button, and when the screen blinked to life, he angrily stabbed at the keypad with his index finger, punching in 911.

The voice of an adult woman, calm and professional, answered, "Philadelphia Police Nine-One-One. What is your emergency?"

"Yeah, some Puerto Rican punk with a gun just carjacked a VW Jetta in Frankford, on Torresdale near the Harding Middle School. Silver four-door with Jersey plates."

The female voice repeated the information back to him.

"That's right," Mariano said.

"Was anyone hurt?" she said.

"Looked like it. But they sped off. You'd better hurry."

"I need your name and—"

Mariano did not listen to the rest of her reply.

He turned over the cell phone, pulled off its back cover, removed the battery, and tossed all the pieces back in the desk drawer.

Ruben Mora's mind spun as he drove down Torresdale Street. His first thought was that he had to get rid of the car and its contents. And rid of it now. But then he got mad, and thought he should drive to Kensington and get his two hundred dollars back.

That jacked-up bastard! he thought as he slowed for a traffic light that was changing to green. *I shoulda known Reggie sold this cheap for a reason!*

He hit the turn signal. But just before he made the turn to go back to Somerset, he realized that his first thought was best. He really had to get rid of the car. He had known that right away at the garage without really thinking about it, because that explained why he had automatically grabbed the dirty shop rags and paint thinner.

He made a hard right, then drove slowly, trying not to draw attention while he looked for the right place.

Two blocks later, after turning onto Hayworth Street and rolling past a yellow NO OUTLET sign, he came to the dead end of the street. Twenty yards ahead was the tall chain-link fence that ran along the Amtrak rails. He pulled to the broken curb in front of an abandoned row house and turned off the car.

He looked in the rearview mirror and then out the windshield. There was no one around. He leaned over and picked up the cans off the floorboard. He opened the one labeled TOLUENE. It felt a little more than half-full. He emptied it on the fabric of the backseat, then tossed the can to the floor.

The harsh odor of the chemical quickly filled the car, and he started to get a headache.

He opened the door and stepped out. He deeply inhaled the fresh air, then reached back inside the car for the acetone. The can was almost full, and he poured about half of that can onto the front seats and floorboard. Then he took two of the shop towels and soaked them with the acetone. He put the now half-full can on the driver's seat and threaded all but a third of one of the shop towels in its mouth. He moved the can to the floorboard of the backseat, then reached for the second chemical-soaked shop towel.

Again, the fumes started to overwhelm him, and he quickly stood and took another deep breath of fresh air.

He glanced around the immediate area as he did. He thought he saw movement, and froze just as a stray dog, a short-legged brown mutt with a drooping spine, ran across Hayworth. Far beyond it, on Torresdale, a taxicab flashed past the intersection.

He quickly turned back to the car and pulled from his pants pocket the disposable butane lighter, then grabbed the shop towel he'd wetted with acetone. When he thumbed the lighter, its flame immediately found the fumes—a soft *Poof!* sound coming from the rag as it was set ablaze. The heat instantly became intense, and he reacted by slinging the lighter and the rag inside the automobile.

They landed on the driver's seat, which immediately flashed up in flames.

He smelled burned hair, and suddenly saw that when the flames had flared they burned his left hand. The cuff of his sweatshirt had also caught on fire and he immediately realized that acetone must have somehow splashed on it.

Frantically, he waved his hand faster and faster, trying to extinguish the fire. But that served only to make the flames worse.

Then, in the back of his mind came a faint chant—and he remembered the firemen who visited his class at Harding Middle School a decade ago and taught the students *Stop! Drop! Roll!* to starve a clothing fire of oxygen.

He stuffed the burning cuff under his right armpit.

The pain to the raw skin of his burned hand was intense. But the flames finally died.

A minute later, Ruben Mora, feeling light-headed, glanced at the blackened sleeve and hand. Then he looked at the fire growing inside the car.

Mesmerized, it took him a moment before he decided that he had to get away before he burned his whole body.

He kicked the door shut and, pulling his stocking cap tight on his head with his uninjured hand, ran down Hayworth Street.

When he reached the corner, at Hayworth Street, he glanced back. The windows of the Volkswagen were filled with a roiling dark black smoke and bright red flames. He heard a small *Boom!* and saw a flash of bright white flame, and guessed that that had been the acetone can exploding.

He snugged at his black stocking cap, winced as he stuffed his hands in his sweatshirt pocket, and then jaywalked across Hayworth Street.

Two blocks up, at Torresdale, he saw a police cruiser speed past, then a couple minutes later another one quickly followed it.

Then, behind him, he heard and felt the concussion of an explosion, and when he looked back he saw a huge plume of black smoke soaring above the roofline of the row houses.

Then he heard the wail of police sirens.

He glanced around the neighborhood, trying to figure out the easiest way to get back down to the corner in Kensington without walking what he guessed had to be three or four miles. He remembered the money he had taken from the VW's ashtray, and decided SEPTA was it.

He pulled out his injured hand and looked at it. It felt as if it was still on fire, even exposed to the frigid air.

And it had begun to throb.

Dammit that hurts! he thought as he went to cut across the middle school playground, headed for the El station that was six blocks away.

[THREE]
Monmouth and Hancock Streets
Fairhill, Philadelphia
Saturday, December 15, 3:32 P.M.

"Is your momma gonna come down here and surprise us?" seventeen-year-old Carmelita Martinez teased Tyrone Hooks, who was sitting naked on the edge of his bed while watching her pull her shirt off over her head.

The cluttered basement bedroom, a crowded space of fifteen by twenty feet, also held a brown couch that faced a flat-screen television against one wall and, against the opposite wall, a wooden desk on top of which was a MacBook computer with a pair of high-end studio headphones and a chromed-mesh Shure professional musician's microphone plugged into it. Also next to the computer was a ruby-red crushed velvet pouch with a string closure and a small, six-inch glass pipe. A wisp of smoke twisted upward from the pipe, the pungent aroma of marijuana hanging in the air.

Carmelita, a petite, dark-eyed, coffee-skinned Dominican with large breasts and full hips that had begun to spread, playfully tossed her top at Tyrone. Smiling widely, she ran her finger along the thin silver necklace that he had minutes earlier taken from the crushed velvet pouch and presented to her.

"She knows to stay in her room upstairs," Hooks said, reaching out to unbutton Carmelita's blue jeans. "Here, let me help you, baby girl."

In the years that Tyrone's grandparents had lived in the row house—his mother's parents, who helped raise him; he never knew his father—the blue-collar neighborhood had begun to fall on hard times as its middle-class jobs slowly disappeared with the closure of the nearby factories.

By the time the grandparents had died, and his mother had inherited the home, a great deal had really changed in the area.

There now was widespread blight, for example, pockets of it severe. Calling the Hooks property a row house was something of a misnomer, as there were no other houses along its row. Twenty years earlier, when Tyrone had been five, a fire had ravaged all the others on that side of the street. Their blackened masonry shells had been demolished by the city, leaving the Hookses' two-story structure standing alone near the corner, with only raw empty lots where the other row houses had once stood.

Over time the demographics of the neighborhood had dramatically changed, too.

Now the vast majority—eighty percent—of Fairhill's residents were Hispanic. While these were mostly Puerto Ricans, there were also many who had emigrated from Cuba and Jamaica and the Dominican Republic. Family-owned businesses in what they called their El Centro de Oro—Center of Gold—catered to them, the markets painted in the same bright yellows and greens and blues as those in the islands. Remarkably, on all four corners at Lehigh and Fifth there were even palm trees—leaning ones made of metal installed to further create a tropical feel.

Carmelita—who had been born at Temple University Hospital's Episcopal Campus, on the outer edge of Fairhill—wiggled her hips as Tyrone tugged down her skintight jeans.

Just as she jumped onto the bed, Tyrone's cell phone—which he had tossed on the couch next to his black Ruger 9-millimeter semiauto pistol when he had undressed—began ringing.

Or, perhaps more correctly, it began rapping.

Hooks had recorded songs he had written on the computer, and from those digital files had created ring tones, then transferred the rings to his cell phone, where he had linked them to the telephone numbers of select members of his crew.

"Damn it!" he said, recognizing who was calling without needing to look at the phone screen.

"Anything wrong?" Carmelita said, watching the skinny Tyrone walk quickly to the couch and grab the phone off the seat cushion.

He ignored her, then snapped at the caller: "You better be calling to say it's done."

Carmelita could hear the male voice of the caller but could not make out what he was saying, only picking up on his tone. He sounded, she thought, excited in a nervous way—maybe even scared.

"Look, man," Tyrone said angrily, his eyes darting at Carmelita then away, "we've been over this. You gotta just do it. You hearing me? 'Cause if you don't, you know what happens."

There was no reply for a moment, then Carmelita heard the caller mumble, "All right."

"Don't say it—do it! Let me know when it's done. No surprises."

Hooks ended the call, and was about to toss the phone back on the cushion when it made a *Ping-Ping!* sound.

He looked at the screen and read the text message: "Yo, King. Bags in AC safe. All good here. TV news keeps showing smash & grab. That dude really dead???"

Tyrone turned his back to Carmelita, then thumbed a reply: "News says 1 dead 1 shot. Stay there. No casinos!! Lay low til I say."

He nodded as he glanced at the crushed velvet pouch and thought: *Lucky they got to the Shore quick. Five-Oh really got to be looking hard for them, especially since he killed that guy. Damn good news that loot's locked up.*

Right after he hit SEND, the phone made another *Ping-Ping!*

"Damn," he said in a hiss, then flipped the switch to silence the phone.

He suddenly felt the warmth of Carmelita's skin against his back, then her arms wrapping around him, her gentle fingers finding his curly black chest hairs. She rested her chin on his shoulder. He could feel her moist breath on his ear.

"You ever shoot anyone, King?" she said.

Hooks jerked his head.

"Why the hell you say that?"

"You rap about it," she said, her tone playful but serious. "You got the nine. Just wonder sometimes if you've done it."

She buried her face in his neck as her right hand slipped down to his belly and then to his groin.

Hooks inhaled deeply.

"Well, baby, I rap about some super-hot sex, too, so what do you think?"

He exhaled as he glanced at the phone screen and saw that the text massage read "Call me QUICK!"

"What's that text about?" Carmelita said.

"You oughta not ask so many questions," Hooks said sharply, turning from the phone toward her.

She stuck out her lower lip in a pout—just as her hand grasped him in a way that left no question she wasn't really pouting.

After a very brief moment he grinned, tossed the phone back beside the pistol on the couch, and said, "But that one's about nothing that ain't gonna wait!"

He then roughly pulled a giggling Carmelita back across the room to the bed.

A half hour later, Hooks hit a speed-dial key on his cellular phone as he watched Carmelita, sitting up in bed beside him, take a fat pinch of crushed marijuana from a clear plastic zip-top bag and refill the bowl of the glass pipe that had been on the desk.

"Don't forget I need you to call your brother after that bowl's burned," Tyrone told her. "I got a job for him."

"What you want with Ruben?" she said, picking up a matchbook from the bedsheet.

"Baby girl, what'd I tell you about asking so many questions?" Tyrone said, then barked into the phone, "Yo!"

"You call that calling me quick?" DiAndre Pringle answered.

"I had something I had to do first."

Carmelita giggled.

"Whatever, Ty," Pringle said.

Hooks guessed that Pringle had overheard Carmelita, and grinned at her.

"Listen," Pringle went on, "I wanted you to call quick 'cause I'd just got an idea for you."

"This about me performing at that Turkey Day gig?"

"No."

"What? I'm still doing the gig, right?"

"Yeah, Ty. But you want to work another gig?"

Hooks looked at Carmelita, grinned, then said, "Depends. I don't know. Might be busy. When?"

"This afternoon."

"Today? You messing with me?"

"No. You heard that the Rev is putting on a rally, right?"

"Rally? About what?"

"About all the killing that's going on. About stopping Killadelphia."

Hooks felt the hair on his neck stand up.

He can't mean what happened this morning.

How'd he know about my boys?

Unless somebody else went and talked . . .

"Going to be lots of people at the ministry here, Ty. And I figured you'd be really good at really amping up the crowd."

Yeah, he does mean my raps.

"How much?" Hooks said.

"How many people?"

"No. How much I get paid?"

"Are you serious? Ain't nobody getting paid. I mean, c'mon, it's for our people!"

Hooks was quiet a moment.

Guess I'm about to get me a good grip for that loot—plenty of benjamins for a while.

And it'd look good if I played that rally.

Might even be news covering it. Get me on TV.

"TV news coming?" he said.

"Yeah. I left messages with 'em all. That *Philly News Now* and Channel 10 called back and said they were sending reporters. Sure there'll be more."

Hooks's eyebrows went up.

"Yeah, man," he said, nodding, "I could seriously amp that crowd up."

"Don't need you to do a whole set or nothing. Just rap one or two songs. Rev Cross doesn't like folks taking over his stage."

Carmelita lit a match, then put the flame to the pot in the pipe bowl. She took a deep puff on the glass pipe and held it in, before holding out the pipe to Hooks.

"So," Pringle said, "whatcha say, King?"

Tyrone Hooks looked at his gold Rolex watch.

"I say what time you want me there?" he said, winked at Carmelita, then took a puff on the pipe.

[FOUR]
Lucky Stars Casino & Entertainment
North Beach Street, Philadelphia
Saturday, December 15, 3:45 P.M.

"The way this ghetto punk strutted out of here, he must've really thought that he'd conned everyone, that we were just gonna swallow this little charade of his," Security Director Sean Francis O'Sullivan said, as he gestured toward the wall of flat-panel monitors showing live video feeds of activity throughout the casino property. One monitor had a sharp freeze-framed close-up image of a smirking Tyrone Hooks as he sat on a Winner's Lounge barstool.

O'Sullivan looked at Homicide Detective Anthony Harris, and went on: "He expects us to believe that, after being in the jewelry store, he just happened to be having a beer while the robbery was taking place downstairs? Innocently playing a couple hands of five-card stud on the video game at the bar? And then that he just happened to leave the scene after it's all gone down?"

"That really is pretty ballsy bullshit, Sully," Harris said, looking from the close-up image and meeting O'Sullivan's eyes. "Almost like he's taunting whoever's watching."

"I'd say more bullshit than ballsy, Tony. I really don't think he's that smart, or that he realizes what deep shit he's in. Because what I do know is that Mr. Antonov is more than a little pissed. He's been in and out of here constantly all day, watching the videos, getting information updates, and saying to make sure that we—meaning me personally—give you everything you need."

Harris and O'Sullivan were in the large security office on the top floor of the casino complex, which was down the hall from the office of the casino's general manager, Nikoli Antonov.

Harris thought the forty-by-forty-foot space—with a small staff busy at a dozen workstations and watching the wall of flat-panel monitors—looked somewhat like the ECC war room at the Roundhouse. O'Sullivan had told him that, while not nearly as impenetrable as the casino's vault room, which had been built in-side a fortress of reinforced concrete walls one floor below ground level, it was highly secure.

O'Sullivan was forty-three years old, tall and fair-skinned, with a smoothly shaven face and scalp and a bushy mustache and goatee and eyebrows that in recent years had faded from carrot-red and added flecks of gray. He wore a nicely cut dark woolen two-piece suit that had been tailored to accommodate the Sig Sauer .40 caliber semiautomatic that Harris knew he carried in a black leather holster on his right hip.

O'Sullivan had put in just over twenty-two years at the Phila-delphia Police Department, leaving as a lieutenant in the Citywide Vice Unit, which fell under Specialized Investigations along with Narcotics, Special Victims, Homicide, and other units.

For someone who had served in such an intense unit of the department—while most officers worked within one of the depart-ment's twenty-five districts, performing the necessary street-walking grunt work, Vice worked big complicated cases throughout the city—O'Sullivan required a challenge after retirement.

He had found that challenge at the casino, he said, "protecting the facility from a constant string of knuckleheads who misinterpret its 'More Money! More Winners!' slogan as an open invitation to rip off the place."

O'Sullivan had replayed for Harris that morning's security camera videos of the flash mob raging through the casino, of the four males in black hoodies and bandannas obscuring their faces while robbing the jewelry store, and finally of Tyrone Hooks. The videos had been made using scores of camera angles to create seamless detailed time lines of each subject's every step at the casino.

The compilation of Hooks began with the cameras first picking him up strutting across the parking lot and entering the revolving doors, then, approximately an hour later, showed him exiting doors to the parking garage at the opposite end of the complex and hailing a taxicab.

"Hooks," O'Sullivan said, "bragged to the bartender that he was some hot-shit hip-hopper going by the name King Two-One-Five, and tried to make himself sound like he was something of a regular big-time gambler. When he flashed that gold Rolex President, the bartender felt obligated to ask about it, and Hooks was quick to pull the wrinkled bill of sale from his pocket to authenticate it was in fact his and that he had paid for it with his winnings . . . and probably flashing how much he had paid for it.

"Clearly he thought," O'Sullivan went on, "that everything he'd done would give him a pretty solid alibi. We know that he knows the casino cameras capture everything, because we have record of him taking our beginner's intro tour, and that's one major point we make to all the newbies. We show them the cameras."

He gestured at the monitors. Tony's eyes went to them.

"We're not actually watching every table in live time," O'Sullivan went on, "but the cameras certainly are, and when someone starts really winning a shitload of money, we say, 'Whoa,' and go to check the forensic recordings."

"How often does that happen?"

"Every damn week. This week we caught this guy—a really bright numbers guy who just graduated from Wharton—counting cards at the blackjack tables. He denied he was doing it. So we showed him the video, then escorted him from the building. We were nice about it. Didn't kick him in the ass on the way out. But a lifetime ban, he got. And we shared his name with other casinos. Now he'll have to figure out some other way to come up with the funds to pay off that massive MBA student loan he probably has."

"Lifetime ban? That's pretty harsh, isn't it? It's not like he was cheating, he's playing smart."

"We're not in this business to go broke, Tony. Look, we make the rules, and one of those is that the odds are in the casino's favor. And we tell people exactly that, especially during that beginner's intro tour—right before we then tell them, 'You don't like it, then start your own damn casino.'"

Harris caught himself chuckling.

"Valid point," he said.

"This ain't a charity nonprofit. We keep track of everything. Which is why this ghetto punk may or may not be aware that we know his real history, how much he's won and lost, what he paid for that Rolex, everything."

"Because he has one of those customer loyalty cards that he put that two hundred bucks on?"

"That's exactly right. The Lucky Stars More Money! Rewards

Program," O'Sullivan said. "For taking the intro tour, he got a debit card with twenty bucks preloaded on it. It's a loss leader—"

"C'mon, that's not really a loss," Harris interrupted. "You're going to get that twenty—and lots more—back because, as you like to say, the odds are in the casino's favor."

"It's not like we make it a secret," O'Sullivan said. "And not everyone who gambles has to join the program and get the card that comes with it. But the ones who like thinking they're getting something for nothing—it's a point for every dollar bet or spent, and the points can be used for booze, rooms, cash back—they're all in. There're even people who don't gamble but want to use just the debit card function and earn points that they can cash in. Almost all gamble, though, either in one of our thirty-two casinos worldwide or on our Internet site. More than fifty million users, and growing."

"And those are prepaid cards, too, right? Meaning the casino gets to sit on all that cash interest-free."

O'Sullivan smiled. "You're right. But that's another point we make on the beginner's intro tour and in the fine print of the user agreement everyone signs to get the card. Remember, 'You don't like it . . .'"

Harris chuckled again. "Right."

"So, anyway, we checked out this punk's account." O'Sullivan looked at his notes. "We know he lost a hundred bucks at the video poker game while he drank a five-dollar Philly Pale Ale."

Harris grunted. "A hipster craft brew? I would've guessed he was more a Pabst Blue Ribbon in the can drinker."

"He probably was, but I bet it was the card. If I researched further back, I could find out from day one all he's ordered—booze, food—and which games he's played, how much he wagers, even which shows, if any, he's seen."

"Remarkable."

"All that data gives our marketing people details that they can use to target customers' likes—then offer them more of that, or even carefully get them to move up to a more expensive level. So he could've started out drinking two-buck PBRs, but at some point the system made him an offer that moved him into the five-buck craft microbrews. I've heard the value of that program—just the user information, the spending habits of those fifty million, not counting the money in the accounts—has been pegged at more than a billion dollars."

Harris shook his head.

"No offense," he said, "but I'm suddenly reminded why I hate these places. People pissing away money they can't afford to. Then pissing away even more trying to win it back."

"To each his own. Nobody has a gun to their head, making them do it." He paused, gestured toward what would be the office at the end of the hallway, then went on: "Which is why Mr. Antonov is not pleased."

"A robbery and a murder in your casino isn't exactly good for business, huh? Not to mention the two hundred grand in jewelry they stole. I wouldn't want to be the one reporting it to Tikhonov."

"No shit, Tony. That's the understatement of the day. And you're getting ahead of me."

Harris knew that Nikoli Antonov worked for Yuri Tikhonov, the forty-eight-year-old international investor who had made his first billion dollars more than a dozen years earlier. In addition to owning almost half of Lucky Stars and a large interest in an entertainment complex being built on just the other side of the I-95 Delaware Expressway, Tikhonov had significant investments around the world.

It was said that Tikhonov's remarkable rapid rise as a successful businessman was in large part due to his having served in Russia's Sluzhba Vneshney Razvedki, the latest incarnation of the external spying and intelligence-gathering agency formerly known as the KGB. Being closely associated with high-ranking politicians in the Kremlin—powerful ones whom he had worked with in the SVR— did not hurt.

Nikoli Antonov was thirty-seven years old. Born in Russia, he was fluent in his mother tongue, but had no obvious accent due to his early years attending a Helsinki boarding school. He looked Western European, and dressed expensively, favoring custom-tailored dark two-piece suits with a crisp white dress shirt, no tie.

O'Sullivan had told Harris, "Mr. Antonov embodies Teddy Roosevelt's 'Speak softly and carry a big a stick.' He can be quietly ruthless." And that Antonov had been sent to Philadelphia by Tikhonov to get Lucky Stars up and running, and then was set to do the same in Macao, where Tikhonov was opening a new casino.

"Mr. Antonov," O'Sullivan went on, "wants to have an acceptable explanation of what happened—and what's been done about it—when Mr. Tikhonov is made aware of the situation."

"He doesn't know?"

O'Sullivan shrugged. "I don't think so. At least not yet. Mr. Antonov is very selective about what he tells me. He's good about just letting me do my job on the straight and narrow. And that's why I wanted to let you in on something—and why I just said you were getting ahead of me."

Harris raised his eyebrows, wrinkling his forehead.

"You've got my undivided attention."

"As I said, Tony, Mr. Antonov prefers to deliver good news to his boss, such as how a problem was addressed and was no longer a problem." He glanced up at the image of Hooks smirking at the Winner's Lounge, then looked at Harris. "I know you have plenty of open cases you're working. Homicide clearance rate is still about—what?—maybe forty percent?"

Harris nodded. "Sometimes a little bit better."

"Still better than Camden's thirty percent, huh?" O'Sullivan grinned, then added, "So if I were you, I wouldn't put too much effort in this job."

Silently, Harris, holding his right hand palm up, gestured with his fingers *Give me more*.

O'Sullivan looked him in the eyes.

"Okay," he then said, "let's say, hypothetically of course, that someone with a real motivation found this golden-voiced rapper first, and then recovered the merchandise, or what's probably left of it, and then made an example of him to others who might think that if a dipshit like Hooks could get away with ripping off a casino, so could they. Go hit the one across the street, or any of the others in Philly or at the Shore."

Harris narrowed his eyes.

O'Sullivan shrugged, and then said: "Ghetto punks are killing each other every day in this city, and there doesn't seem to be an end to it." Then he added, his tone dripping with sarcasm, "I've heard there's even a name for it—Killadelphia?"

Harris pursed his lips, then nodded.

"Yeah. I may have heard that, too," he said, adding his own sarcasm.

"That may be job security for you," O'Sullivan said. "But when those ghetto punks bring their shit into my casino . . ."

After a moment, Harris said, "Kind of hard to be surprised it happened, no? They built this fancy place with lots of money in the middle of a really rough part of town, not to mention right across the bridge from Camden. That's like dragging a carcass of raw meat past a pack of starving dogs."

"Tony, those animals this morning killed a poor bastard just trying to make a living selling watches. And they may have killed a beautiful, innocent young girl."

After a moment, Tony sighed disgustedly.

"I hear you, Sully. And agree. But—"

"No buts," O'Sullivan said sharply. "Being a wild dog, particularly a starving one, to use your analogy, usually does not end well."

Harris raised his eyebrows again.

"That mean what I think it means? You'd be party to that, Sully?"

O'Sullivan shook his head.

"Not only no, Tony—*hell no*. You should know me better than that. Never. That's why Mr. Antonov ordered me to give you everything you ask for—copies of the videos, everything—on the level . . ."

His voice trailed off as his eyes scanned the room. Then he motioned for Harris to follow him across the room.

"Look, Tony," he said quietly a moment later, "I'm going to do everything in my power to help you do your job. But that doesn't mean other gears aren't turning. I don't know for a fact that they are—on my mother's grave, I swear it—but I do know that I cannot control what others do. Just as you can't."

"And what do you mean by that?"

"Remember the Frankford Five guys? Shaking down the dealers they were supposed to be arresting? And then that rookie kid walking his Fifteenth District beat actually caught one of the dealers dealing, and when he cuffed him the dealer announced that he was untouchable, and why."

"Yeah, and then the rookie, trying to do the right thing, told his superior in the Fifteenth."

"And next thing the kid knows," O'Sullivan picked back up, "the dirty guys are calling him a gink, and even though no charges stuck, the kid spent every day looking over his shoulder, then finally felt he had to quit the department."

"I hate that gink term, Sully. The kid wasn't ratting out those dirty guys. He did the right thing. Those scumbags got lucky that nobody believed the dealers, who kept changing their stories. That's why no charges stuck, and why they kept their damn badges, not because they weren't dirty."

O'Sullivan grunted. "You're right. Trouble was, the kid still paid the price. But it makes my point, and you and I've seen this, that things are not always black and white, not always that right and wrong."

Harris met his eyes for a long time.

"We go back a long way, Tony. I'm just giving you a friendly heads-up. I'm not saying that I know something is going to happen to this ghetto punk—"

"The hypothetical one?" Harris interrupted.

"—this hypothetical punk," O'Sullivan went on, "but no one would be surprised if the shooter and everyone else involved suffers the consequences of their actions. And—who knows?—worse comes to worst, you might just get them handed to you on a silver platter. Add one more to the closure rate, you know?"

Harris looked at him for a long moment.

"You understand, Sully," Harris then said evenly, "that I'm going to have to share this with Matt Payne. And you know he has the personal ear of the white shirts with stars on their shoulders."

"That's right—Payne got himself promoted to sergeant, didn't he? Passed the exam at the top of the list. Super-smart guy. I always thought the bastards who called him a Richie Rich playing cop were just crumbs being petty pricks. His old man and uncle were damn good cops."

He paused, then went on: "Tony, I fully expected you to send what I told you up the chain—I certainly would do the same in your shoes—but now that I know it's going to go to the Wyatt Earp of the Main Line, hell, that tells me the odds of this ghetto punk getting his due just got better."

Five minutes later, Sully O'Sullivan, his arms crossed over his chest as he looked up at the security room's wall of monitors, watched Detective Tony Harris walking through the revolving door and out of the casino.

O'Sullivan was not at all surprised to see Harris holding his cellular phone to his head with his left hand while he cupped his right hand over his mouth so that what he was saying could not be overheard.

VII

The enormous black thirty-six-year-old homicide detective standing at the two-way mirror of the Homicide Unit's Interview Room
II turned at the sound of the door opening.

Harold Kennedy nodded as Sergeant Matt Payne entered the
small, dimly lit viewing room.

"Hey, Sarge," he said.

"I miss anything, Hal?" Payne gestured toward the interview
room on the other side of the two-way mirror. "How's he doing in
there?"

Payne saw that Detective Dick McCrory was in the slightly
larger—ten by twelve feet—harshly lit room with a male teenager.
McCrory stood leaning against the far wall, looking down at the
teen, who was seated in one of two metal chairs, both of which
were bolted to the floor on opposite sides of a bare metal table,
also bolted to the floor. A manila folder was on the table, next to
an open plastic bottle of water.

Payne studied the unkempt teenager, who was handcuffed to
the chair, one cuff on his left hand and the other around a thick

bar on the seatback. He had matted hair and filthy clothing—a black sweatshirt, ragged blue jeans, scuffed leather boots. The hood of his sweatshirt was down, exposing a hard face with hollow eyes behind thick black-framed eyeglasses and framed by a scraggly beard.

Kennedy's massive shoulders shrugged as he raised his eyebrows, making a look of frustration.

"So far it's looking like you wasted your time coming. All I can say for certain is the kid's got a clear case of rectal cranial inversion."

Payne grunted.

"Don't they all have their head up their ass?" he said, then added, "So, this guy is supposed to be our big lead, but now my time's wasted?"

Kennedy grimaced.

"Key word *supposed*. Say hello to eighteen-year-old Michael Hayward, aka Jamal. Turns out Antwan 'Pookie' Parker lied—"

Payne, making his eyes wide in mock horror, slapped his hand to his chest and said, "A CI lied? I'm shocked!"

"And—brace yourself—one of the things he lied about was this guy wanting to see the famous Wyatt Earp of the Main Line."

Payne thought: *I knew the bastard was blowing smoke.*

He said: "Well, in addition to being shocked, now Jamal the Junkie has really hurt my feelings."

Kennedy chuckled.

"What's more," Kennedy went on, "Jamal said he doesn't have a clue who the famous Wyatt Earp of the Main Line is. In fact, with his high level of maybe an eighth-grade education—he got thrown out of Mansion barely into his first year—it wouldn't surprise me if he ever heard of the actual Marshal Earp and/or the Main Line."

"Mansion"—Strawberry Mansion High School, its student body of four hundred coming from deeply impoverished families—struggled to overcome a reputation as one of the most dangerous schools in the entire United States. The addition of metal detectors manned by armed school police officers, and the running of students through them throughout the day, had helped create a somewhat safer learning environment. But that hadn't stopped the fights in the hallways and the cafeteria from breaking out daily.

"When we frisked him," Kennedy went on, "he had that belly pocket full of packets of smack and pills. And in his waistband there was a .40 cal semiauto, a Smith & Wesson M-and-P with—get this—only one cartridge. The fifteen-round magazine was empty. When I asked him about it—while doing my little show you said to do—he told me that one bullet was all he had left."

"Did Jamal get tested for gunshot residue?"

"Yeah, and there was none on him. And it's not like he washed his hands and clothes of it. I mean, look at him. Washing would have actually cleaned some part of him. And I'm not going to ruin your day and describe what we saw passes for a toilet on his street."

"The street probably is the toilet."

Kennedy grunted.

"Right. Close enough . . ."

"Well," Payne said, pointedly getting back on topic, "if there was no GSR on him, then someone cleaned the gun."

"Yeah, but only wiped down the exterior. When I glanced

down the barrel, the bore was filthy. Someone ran a lot of rounds through it. Way more than just the one magazine."

"He say where he got the gun?"

Kennedy shook his head.

"He hasn't really said anything. But I'm betting it was from Pookie. He has a reputation for that. Where Pookie got it is another story. We do know that the street and sidewalk at the scene of Dante's drive-by was riddled with .40 cal casings."

"And nine-millimeter, right?"

"Right. And there was plenty of lead recovered, by the Crime Scene guys and a couple during Dante's autopsy. That'll keep ballistics busy looking for a match. Especially if they find any of the recovered .40 cal bullets are full metal jackets that had been scored."

"Cut so they can flatten more like hollow points?"

Kennedy nodded. "Looks that way. That's what the lone round in Jamal's gun had. Obviously, a match won't point to the shooter, but it would at least place the gun at the scene."

"Sounds like it would be a helluva lot easier having a heart-to-heart chat with ol' Antwan 'Pookie' Parker and getting him to confess," Payne said, then glanced above the mirror.

Mounted on the wall at the top of the mirror's window frame was a twenty-inch flat-panel monitor. There were six images, two rows of three, on it, the cameras of the interview room showing its entire interior from various angles. A line of text at the bottom of each image had a date and time stamp and showed the names of the officer conducting the interview and the person being interviewed. All of it was being digitally recorded.

Payne looked at Jamal through the two-way mirror. He knew

that the thermostat for the interview room was generally set around sixty degrees. Yet the teenager had beads of sweat on his forehead and the armpits of his sweatshirt were darkened by more moisture.

"What's Jamal the Junkie on?" Payne said.

"We thought smack. He's pretty much got needle tracks on his needle tracks. But he said he smoked some wet. Whatever he took, we didn't get much out of him on the drive over here. Dick wanted to see if he'd open up to him in here—and to you, but that was before we learned Jamal doesn't know any Marshal Earp exists. Now we're just about to hand him over to the Detention Unit—let him dry out downstairs and try again later."

"Look at that body language," Payne said. "He's closed-off, defensive. Legs crossed, his free arm hugging his chest. And he's clearly anxious—he's about to chew off his lower lip."

"Uh-huh. He'd probably really be a basket case if it wasn't for the drugs making a zombie of him."

Payne reached toward the control panel and turned up the volume to the interview room microphone. From the speaker in the ceiling came McCrory's voice: "Okay . . . remember me asking, back in the car, how familiar you are with McPherson Square, Jamal?"

"With what?"

McCrory pointed at a sheet that was a desktop computer-printed map, his fingertip touching a square that had been marked in yellow highlighter.

The park—off Kensington Avenue, at F and Indiana, just two blocks from an elementary school and another two from a magnet middle school—was well known as an open-air market for the dealing and consumption of drugs.

When police patrolled it, the junkies slipped away into the shadows, looking like so many cockroaches suddenly exposed to light, and leaving the park grounds littered with empty glassine packets and dirty syringes. When the patrols left the park, the waves of junkie zombies rolled back in for another high.

Not all fled. Some were so severely wasted—it was not uncommon for the heavily addicted ones to shoot up ten to twenty hits of heroin a day—that they could not move, and simply sat or lay on park benches in a drug-induced state that bordered on the comatose.

The police found the park environment, as hopeless as it seemed, was preferable to the days of widespread drug dens in abandoned row houses and factory buildings. There the addicts would shoot up crack cocaine and heroin out of sight—but would then frequently simply disappear, their bodies discovered days or months later, if ever.

In the open, however, the officers—as well as various teams of volunteers, often those who had sons and daughters lost to the drugs—could approach those in and near the park and try talking them into attending a substance abuse program—detoxifications with the synthetic opioids Suboxone and Methadone—like the one at the addiction hospital across from nearby Norris Square.

The odds were great that the addicted, absent professional help would—sooner or later but most likely sooner—join the hundreds who died each year in Philly either from an overdose of heroin or, indirectly, from the violence associated with it—being killed in a robbery, for example, or in the course of performing sexual acts, as they tried to raise cash for their next high.

"Uh-huh," Jamal said, nodding. "That's Needle Park."

"So McPherson—what you call Needle Park—that's Antwan's turf, right?"

"Antwan?"

"Antwan—Pookie."

Jamal nodded again.

"I've seen Pookie there, if that's what you mean—"

"Then it's his turf?"

Jamal shrugged. "But I see lots of folks there."

"Pookie work for anyone?"

Jamal again shrugged, then tried looking McCrory in the eye but looked away and said, "Guess you'd have to ask him about that."

McCrory shook his head.

"So," he pursued, "you see Pookie there working the park. And then along comes Dante Holmes. Was he trying to move in, work it, too? And that got him capped?"

Jamal, nervously chewing on his lower lip, did not reply.

"Okay," McCrory then said, opening the manila folder on the table and placing a series of photographs before Jamal. The top one showed the street view of a row house with police line yellow tape strung from the porch out to the street. Evidence markers, inverted yellow plastic Vs with black numerals, filled the marked-off area.

"This is where the drive-by shooting took place," McCrory said. "On the front stoop . . ."

Jamal's eyes darted to the photograph, then looked away.

". . . of Dante's grandmother's house in Kensington, on Clementine at E Street. Five o'clock on a Friday afternoon. Yesterday. Grandma happens to look out her upstairs bedroom window when a Chevy Impala with tinted windows comes rolling up Clementine and stops shy of her house. It's dark already, but she can just make out the car's front passenger window opening, and she sees a guy waving Dante to come over. Dante, probably thinking he's about to move some product, starts walking toward the Impala. Then the back passenger window goes down and a hand reaches out with a semiauto. The night lights up with muzzle flashes as both passengers start firing multiple shots, at least twenty-five, at Dante. Grandma says that it looks and sounds like really loud Chinese firecrackers going off. Then the car speeds off. And Dante's down. Three rounds, two to the chest, one to his thigh. He never had a chance. And right in front of his grandma."

McCrory paused to let that sink in, then went on: "That's bad enough. But what's worse: most of those bullets skipped past Dante, some going into a neighbor's row house. You have any family, Jamal, any brothers or sisters?"

Jamal, stone-faced, did not respond.

McCrory flipped to the next photograph. It showed three evidence markers—one by a large dark stain on a threadbare couch— in the living room of a home.

"Okay," he said. "Well, this is where a ten-year-old girl was watching TV after school with her little brother. She takes one of those bullets to the head. Now she's still in intensive care, and not looking like she's going to make it. And Dante, he's dead."

McCrory stopped and cocked his head.

"Look at me, Jamal. You following all this?"

Jamal glanced at him, then looked back at his feet.

McCrory went on: "It's important that you do. Because it's my job to find out who's responsible, and I'm telling you now that I don't give up. Nobody deserves to die that way. Especially an innocent little girl."

He paused to let that sink in, then pointed at the evidence markers in the photo of the street scene.

"See these? They're .40 cal casings. These and the bullets that were collected at the drive-by can be matched to the gun that fired them. And if even one was fired by the gun you had on you . . . then you need to start talking, Jamal."

Jamal glanced at the photograph, then stared at his feet a long moment, anxiously crossed his legs the opposite way, then back again. He met McCrory's eyes, and sighed.

"Told you I don't know no Dante," he finally said.

"So you keep saying," McCrory said, his tone disgusted. "Not knowing him and shooting him are two different things. I can imagine that you don't know the little girl, either. But that doesn't change the fact that she may die."

"I didn't shoot nobody. That gun I got so I can defend myself. There're crazy folks out there, shooting you for no reason. But that ain't me."

McCrory picked up the stack of photographs and began laying them out on the table so that they were all visible at once.

In the viewing room, Payne grunted, then glanced at Kennedy.

"Don't know about you, Hal, but I say he's lying."

"How can you tell?" Kennedy said. "Because his lips are moving?"

"He may not have pulled the trigger, but he knows who Dante is and/or knows who did it. And you nailed it—we're wasting our time with him right now."

Payne then reached into his suit coat pocket and produced a folded sheet of paper.

"Show this to Jamal the Junkie," Payne said, handing the sheet to Kennedy. "Just to throw him off. Maybe it'll jar loose that rectal cranial inversion."

Kennedy unfolded the sheet and saw that it was the Wanted flyer of the heavyset male suspect in the LOVE and Franklin parks murders. He shook his head as he looked at the cold, empty eyes and the spread of tattoos—the inverted heart under the left eye, the inverted peace symbol under the right one, "Family" inked in tall, dark lettering across his throat.

"What've we got to lose?" Payne said. "I just want to watch his reaction—if any—to seeing the doer."

Kennedy left the viewing room and, a moment later, Payne heard him over the speaker knocking twice on the interview room door. McCrory cracked open the door, leaned toward it to listen as the Wanted flyer was passed inside, then nodded and closed the door.

Payne watched McCrory glance over the flyer, then extend it toward Jamal.

"What about this guy, Jamal?" McCrory said, his tone sarcastic. "Don't know him, either?"

Jamal didn't move to take the sheet, and McCrory put it on the table on top of the other papers before him.

As Jamal focused on it, his eyes grew wide and he wrinkled his forehead. He quickly tried to mask his reaction by taking off his glasses, then running his hand over his face and rubbing his eyes.

"So you do know him?" McCrory asked, making it more a statement.

Jamal's body slumped as he shook his head.

"What?" McCrory said.

Jamal shook his head again, and, apparently thinking he was being clever, looked at McCrory and said, "Who is he? What'd he do?"

Payne grunted.

"At least he's consistent with his lying," he said.

McCrory had come to the same conclusion.

"You're lying, Jamal. Who is this guy? How do you know him?"

Jamal looked at his shoes for a long moment.

"C'mon, Jamal. Talk to me. You're looking at some serious time already with a gun charge on top of possession with intent to distribute . . . or worse."

After a moment, Jamal sighed.

"He's one I've seen at Needle Park, too," Jamal said. "I don't know him. But a guy I did know there said stay away from him. Said he's a really bad dude. Angry at everything, you know?"

Jamal's tired voice trailed off, and he began to rub his face again.

"What's the guy's name who told you that?"

Jamal shrugged.

"Harvey? Javier, maybe? Heard he OD'd. He didn't say this guy's name, just called him *la gente loca* . . ."

"'Crazy people'?" Payne said, making the translation from Spanish. "I'll be damned!"

He reached to pull out his cellular telephone, then felt it vibrate. When he checked its screen, there was a text from Kerry Rapier: "The mystery of Where's Waldo solved! At least the where part . . ."

"Jesus!" Payne blurted, then looked at Kennedy and said, "If you'll excuse me. I should be right back but might not. Nasuti and Lucke own the LOVE and Franklin parks murders. Let them and me know what else that bastard says about that doer, and also when you've got Pookie coming in for that heart-to-heart talk."

"Will do, Sarge," Kennedy said, crossing his arms over his massive chest. "We've already texted Pookie. Just waiting to hear back."

"Good luck with that."

"Oh, you can count on it that he'll be in touch. The bastard thinks he's due a payday for ratting out this knucklehead to us."

[TWO]

As Payne stepped outside the viewing room, using his shoulder to push the door closed, he finished what he had started to do when Kerry Rapier's text interrupted him: alert Nasuti and Lucke about what Jamal had said. Then he tapped the key on the screen to call back Rapier.

"Thought that'd get your attention, Marshal," Rapier said, by way of answering the call. "We found the car, and just waiting on a positive ID on the victim, too."

"Where?"

"Off Torresdale, some blocks up from Harding Middle School. The VeeDub initially was reported to nine-one-one as having been carjacked."

"You've lost me. Waldo's buddy said it was taken from them at gunpoint, before Waldo got whacked."

"Right. But then a couple hours later an anonymous adult male called in to nine-one-one and said that a Puerto Rican with a gun had just carjacked a silver VeeDub Jetta with Jersey plates on Torresdale. A couple of marked units responded, and as they searched the area, there suddenly was a black plume rising over by the commuter train tracks.

"When they got to the fire, right before the fire trucks, they saw that it was a VeeDub and that it was completely engulfed in flames. Windows were either blown out or melted."

"Nice."

"There's no question that the fuel tank blew up, but they also found remains of two metal cans, one that looked like it exploded, and it's believed these were the accelerants. And the gas in the tank. It was a superhot fire."

"And the body?"

"There's not much left of it. Not a completely charred skeleton but close. Apparently when the gas tank cooked off, it blew the body up into the trunk lid, which may or may not have been simultaneously blown open."

"Well, it's logical that it's Waldo. The shooter likely just stuffed him in the trunk and then torched the evidence." He paused, then said, "Didn't Waldo's buddy say the shooter was a skinny black guy?"

"Yeah, and his drug dealer partner was a big black guy with a bald head and meth mouth. And the young kid delivering the product was also black."

"But the nine-one-one caller said the carjacker was Puerto Rican?"

"And near Harding Middle School, which is approximately four miles from where Dan said he saw Billy killed. They ran the

Jersey plate, and it belongs to a Chevy. The Penn plate that was under the Jersey one is registered to the Jetta, and in Billy's father's name."

"You have someone running down surveillance camera footage in the area?"

"Already on it before I texted you."

"Good man."

"One more thing, Marshal."

"What?"

"Chuck Whaley's headed to the location of the car fire since they found pretty much nothing but blood at the site of the killing. The Crime Scene guys have already wrapped up."

Payne grunted derisively. "Great. Make sure he gets all you've got. He'll need all the help he can get."

"Done. Anything else?"

"No . . . wait. Yeah, there is. You have access to the recording in Homicide's interview rooms, right?"

"Uh-huh," Rapier said, and Payne heard the sound of rapid typing in the background. "Punched it up now. Michael Hayward, aka Jamal. That's one filthy person."

"Yeah. Jamal the Junkie. McCrory and Kennedy brought him in on the Dante Holmes drive-by, and he just now said he's seen the doer in the park murders at McPherson Square in Kensington. But then again he's been consistently lying for at least the last hour."

"That's a great break, if true. You believe it?"

"Hell if I know. I *want* to believe it, so we can grab the bastard. I was giving Nasuti and Lucke the heads-up when you texted. They can broadcast the info with a Flash, and then see if any of our blue shirts who patrol the park—who probably haven't seen the Wanted flyer yet, otherwise they'd have already made him and tried running him to ground—can ID the doer. All of which hinges on if Jamal the Junkie isn't lying—again. And, if he actually is telling the truth, if the doer's been seen anywhere near the park."

"So, what is it you need me to do?"

"Right now, just make sure everyone's getting all updates and that there're backups of backups of that interview recording."

"Oh ye of little faith, Marshal. Redundancy is my middle name."

[THREE]
SEPTA Somerset Station
Kensington Avenue, Philadelphia
Saturday, December 15, 3:12 P.M.

Transit Police Officer Thelonious "Theo" Clarke, a beefy five-foot-ten twenty-one-year-old African-American, stood near the concourse exit as he scanned the crowd stepping off the just-arrived southbound train.

Clarke had served six months on the force of three hundred that policed the Southeastern Pennsylvania Transportation Authority mass transit system, the trains and buses of which servicing, as its name suggested, the City of Philadelphia proper as well as the surrounding four suburban counties.

If there appeared to be some similarities with the Transit Police and the Philadelphia Police Department, that was not by coincidence. SEPTA's officers went through the same Philadelphia Police Academy training as did Philly's officers. Thus, it was not unusual for SEPTA's officers to later join the PPD, which, with manpower of more than six thousand, was approximately twenty times larger in size.

And, while not nearly as common, the reverse of PPD cops joining the SEPTA force also was true—right up to the top cop.

The police chief of SEPTA had served, prior to his transfer, as head of the PPD's elite Highway Patrol Unit. Like many cops in both departments, it was said he had multigenerational blue blood running in his veins. The chief could in fact count on the fingers of both hands how many family members served in, or had retired from, the ranks of the Philadelphia Police Department, uncles and cousins and nephews and nieces—and his father, who had retired after rising to the level of deputy police commissioner.

While Clarke liked that—he devoutly considered his brothers in blue to be family—he was the first of his biological family to become a law enforcement officer.

Theo had grown up in Spring Garden, a tough section of the city wedged in just north of the wealth of Center City. In his senior year of high school he learned that one could apply to the Philly police at age nineteen, but that PPD required sixty hours of college credits, or a mix of education and experience that could be military service or two years in the Police Explorers Cadet Program and hundreds of hours of training.

His joining the army or navy simply was not a viable option because he needed to be near home to help care for his mother, who suffered from diabetes and could not get around by herself. So he had enrolled in Community College of Philadelphia to acquire the necessary credits—then about a year thereafter, while talking to another student as they scanned a bulletin board in the school's Career Center, learned that SEPTA required only a high school diploma or General Equivalency Diploma.

Theo Clarke, anxious to do something job-wise, thought that he could put in time as a SEPTA transit officer—policing was policing, he decided, and he would get to go through the police academy same as the others—and continue with school and then at some point possibly look at transferring to the PPD.

He found that he actually liked being a SEPTA transit officer, especially because transit cops had authority all across the mass transit system, not just limited to one small area of the city.

While pursuing and arresting people who jumped over the turnstiles to evade paying the subway fare did get somewhat repetitious, he found that it could occasionally get interesting.

The bad guys whom the SEPTA police chased on the trains were, after all, if not the exact same bad guys who the Philadelphia Police Department chased—and oftentimes they were—then they could be equally as bad. They committed the same crimes— assaults, robberies, illegal drug sales, and the like. They just happened to do it on SEPTA property.

And of course there always was the steady stream of fare evaders.

The philosophy of the SEPTA police chief was that the bad guys—and, too often, the bad girls—who jumped the turnstiles were of course guilty (a) of theft of service but also (b) of being generally up to no good. They weren't, to put a point on it, jumping the turnstiles during their commute to and from work or school—they were looking for an opportunity to commit a crime.

Thus, it wasn't just a philosophy—and when the chief mustered his SEPTA patrols to crack down on fare evaders, there followed an immediate drop in the rates of other more serious crimes committed on the mass transit system.

Which was why Transit Officer Theo Clarke often found himself watching, as now, the crowds embarking and disembarking the train cars at the elevated Somerset station.

This being Kensington, he knew it was only a short matter of time before he would nab some miscreant leaping over—or, his favorite because they looked so ridiculous, crawling under—the rotating arms of a turnstile.

And, also entirely probable, committing a worse offense.

Clarke had been standing by the concourse exit for not even ten minutes when his eyes caught sight of a male walking in a crouch at the back of the last group exiting the train.

His first thought: *That dude's hiding something that's making him walk that way.*

Clarke saw that the male was short, maybe five-four, and chunky. He looked Hispanic—*Probably Puerto Rican,* Theo thought—and maybe around his own age. He wore a black stocking cap pulled low on his head. He had on a gray sweatshirt—the right cuff of which he suddenly realized was blackened.

Like it's been on fire. What's up with that?

Transit Officer Clarke started walking toward him to get a closer look, and then saw that the male was very carefully cradling his hand—*That's why the dude's walking funny*—and that the flesh of the hand was a bright red with black streaks.

Clarke intercepted him.

"You okay?" Clarke said. "What happened to your hand?"

When the male looked up and saw a uniformed policeman looming over him, his tired eyes grew wide.

Clarke knew that wasn't an unusual reaction to occur in Somerset station, where he figured at any given time a majority of people could be under the influence of some drug, legal or illicit, and thus Clarke, though remaining cautious, did not immediately read anything into it.

The injured male, whose arm with the burned hand then began shaking uncontrollably, did not respond to his questions.

"What's your name?" Clarke pursued.

"Juan," Ruben Mora lied.

"You really need to get that injury looked at, Juan," Clarke said, then pointed past the concourse exit. "There's a hospital ER just a few blocks away."

For Clarke, it unfortunately was a regular occurrence to come across someone who had overdosed—not necessarily on the El, though that of course had happened. Just two days earlier he had had to administer a prefilled syringe of naloxone hydrochloride that he recently had begun carrying as part of his kit to a nineteen-year-old white female—the naloxone blocking and reversing the effects of opioid painkillers, such as Oxycontin, and heroin—and then had EMTs transport her the short distance down Kensington Avenue to the emergency room at Temple University Episcopal Hospital on West Lehigh Avenue.

"Yeah, it hurts bad," Ruben Mora said.

Mora then looked from Transit Officer Clarke to his burned hand. Then all at once his eyes drooped, his shoulders slumped— and he collapsed to the ground.

"Damn!" Transit Officer Clarke blurted.

He quickly knelt and then lifted Mora off the ground. He threw him over his shoulder in a fireman's carry and began trotting toward the exit, calling out, "Make way! Clear a path!" as he went.

After maneuvering down the stairs and reaching street level, Clarke carried Mora to the marked Ford Crown Victoria that he had left parked in the spot at the curb marked OFFICIAL SEPTA USE ONLY.

Transit Officer Clarke opened the Police Interceptor's back door behind the driver's, then squatted and carefully leaned forward, dropping Mora onto the backseat. He then hopped behind the wheel, activated the emergency lights and siren, then looked over his shoulder as he yanked the gear selector into drive.

"C'mon, c'mon, make a hole!" Clarke said, stabbing his right index finger at the control panel button between the seats that added a louder *BRAAAAP! BRAAAAAP!* horn sound to the *Woop-Woop!* of the siren.

At the third *BRAAAAP!* a delivery van braked hard, creating an opening, and Clarke caused the Ford's rear tires to squeal as he took it, the engine roaring as he accelerated down Kensington Avenue.

[FOUR]
Office of the First Deputy Police Commissioner
The Roundhouse, Philadelphia
Saturday, December 15, 5:15 P.M.

"The difference with the murder of the reporter and his wife," Matt Payne explained to First Deputy Police Commissioner Dennis V. Coughlin and Lieutenant Jason Washington, "beyond it being a slaughter—terrible word, but that's exactly what they did to the O'Briens—is that those responsible wanted everyone to know they did it. They basically left a calling card saying, 'Hey, we did it before, and we'll do it again.'"

Washington shook his head. "Mickey O'Hara said this cartel—"

"The New Acuña Cartel, Jason," Payne provided.

"—this New Acuña Cartel did the same to another reporter who worked for O'Brien in Texas?"

Payne nodded. "Tomas Rodriguez, thirty-five, a husband and father who fled Acuña with his family after the cartel tortured and killed his photographer, and then hung his body with a note saying, in essence, 'We warned you. Stop the reporting. Or else.' The cartel hunted down Tomas and his family in San Antonio. Left his bloody head on his laptop with a note, and I quote verbatim, 'The sins of the father shall be visited upon the son.' I saw the photograph of it. Those are images you never forget."

"My God," Coughlin said. "The butchering of human beings is beyond simply uncivilized. It's savage . . . barbaric."

"And tragically it's starting to happen more and more," Payne said. "I've certainly seen more than I ever expected." He paused. "So we basically know who's responsible. But, and I'm getting this from Jim Byrth, the cartels are hiring hit squads."

"Contract killings?" Coughlin said.

Payne nodded. "And these squads are more or less expendable. They live or die at the will of the cartel. That's what Jim Byrth says the Texas Rangers found when they investigated the murder of the Rodriguez family."

"I don't think I follow you," Coughlin said. "What exactly did they find?"

"Same as we found here in University City. The doers made no effort to hide any evidence. They didn't try to cover their tracks— literally, there were bloody boot prints all over the scene. And fingerprints, there and in the truck they stole from the pest control company that was found abandoned blocks away."

"And?" Coughlin pursued.

"And we may very well find these killers, matching them to those bloody fingerprints."

"I'm repeating myself, 'And?'"

"And, like Byrth said of the killers of the Rodriguez family in San Antonio, they'll be found dumped on a roadside with a single bullet wound to the back of the head."

"Executed."

"And so we have the killers positively identified—and can give the families of the O'Briens their closure—but we do not have who hired them to make the hit. So we have closed one case without an arrest—"

"Some in the business call that solving crimes by eraser," Washington said.

"—but wind up with what will no doubt become a cold case on the killers' killer. Meanwhile, the cartels are still calling in hits. And they have an endless pool of hit men. Byrth said the ones who killed Tomas were in the Tejas Familia prison gang. They'd been recently released, and probably working off debt accumulated while in jail."

Payne paused, then added, "This is usually where I make the wisecrack that that's what's known as job security in our business. Except the next one they've threatened is Mickey O'Hara."

"And he said he's not worried," Washington said, incredulous.

Payne shook his head. "He said O'Brien had more material beyond the heroin story, and was going to run it."

Payne gestured at the photograph that was on the desk that showed Tyrone Hooks viewing the glass display cases in the casino jewelry store.

"Meanwhile, we have this bastard casing the place approximately fifteen minutes before the robbery. And there's video, sharp and clear, of the whole thing going down. But these guys were very good. First, they entered from four different directions, and as they did, they (a) kept their hoodies up and (b) kept their heads down so that their faces were not visible to cameras, then (c) quickly converged at the retail mall and pulled bandannas over their faces. So all we've got is four guys in black outfits robbing the jewelry store."

"And this Tyrone Hooks character," Coughlin said, gesturing at a photograph on his desk.

Payne nodded.

"Who," he said, "is now pretty much a dead man walking, according to Tony Harris. If Sully O'Sullivan is to be believed, and I see no reason not to. We need to bring Hooks in—if only for his own safety—except we don't dare try to grab him at the rally with this crowd around."

He motioned in the direction of the Executive Command Center and added, "Looking at the rally site, we've gone over every viable scenario, and it would be suicide to try."

Next door, two of the three banks of flat-screen monitors in the ECC showed various views of the Stop Killadelphia Rally at the Word of Brotherly Love Ministry in Strawberry Mansion. The vast majority of these were proprietary feeds from police department cameras—from those on the undercover PECO van to the tiny ones affixed to the helmets of the four Mounted Patrol Unit officers watching the crowd. The third bank of nine monitors showed the live feeds of the news media covering the event.

"While you can't slay the dragon until you lure it from its cave," Payne said, "no one can touch Hooks in that contentious crowd."

"Which is why I'm glad you decided not to attend the rally, Matty," Coughlin said. "Wise decision."

"The last thing I intend to do is give Skinny Lenny the satisfaction of me backing down," Payne said, "but I faithfully took heed of Jason's warning that Public Enemy Number One being there would probably be the spark that ignited the powder keg— or words to that effect. And that igniting that keg would play right into Lenny's hand, which would be worse than me backing down."

He paused, then added, "I don't get it."

"Don't get what, Matty?" Coughlin said.

Payne shrugged. "All the posters of dead bad guys, all the protesting over dealers taking each other out."

"You don't?" Coughlin almost snapped, his tone incredulous.

Payne shook his head. "They're making it out like it's a bad thing. The miscreants all had long lists of priors. You'd think they'd be thanking us."

Coughlin grunted. Washington silently shook his head.

"The innocent victims, the anger over their loss, that I get," Payne said. "But here's Lenny lumping them all together—and sharing the stage with this thug Hooks. That I really don't get. Anyway, all our guys are in position to grab Hooks—but right after the rally, and away from the view of the crowd."

"What's the latest estimate of crowd size?" Washington said.

"Between twenty-five hundred and three thousand. And growing."

"Carlucci suggested we send up Tac Air," Denny Coughlin said. "It took some doing, but I talked him out of it. We don't need the presence of a helicopter giving the suggestion of an occupying force. I told him that the helos are on standby and if necessary can be there in minutes."

The Aviation Unit's tactical aircraft—"Tac Air"—had added, with the help of Department of Homeland Security federal dollars, a pair of Airbus AStar helicopters to its fleet of Bell Rangers.

"Good idea," Payne said. "Ghetto birds hovering overhead screams police militarization, which would only give Lenny something else to scream about."

Coughlin made a sour face.

"'Ghetto birds'?" he parroted. "So now we have heard from the peanut gallery. Thank you for your colorful input, Sergeant Payne."

Payne grinned.

"My pleasure, Uncle Denny."

"For being Public Enemy Number One, you certainly seem terribly cheery," Coughlin added. "And your use of that term suggests to me that you might actually be spending some time walking the beat."

Payne shrugged. "A little."

"Community policing," Washington said. "Winning one heart and mind at a time?"

"Something like that."

"Speaking of which, Matty," Coughlin said. "Is there any truth that there's some new mentoring program—an *underground* program—in Kensington?"

"Rumor has it," Washington added, "that there's a certain Homicide sergeant who's quietly funding it."

"Really?" Payne said. "Well, you know what President Truman said, 'It's amazing what you can get done if you don't care who gets the credit.'"

Washington's eyes looked warm and thoughtful as he nodded. *He's always up to something, living by the motto It's better to beg forgiveness than ask permission* he thought, and was reminded of the previous week, when he went with Payne to the Executive Command Center.

And some things he's up to play out better than others . . .

When Washington and Payne had entered the ECC, Kerry Rapier had greeted them, then pulled off his jacket.

"Thanks for the shirt, Marshal," Rapier told Payne.

"They came!" Payne said, then looked at Washington to explain. "I had T-shirts made with this on the back . . ."

Washington looked at the bold print on the shirt. It read *There is no hunting like the hunting of man, and those who have hunted armed men long enough and liked it never care for anything else thereafter.*

"I saw the quote when we took a tour of Hemingway's house in Key West. Apparently ol' Ernie wrote that in a magazine essay in 1936."

Payne motioned again for Rapier to turn, and when he had, Payne pointed and said, "And had that printed on the front."

Over the left breast was the silhouette of a grim reaper shouldering a scythe and, circling it, the words PHILLY PD HOMICIDE UNIT—OUR DAY BEGINS WHEN YOURS ENDS.

Washington met Payne's eyes.

"Matthew, pray tell, when you have your wild ideas, is there any type of filtering process that occurs before you act? Some method of vetting that, perhaps, evaluates the pros and cons? Or is it simply the result of a stream of consciousness?" He paused, made a thin smile, then added, "Not that that query is to mean that I am suggesting anything . . ."

"Do I detect a modicum of dissatisfaction?" Payne said, his tone mock-indignant. "Stream of consciousness—as I would expect one known respectfully as the Black Buddha to recognize—is given credence in the earliest Buddhist scriptures, notably Theravada, ones dating back to long before the birth of Christ. It was passed down the ages with the scriptures, first orally then as written text in the Pali language. Personally, I feel anything that survives that long must have its merits. So, yes, I do indeed embrace stream of consciousness."

"Here's more of that stream of consciousness," Rapier then

said, reaching under the desk and producing a cardboard shipping box. "This also came for you while you were gone."

"This what I think it is?" Payne said, looking at the mailing label. "It is!"

He pulled out a tactical folding knife from where he had it clipped inside the right front pocket of his pants. Then, in rapid fluid motions, he flipped open the knife's blade with his thumb, slit the packing tape, then closed the knife and clipped it back in his pocket. He opened the box flaps and removed a half-dozen cellophane-wrapped decks of playing cards.

He handed one pack to Washington.

"There," Payne said, smiling. "Now the Black Buddha cannot say I never gave him anything. And perhaps this will allow you to look favorably, if only a little, at my unfiltered wild ideas."

Washington looked at the pack for a moment. On the front of the box was the logotype of the Philadelphia Police Department, and under that: HOMICIDE UNIT COLD CASES.

He pursed his lips and nodded approvingly as he glanced at Payne, then peeled off the cellophane wrapper.

"Read the back," Payne said.

Washington flipped over the pack, and saw:

THIS DECK OF CARDS FEATURES FIFTY-TWO HOMICIDE COLD CASES AT THE PHILADELPHIA POLICE DEPARTMENT. THESE CASES REMAIN UNSOLVED. IF YOU RECOGNIZE ANYONE AND CAN PROVIDE INFORMATION ON

THEM, PLEASE CONTACT US. YOU CAN REMAIN
ANONYMOUS, AND YOU COULD BE ELIGIBLE FOR A CASH
REWARD UP TO $20,000.
CALL US AT 215-686-TIPS (8477) OR TEXT PPDTIP
(773847) OR TIPS@PHILLYPOLICE.COM OR
PHILLYPOLICE.COM/SUBMIT-A-TIP.

"Interesting," he said, then opened the top flap and pulled out the stack of cards and picked one.

It was the queen of spades and, as was common to standard playing cards, the card's back was identical to all the other cards in the deck. In this case it was the blue uniform patch with gold stitching in the shape of a badge that read PHILADELPHIA POLICE, HONOR, INTEGRITY, SERVICE.

The face of the card, as also was common to standard playing cards, had a black "Q" and a black spade in the upper-left and bottom-right corners. But instead of an image of a queen in royal garb, the center of the card had text and a color photograph.

Under the headline UNSOLVED HOMICIDE was the picture of an attractive brunette, under which was written "Jennifer Ann Dusevich, White Female, 32 years old, found 11/10/81 deceased in a wooded area of Point Breeze near the Delaware River just north of O'Maddie's Pub on State Road." And then it repeated the cash reward and the police department contact information.

"Quite clever, Matthew," Washington said, tucking the card back in the deck and the deck back in its box.

"Thanks. While modesty of course overwhelms me, I do think

it is a brilliant idea. People with a lot of time on their hands—oh, say, bad guys, and people who associate with same—like card games, and while they're playing, they just might have their memories jarred. I'm having boxes of these shipped to our jails and prisons and to our parole officers, getting them literally into the hands of those who would know. The hard part was which of the hundreds of cold cases from over the years to feature. I've got another two sets of fifty-two cases ready to go to print."

Washington nodded.

"I was about to ask," he said, "if you paid for this. But here we have the small print: 'This project funded as a community service by CrimeFreePhilly.com and PhillyNewsNow.com.'"

Payne said: "The families like that Dusevich girl's deserve knowing. She deserves it."

Washington nodded solemnly.

"To coin a phrase," he deeply intoned, "we do speak for the dead, don't we?"

Payne reached in the box and produced more cards.

He handed a stack to Washington, who saw that they were approximately the size of the playing cards but distinctly different.

"And I got the printer to throw in a bunch of Miranda cards for the unit," Payne said. "After reading from them—'You have the right to remain silent,' et cetera, et cetera—the miscreant then signs and dates it. And on the back, it's in Spanish. This way the rights can be read word for word off the card, then the suspect acknowledges that by signing off on it. No defense attorney would have a chance accusing one of our officers taking the stand that he hadn't read the doer his rights."

Washington nodded, then said, "Very thorough. Excellent ideas. Your other stream of consciousness notwithstanding."

And now, Washington realized, Payne was again explaining what else he had working that was above and beyond what the job required.

"First, Uncle Denny, I would not call the mentoring program 'underground,'" Payne said. "Maybe a better description would be 'below the radar,' which, for now at least, lessens the chance of retaliation from those who think, with their warped reasoning, that those trying to better themselves are traitors to those in the hood who don't."

He paused, then went on: "And it's not about the money. It's about reaching the individual. These kids are terrified to go to school—if they even make it there. Fights break out if someone looks crossways at another, on a sidewalk or in a school hallway. And the troublemakers don't care if there's an officer there—getting hauled out of class in handcuffs just adds to their street cred. So, we give those who want to break the cycle a second, even third chance. Help them live to see age twenty—and hopefully thirty and beyond."

"You're right, Matthew. We're doing more—have to do more, especially in today's lawless environment—than simply fighting crime."

"And last thing I want is to take credit for it," Payne said. "Lots of others are involved. Everyone just trying to reach out to those who have nothing, give them some hope."

"Would these others involved include Francis Fuller?" Coughlin said.

Payne grunted.

He said: "Why would Five-Eff—"

"'Five-Eff'?" Washington interrupted, raising his eyebrows. "Where have I heard that?"

Payne grinned and nodded, then explained, "I've never been a big fan of Fuller. I admire his ability to seemingly mint money, but not his method of doing it. He and I have had our differences for years. So while some call him Four-Eff, shorthand for Francis Franklin Fuller the Fifth, I added one more—"

"Ah," Washington again interrupted, "I believe I know what your fifth *F* might be. And I remember why it's vaguely familiar."

Payne smiled.

"Then I take it that you've heard of Fucking Francis Franklin Fuller the Fifth?" he said rhetorically.

That triggered a deep chuckle from Washington.

"Yes," he said, "and I actually heard it from our beloved mayor."

"And Hizzoner heard it from me," Payne added.

"Did he really?" Coughlin said, his tone suggesting disapproval.

"It was a slip of the tongue for the mayor," Washington said. "At least at first. After he realized he'd said, 'Five-Eff,' he added, 'That Matt Payne is a bad influence. He's used that enough that now I've picked it up. But I cannot blame him. Mostly because I agree with him. Five-Eff is . . .' And then he enthusiastically repeated the entire name."

"And one of the reasons that I gave ol' Francis that indelicate sobriquet," Payne went on pointedly, "is because his companies— and thus Five-Eff himself—shamelessly suck at the taxpayer teats. What did he get for building that shiny new high-rise over on Arch Street? The city and state kicked in some fifty million bucks for the development, on top of another fifty mil in tax abatements. Not bad for a guy whose personal fortune is some two thousand million dollars."

"The argument," Coughlin put in, "is that the building and the companies established therein are going to bring more jobs to our fair city."

"Yeah. But to only Center City," Payne said. "Meantime, today, with Philly having more people in deep poverty than any other major U.S. city, the only skills the thugs have learned revolve around selling dope—and worse."

"You allow Fuller no points for the funding of Lex Talionis?" Washington said.

"The last thing that Five-Eff is, Jason, is altruistic. That bad-guy bounty of twenty grand that he pays is a personal passion for him. What happened to his family was absolutely terrible. But, as we all well know, that is what's happening every day to those trapped in Philly's decaying neighborhoods."

Washington was nodding.

He said: "And his wife and daughter, caught in the crossfire, became collateral damage of what essentially was just one day's battle for turf. The next day comes another, and the next day . . . It is indeed tragic."

"Which is why," Payne went on, his tone bitter, "someone needs to get around the incompetents and thieves on the city council—the ones who would have us all be mushrooms, kept in the dark and fed a steady diet of manure. We need to connect directly with those who desperately need help. It's been more than a hundred years since that journalist—Lincoln Whatshisname . . . Lincoln *Steffens*—wrote about graft in America's big cities and said it was the worst here."

"'Philadelphia: Corrupt and Contented,' he called it," Washington said.

"Exactly, Jason. And nothing's changed with that. A century later, look where we've come."

Washington nodded again and thought, *No surprise he's taking this on personally. Matthew has always thought ahead of the conventional wisdom. The word* wisdom *being used loosely.*

"Impressive," Washington said.

"Don't encourage him, Jason," Denny Coughlin said. "Matty's ego is enormous enough as it is."

Payne looked at Coughlin. He saw that he was smiling.

Payne returned it, then said, "Thanks, Jason. But not really. More like just common sense. We're looking at it as another part of the business of fighting crime—that is, hopefully stopping future criminal acts. We know that our typical murderer and victim is a black male, eighteen to thirty-four years of age, with at least one prior arrest. If, instead of putting the guys on probation and then just throwing them back into their old hoods—where possibly, if not probably, they fall back into their old ways—if we can help them find suitable housing and learn a marketable skill, they may not commit a second—or tenth—crime. And/or get killed."

"Seems like a long shot," Coughlin said, "but a worthy one."

"Something has to change," Payne said. "Granted, the odds of failure are high for the hardest cases, but some, especially the younger ones, you can reach. And then there's Pretty Boy—"

"Pretty Boy?" Coughlin said.

"Detective Will Parkman—he got that handle from his fellow marines, who apparently have a warped sense of humor, as even he admits 'pretty' is the last word that comes to mind when you see him. I give Parkman a world of credit. He quietly sponsors an academic scholarship in criminal justice at La Salle, and has arranged for others to sponsor ones there, and he mentors as many students as he can."

He looked between Coughlin and Washington.

"That," Payne said, "is the winning of hearts and minds, and more than one at a time."

Payne then glanced over at the television screen.

"Oh, good," he said. "Looks like it's showtime! Care to join me in watching all the rally festivities on the video feeds next door?"

VIII

[ONE]
North Twenty-ninth and West Arizona Streets
Strawberry Mansion, Philadelphia
Saturday, December 15, 5:40 P.M.

Reverend Josiah Cross, in his signature flowing black robe and white clerical collar, stepped onstage just as the rail-thin Tyrone "King 215" Hooks shouted out the last refrain of his "Beatin' Down The Man."

Using the profane language of the street, the rapper's song preached that they had failed at overcoming the oppression by The Man through peaceful methods and encouraged not only responding in kind in the event that The Man used violence—but also preached instigating it.

The oppression by The Man, according to the hip-hop lyrics, occurred every day in the form of any police action, but particularly a shooting—thus justifying the title and refrain of the song:

"To our brothers the fuckin' Five-Oh daily rains / Nothin' but nines to our young brains / We got to get beatin' beatin' beatin' / Get beatin' down the man!"

The music—mostly a deep bass beat blaring from the pair of heavily amplified speakers on either side of the podium—was replaced by loud applause and cheering from the crowd that packed the streets. Cross estimated there to be at least a thousand people, maybe even a couple of thousand.

Most of those in the crowd appeared to be in their twenties and thirties, about a third of whom were white, with the majority a mix of those with darker complexions.

Directly in front of the stage, facing the crowd and standing shoulder to shoulder, stood a line of a couple dozen people who wore over their coats and sweatshirts the white T-shirts with STOP KILLADELPHIA! in bold lettering on the front and back, the STOP printed in bright red ink and the KILLADELPHIA! in black. A cameraman from a local TV news station, moving slowly in a crouch down the line, captured video of them with Hooks strutting onstage in the background above them.

Hooks, now holding his chromed-mesh microphone triumphantly over his head, took a grand bow as Cross, his robe flowing, swept across the stage toward him.

Cross carried his own microphone and put it close to his mouth as he waved his free arm over his head to draw the crowd's attention.

He loudly announced, "Let's give Philly's favorite hometown artist another big round of applause for that very gifted performance."

Cross, startling Hooks, then grabbed his outstretched hand and added, "Sisters and brothers, King Two-One-Five!"

Hooks recovered, and did a short celebratory dance that consisted of jumping up and down a few times, and bowed again.

Cross then proceeded to carefully tug him in the direction of the end of the stage. When Hooks felt the tug, but in the excitement of the moment did not initially move, he suddenly felt a sharp pain in his rib cage. He looked at Cross, but could not tell if the elbow, hidden from view by Cross's flowing black garment, had been thrown intentionally or not.

As Hooks hopped down from the stage, Cross quickly swept back across it to the podium and placed his microphone beside the dozen others already there that belonged to the news media. Draped above and behind him, tied across the red faux pagoda roof, there was a white banner emblazoned with the same red and black STOP KILLADELPHIA! as the T-shirts.

Cross gripped the top of the lectern with both hands and quietly scanned the crowd, making eye contact as he did so.

As the people became more quiet, he then leaned forward.

"This, my friends," he intoned in a booming voice, "is both a very sad day—we mourn those who were killed today and pray for their souls, and"—he paused as there came a wave of people saying "Amen!" then went on—"and it is an uplifting day because all of you have gathered here to help"—he gestured dramatically at the banner behind him—"to *Stop Killadelphia!*"

The crowd applauded. There were more amens.

Cross waited until the crowd again became quiet, then deeply intoned, "Seventeen thousand! That's how many citizens of this city have been shot in the last decade! They are our brothers and sisters, sons and daughters, mothers and fathers, aunts and uncles— loved ones all. *Seventeen thousand* in ten years! That equals four of God's children each day. Four a day, I say!"

Cross then formed an imaginary pistol with his thumb and index finger and, as he repeated *"Pow!"* two times, mimed firing at the line of people before the stage wearing the STOP KILLADELPHIA! T-shirts.

With the first *Pow!* the third person from the far end fell to the ground, his arms flailing in dramatic fashion. At the second *Pow!* a woman at the opposite end of the line dropped to the ground, her arms flailing also in dramatic fashion.

A couple of TV news cameramen from different stations swept in for close-up shots as this was repeated twice more.

"That was yesterday," Cross then loudly proclaimed, and again repeatedly mimed firing with his imaginary pistol, only this time in rapid fire: *"Pow-Pow-Pow-Pow!"*

And four more wearing the STOP KILLADELPHIA! T-shirts reacted theatrically as they fell to the ground.

"And that was today!" Cross said, his voice booming.

An anxious murmur arose from the crowd.

He paused, and slowly looked around at the people.

"And what do you think happens tomorrow?" he then said softly, drawing out the words as he dramatically raised both hands over his head. "Tell me what happens tomorrow?"

"Four more!" a middle-aged woman in the crowd yelled, smiling broadly at being so quick with her answer.

"No!" Cross called out in almost a shout, pointing his finger at the woman.

Then he wagged his finger at the whole crowd as he went on: "Oh, no, no, no! That is what is expected. That is what's always been expected. And that is why we are here today—to Stop Killadelphia!"

He swept his arms, motioning toward the crowd as a whole.

"It is time for all of us to do something, not simply accept the same to happen again and again. It is time to rise up"—the eight people who had fallen to the ground after being "shot" now stood, arms held triumphantly above them, joining the raised hands of the others in the line—"and take back our neighborhoods, take back our city."

There came another wave of cheers, and when that quieted, a chorus of amens could be heard.

"It's no news when I tell you that we're not safe on the streets of our neighborhoods, that we're not even safe in our own homes," Cross said.

There was a murmur from the crowd and he saw a lot of people nodding in a solemn fashion.

"And why do you think that is?"

He gestured at the Stop Killadelphia! banner.

"I want you to think of something," Cross then said. "There's no jobs here. No work. So our children, desperate, look for a way to make a buck. And that's what? It's drugs.

"Now, have you ever wondered what's the real reason why drugs arc not legal? Have you?

"Yes, there's talk in City Hall about legalizing marijuana—even talk about cocaine—and selling it like alcohol, including those same folks in City Hall collecting taxes on it. But there's only just talk."

He paused, looked across the crowd, then went on: "Think about this: Even though they have signed a city ordinance that lets you have up to an ounce of marijuana, you still get fined twenty-five dollars if the police find you with it. You get caught smoking it in public, it's a hundred-dollar fine. And if they catch you buying pot—and especially selling it—you're gonna get thrown in jail!"

He paused for a moment, then added: "So, it really ain't legal, is it? The Man, as King Two-One-Five raps, still be raining down on us."

He swept his arms across the crowd.

"And do you want to know why that is?" Cross then said, carefully drawing out his words. "Well, let me tell you why. It's because illegal drugs is a way to keep our young men killing one another."

A murmur rose from the crowd.

"That's right!" Cross went on, his voice booming. "They want us to stay here in the hood, selling to one another, getting hooked on smack and crack, and then either dying of overdoses, or going out in a gunfight."

"Beat down The Man!" a young male shouted from the crowd.

Cross nodded as he added: "And when someone needs money, you don't see them going into Center City or out to the fancy Main Line. No, the home invasions are happening here.

"These crackheads and junkies, they go into the homes of hard-working neighbors who they know aren't going to call the police."

He pointed off into the distance.

"Our neighbors over in Fairhill and other areas where people are coming to live from other countries, they are easy targets. They are getting robbed and raped in their own homes, but they don't report it because they're afraid to go to the police.

"And so every day four folks get shot. Every day! It's a Wild Wild West culture."

He then grasped the lectern with both hands, leaned into the microphone.

He evenly added, "And, as I said for the last four years serving on the Citizens Police Oversight Committee, that Wild Wild West culture must stop! The police department must set the tone, make an example. And today I say that must be done now, beginning with the one we have come to associate with that Wild Wild West culture"—he pointed to the front of the lectern, to the poster that had been attached there—"Public Enemy Number One, Sergeant Matt Payne, the so-called Wyatt Earp of the Main Line!"

The crowd roared.

After a long moment, Cross motioned with his hands to quiet the crowd, then went on: "And to show my dedication to our cause, I am resigning from CPOC! I will not be part of the problem. I want to be part of the solution that we . . . *Stop Killadelphia!*"

The crowd roared again.

Just then, Tyrone Hooks jumped back onstage with his microphone—the crowd roaring even louder—earning him a glare from Josiah Cross.

"Yo, Yo, Yo! Payne Must Go!" Hooks shouted into the mic, playing to the crowd, pumping his left arm in rhythm and encouraging them to join in.

"Yo, Yo, Yo! Payne Must Go!" a few in the crowd chimed in.

"King Two-One-Five, sisters and brothers!" Cross said, trying to mask his displeasure while at the same time sharing in the applause, dramatically sweeping an arm toward him.

"Yo, Yo, Yo! Payne Must Go!" Hooks shouted again, fist pumping.

There was applause, then the crowd enthusiastically pumped

fists in the air and more began chanting, "Yo, Yo, Yo! Payne Must Go!"

Cross went over to Hooks and again reached up and took his outstretched hand in his.

And then there suddenly came from somewhere in the crowd the popping sound of actual gunfire.

Both Cross and Hooks went down, crumpling to the deck of the stage.

People screamed and then began shouting as the crowd started fleeing in all directions.

Hands reached up and quickly pulled Cross and Hooks from the stage. They then disappeared with a small crowd through the red door of the ministry.

[TWO]
Philly News Now
Center City, Philadelphia
Saturday, December 15, 6:15 P.M.

Michael J. O'Hara was sitting at his office desk, his fingers flying over the computer keyboard.

He stopped for a moment, hit the keys that would save what he'd just written, then put his hands together as if in prayer and tapped his fingertips as he reread it:

HOT HOT HOT—Proofread for typos only then
IMMEDIATELY CROSSPOST on website and TV
newscast!!! -O'Hara

Breaking News . . . *Posted [[insert timestamp]]*

Double Murder in University City

Police Report: Young Couple Brutally Killed This
Morning

PHILADELPHIA, Dec. 15th — A husband and wife in
their early twenties were found murdered in their
home in the 3000 block of Powelton Avenue early
this morning, according to a Philadelphia Police
Department spokesman. Names are being withheld
by police as the criminal investigation
continues.

Based upon initial eyewitness reports, an
anonymous police source said, a pest control
company's truck was seen parked at the address
this morning, and detectives have determined that
the assailants had gained entry to the home
after stealing that vehicle and workmen's
clothing from Pete's Pest Control. The vehicle
was found abandoned a half-mile from the crime
scene. It contained what is believed to be the
weapons used to commit the crime as well as the
stolen workmens' jackets, all of which had been
bloodied.

According to the police source, while a motive
remains unknown, there was clear evidence at the

scene that the couple was targeted because of the husband's employer. The source, due to the nature of the crime and its ongoing investigation, was unable to provide more information at this time.

Police are asking that anyone with any information please contact Sergeant M. M. Payne of the Philadelphia Police Department's Homicide Unit at 215-686-3334, at M.M.Payne@Phila.Gov, or anonymously at phillypolice.com/submit-a-tip. Individuals who provide information that leads to an arrest are eligible for cash awards of up to $20,000.

Updates to this story will be posted as soon as available.   —Staff Report

O'Hara looked up and across the newsroom—past the plain-clothes policeman whom Matt Payne had insisted sit on O'Hara for at least the immediate future—and over to O'Brien's desk.

He felt his throat tighten and his eyes tear up.

He swallowed hard, looked back at the computer, and angrily smacked the ENTER key, sending the article to the copy editor's desk.

Then he went to his backup e-mail program and opened the e-mail that he had forwarded there that morning, the one that had caused him to drive over and check on Tim O'Brien.

His eyes dropped to the pop-up window filling the screen:

From: O'Hara, Michael <m.j.ohara@philly.news.now>
Date: 15DEC 1155AM
To: Mick Off the Grid <irish.ayes@skyservers.net>
Subject: cartel backup file
Attachments: 1

BEGIN FORWARDED MESSAGE:

From: O'Brien, Tim <typos2go@auto-send.com>
Date: 15DEC 1145AM
To: O'Hara, Michael <m.j.ohara@PhillyNewsNow.com>
CC: O'Brien, Timothy <t.s.obrien@PhillyNewsNow.com>
Subject: cartel backup file
Attachments: 1

Buenos Dias/Noches, El Jefe . . .

Or maybe it's not so bueno—no matter what time of day it is—for your wandering scribe.

You will no doubt note that this is being sent from my auto-send account. As I explained over those many pints of Kenzinger and Walt Wit at the pub, if you're getting this, then I've either overslept and not had a chance to reset the send clock . . . or I've gone over to the Isle of the Blest.

In either case, attached as insurance is a file containing the working material for what I have been doing when not downing pints or chasing my lovely lass of a wife. You're welcome, in either case, to have a look at it.

This is some serious shit, El Jefe. Bigger, I'd suggest, than the piece on the heroin ring in Strawberry Mansion that ran today (I'm typing this Friday).

Clearly the piece isn't ready for publishing. But I'm of course confident you can get it there in my absence. Ones to follow may require heavier lifting on your part.

Tim.

P.S. If I have been whacked—or hit by a bus or whatever—remember that in this Irish afterlife paradise here, I am enjoying, among other things, "endless stocks of meadow and wine." Please remind my beloved Emily of that, and that I love her. I know that you'll see that she's taken really good care of. Peace, my friend . . . (Of course the next sound you hear will be my belch as I walk up behind you, alive and well. I hope.)

O'Hara felt the tears start streaming down his cheeks.

Godspeed, Tim.

May you now rest in peace with your beautiful bride . . .

Jesus! That was one thing we didn't consider, and should have.

Tomas was whacked with his wife and kids. Why wouldn't we think they'd do the same here?

Answer: We weren't believing it would happen.

But it did.

And we did make a plan to provide for Emily if Tim were killed. Which now is moot.

He wiped his eyes, then clicked on the file.

O'Hara's bushy red eyebrows went up as he read O'Brien's work again—it came as no surprise that the piece was a fairly clean first draft, and had three pages of source material, including contact names and numbers—and slowly nodded.

When he'd finished, part of his conversation with Matt Payne at the University City bar earlier flashed back . . .

"After this, Mick, you're going to run O'Brien's next piece?"

"Well, the bastards can't kill O'Brien again when it does."

"That's a bullshit answer and you know it. They can kill you. Jesus! I'm having an undercover sent to sit on you."

"You don't need to, Matty. Don't."

"And one for your mother, too. An unmarked unit parked on her street twenty-four/seven."

"Oh, God! I completely forgot about her!"

"Okay, then. It's not up for debate. You've got to be worried, Mick."

"Worried? Hell yeah. I am worried. But if we give in, Matty, the bastards win. And they get away with . . . with what they did to the O'Briens."

O'Hara picked up off the desk the mug of coffee that he'd spiked with a heavy pour of Irish whisky, and took a gulp.

Then, hands back to the keyboard, his fingers flew as he began editing the piece, preparing it for publication.

[THREE]
Office of the Mayor, City Hall
1 Penn Square, Philadelphia
Saturday, December 15, 6:15 P.M.

"Clearly, Mr. Mayor, we knew something had to be up when Cross did not get in touch with me after Badde promised that he would," Edward Stein said. "However, I damn sure did not expect that Cross would double-down on his attacks on the police. And now he's sowing these seeds of revolt that the lawlessness is intentional? That we want the killings to continue as some sort of self-perpetuating control?"

Mayor Jerry Carlucci's eyes went from Stein to James Finley, who was anxiously pacing in front of the television.

"Something is going to have to give," Finley said. "We need to contain this before something blows up."

"*Before* it blows up?" Mayor Carlucci said. "What do you call this lawlessness, this mayhem?"

He pointed at the flat-screen television on the wall of his office. It showed live video from police department cameras at the scene of what an hour earlier, before the gunfire, had been a more or less peaceful rally.

Now the view of the immediate area looked like a war zone.

After the shots had been fired, and Reverend Josiah Cross and Tyrone "King 215" Hooks had been whisked behind the red door of the ministry by deacons, those in the crowd who had not fled for their lives then set about trying to destroy everything in their path.

As police officers—ones in uniform and at least ten others in plainclothes, having slipped over their coat sleeves elastic armbands embossed with representations of the blue and gold police insignia—attempted to control the raging crowd, the protesters began throwing anything from bricks to metal pipes to glass bottles.

With that, the officers moved in and started handcuffing the worst offenders, then taking them to the nearby white panel vans that had just begun arriving.

A chunk of jagged concrete taken from a pothole on Twenty-ninth Street struck one of the horses of the Mounted Patrol Unit. Hit between its left eye and ear, the horse reacted violently, roaring in pain as it reared up on its hind legs, throwing the officer from the saddle. The enormous animal shook its head, then became unstable and crumpled to the ground, landing on its side on top of the thrown officer.

About the same time, the stage and the posters showing those killed in Philadelphia were toppled, then set afire.

The yellow rental van with the vinyl sign promoting FEED PHILLY DAY was broken into, first the cab and then the cargo box. When they found that there was nothing but empty cardboard boxes in the back, they attempted to steal the entire van, and when that proved unsuccessful, they threw a flaming poster on the fabric seat, setting it on fire.

Two other protesters, meanwhile, ripped the rubber hose from the gasoline tank that was used to fill it, then stuffed a Stop Killadelphia! T-shirt in the opening, waited a moment for the cotton to become saturated with gasoline, then set the makeshift wick aflame.

The entire truck cab was engulfed in flames a minute later, and then the front tires caught fire, the burning rubber sending up an even denser black smoke.

After turning over two cars parked along Twenty-ninth Street and setting them aflame, other protesters tried moving toward the PECO van parked nearby, but were turned away by uniformed officers who were forming a loose but effective perimeter.

A dozen units of the Philadelphia Fire Department, engines and ladders and medic units, swarmed in to reinforce the two fire trucks and ambulances that had been pre-positioned for the rally.

Police cars—at least fifty, their emergency lights flashing—were visible as far as the eye could see.

"We've been damned lucky there haven't been flare-ups in other parts of town," Mayor Carlucci said.

"And that's my point: We cannot afford for it to get any worse," James Finley said. "Something has to give."

"Such as?" Carlucci said.

"There needs to be a real sacrifice," Finley said, "one from a public relations standpoint. One of the police department appeasing the citizenry."

"Such as?" Carlucci repeated, his tone angry.

"You said Matt Payne doesn't need this job," Finley explained. "Can't he be convinced to fall on his sword—"

"What the hell!" Carlucci blurted.

"For the greater good."

Carlucci's face turned red.

"That is outrageous!" he said. "Payne has done nothing wrong! I won't stand for him being railroaded out. He'll be made a scapegoat over my dead body."

Carlucci looked between Stein and Finley.

That wouldn't disappoint you in the slightest—you would get me and Payne out.

Is that what you're going to report to Francis Fuller?

Five-Eff and Payne are not exactly the best of buddies.

"It would be symbolic," Finley said. "Symbolism is good in a crisis."

"That symbolism, as you call it," Carlucci snapped, "would make Payne a lightning rod. And make cops in general targets. It sends the wrong message."

"If you're worried about Payne," Finley went on, "give him some desk job in your administration. Make him City Inspections Czar or something. I don't know. Anything harmless so that you can just tell the people of this city—and beyond—that he no longer carries a badge and gun."

The room was silent for a long moment.

"What about DPR, Mr. Mayor?" Edward Stein then said.

"DPR!" Carlucci blurted. "That's purgatory."

"What's DPR?" Finley said. "Purgatory sounds to me like it would work great."

"Differential Police Response Unit," Stein provided. "When police officers get involved in an OIS—or some other possible infraction—they're sent to DPR temporarily and assigned a desk. They're kept busy with administrative duties, mostly monitoring surveillance cameras, answering anonymous callers who are reporting drug activity, handling four-one-one calls, and sending the important ones to the nine-one-one call center. Those who are deemed unfit to walk a beat get sent there permanently, hoping that they get the message and quit the department."

"No way in hell, so to speak, would Payne put up with that transfer," Carlucci said. "He would quit first."

Carlucci saw Finley's eyes widen.

"Then problem solved!" Finley said. "It's win-win."

Carlucci appeared to be taking great pains not to really lose his temper.

"For the record, Mr. Mayor," Stein said, hoping to calm the waters, "I simply was suggesting he go there temporarily. Since it's more or less general knowledge that most officers involved in an OIS get parked there while Internal Affairs and the DA's office review their shooting, it would make perfect sense that that's where he's been put. Both realistically and symbolically."

"Let's get something clear," Carlucci said icily. "You want some symbolic act, find another one. Payne is off-limits."

The large black multiline telephone on Carlucci's desk began to ring. Carlucci's eyes automatically went to the screen on it, and he saw that the caller ID read LANE, WILLIAM MOBILE.

"Hold on," Carlucci said, then snapped up the receiver.

"Yeah, Willie? You get my message? We've got a bit of a problem, to put it mildly."

Stein and Finley watched closely as Carlucci, hunched over his desk and anxiously rubbing his forehead, listened to the president of the city council for a moment.

Then they saw Carlucci immediately sit upright and look between the two of them.

Finley thought he detected a slight grin—but then it was gone.

"Hold one, Willie, I'm going to put you on speakerphone," Carlucci said, then stabbed a button on the desktop phone with his index finger, and dropped the receiver back in its place.

"Mr. Mayor?" William G. Lane's gravelly voice came across the speaker.

"Yeah, I'm still here, Willie. As are Edward Stein, Esquire, and Mr. James Finley. I trust you've made their acquaintance."

"Yes, Mr. Mayor. How are you, Ed? James?"

"Hi, Willie," Stein and Finley said almost in unison, and in a monotone.

"How can I be of service?" Lane said.

"Willie," Carlucci said, "James just now said that considering the situation we find ourselves in, some real sacrifice needs to happen to calm our citizens. And Ed concurs."

"I can understand that, Mr. Mayor," Lane said.

Carlucci saw that Finley's expression suddenly visibly brightened.

"And—" Finley began.

"Some sort of symbolic act, James said," Carlucci interrupted. "And I'm very much in agreement."

Carlucci almost grinned once more when he saw the shock on Finley's face.

"What did you have in mind?" Lane said.

"We thought—" Finley began again.

"Actually," Carlucci interrupted again, "what I had in mind was a multifaceted act, two parts, for now, the second dependent on how the first plays out."

"I see," Lane said. "And they are what . . . ?"

"First, we get to Councilman Badde and have him find Skinny Lenny—"

"I'm sorry," Lane said. "'Skinny Lenny' is who?"

Carlucci could tell by the looks on Finley's and Stein's faces that they did not recognize the name, either.

"Oh, I thought that you knew Reverend Josiah Cross's given name was Leonard Muggs. His street name, up until he got sent to the slam for stealing a neighbor's welfare checks, then beating him, was Skinny Lenny."

He paused to let that sink in.

"I'm afraid that this is news to me, unsettling news," Lane said, the surprise evident in his tone. "And he's now chairman of CPOC?"

"If not for the extenuating circumstances we find ourselves in," the mayor went on, "I certainly would not bring up that history. He has, after all, paid his debt to society and, at least on the surface, tried to find a better path in life as a man of the cloth. But, as I said, these are extenuating circumstances, and we need Badde to get Skinny Lenny to renounce that incredible notion—I cannot believe that I am actually repeating this outrageous nonsense—that we allow illegal drug activity to flourish as a method of population control. The very suggestion is reprehensible, wouldn't you agree, Willie?"

"Of course."

"I thought you would," Carlucci said, somewhat piously. "And so, if Badde is unable to persuade Reverend Cross to do that, then Badde is to immediately remove Cross as a CPOC member. This could coincide—key word 'could,' I yield to James and Ed on what they believe is the best timing—with the announcement that I am making provision for four more seats on the CPOC board. We are creating a short list of citizens who would make strong additions."

Carlucci looked at Stein, who, having been caught off-guard by Carlucci's announcement, was rapidly handwriting notes on his ledger.

Stein looked up and raised his eyebrows.

"Didn't Cross," Willie Lane said, "actually proclaim at the rally that he was resigning his CPOC position? That leaves Badde with no leverage on him. Basically Cross is saying, 'You can't fire me— I've quit!'"

"That's a bullshit bluff on Lenny's part!" Carlucci snapped. "He doesn't have a pot to piss in. I can guarantee that he is not walking away from eighty grand a year."

There was a long silence, and then Carlucci, in a measured tone, went on: "Now, part two, should Councilman Badde, for whatever reason, not see the wisdom in the course of action you've suggested to him, then I believe that the president of the City Council should announce to Badde that he will immediately be transferred from his seat on the Committee for Public Safety, which of course would have immediate effect on any and all of his appointments in such capacity."

Looking pleased with himself, Carlucci then laced his fingers and put his hands behind his head as he casually leaned back in his high-back leather chair. He looked between Finley and Stein.

"If that two-by-four whack between the jackass's eyes doesn't get his attention," Carlucci said, "then we can threaten his other committee memberships, whatever they may be. And, Willie, when I say 'we,' I mean that you can say that I am forcing your hand on this, which would absolve you. How does that sound, Willie, for starters?"

There was a long, awkward silence.

He has to see this as a chance to undermine Badde's future as a potential mayoral candidate, Carlucci thought.

I'm handing him a slam dunk.

"Any of that," Lane then said, "certainly could be considered either a sacrificial or symbolic act."

"I'm pleased that you see it that way, too."

"I will reach out to Councilman Badde, Mr. Mayor," Willie Lane finally said. "Do we know if Skin—if Reverend Cross was injured in that shooting at the rally?"

"Our best information right now is, no, he was not shot. But we are not certain. Nor do we know about that rapper singer's condition. Which is why you contacting Badde is crucial," Carlucci said, then leaned forward, his finger hovering over the desktop telephone. "Let me know soonest."

"I'll be in touch."

Carlucci stabbed the SPEAKERPHONE button, breaking the connection.

[FOUR]
The Roundhouse
Eighth and Race Streets, Philadelphia
Saturday, December 15, 6:20 P.M.

Matt Payne, holding his hand up to shield his face, was slumped in the front passenger seat of Tony Harris's Ford Crown Vic, the unmarked Police Interceptor coated in layers of gray grime. Payne tried not to make eye contact with any of the protesters on the sidewalk as Harris turned out of the parking lot. The black smoke from the fires in Strawberry Mansion was visible in the sky in the distance, and Payne believed that there was a very real possibility these protesters were angry enough to overturn the car—and worse.

Harris accelerated hard as he headed for North Broad Street, then Ridge Avenue, which would take them northwest to North Twenty-ninth Street. Payne sat back up in his seat, then began scrolling through messages on his smartphone.

The female dispatcher on the police radio was rapidly, but professionally, broadcasting updates on the unrest in Strawberry Mansion. There came a long pause, which she broke by automatically adding a filler safety message: "When exiting your cruiser, always turn off the engine and take the keys."

Payne and Harris exchanged glances.

"Might want to keep that in mind, Detective. I understand there might be a criminal element where we're headed," Payne said drily, turning back to his phone.

Harris snorted. He then felt his cellular phone vibrating. When he checked the caller ID, it read NUMBER BLOCKED.

He reached over and opened the glove box, where the unmarked car's radio was concealed, and turned down the volume as the dispatcher announced, "Safety is a full-time job. Don't have a part-time attitude. The time is . . ."

"Yeah?" Harris then answered the call, his tone annoyed.

Matt Payne, picking up on that, looked at him out of the corner of his eye.

"Hey, Sully," Harris said. "What's up?"

Now Payne turned his head to look at Harris. Harris shrugged his shoulders at him as he nodded.

"Tell him I want to talk to him," Payne said.

Harris raised his index finger in a *Hold one* gesture.

"All right, Sully. Get back to me if you hear anything." He paused, then added, "If I can. No promises."

Harris met Payne's eyes as he broke off the call.

"I said I wanted to talk to him," Payne repeated. "What'd he want?"

"Sully says the rally shooting was not his guys in the crowd."

"His guys? In the crowd? I thought he said he had nothing to do with the hypothetical whacking of Hooks and Company."

"He still maintains that. These guys, he says, were doing recon work. He had two there. One was actually Lynda Webber, who used to work for him in Vice. After she got back from two tours in Iraq with army intel—she's a captain in the reserves—Sully hired her away. Really razor-sharp mind. I actually saw her in the crowd on the video feed."

Harris chuckled as he honked the horn to pass a slow-moving pickup.

"What?" Payne said.

"Shouldn't tell you this, but what initially drew my eye to her was that there was a group of young white women in a clump, all with their politically correct looks of moral outrage, and furiously pumping those posters of the murder victims over their heads. One, projecting the angriest outrage and loudly leading that 'Yo, Yo, Yo! Payne Must Go!' chant, held a poster of Public Enemy Number One."

Payne grunted. "So she was carrying mine."

Harris chuckled again. "Guess Lynda felt that gave her a really solid cover."

"Glad I could help in some small way."

"So, Sully claims they were just there to keep an eye on Hooks, gather intel, follow him if necessary. The last thing he said would happen was for Hooks to be whacked like that. If that's what happened."

Payne looked at Harris and said, "Because it would not give them a chance to recover the stolen jewelry and, more important, it would not be the punishment that would make an example of why one does not rob their casino."

"Almost word for word, more or less."

"What did I miss? What wouldn't you promise?"

"If we found Hooks and/or Cross dead or alive."

When they pulled up to the scene, Payne saw that there was now some semblance of normalcy—or what passed for normalcy in that part of the city.

The raging fires had been brought under control, although smoke still rose from the rented panel van. Two fire engines were pulling away, and the last ladder truck was being packed up in preparation of leaving. Only one fire-rescue ambulance was in sight. And Payne also noticed that the PECO undercover van was still in its place, and in one piece, parked just off Twenty-ninth Street.

Then, parked just ahead of the PECO van, Payne saw a Ford Explorer wrapped in the logotype of *Philly News Now* and, near it, the logotype of *Action News!* on a Chevrolet Suburban. And there

was an assortment of what looked like rental sedans, all with plac-
ards on their dashboards that read WORKING MEDIA and/or a station's logo.

Standing next to the Suburban was a five-foot-tall buxom brunette reporter wearing high heels with her blue jeans. She had on a
bright red knit sweater with a string of pearls. And an *Action News!*
ball cap with her hair in a ponytail poking out the back.

Payne sighed.

"What?" Harris said.

Payne nodded toward the reporter.

"Wonder Woman, our fair city's Super Anchor, is here."

"What do you know about her?" Harris said, then grunted.
"Besides that she wears pearls and heels in the hood."

"For starters, that she's dangerous. So don't say a word to her.
Let me do all the talking."

Harris put the Crown Vic in park, then looked askance at
Payne.

"You're serious, Matt."

"As a heart attack."

"Not a problem. With the exception of O'Hara, I hate dealing
with those media types. She's all yours, boss, Sergeant, sir."

"Good. She's out to prove herself, and as Mickey told me last
week, it's not exactly pretty."

The previous Saturday night at the Union League in Center City,
two blocks down Broad Street from City Hall, the Honorable
Jerome Carlucci had held his annual charity event in the Lincoln
Hall ballroom to raise funds for holiday gifts for the needy.

Payne's attendance had come under some pressure—"Uncle Denny couldn't make it," he had told Mickey O'Hara, "and when he asked if I could, I knew by his tone, not to mention he was holding out the tickets, that that was the same as him saying I would, and so here I am under durance vile"—and he had spent a majority of time holding court at the League's ornate dark oak bar with O'Hara.

Both were in black tie and drinking Macallan eighteen-year-old single malts mixed, at Payne's instruction, with a splash of water and two ice cubes, and, because he was a member of the Union League, billed to his house account.

As Payne tilted his head back to drain his second drink, he absently looked up at the television above the bar.

It was tuned to the newscast of Philadelphia Action News. A perky-looking buxom thirty-year-old stood outside a Center City diner, her brunette hair in a ponytail poking out the back of a ball cap with the *Action News!* logotype across its front. The line along the bottom of the screen read RAYCHELL MEADOW INVESTIGATES.

"Why is this chick wasting time with Little Pete's?" Payne said. "I thought it was closing because the building it's in is set for demolition."

An eccentric dive diner, Little Pete's, at Seventeenth and Chancellor, around the corner from the Union League and across the street from the storied ninety-year-old Warwick Hotel, was an institution in its own right, having served in Center City around the clock, twenty-four/seven, for nearly four decades. And, judging by just the well-worn white-specked emerald green Formica tables, it more than looked its age—it appeared to have not had an update of any note since the doors first opened.

That, of course, was part of its charm. The fact that Little Pete's served hefty portions of its greasy spoon staples—bacon-and-eggs to lox to scrapple to gyros—certainly was another. As were its lively servers, who addressed patrons as "hon"—even the obnoxious drunk ones feeding their munchies at three A.M.—and made sure that when ordering, patrons knew that Little Pete's embraced In God We Trust—All Others Cash Only. Thank You Kindly. Hon.

"Raychell was anchor at one of the network TV affiliates in Missouri's capital," O'Hara said.

"St. Louis?"

O'Hara raised a bushy eyebrow.

"Not very big on geography, eh . . . ?"

Payne shrugged.

O'Hara went on: "Me neither. I had to look it up. Jefferson's the capital. It's tiny, so it shares its market with Columbia. Together they're somewhere in the mid-hundreds, maybe one-sixty, market-share-wise."

"While Philly is number four in the country."

"Right."

"And she catapulted into the hottie hot seat here because . . . ?"

"Oh, I'm not going to give this to you, Matty." He smiled. "You've gotta work for it. This is too rich."

Payne grunted.

"Okay, give me a clue."

"Who was the attorney general of Missouri?"

"What? I don't know the damn capital. How the hell would I know that? *Why* would I know that?"

"Perhaps because you know his former chief of staff."

"I do? The Missouri AG's chief of staff? How is that possible?"

"Former, and now current chief of staff for the attorney general for the Commonwealth of Pennsylvania."

O'Hara looked across the bar. Payne followed his eyes and saw a pale-faced chubby-cheeked thirty-something with horn-rimmed glasses and a suit that dripped Ivy League having an animated conversation—*He acts like everything he says is hilarious,* Payne thought, *but only he's laughing*—with Edward Stein.

Payne was aware that Frank Fuller had hired Stein away from his father's law firm—his father, indicating his displeasure, had told him that—and Stein, at Fuller's pleasure, was on loan to serve as Carlucci's chief aide. The latter information having been provided by Denny Coughlin.

"So," Payne said, "Daniel Patrick O'Connor is somehow connected. I do know that he and Stein, who until recently worked at my old man's firm, were in the same Penn Law class. And that connection is?"

"Who owns the affiliate station, the perpetually-last-in-the-market affiliate that gives us the riveting *Action News!*?"

"I'm guessing the same sonofabitch who bankrolled the attorney general's run for office."

O'Hara nodded as he sipped his drink.

"With dark money, of course . . ." he then said.

Payne knew that the "dark money" of well-heeled donors—individuals to teamster unions—was funneled through third-party political action committees in order to mask its source. And, for reasons that baffled him, was fully allowed by Pennsylvania law.

Payne nodded. "Which is legal, of course, but despicable. Which is why corruption in this state is off the chart."

"Pay to play . . ." O'Hara said, nodding, then added, "Five-Eff ring a bell?"

Payne sighed.

"Tell me you're yanking my chain."

"Good ol' Frank, as you refer to him on days you're not in a foul mood, tried to foist Wonder Woman on me at *Philly News Now*—which, incidentally, is how I came to research the Missouri capital—and I put my foot down. So he bumped her down the ladder to be a weekend anchor on *Action News!*"

The image on the TV screen transitioned to the station anchor desk, where the same buxom reporter, now with her thick brunette hair down to her shoulders and wearing an expensive outfit, sat with a TV monitor behind her showing the image of her in ball cap confronting the restaurant manager. At the bottom of the screen was a text box with ACTION NEWS ANCHOR RAYCHELL MEADOW.

O'Hara jerked a thumb at the screen.

"This is all for show," he said, "for inflating Raychell's ratings to hopefully get the station out of last place and get her to the next step of her career. Little Pete's is clean. I had it quietly checked. Clean enough, anyway. The city inspectors found a few things. But every restaurant fails some part of the inspection. There're eight violations each year for the average Philly eat-in restaurant. My bet is some wise-guy city inspector got told to go fuck himself after he thought he could shake down Pete's by threatening a bad inspection—one violation was 'mouse droppings'—and then made sure she got her hands on it."

O'Hara made a face and shook his head.

"So there's your investigative mouse-shit journalism," he said.

Payne raised his eyebrows.

"Okay," Payne said, "but I'm not making the connection. I need more dots."

"Who did POTUS just propose to make his next AG of the United States of America?"

"Jesus H. Christ . . . !" Payne blurted.

"No, not even He is forgiving enough to work for this POTUS," O'Hara quipped.

Payne finished: ". . . The previous attorney general of Missouri! You simply said the AG."

O'Hara smirked.

"I said you'd have to work for it."

"And now Daniel Patrick O'Connor is here . . . and headed for Washington."

"Final clue: as soon as Five-Eff gets O'Connor's wife a job there."

O'Hara looked up at the buxom brunette *Action News!* anchor.

"Jesus H. Christ!" Payne said again, this time his tone disgusted. He looked back across the bar. "Raychell Meadow is O'Connor's wife?"

O'Hara made a false smile, then drained his drink.

"On the face of it," Payne said, "it stinks that a high-ranking political operative in a powerful state is married to a talking head of a TV news team in the fourth-largest media market. Even if that station's dead last in ratings. It's a whole other stink that they're both owned by Five-Eff."

Payne drained his Macallan and waved to the bartender for two refills.

"Of course," Payne said, dripping sarcasm, "I would never expect that either would violate any ethics by discussing confidential work—or worse—over the dinner table."

"You mean such as going easy on covering certain politicians, and harder on others?" O'Hara said. "Or getting court-sealed documents on the opposition leaked to the station? Why, now that just would not be proper."

Payne looked at him.

"Like that health inspection on Little Pete's. You got a copy 'leaked' to you, too, didn't you?"

"Matty, I get all kinds of possible scoops secretly fed to me. Hell, I've gotten tips from you and others in the department. But, like with Little Pete's, I verify them independently and then only report them if there is no legal or moral obstacle. But the vast majority of 'scoops'—with the notable exception of that from present company—are tainted. They're trying to play me, just as they're using Raychell. The difference is, as our Texas Ranger friend likes to say, 'This ain't my first rodeo.'"

After a moment Payne added, "How do you reconcile that in your mind, Mick? I mean, knowing you're ultimately working for Five-Eff?"

O'Hara watched as the bartender placed two fresh Macallan single malts before them. He then picked up his and held it toward Payne in a sort of toast.

"Matty, I thought you knew: My heart is made of gold, my intentions pure. I'm simply not for sale. I devoutly believe I'm the lone noble knight on his white steed fighting the good fight."

Payne met his eyes and nodded slowly.

"One who embraces," O'Hara added, gesturing with his drink, "what Sun Tzu wrote in *The Art of War*: 'Keep your friends close, and your enemies closer.'"

Payne, putting his drink back on the bar, saw that the bartender had left on the bar, next to a stack of cocktail napkins and short plastic straws, the TV remote control. He reached for it, then thumbed keys to change the channel to *Philly News Now*. Then he slipped the remote in the pocket inside his dinner jacket.

"There," he said, smiling broadly. "That's better."

He saw, almost immediately, Daniel Patrick O'Connor's head jerk as he looked toward the TV. O'Connor made a face, then began motioning for the bartender's attention.

As Payne and Harris approached the yellow crime scene tape, Raychell Meadow came clomping up in her high heels toward them.

"Sergeant Payne!" she called out, holding on to the brim of her *Action News!* ball cap. "It's good to see you again! Can I have a moment of your time?"

Again? We've never met, Payne thought.

She held out the microphone, sticking its black foam tip to just beneath his chin. Her video cameraman came in close with his lens, framing Payne with the smoldering stage in the background.

"What is your comment," Raychell Meadow said, "on being declared Public Enemy Number One by Reverend Josiah Cross, who now appears to have been shot after publicly demanding your resignation from the police department?"

Payne looked her in the eyes, made a thin smile, then turned to Tony.

"Detective Harris, feel free to speak with the lady. Or not . . ."

Payne then smoothly ducked under the yellow police line tape and began marching purposefully toward the red door of the ministry, where some of his small crowd of undercover officers stood. He saw, on the smoldering stage, the lectern with his burned poster.

"Sergeant Payne!" Raychell Meadow called.

Payne, without turning or breaking stride, held his right hand up to shoulder height, fingers spread wide.

Harris thought: *Is he about to fold everything but his middle finger . . . on camera?*

Payne waved once, then put his arm back down to his side.

Raychell Meadow looked at Harris.

"Detective?" she said. "What do you—"

"No comment."

And then he ducked under the yellow tape and moved with purpose to catch up with Payne.

[ONE]
Queens Club Resort
George Town, Grand Cayman Islands
Saturday, December 15, 6:35 P.M.

"I'm going to kill him!" H. Rapp Badde Jr. shouted right after snapping closed his Go To Hell flip phone and then almost throwing it out into the shimmering Caribbean Sea.

The sun hung low in the western sky, an enormous sphere slowly sinking toward the horizon. Its rays, bathing everything in golden hues, cast long shadows across the five-star resort.

Guests of Queens Club, most carrying drinks, were gathering up and down the sugar-white sand beach to await what promised to be yet another glorious tropical sunset.

Kicking at the beach sand in frustration, Badde shouted, "Goddammit!"

His voice caused heads to turn—just in time to witness him make a fist with his free hand and punch the thick trunk of a tall palm tree.

"Damn it, that hurt!" Badde blurted, frantically waving the hand.

A young mother, holding the hands of children as they walked nearby, said, "Come on, kids, hurry this way!"

She tugged them toward the beach as the children stared wide-eyed over their shoulders at the madman who had hit a tree after yelling into his phone.

Badde, a half hour earlier, watching large yachts moving off in the distance, had already been imagining himself counting his soon-to-be new wealth on his own luxury vessel.

Now I can forget that—I'm on a sinking Titanic.

It's about to all go to hell . . .

They had all gathered near the resort's seaside tiki bar in one of the twenty private cabanas. Each cabana had a frame fashioned of rough-hewn palm tree trunk, a roof of fronds, and walls of heavy white cotton duck fabric that undulated with the breeze.

Above the doorway, which had its two panels of white cotton duck tied back, was a hand-carved sign with brightly painted letters that read JOLLY MON CABANA. Inside, the cabana held six chaise lounges topped with thick royal blue cushions, a low bamboo table, and four armchairs arranged around a table topped with a soaring birds-of-paradise floral centerpiece. Broad fan blades made of woven palms hung from the raised ceiling and undulated, adding to the cool ocean breeze.

Janelle Harper sat at the table across from Rapp Badde. Each had a tall, icy glass filled with locally crafted Governor's Reserve dark rum, tonic water, and a lime wedge.

Sitting between them was Miguel Santos, a beefy Hispanic in his late twenties who had his big hand wrapped around a dripping wet bottle of Red Stripe beer that he had just pulled from a cooler of ice.

"Mike" Santos, the chief executive officer of OneWorld Private Equity Partners, had a chubby face with dark eyes and thick wavy black hair, combed back and reaching his collar. He wore a tight-fitting black T-shirt with faded blue jeans and, despite it being a tropical island, black pointed-toe Western boots, which now had a dusting of white sand.

"I'm glad you two could get away on such short notice," Santos said. "In addition to executing the contracts here, this gives me a chance to share with you both a detailed tour of what we hope to do with the casinos."

"We're quite happy we could make it," Jan said politely. "And thank you for sending the jet."

"The view here is a helluva lot better than back home," Badde said, flashing his toothy politician's smile. "Do you have any idea how miserable the snow and cold have been in Philly?"

Santos chuckled.

"Yeah, Rapp, it's already damn cold in Dallas, too," he said, and turned to Harper. "Which is partly why my partner is unhappy he couldn't make the trip. And Bobby was looking forward to meeting you, Jan. He speaks highly of your skill in reviewing the contracts."

Janelle Harper had graduated from Temple University's Beasley School of Law two years earlier.

"That's very kind," Jan said. "Thank you."

"You're welcome," Santos said, and smiled warmly at her.

Badde's eyes darted between the two as he tried to discern if there was something he was missing in their exchange.

Badde had met Santos, along with his partner, a lawyer by the name of Robert Garza, a month earlier in their offices in Uptown Dallas. OneWorld Private Equity Partners occupied the penthouse, on the twenty-fourth floor of its building. The partners had explained that they had arranged the financing for the entire complex, which was owned by the same clients who owned luxury resorts worldwide, including Queens Club, for which they had also arranged the financing.

Badde remembered them saying that China Global Investments owned Yellowrose, one of the foreign conglomerate's four significant companies in the hospitality market.

"We packaged Yellowrose, then sold it to them, and continue to help them expand it," Garza had told him.

Robert "Bobby" Garza, thirty years old, was a tall, light-brown-skinned man with a neatly trimmed goatee and a smoothly shaven scalp. In contrast to Santos's jeans and boots, he wore crisp slacks and a white dress shirt. He was a *Tejano*—a Texan of *criollo* Spanish descent—his family having lived near San Antonio when the area was still Mexican territory and called *Tejas*.

Santos's family, meanwhile, was from Colombia, and had cattle ranches there, as well as in Argentina and Brazil. His father had sent him to boarding school in San Antonio at age thirteen—where he and Garza first met—then he went on to graduate from the Ranch Management program—"with an MBA in Cow Shit," he said—at Texas Christian University in Fort Worth.

"Rapp said you started out as a cattle rancher," Jan Harper said to Santos. "How did you wind up . . . well, here?"

"Jan, where one finds cattle, one also finds cow pies—"

He paused when she shook her head at the unfamiliar term.

"That's cow shit, honey," Badde put in, then in an attempt to illustrate, held his hands up about a foot apart. "When they go, it's pretty wet, and it makes a big brown—"

"I get the picture, Rapp," she interrupted.

"My apology, Jan," Santos went on. "I shouldn't have started with that. It's just that I felt comfortable enough in your company to use my usual explanation."

She smiled. "No apology necessary, Mr. Santos."

"Please. As I said, it's 'Mike.'"

He smiled warmly again.

"Mike," she said, and also smiled warmly.

Badde looked somewhat suspiciously between them again.

He thought: *I made a point to call her "honey"—for his benefit as much as hers—and she about chewed off my head with that reply.*

Santos went on: "What I meant to say was that I grew up working on the ranch, and didn't want to spend the rest of my lifetime around the odor that seems to permeate everything."

She nodded and smiled.

"But," he continued, "a bigger reason was that after graduating TCU, I still was a Colombian national with a just-about-expired student visa. If I wanted to stay in the States—legally stay in the States, since many simply overstay their visas after they expire and risk deportation—I needed a Plan B. I had my MBA, and crews running the ranch, and decided venture capital looked appealing. When Bobby was in law school, he was learning the ins and outs of the United States Citizenship and Immigration Service's visas."

"The HB ones we talked about, right?" Badde said.

Santos, being careful not to directly correct him, said, "Right. The specialty occupation H-1Bs are for architects, doctors, engineers, fashion models. They're good for three years, with a three-year renewal. H-2Bs are the seasonal jobs, like for migrant farm workers. And he was introduced to the EB-5 green card program that fast-tracks you to permanent resident status. He told me about it, and we decided to start OneWorld Private Equity Partners. One of the first things OneWorld did, as a test case you might say, was to get me my citizenship through the EB-5."

"You mind me asking what you did to qualify for the program?" Badde said.

"Not at all. I thought we'd touched on that in Dallas," Santos said. "I created the ranch on the Texas border. I had the two already, then bought three smaller ranches and combined them all to create Rio Grande Organic Farms. We grow citrus—grapefruit, oranges, lemons, limes—and run an average of two thousand head of cattle."

"How did that qualify for the EB-5?" Badde said, then chuckled. "Correct me if I'm wrong, but you can't count the cows, right?"

Santos smiled.

"You're right. But any foreign national investing at least a million dollars in a U.S. business that creates and maintains at least ten jobs for existing Americans, plus ones for himself and his family members, gets a green card for himself, his wife, and his kids under twenty-one. Which is what we did."

"You're married, Mike? And have children?" Jan said.

Santos looked at her and shook his head.

"Still looking for the special someone," he said.

"Mike, have you ever heard that marriage is like a deck of playing cards?" Badde said.

"Rappe . . . ?" Jan said, her tone warning.

"No, can't say that I have heard that," Santos said.

Badde grinned.

"Yeah," he said, "in the beginning of a marriage you just need two hearts and a diamond . . ."

"Ha," Santos said.

". . . But in the end you want a club and a spade."

Jan shook her head.

Santos chuckled.

"Duly noted," he said.

He turned to Jan, then added, "With Rio Grande Organic Farms, I added more than fifty full-time positions. Not counting the seasonal jobs, which require the 2B visas for those who aren't citizens."

He paused and looked at Badde.

"Did you know demand for 1B visas runs in the six figures, but only sixty-five thousand are issued? Meanwhile, the U.S. never issues all ten thousand EB-5s that are available each year. Which we are going to change."

Santos then gestured, holding his arms wide.

"Anyway, so here I am," he said. "And here we are."

"Interesting," Jan Harper said, sipped her rum, then added, "And there are some five hundred banks here, is that right?"

Santos nodded.

"Correct. Which is why OneWorld does all its business here. As you probably know, the Caymans are called the Switzerland of the Caribbean. For a couple main reasons. One, it has those five hundred–plus banks you mentioned. And, two, it has the confidential Relationships Preservation Law—in which Section Five imposes criminal penalties—fines and imprisonment—if someone attempts to share confidential information. That of course includes where funds come from and where they go, but everything else, too, including the names of the officers of a company."

"Remarkable," Jan said. "And it's certainly kept everyone who's investing with Diamond Development happy."

Santos nodded again.

"That is why all our investment vehicles for Diamond Development are FINS—Focused Investment Niche Strategies. They're highly diversified, include many EB-5s, and, being Cayman-based, the lid on them is kept tight."

"Rapp," Jan said, turning to Badde, who was draining his glass of rum with his straw, "that's what I was talking about with Yuri. Reassuring him of the confidentiality and stability of the investment . . ."

The Philadelphia Economic Gentrification Initiative's first project had been to replace an abandoned factory on the banks of the Delaware with the new Lucky Stars Casino & Entertainment facility. Diamond Development—forty-nine percent was owned by Yuri Tikhonov through shell companies; minority-owned companies, including Urban Ventures LLC, which Badde had a small piece of, held the rest—was constructing a new indoor sports and live music coliseum that could fit sixty thousand fans under a retractable roof.

Jan went on: ". . . especially since PEGI cuts through the red tape to get the EB-5 applicants approved. That's critical. A typical investor could expect a seven to ten percent return on investment. A foreign national wanting U.S. citizenship will settle for around two percent—if they're assured the project has Fed approval."

"Exactly," Santos said. "It's equally critical for those borrowing the money, because they're paying less interest." He grinned. "Which of course allows for higher profits."

Badde nodded.

"And that's damn cheap ROI," Santos added.

"ROI?" Badde said.

"Return on investment. Rapp, your hotel project is going to get a mighty sweet ROI."

Badde grinned, then flashed his full toothy smile.

Then he felt his Go To Hell flip phone vibrate. He looked at the caller ID. It read gibberish: #01-0K0-30X-V34-X%K.

He ignored it.

[TWO]
Strawberry Mansion, Philadelphia
Saturday, December 15, 6:55 P.M.

"How long do we gotta stay down here?" Tyrone Hooks said, trying hard not to shiver as yet more cold water dripped on him from the roof of the tunnel.

Hooks could just barely make out in the dark tunnel the form of Reverend Josiah Cross sitting on an empty plastic milk crate. Both Hooks and Cross were wrapped in thick woolen blankets.

"Shhhh," Cross said, glancing up at Hooks, who was standing. "Keep your voice down until we get to where it's all clear."

"I don't know how much more of this cold I can take," Hooks said.

"Cold I can deal with," Cross said, then chuckled. "But that stinking smell of yours got old a long time ago."

"Said I was sorry. Never been shot at before."

Tyrone Hooks was no stranger to the sound of gunfire—for as long as he could remember, he had heard shots in his neighborhood on a regular basis, sometimes every night on weekends—and at the rally there had been no doubt in his mind that he was hearing shots fired in the crowd.

The real trouble was that he saw the black guy—he stood by a group of white people—aim and fire at him. Which had been why he automatically dropped to the stage.

He'd seen that Reverend Cross had done the same, and as Hooks tried to think quickly about what to do next—how to get the hell away from what he expected to be more bullets aimed at him—he suddenly felt a big hand roughly grabbing the back of his hoodie and dragging him from the stage.

Once on the sidewalk, his heart feeling as if it could beat through his chest at any second, he struggled to get to his feet. When Hooks looked up, he saw DiAndre Pringle pulling Reverend Cross from the stage and then dodging those rushing past as he tugged Cross toward the red doors of the ministry.

Pringle looked back over his shoulder.

"This way, Ty! C'mon! Move your ass!" he called to Hooks.

Hooks felt a hand on the small of his back pushing him toward the doorway.

Once they were all inside, and the red door was slammed shut, Hooks followed Cross and Pringle across the big room and to the staircase at the back of the row house.

Outside, the police sirens, more and more of them, were getting louder.

"Keep up, Ty," Pringle said, and led them quickly down the wooden steps into the basement.

At the bottom, behind the back staircase, was a heavy wooden panel with shelving, made to look like the rest of the wood paneling of the basement. It was about the size of a narrow door—and, Hooks saw, for a reason.

Pringle gave a hard push on the left end of the panel, and it slid to the right, revealing a passageway with a raw earthen floor, walls reinforced by wooden beams, and a ceiling of chipped stone.

"Here, Rev," Pringle said, handing Cross a small flashlight.

"What the hell is this?" Hooks said as he looked at where the dim beam lit the darkened hole.

"It began as an escape route, Ty," Pringle said, "and it stored homemade moonshine and beer during Prohibition."

"Escape from what?"

"From the cops, man!" Pringle said. "Just like now. Now stop fucking talking and get going!"

He shoved Hooks through the opening and slid shut the panel door.

Hooks looked down into the tunnel.

Cross, the dim flashlight beam bouncing off the rough-cut rock and the wooden beams, was leaving him behind.

Damn it!

Tyrone Hooks then noticed a familiar sickly sweet smell, and about the time he realized what it was, he sensed a very warm, moist spot in the back of his briefs.

Oh, man! I don't remember doing that!

But . . . I almost died!

Pulling out his cell phone, he lit up the screen, cursed that he had no service, then held the phone out before him, its light casting a green glow down into the tunnel.

He tried opening the panel door behind him. It did not budge.

Damn. Locked . . .

Carefully, awkwardly, he rushed to catch up with Cross.

Five minutes later, Tyrone Hooks and Josiah Cross were standing before a wooden wall—what looked like a dead end—with empty plastic milk crates stacked next to it.

"Now what?" Hooks said. "We're trapped?"

"No," Cross said.

Hooks tapped his phone to light up the screen again.

"And there's still no signal down here," Hooks added.

He waved the screen light of the phone around at the stack of crates and then the wood panel that capped off the tunnel.

"What is this place?"

"What DiAndre said. An escape route back when booze was illegal. For when the cops cracked down on the market selling moonshine—at least the cops who didn't take an envelope of cash, and maybe a bottle or two, to look the other way."

"What market?"

"It's now a bodega, but same thing then. Selling whatever people wanted, legal or not."

Cross shone his flashlight on the plastic crates and reached down. Hooks saw that not all the crates were empty. Cross removed a large blanket from one and handed it to Hooks.

"We'll be here a little while, so better wrap up," Cross said.

As Hooks did so, Cross sniffed once, then again, and added, "What's that stink from? Is it that blanket?"

Cross pulled out another blanket, sniffed it, and said, "This one's okay."

Hooks did not say anything.

After a long, quiet moment, Cross began chuckling.

"Oh, man, don't tell me . . ." he said.

"I ain't ever been shot at before," Hooks said quietly. He sounded deeply embarrassed.

"Shot at!" Cross parroted, then could not contain himself. He laughed so loud it echoed down the tunnel.

"What's . . . what's so damn funny? Those bullets went right past me!"

After a moment, Cross forced himself to stop laughing.

He said: "It's just that the big badass rapper singing about capping the police hears a gun go off and shits his pants!"

"Fuck you," Hooks said meekly.

"And I shouldn't say . . ." he began, chuckling again. "Oh, this is funny . . . but it wasn't . . . it wasn't . . ."

"It wasn't what?" Hooks said.

"He was shooting blanks!"

Nearly three hours later, a grinding sound startled them. The wooden wall that had looked like it could be a dead end started moving, sliding to the side like the one under the ministry's row house.

Light flooded into the dark tunnel.

Hooks squinted as his eyes adjusted enough to see Cross quickly get up from the plastic crate and then slip through the opening.

Hooks heard DiAndre Pringle's voice: "What was so funny, Rev? The guys said they heard you all the way upstairs. *Ugh.* And what the hell is that smell?"

"Tell you later," Cross replied. "Everything okay?"

"Yeah, Rev."

"Then let's get upstairs."

"C'mon, Ty," Pringle called.

Hooks paused a moment to let them get a head start, then went through the opening.

On the other side of the panel was another basement, packed with shelving and cardboard boxes carrying everything from potato chips to Tastykakes to cases imprinted with VIKTOR VODKA— SIX (6) 750-MILLILITER BOTTLES in large red Cyrillic-like lettering. Hooks, who drunk cheap liquor, knew that, despite the genuine-looking "Imported Russian Spirits," the small print on the back of the clear plastic bottles, also in red Cyrillic-like lettering, stated that the cheap booze had been made in a Kensington distillery.

There were also cases of Pabst Blue Ribbon in cans stacked

next to cases of forty-ounce bottles of Colt 45 malt liquor. The latter was a favorite of Hooks's—he liked to call it "liquid crack"—because it was beer brewed with more sugar to create six percent alcohol for a stiffer, and cheaper, kick.

He watched Pringle and Cross disappear up the back stairs.

As Hooks passed one stack, and no one could see, he grabbed a bottle and stuffed it in the belly pocket of his hoodie.

Need this to help me calm down.

The back stairs led up to the street-level floor that was the bodega.

The top of the stairs opened into the back storeroom, which Hooks saw had a half-bath with a filthy toilet and sink—its door was open, the light burning—and on the opposite side of the room a second staircase leading up to the next level.

Hooks started to head for the half-bath, but Cross pointed to the staircase.

"No, use the one upstairs," he said. "Follow me. But be quiet!"

After ascending the second set of stairs, Hooks saw that the next level was a full two-bedroom apartment. It had a living room area with a dirty gray fabric couch and a fairly new flat-screen television, a small kitchen with a wooden table and four chairs, and a single full bathroom.

"In there!" Cross said, pointing into the bathroom as he headed for one of the two windows that overlooked North Twenty-ninth Street.

Cross, standing to the side of the window, carefully pulled back the outer edge of the curtain and scanned the street.

A single marked police cruiser was parked in front of the mis-

sion, its overhead red-and-blue lights pulsing. Maybe a dozen uniformed police officers were milling about.

"There's only the one car," Pringle said. "That Sergeant Payne
said there'd be one there until you turned up. Dead or alive, he
said."

"Really? We can use that," Cross said, turning to look at him.
"And what did you tell our Public Enemy Number One about
what happened?"

"Like you said: not a thing. Let them have a look around—
they said they were going to even if I didn't—but then I didn't say
anything. And they found nothing."

"Good job. You bring your computer pad?"

"Yeah, and I already got the next one set up—*asterisk-March-
ForRevCross*—with the Liberty Bell labeled BEATDOWNTHEMAN
on the *Philly News Now* website." He paused. "But there's something you got to know about the rally. Here. Wait. Hear it from
Smitty, Rev."

Pringle pulled out his phone, and a moment later said into it,
"Tell Rev what you said."

Cross took the phone.

"Smitty," he said, "what the hell is going on?"

"Hey, Lenny, look," Smitty Jones began, "I did what I was told
to. But I thought I was the only one."

"What are you talking about?"

"I was in the crowd, right where I was supposed to be in front
of the stage, and waiting for you to finish your speech, before, you
know, before shooting those blanks I got at the sporting goods
store Chester." He paused, and chuckled, then said, "You know,
when I was buying them, the kid behind the counter asked me if I

was getting them for horses or dogs, and I said, 'What?' and he said, you know, there's small blanks—ones that don't make too loud a bang—for training a horse or hunting dog, to get used to hearing a gun going off—"

"Smitty—" Cross said, trying to interrupt.

"—I said I wanted the louder blanks. You believe that, Lenny? That's what those rich folks do. Shoot fake bullets to get used to the sound. I about said just come on in to Philly, 'cause we're used to lots of shooting going on—"

"Smitty!" Cross snapped. "Tell me what the hell happened in the damn crowd!"

"Oh, yeah," Jones said after a moment. "Sorry. So, like I said, I was doing what I was told, waiting for you to finish your speech—gonna shoot when you said, 'I won't be stopped'—but then King Two-One-Five jumped up on the stage and started getting the crowd chanting. I was afraid I missed when I was supposed to shoot, so I got out the gun and—*BAM! BAM! BAM!*—some bastard starts shooting next to me. Couldn't see who—bunch of white folks there holding posters. So I aimed at King and started squeezing the trigger."

"Someone else was shooting?" Cross said slowly.

Cross's eyes shifted to DiAndre Pringle, who was shaking his head.

"It was just supposed to be Smitty alone," Pringle said.

"Yeah, it was someone," Jones said, "but I dunno . . ."

"I'll call you back, Smitty," Cross said, then broke off the call and handed the phone back to Pringle.

"Who you think it was?" Cross said.

"No idea, Rev," Pringle said, shaking his head. "Except it could be anyone."

Cross glanced at Hooks, who was thumbing a message on his cellular telephone.

So, Cross thought, *he didn't shit himself? No, he did do that. He said he saw the gun.*

But they were shooting at him?

Or me, too?

[THREE]

Queens Club Resort

George Town, Grand Cayman Islands

Saturday, December 15, 7:35 P.M.

"Here's Illana now, right on time," Mike Santos announced as the stunning tanned blonde appeared through the white canvas flaps of the Jolly Mon Cabana.

Rapp Badde saw that she carried a stack of manila folders. He also noted, appreciatively, that she had changed from the nautical-themed outfit of tight navy shorts and sheer white captain's shirt into a melon-colored linen sundress.

Illana put the folders on the table between Badde and Janelle Harper.

Santos looked at Jan and said, "These you'll of course recognize as the contracts that I sent up for your review last week.

"Rapp," Santos then said, "if you're ready to sign, we can move forward to more important things. Like celebrating."

As if on cue, the white cotton flap of the cabana was pushed aside again, and two very attractive females who looked like younger versions of Illana carried in a polished stainless steel insulated tub containing three bottles of champagne on ice and a serving tray holding champagne stems and an assortment of sushi, sashimi, and raw oysters on the half-shell.

"A little something to celebrate with while the ink is drying," Santos said, smiling broadly. "It's a tradition for us. And after we celebrate, tomorrow I will show you the plans for the casino."

"I like it," Badde said, and turned to Janelle. "You want to hand me a pen, so I can get this done?"

Illana popped open the first bottle of champagne and poured everyone a full stem. After Santos had made a toast—"To the success of Philly's newest and finest luxury hotel and its developers"—and they touched glasses, Santos reached into the pocket of his shirt. He came out with a small cell phone, looked at its screen, thumbed it, then looked up at Rapp Badde and Jan Harper.

"You'll excuse me a moment, please," Santos said, standing.

He put the phone to his head as he carried the champagne stem out of the cabana.

Rapp and Jan exchanged glances when they heard Santos say, "Talk to me, Bobby. What the hell is going on?"

Badde shrugged, then drank half of his champagne. He looked at the tray of food, and proceeded to eat two pieces of the tuna sushi—selecting them over the sashimi only because the pieces were on rice—he wasn't sure about simply eating slices of raw fish.

And then, feeling adventurous after swallowing the sushi without incident, he tried one of the half-shell raw oysters.

"You sure you want to do that?" Jan Harper said, right before he slurped it from the shell—and began gagging.

She gestured toward his champagne stem.

"Oh, for Christ's sake, Rapp. Just wash it down."

He did, emptying the stem. Then he burped.

"Nice," Jan said, shaking her head, disgusted.

As Badde reached for the champagne bottle, his Go To Hell cell phone began ringing again. He refilled his stem, then looked at the caller ID. It again read gibberish: #01-0K0-30X-V34-X%K.

He looked at it a long moment, considered ignoring it, began to answer it, then finally decided to let the call go to voice mail. Almost the moment after it did, the phone began ringing again, and again the ID came up as gibberish.

"Damn it," he said, then quickly left the cabana.

He walked about ten yards over to where a pair of tall palms leaned against each other, flipped open the phone, and barked into it, "What?"

"Councilman Badde," an adult male said, his tone calm, with no indication he had taken any offense over how his calls had finally been answered. "We have a mutual friend, one who has asked that I get in touch with you."

Well, that's how this guy got my private number. But who?

"Who is this friend?" Badde said.

"I believe you will be able to figure that out in due time."

What kind of accent does this guy have? Badde thought.

Badde was quiet a moment, then said, "What is this about?"

"A matter of mutual concern. We are in the process of recovering some valuables that belong to us."

"What kind of valuables?"

"Perhaps you have seen the news today about the robbery in the casino."

Robbery? What robbery? All I've seen is Lenny's craziness.

"I'm afraid I don't know what you're talking about."

"I see," the male voice said.

There was a long silence.

"You know my name," Badde then said. "What's yours?"

"That is immaterial right now. You are aware, I trust, of your friend Reverend Cross's rally today?"

I wouldn't say he's exactly my friend these days.

But where are you going with this?

"Yeah," Badde said, "I know of it."

"And that he had a musician perform?"

"I do not know the details of who was at the rally."

"Well, I do. And the musician who performed during it is a young African-American named Tyrone Hooks. He goes by the stage name King Two-One-Five."

"Okay, so this rapper, why is he relevant . . . ?"

"You do not know Hooks?"

"Never heard of him."

"I will have to take you at your word on that."

Well, you just do that, Badde thought, *fuck you very much . . .*

"What the hell do you want?" Badde snapped.

"It's what *and* who. As I said, we intend to recover the stolen valuables. But in order to do that, we first need to find Tyrone Hooks."

"Okay. And?"

"And the last time that Hooks was seen, he was in the company of Cross."

"What, assuming it were possible, is it that you want me to do?"

"It is very important that I find Hooks immediately. I need you—our mutual friend needs you—to find Cross and then find Hooks."

There was a long pause, then Badde said, "Fine. How do I get in touch with you when I do?"

"I will call back in thirty minutes. Every thirty minutes."

"Fine. Okay," Badde said, as he looked at Jan exiting the cabana while holding her cell phone.

As she approached him, he saw that she was looking at it, then apparently letting the call go to voice mail. After a moment she went to listen to the recording and raised her eyebrows as it played.

A moment later Badde almost spilled his champagne when he heard Jan gasp audibly as she held her phone to her ear.

She broke the connection and leaned in toward Badde.

"That was Raychell Meadow. She's the fifth reporter who's been calling, asking for a comment—one from you, but she would settle for me speaking for you—about the apparent shooting of Josiah Cross after he called Matt Payne Public Enemy Number One."

Badde, his eyes wide, did not immediately respond. Instead he drained his stem, then burped.

After a moment's thought, he shrugged, and then said, "Between you and me, Skinny Lenny is not shot, but him being out of the picture would not be a bad thing—"

Badde felt his Go To Hell flip phone vibrate, and saw that the caller ID read PHILA MAYOR'S OFFICE.

Probably that Stein guy. He, and Carlucci, can kiss my big black ass.

He pushed the key, sending the call to voice mail.

"What do you want to tell Raychell and the others?" Jan Harper said.

"What I want to say and what I am limited to saying are two completely different things. You're the lawyer. Why don't you earn your keep and come up with a clever quote that says nothing?"

Jan narrowed her eyes at him as she sipped her champagne.

Just as he slid the Go To Hell phone back into his pocket, the smartphone with his general number began to vibrate. Without looking to see who was calling, he immediately pushed the key that sent the caller into voice mail; a moment later, a short vibration signaled that the caller had left a message.

Curiosity caused him to glance at the screen. It read WILLIE LANE, 1 VOICE MAIL MESSAGE.

He pushed the key to play the message, then put the phone to his head.

He heard City Council President William Lane's gravelly voice: "Rappe, it's Willie. I need you to call me *yesterday*. It's an extremely important matter. You should have my numbers, but just in case, these are my office and cellular . . ."

Oh shit! Badde thought as the numbers were repeated.

"Yesterday"?

Willie sounds pissed.

Then the phone rang again.

He checked its screen.

Willie again? He must really be pissed . . .

H. Rapp Badde Jr., using the hand he had not punched the palm tree with, pushed the white canvas flap aside and entered the Jolly Mon Cabana. Janelle was gone, and Santos was on his cell phone.

Santos glanced up at Badde, then said into the phone, "I'll get back to you."

He ended the call, stood, and walked over to Illana. He leaned in close, putting his right cheek next to hers.

"Illana," he said softly, "put those in the safe in my office for now."

She nodded, and quietly replied, "Yes, sir, Mr. Santos."

With the folders against her ample chest, tightly beneath her crossed arms, she made a thin smile at Badde, and then turned and walked out of the cabana.

What the hell just happened? Badde thought, his stomach suddenly in a knot.

"We seem to have problems," Santos said.

[FOUR]
McPherson Park
Kensington, Philadelphia
Saturday, December 15, 9:35 P.M.

After exiting the Delaware Expressway just past all the blinking bright lights of the two enormous gambling casinos, Piper Ann Harrison glanced at the clock in the dash of her five-year-old silver Toyota Prius and then sighed heavily.

I really don't have time for this, Piper Ann thought.

The twenty-one-year-old college student, pale-skinned, her jet-black shoulder-length hair highlighted with streaks of purple, wore a silver stud in her right nostril. She had three other piercings in each ear, though these were now vacant.

At five-foot-five and one-ninety, she embraced what she called her "healthy earthy look," though she still occasionally complained about being at least thirty pounds overweight.

I should have just stayed home and finished packing, she thought, then glanced in the rearview mirror. The two big cardboard boxes of sandwiches and hot chocolate were visible on the backseat.

But I just couldn't let all that go to waste. And it's definitely needed . . .

Each of the boxes contained a stainless steel thermos full of hot chocolate, twenty insulated foam cups, and twenty ham and twenty Swiss cheese sandwiches. Each sandwich was on whole wheat bread with low-fat mayonnaise and individually wrapped in cellophane with a business card included. There was an additional stack of about forty cards wrapped in a rubber band in the box.

The cards all read:

```
          PATHWAYS PREVENTION

     HELP & HOPE FOR WHEN YOU ARE READY

     FREE COUNSELING!  FREE MEDICAL CARE!

   CLINIC OPEN TUESDAYS-SUNDAYS 8AM-6PM

        DIAMOND & N. HOWARD STREETS

   HOTLINE - 215-555-1567 - ANSWERED 24/7
```

Piper Ann had decided that, before traveling on a mission trip to the Republic of Cuba with her professors in the Graduate School of Social Work and Social Research at Bryn Mawr College, she would dedicate part of what she called Winter Break—she shunned the idea of Christmas—to helping the city's local homeless population, many of whom were known to have severe drug addictions.

Working on a double major, in Spanish Studies and Social

Work, Piper Ann had discussed her idea with one of her professors. He in turn had put her in touch with the free clinic, which was about a dozen miles from her small, expensive (fewer than 2,000 students and an annual tuition of about fifty grand) private women's liberal arts school in suburban Philly.

When she contacted Pathways Prevention, one of the staffers—a former addict by the name of Jimmy "Bones" Packer, an extremely skinny thirty-two-year-old who looked fifty—suggested she adopt McPherson Square, and offered to give her a tour at her convenience.

"Needle Park ain't as bad as some folks think," Bones had told her as he gestured toward it on a cloudy gray Wednesday in early December. "It's gotten better than it was years ago. But it still ain't pretty. Fact is, probably won't ever be. There's always gonna be addicts because people always gonna have problems they want to forget. And of course the drugs just make them feel better. We're trying to help one person to cope, one day at a time, and hopefully get help. Like I got help."

As they walked, Piper Ann saw that McPherson Square covered an entire city block. Sidewalks lined all four sides. It was studded with mature trees, and the pathways cutting across it created a giant X with two concentric rings. In the center of the X, wide steps led up to a branch of the Free Library of Philadelphia.

As they approached the library, two girls around age ten were sitting on the steps and playing a frenzied game of Go Fish.

When Piper Ann looked at the back of the cards, she did a double take.

"Is that what I think it is printed on those cards?" Piper Ann quietly asked Bones.

He looked down at the cards, saw the familiar design, then pointed across the park. A white panel van was parked on the sidewalk. On its doors it had the same image the cards did—the logotype of the blue-and-gold Philadelphia Police shield.

"The cops have been giving them out," Bones said. "That van's from the Twenty-fourth Police District. They keep a pretty steady presence here, both walking and biking the beat, and the druggies, no surprise, keep clear of them. Those playing cards are an interesting idea. We thought about having the clinic make some up. Be better having the clinic info. Kids looking at photos of murder victims probably ain't the most ideal."

"No kidding."

Bones shrugged. "But since their mothers are here watching, I'm betting the lady in the library gave the deck to one of the mothers. These people don't have nothing. Absolutely nothing. And a free deck of cards is exactly that—a free deck of cards. Cheap entertainment."

Piper Ann saw that there was a small playground nearby, and smiled at the sight of two young mothers watching six little children running from one piece of equipment to another.

"And there's one thing you gotta watch for," Bones said, and nodded in the direction of the playground.

"What?" she said, and then saw a rough-looking white male, tall and walking with a stoop, approaching the playground. "Is that guy going to do something?"

One of the mothers, a Latina of medium build, saw the man, went over to a park bench by the playground, and picked up what looked like a large glass jar. She carried it toward the man.

"What's with the jar?"

"The deal is," Bones said, "since you can contract HIV and hepatitis from reusing a dirty needle, the free clinic gets funds to distribute sterile ones. We give out plenty, but there's still room for guys like Jumper there."

"That's his name?"

"It's what he goes by. You're gonna come to know, over time, many of the park's regulars. Some of them are not much older than you. He's one. And you'll learn it's common for many to hide behind street names—there's Jumper, and over there are Ace and Wildman"—he pointed to them—"and then there's others who go by regular names—that's quote Amy and Bud unquote on the bench there—but that's not their real names. Because they're really embarrassed to be out here, they use an alias."

Piper Ann looked at the couple. "Amy" appeared to be asleep. *And it's the middle of the day,* she thought.

"So Jumper there," Bones went on, "he works the system. He's a dealer. Those young mothers? They bring rubber gloves and a jar to collect the used needles from the park so their kids don't get stuck by them. Some mothers will just toss the jar of dirty needles in the trash can. But Jumper will buy them."

"Really? Why?"

"Because he knows that the free clinic will swap old needles for new sterile ones. Sometimes he'll do the needle exchange when our mobile clinic van comes by. But if he goes to the actual clinic, where we offer counseling and free medical care, he can get the doc to prescribe Sub."

"Suboxone? The methadone-like pill?"

"Yeah, for fighting the symptoms of withdrawal from the opiate. Jumper can get a three-month supply, then sell the pills on the street for ten or so bucks each, pocketing about a grand. And for those doing dope, he sells 'the works'—the sterile needles—for a buck each."

Piper shook her head.

"That doesn't seem right."

"The addicts are too lazy to do it themselves. Or too fucked up—pardon my language."

She waved her hand.

"No worries. I've heard the word a couple times. It seems appropriate here, I guess. But they could get their needles for free."

"Sure they could," Bones said. "But Jumper provides a service. Sells the smack for ten bucks, then the needle for another buck. Kinda like, You want fries with that? Capitalism at its best."

Piper Ann grunted derisively.

"Maybe I'll bring the needles," she said, "and give them away."

"Uh, I wouldn't do anything until you learn more. Depending on the person you're cutting out, doing that could get you killed."

Piper Ann met Bones's eyes, made a face, then nodded.

"Like I said," Bones went on, "the park's not anywhere near perfect, but it's better than it was." He motioned at the SEPTA station. "Used to be, just to avoid the drug-dealing and drug-using there at Somerset Station, people would walk the dozen or so blocks to the two other nearest stations, Huntington and Allegheny." He chuckled. "Hookers are a big problem at Huntington, but I guess that's easier to deal with."

"What's going on with Amy?"

Bones looked toward the park bench. He saw that Bud just sat there. But Amy was now awake and clearly trying to hold her head upright. She was unsuccessful. Her chin dropped to her chest, and then she did not move.

"What do you mean?"

"Is she hypoglycemic?" Piper Ann said.

"That's not a diabetic shock. She's been doing it almost ten minutes. And look at Bud. He's not worried. If it was suddenly something new she was suffering—and there's a lot of that these days—he'd be screaming bloody murder."

"Then what?"

"Doper dip. Heroin nod."

"Oh my God. She's so young."

"Your other clue is her hair, her clothes—she's a mess." He looked at Piper Ann. "You'll get used to it."

"You said there's a lot of suddenly new stuff?"

He nodded. "Follow me."

As Bones led Piper Ann to the rear of the Free Library, she looked around and realized that she was really not all that surprised at what she saw.

It reminded her of another mission trip she had taken, to New Orleans to help rebuild homes. She found the misery in that southern city—the poverty, the drugs, the crime—was not at all unlike what she had learned existed in clear view in Philly.

And, when her classmates had gone to the jazz clubs on Frenchman Street, which was in a rough section just outside the French Quarter, they'd heard Glen David Andrews and his high-energy brass band perform. Andrews, who talked about being in rehab for his heroin addiction, was a champion for rising above. And his songs carried the message. In one tune, "Bury the Hatchet," with a trio of trumpets backing him on his trombone, he sang: "How come children know how to work a nine-millimeter but can't work a geometry problem? Illiteracy is not cool . . ."

It's like everyone knows this is going on, she thought. *One big dirty secret . . . but it's hardly a secret.*

Near a bench on the backside of the Free Library, Bones bent to the ground and picked up one of the thirty or more discarded plastic pouches that lay in a pile.

Piper Ann saw that they were colorful, and, surprising her, looked kid-friendly. The big yellow letters read ROCK CANDY.

"You're familiar with MDMA?" Bones said.

"A little."

"In large part due to it being illegal, MDMA is dropping in popularity," Bones said, then gestured with the brightly colored pouch. "The other reason is that these designer drugs are taking its place."

"Designer drugs?"

"MDMA is short for methylenedioxy methamphetamine. Better known as Molly or Ecstasy. The meth creates euphoria by messing with the serotonin and dopamine levels in the brain. Dopamine affects the reward centers of the brain. You know, like when you feel pleasure."

"Like booze?"

Bones nodded. "Alcohol produces, say, a hundred or two hundred units of dopamine. Cocaine takes it up to three-fifty. And meth creates extreme euphoria—in excess of a thousand units. Small wonder folks get addicted. Lord knows I did. You just want more and more."

After a moment she said, "What about Spice? Is there much here?"
Bones raised an eyebrow.

"I've never used," she said. "Not after the stories I heard."

"Smart girl," Bones said. "Spice I hope is on its way out. Dealers bought the synthetic marijuana in powder form, mixed it with rubbing alcohol or, preferably, acetone, because it evaporates rapidly, then sprayed it on tobacco or some other leafy material, like herbs, with a bit of spearmint added for smell and flavor.

"What's dangerous about Spice, as well as most street drugs, is there's no quality control—could be a little of the drug, could be a lot—so users never know exactly what they're ingesting. It was flying off the shelves in head shops, even online, for thirty-five bucks for three grams. But now the DEA has labeled the five active chemicals in it as Schedule One controlled substances."

"Then what's all that?" she said, pointing at the bags on the ground.

"So now along come these new ones. They're synthetic versions of cathinones, which occur naturally in the khat plant. They can be swallowed, smoked, snorted, injected. They're so new—Chinese 'design' them as variants to older ones, which is why they're called 'designer'—that laws can't keep up with the changing chemical makeup. Like the ones they called 'bath salts' and 'potpourri,' these make folks paranoid. They hallucinate. But what's worse is that they can cause the user to get hyperthermia—their body temperature soars over a hundred degrees."

He held up the Rock Candy packet.

"This is it. Also called Grrr-ravel. And other names. It looks like tiny rocks."

"But the package label says Not for Human Consumption," she said.

"It's an attempt to get around the law. They did the same with bath salts—which were made from a cathinone derivative called MDPV, now banned—but despite the warning, everyone knew their real purpose. It damn sure wasn't bathing. Gravel is in the same cathinone family, but the alpha-PVP isn't—yet—illegal."

He paused.

"They should just call it Guinea Pig. It's anyone's guess what's in it, and what it's going to do. So every time a user takes it, they're turning themselves into a guinea pig. I heard someone, not exactly kindly, call them a new kind of reverse eugenics."

She shook her head.

"Darwin's survival of the fittest."

He nodded, then added, "Cruel, but in many cases not entirely wrong. Their life expectancy is tragically short. I got lucky I got clean."

"Where do they get these?"

"The better question might be, 'Where can you *not* get these?' They're everywhere, because they're legal. China, and increasingly Pakistan—they're creating ones so fast that there's not a scientific name for them.

"The DEA says there are more than a hundred and fifty thousand of these chemical manufacturing facilities in China alone. They also admit we're not going to arrest or legislate our way out of this."

Piper Ann was silent a long moment.

"Surreal," she finally said.

"Yeah, surreal and worse. And so we have the free clinic. Like I said, one person one day at a time."

———

Piper Ann Harrison reached over and turned off the radio in her Prius, and sighed heavily again. She had been listening to the news on WHYY, the public radio FM station, then pushed the button for the University of Pennsylvania's WXPN.

They were playing a music program of classic jazz. Coming from her speakers was the sound of John Coltrane on the saxophone. The horn was soothing, especially compared to the news that WHYY had been broadcasting about the rally in Strawberry Mansion.

The WHYY reporter had hesitated to call it a riot, but from her description of burning cars and mayhem, not to mention the shaky tone of the reporter's voice, a riot was what it sounded like to Piper Ann. It all had made her very nervous, and gave her all the more reason to hurry and get the delivery of the sandwiches behind her.

Because of that disturbance, she had had to go out of her way to avoid that part of town. Every other time she had made the drive to Needle Park, she had gone down Lancaster Avenue, then taken Girard Avenue across the Schuylkill River and all the way into Fishtown, then cut up to Front Street to reach the park in Kensington.

But that route took her right past North Twenty-ninth Street.

Taking the expressway now had been frustrating—she really had hoped to already have been there and back—but decided the inconvenience was worth it to avoid the problems in Strawberry Mansion.

Piper Ann turned up the volume on the radio. John Coltrane's horn, playing "My Favorite Things," was almost hypnotizing. She dug in her purse and produced a cigarette and lighter.

After her first puff, she pushed the button that opened her sunroof. She could feel the bitter cold air, and tilted her head back to exhale the smoke out the opening.

Sooner I get this done, the sooner I can get home.

And the sooner I'll be enjoying the warm Caribbean sun in Cuba.

She pressed harder on the accelerator, and the hum of the electric motor grew slightly louder as the seventy-four-horsepower gasoline engine kicked in with extra power.

Ten minutes later, she approached McPherson Park.

She saw that, despite the winter weather, the park was busy as usual, with many people milling around its center, near the Free Library.

Well, I feel better now that I came.

I can just leave the boxes of food up at the library, then take the empty thermos and head home.

Speeding up to make it through the changing traffic light at F Street, she suddenly heard through her open sunroof the sound of a male screaming.

She quickly turned off the radio.

She turned her head, trying to find him.

And then she noticed movement out of the corner of her eye— someone running out of the shadows and down the slope of the park toward the street.

It appeared to be an enormous human figure, with a mop of dreadlocks.

Then she heard him scream again. The tone was one of sheer terror, and she could now make out exactly what he was screaming.

It sent a chill through her.

"They're here! They're here! Save me!" he screamed.

When she turned, she saw that the enormous human, despite the bitter cold, had absolutely no clothes on.

Then she screamed as the enormous naked male suddenly ran in front of her Prius.

She slammed on the brakes.

The tiny car shuddered when the man bounced off the front bumper, then slammed across the hood.

In that instant, she saw the terror in the man's eyes, and the heart and peace symbol tattoos on his face, and, finally, the *Family* tattoo across his throat.

And then he hit the windshield, and it shattered, and then began to become coated in red.

Everything went silent.

Piper Ann began sobbing.

[ONE]
Word of Brotherly Love Ministry
Strawberry Mansion, Philadelphia
Saturday, December 15, 10:02 P.M.

Matt Payne found the doors locked on the Police Interceptor, leaned against its front right fender and turned up the collar of his suit coat in a futile attempt to block the icy wind. He surveyed the smoldering blocks-long scene while waiting for Tony Harris to catch up—*What the hell's taking him so long? I'm freezing*—then noticed a strong smell.

"Jesus!" he said aloud.

And then he realized the source: His clothing reeked of everything that had been set afire, especially the heavy odor of burned rubber tires.

Another good reason to get the hell out of this suit . . .

After ducking under the yellow crime scene tape when they'd first arrived in Strawberry Mansion, Matt Payne thought that he might have been a bit overly critical—*Okay, so I was more than a little bit, but screw ol' Raychell*—since his tailored suit and tie was just as sartorially out of place in the hood as the pearls and high heels he had just mocked the *Action News!* brunette reporter for wearing.

Consequently—worse—the suit also turned him into an obvious target.

There may as well be a blinking neon sign above me with an arrow pointing at my back: LOOK! PUBLIC ENEMY #1 RIGHT HERE! SHOOT ME!

Those death threat postings are probably coming from chickenshit keyboard warriors.

But all it takes is one bullet from some emboldened bastard to ruin your day.

Walking toward the red front door of the mission, he scanned the area and felt some comfort in the fact that there were uniformed officers all over the scene.

Only a fool would try something now.

Trouble with that is, this city proves itself to be full of fools with nothing to lose.

He saw that smoldering mounds of debris, including one topped with a charred lectern and what was left of the poster of Public Enemy Number One, were in every direction. And there were broken beer bottles, the glass shards scorched by intense heat, indicating Molotov cocktails.

And some of those same fools came prepared to cause trouble.

And—big surprise—did . . .

At the curb on the corner, there was a vile-looking heap of muck that had been left beside a storm sewer opening. Indistinguishable bits and chunks of trash poked out of the crude sludge.

Looks like the Crime Scene crew checked the storm sewers for evidence.

God-knows-what all winds up down that drain.

That's some really foul-looking stuff . . . almost like it could be hell's version of a Ben & Jerry's Chunky Flavor of the Month.

He stepped carefully, making a wide arc around the pile.

Ahead, a half-dozen plainclothes officers were standing in front of the red door of the former row house turned Chinese restaurant turned church.

Payne recognized most of them, some by face and others by name, including Harvey Simpson. The thirty-two-year-old detective had been in the old PECO van running surveillance when Payne tapped him to coordinate the operation to grab Tyrone Hooks after the rally—before anyone else could, if Sully O'Sullivan's warning held true.

Simpson wore a faded blue winter coat with diamond-shaped stitching. An oval white patch with red cursive lettering was on each breast, the left one reading *Carlos* and the right one *Doylestown Moving Co.*

It was the polar opposite of what Payne was wearing.

For cops wanting to blend in with crowds, outfits like Simpson's were common—the average civilian tended to take things at face value—although at this moment Simpson had intentionally blown his cover. His jacket was unzipped and his holstered Glock 9-millimeter pistol and police department shield next to it were clearly visible on his right hip.

The small group began to disperse, the men greeting Payne as they went.

"Hey, Sarge," Simpson then said. "Let me say again I'm sorry we let that bastard Hooks slip away. The team was in place, ready to grab him right after the rally, and now they're really damn disappointed—"

Payne held up his hand.

"Don't sweat it, *Carlos*," Payne said with a smile. "How the hell could you know that shooting would start? I sure didn't."

After a moment, Simpson said, "I guess you're right."

"Keep the faith, Harvey. We'll get the bastard. So, what's the latest?"

Simpson took out a small spiral notepad from the pocket under the *Doylestown Moving Co.* patch. He flipped a few pages, then read his notes.

"So far," he then said, "there's been exactly twenty-seven arrested for the usual—disorderly conduct, resisting arrest—and, surprisingly, a handful of charges—six, to be precise—for assault on a police officer, including the miserable prick who assaulted the horse with that piece of concrete. All those miscreants filled up three paddy wagons fast—"

"You're not supposed to say that," Payne interrupted.

He looked up from his notepad.

"Miserable prick? Or miscreants?"

"Neither. You can't say paddy wagon. It offends our Irish friends."

Simpson let loose a Bronx cheer as he tucked the notepad back in his shirt pocket.

"You know I'm part Irish, right, Sarge?"

"As am I—and, it sometimes seems, half the department," Payne said, and grinned, then in a serious tone added, "How is our Mounted Patrol guy?"

"Hampton is ten kinds of pissed-off. He ain't happy he got a broken leg from the fall. But he's really furious about his partner— the four-legged one—getting hurt. Other than that, he's okay, I guess."

"And what about the horse?" Payne said.

"His name's Wyatt—"

"As in . . . ?" Payne interrupted.

"Yeah. As in Earp."

"You're not pulling my chain . . ."

"You're an Eagle Scout, right?"

Payne nodded. "Proud of it."

"Then Scout's Honor—I made it to Life rank—it's meant as an honor, like they say yours is. But no direct connection to you. Anyway, they had to tranquilize Wyatt. The vet came and carried him back to his shop. They're saying he should be okay."

Tony Harris walked up.

"Hey, Harv," he said.

"Just in time, Tony. I was about to tell Matt the interesting—"

"Hold that thought," Payne interrupted, holding up his index finger. He looked at Harris. "What did you say to Wonder Woman Ace Reporter back there?"

He gestured toward Raychell Meadow, who was doing a live shot with the cameraman back at the yellow police tape. Nearby, more bright lights illuminated another five television reporters and camera crews as they jockeyed for their angles.

"Not a damn thing. I followed your lead, Sergeant Payne . . . Fearless leader, sir."

"Good," Payne said, and looked at Harvey. "For future reference, Detective, should you find yourself so confronted, that is how one effectively handles the media."

"Don't say a damn thing?"

"Exactly. Now, Carlos, you were saying . . . ?"

Detective Harvey Simpson, grinning, shook his head.

"Okay, so, here's the deal," he said. "The Crime Scene guys were unable to find any weapons—"

"And they clearly made a damn thorough search," Payne interrupted, tilting his head toward the pile of filth that had been dredged from the storm drain.

Simpson went on: "They did collect the usual spent casings on the street in the general area where the shooter—make that shooters, plural—"

"Plural?" Payne said.

Simpson nodded. "Plural. That's what I meant by *interesting*. There were live rounds *and* blanks fired."

"Blanks?" Harris parroted.

Simpson nodded.

"I'll get to that in a moment. I say *general area* of where the shooters would have been in the crowd because who the hell knows how many times the casings were kicked as people fled. All were flattened in some way, both from the .38 cal live rounds and from the nine-mil blanks. But the only bullet holes that were in what we gauged to be the field of fire, which is to say the row houses here"—he made a sweeping motion in the direction of the red pagoda roof—"were not from today."

"Old ones, huh?" Payne said. "I'm shocked—*shocked*—there's been gunplay in the hood."

Simpson pointed at a spot on the exterior wall under the red pagoda roof.

"There's one we found. They're all like that—painted over. No telling how old they are."

"Actually," Payne said, "I'm more shocked there really aren't any fresh ones."

"So," Harris said, "if we know there were live rounds, but no evidence of them, then the bullets had to go up and over the roof?"

Payne nodded, adding: "And the trajectory of those bullets going up and over the roof would also go up and over anyone standing on the stage."

"So, then, no one got shot," Harris said.

Simpson raised his eyebrows.

"That's my bet," he said. "At least no one onstage got shot. Depending on the angle, a round could have gone a couple hundred yards thataway"—he pointed to the north—"or even farther. And then have landed god-knows-where—what goes up must come down—maybe in the street, in the side of a building, the roof of a row house."

"Same old story," Harris said. "Unless the round actually strikes something that someone notices—say, a bedroom window, a car door—"

"A person," Payne interjected.

"Or even a person," Harris repeated, shaking his head, "then fat chance recovering it."

"What about the blanks, Harvey? How do you know for sure that they were blanks?"

"The brass casings on blanks are crimped differently, because they don't have a lead bullet."

"Tell me more," Harris said.

"You know that there has to be a seal on a round of ammo," Simpson said, "or else there's no explosion."

"Yeah," Payne said. "Otherwise, when the gunpowder ignited, it would just burn in the brass casing but make no sound."

"Right," Simpson went on. "So, instead of a lead bullet, blanks either have some type of plastic cap, which disperses more or less harmlessly after leaving the muzzle, or the top of the casing is crimped tightly closed, which is instantly obvious. No question whatever that both live and blank rounds were fired."

Payne looked at Harris. "The question is, why both?"

"I'm beginning to think Sully's people, or at least the ones he says are doing the casino's dirty work, actually did do it," Harris said, "which is why he called and denied it."

"But, again, why? He—along with everyone else who does not know that blanks were fired—assumes the rounds were lethal ones." He paused, scanned the area, then added, "Which may be exactly what Skinny Lenny wants."

"You think Cross staged this, Matt?"

"I think anything is possible with that false prophet sonofabitch, who I think doesn't really give a rat's ass about the killings so much as how he can leverage them to his own advantage."

Payne turned to Simpson.

"Who's in here?" Payne said, gesturing toward the red door.

"Not Cross or Banks. They let us search it and the Fellowship Hall."

"Who's *they*?"

"Mostly the chubby bastard who says he's in charge—wait till you see the shirt he's had on all day, you're gonna love it—gave his name as Deacon DiAndre Pringle. But that's about all he said. I ran his name. Just last week he got one of the new citations for possession of pot. But, other than that, nothing."

Simpson nudged open the door with his toe.

"Have a look."

[TWO]

After entering the ministry—followed by Harris and with "Carlos" Simpson bringing up the rear—Payne scanned the large main room with its gold-and-black-patterned wallpaper and red-painted trim.

There were a half-dozen young men picking up the hundred or more brown folding metal chairs scattered across the floor, many knocked onto their side, others folded flat. A crucifix crafted of rough-hewn timber was hanging at an odd angle on the wall.

To one side of the room, where the outlines of lettering that spelled BUFFET had been pried off, were black cubes like the ones outside, now burned, that had served as the stage for the rally.

These were stacked to form two tiers, each level holding more of the brown folding chairs.

"That's him," Simpson said, looking toward an overweight black male in his mid-twenties sitting at the end of the first tier.

DiAndre Pringle had his tablet computer in his lap and was rapidly typing.

Payne grunted derisively when he saw Pringle was wearing a long-sleeved yellow T-shirt with WARNABROTHER on the front.

As Payne approached him, Pringle looked up, and his big brown eyes grew wide.

Pringle said, "You're . . . you're—"

"Apparently Public Enemy Number One," Payne offered, "if Skinny Lenny is to be believed. I want to talk to him now. Where is he?"

"Who's Skinny Lenny?"

"Oh, come on. Your boss, Cross. You know that his real name is Lenny Muggs."

"Muggs? That's shit. I don't believe you."

"And that's pretty sharp language there for a deacon, DiAndre. Where did you say you attended seminary?"

Pringle did not reply.

Payne went on: "Yeah. I thought so. Listen, you don't have to believe me. Just tell me where to find him."

Pringle studied them, then after a moment announced, arrogantly, "In a safe place, because you're trying to kill him."

"What are you talking about?"

"The shots fired from the crowd?" Pringle said. "They were clearly a planned assassination attempt on Reverend Cross."

"Are you crazy? By who?"

"By you. The Man. He said he's lucky to be alive—"

"How badly is he hurt?"

"Which is why Reverend Cross has gone into hiding," he said, evading the question.

Payne sighed audibly.

He exchanged glances with Harris and Simpson, both of whom had looks that said *This is bullshit.*

"Okay," Payne said to Pringle. "Enough. We did not shoot Lenny—if he was even shot. And what about Tyrone Hooks?"

"You mean King Two-One-Five?"

"Okay, sure, King Two-One-Five. Don't tell me—he was shot, too?"

Pringle met Payne's eyes.

"Everybody saw it here, and on their TVs and all," he said, pointing at his pad computer. "Got shot right after rapping 'Beatin' Down the Man' and 'Payne's Gotta Go.' That's why he's gone hiding, too. Go figure."

"And I guess the two of them are now sitting in this safe house of theirs, tending to each others deadly wounds?"

There came no reply.

Payne locked eyes with Pringle, then after a long moment just shook his head.

You sorry sonofabitch! Payne thought.

Payne felt his phone vibrate, then looked at its screen, then looked back at Pringle.

"Thanks for your time, *Deacon*," Payne said, and handed Pringle his business card. "Tell Lenny he'd better call me. Tell him I know a couple good doctors if he needs them to tend to those wounds. And tell him that Public Enemy Number One said there's going to be a police presence out front until he turns up, dead or alive."

Payne looked between Harris and Simpson.

"Let's get the hell out of here, gentlemen," he said.

Simpson gestured at Pringle's chest.

"Nice shirt, by the way," he said, then smiled. "FOAD."

Pringle looked up at the big black cop. "Foad?"

Simpson nodded.

"Just a technical term used in police work."

Payne and Harris exchanged glances and grinned.

Both were familiar with the acronym for *Fuck off and die.*

Tony Harris finally returned to the Crown Vic, where Payne now sat on the front fender, arms crossed over his chest.

"Sorry to keep you waiting," Harris said. "Nature called, and you know you can never be sure if there'll be another restroom downrange." He then made a grand gesture of unlocking the vehicle, and added, "Don't forget what our friends on police radio said about keeping the car secure . . ."

After they got in, sitting on the seat belts that they had left buckled, Harris snapped his cell phone in the spring-loaded polymer mount he had clipped to the air vent on the dashboard.

"Think you can get the heater going sometime this year?" Payne said, rubbing his hands together.

As Harris turned the ignition switch, his phone began ringing and the screen glowed. BLOCKED NUMBER popped up on it.

Payne reached to the dash and pushed the air temperature control as far in the red as possible and bumped up the fan speed. He felt cold air blow on his ankles.

"What's up with all these damn blocked numbers?" Harris said, then tapped his fingertip on the SPEAKERPHONE button and answered the call with "Yeah?"

A woman's voice, her tone even, said, "Okay, Harris, you never heard me say this . . ."

Payne motioned toward the phone and mouthed, *Who?*

There was a lot of background noise on the call, and Harris shrugged as the phone screen dimmed.

". . . but," she went on, "Hooks has—make that Hooks *had*—jewelry from the casino robbery in his mother's house. There's still a lot missing, but we're pretty sure we now know where it's stashed at the Shore."

"Who is this?" Harris said.

"Thank me later," she said, clearly avoiding the question, then went on: "We finally ran down enough leads—his girl Carmelita is a lively one once she gets talking, though she has the vocabulary of a longshoreman, both in English and Spanish—and had a look. You might want to visit his house—actually, the place belongs to his mother—which is at Monmouth and Hancock. You can't miss the place. It's got a small cabin cruiser in the side yard, which isn't really a yard but where a row house once stood."

"A cabin cruiser in Fairhill?" Harris heard himself automatically reply. "What the hell?"

The female caller laughed.

I know that laugh . . .

"That was pretty much my first thought," she said. "But it's not what you're thinking. It's on the ground, on its keel, listing to one side."

"What's it doing there?" Harris said, hoping the more she

talked, the better his chances of confirming he recognized the voice.

"The goats use it as a makeshift barn," she said, and laughed again, "when the chickens let them. Welcome to 19133, poorest ZIP code in town. For the record, I had no part of what was done there or getting the girl to talk; I just connected the dots. Anyway, I'll check back if I learn more. Later . . ."

Payne raised his eyebrows as he watched the phone screen light up and CALL ENDED appear onscreen.

Payne looked at Harris.

"Nice source," Payne said.

"Yeah. That was Webber. That laugh of hers is hard to miss."

"Is she credible?"

"Oh yeah. Quite."

"She's working for Sully, right?"

"Maybe he told her to give us that."

"What do you think she meant by she had 'no part of what was done there'?"

Harris grunted.

"Good question. Which may be why her first words were that we didn't hear it from her. Not sure we want to know."

"Well, then, let's go find out," Payne said. "We can sleep when we're dead."

Harris put the car in gear.

"Or when Tyrone Hooks is . . ." he said.

[THREE]
Monmouth and Hancock Streets
Fairhill, Philadelphia
Sunday, December 16, 1:25 A.M.

It took not quite ten minutes to drive from the Word of Brotherly Love Ministry at North Twenty-ninth and Arizona to Monmouth and Hancock in Fairhill, a distance of a little under three miles.

The "small cabin cruiser" was about twenty-five feet long and right where Lynda Webber had said, sitting on the ground on its side next to the row house and behind a patched-together chain-link fence. Ragged-looking chickens were scattered around the yard.

As Payne and Harris started up the sidewalk, Payne saw that the birds were pecking around trash that littered the ground—cigarette butts, empty plastic baggies stamped with street names for heroin, even a discarded condom.

At the front door, which appeared to have been kicked in and now was slightly ajar, a dim light burned just inside.

They heard a woman sobbing softly on the other side.

Harris and Payne pulled their pistols out.

Harris then rapped hard with his knuckles on the door, announced, "Police!" and then cautiously pushed on the door.

Hinges groaned as the battered wooden door swung inward.

A skinny black woman, wearing a thin faded blue bathrobe, sat cross-legged on the bare wooden floor, her elbows on her knees and face in her hands.

"Police, ma'am," Harris said, his eyes darting between her and the living room behind her. "You okay?"

After a moment, she slowly looked up. Payne guessed she was maybe forty years old, but could easily be mistaken for sixty.

Or older.

"Can we come in?" Payne said.

Between sobs, she said, "Why . . . why not? All those others that just left did."

Payne saw that the living room was a mess. The couch had been turned upside down, its cushions sliced open, the stuffing seemingly everywhere. Cabinet doors and drawers were open, their contents scattered.

"What's your name, ma'am?" Harris said.

"Jolene," she said. "Jolene Hooper."

"How are you related to Tyrone Banks?"

"He's my boy."

"Hooper, you said?"

"That's my married name . . . first husband, not Tyrone's daddy."

"Where is Tyrone?"

She made what sounded like a sarcastic chuckle.

"That's what they wanted to know, too," she said. "He ain't here. But being gone at this hour's normal."

"The people who did this to your house, you mean?" Payne said.

"They say they were looking for Tyrone and the stuff they say he stole."

"How many people?" Harris said. "What did they look like?"

She looked up at them, her face almost contorted.

"You serious, man? I don't know who they was, but I do know they can come back. I ain't getting no stitches."

"Anyone else in the house?" Harris said.

"Not no more."

"You mind if we look around?" Payne then said.

"Do what ya gotta do."

She pointed to the stairs that led to the basement.

"His stuff is down there. I keep to myself upstairs."

Payne, holding his Colt alongside his leg, moved quickly to the stairway, then raised the pistol chest high, sweeping the space as he descended.

The lights in the small basement were still on—a pair of dusty bare bulbs in an overhead fixture that was missing its glass bowl—and Payne stopped at the foot of the stairs.

The room had been gone through like the upstairs. The drawers of the desk were all pulled free and dumped on the floor. The entire cover of the mattress had been cut away, leaving exposed a skeleton of wire springs.

Payne, about to turn and go back up the stairs, noticed on top of the desk, next to piles that he figured had to have been dumped from a drawer or two, that there was a ruby-red crushed velvet pouch with a string closure. He stepped closer and saw that it was imprinted with WINNER'S PRECIOUS JEWELS

The pouch was flat, and he took an ink pen from his pocket to pull back the opening and check inside. It was empty.

After checking the top floor, which also had been ransacked, Payne found that Jolene Hooper was still talking to Harris. She stopped as Payne approached.

"Just more of the same up and down," Payne said to Harris.

"Told ya," she said, then looked back at Harris. "They said that robbery happened yesterday morning, and Tyrone ran it. Said a man got killed. But I told them that I know that ain't right."

"You told them what's not right?" Harris said.

She looked at Harris with a sudden renewed strength, and said, "It ain't right 'cause my boy would never do that. And I know he didn't do it 'cause he was right here at home. With me. Had, uh, he had one of his girlfriends with him down there. She can tell you, too."

Nice try, Payne thought. *But we've seen the evidence.*

You're lying to cover his ass, and the girlfriend will lie, too.

"Where is Carmelita?" Payne said.

"Who's that?"

"Tyrone's girlfriend," Payne said.

She shrugged. "Don't know that one."

"Ma'am," Harris said, "I caution you that it's considered obstruction of justice to make false statements to a police officer."

"What's that mean?"

"Lying to the law is illegal," Payne said, as he walked toward the front door.

"I ain't lying! No way my boy was there."

Payne saw Harris pulling out his smartphone.

"Let me show you something," Harris said. "I'd like to hear your thoughts on this video. It was taken off the casino cameras . . ."

As Payne went out the door, he thought, *Waste of time, Tony. I can already hear her saying, "Who knows when that was taken? He likes gambling. That could be long ago and they changed the date . . ."*

Matt Payne stood on the trash-strewn sidewalk. He looked at a scrawny white goat that had just bleated at him from behind the chain-link fence while he waited for Tony Harris to come out of the row house. Mentally debating what their next steps should be—*Going home is sounding like a real winner*—he then glanced at his watch and was somewhat surprised to see it was just about three o'clock in the morning.

Feels more like it should be at least dawn.

His cell phone then rang, which did not surprise him. He didn't bother looking at the screen as he pulled it from his pocket.

He answered it: "Public Enemy Number One, how can I help you?"

Payne heard a chuckle at the other end, then, "Hey, it's Hank Nasuti. I heard you were still out on a job."

"Jobs—plural—actually. But, then, it is Saturday night, so no doubt more on their way. What's up, Hank?"

"We got the doer in the LOVE and Franklin parks killings."

Payne was quiet a moment as his tired brain processed that.

"No shit?" he then said.

"No shit."

"Where are you?"

"Where you said he'd been seen. Kensington. McPherson Square."

So, Jamal the Junkie wasn't lying, Payne thought. *Can thank Pookie for that—for once, a CI comes through.*

"We're maybe a half mile out. Be there shortly."

"Ah, behold the urban beauty that is Needle Park," Matt Payne said as they pulled up, the strobes from the emergency light bar on the tow squad wrecker pulsing in the dark. Then he yawned.

The wrecker was parked up on the sidewalk, near the Twenty-fourth Police District's white panel van. A totaled subcompact sedan had been winched onto the wrecker's flatbed.

No loss there—just another ugly Prius, Payne caught himself randomly thinking.

Why can't a manufacturer design a good-looking small hybrid? They make plenty of other decent cars. You almost think it's done on purpose.

That's it! It's reverse snobbery! The owners like the fact that the crappy styling stands out in traffic.

"Lookit me! Goofy, sure, but getting great gas mileage!"

Wait. Why do I care?

I must be getting punchy . . .

But it really is ugly.

In the light of the red and blue strobes, it was clear that the car's windshield was completely shattered and caved inward.

And now coated in the blood of a murderer.

Payne pointed.

"There's Nasuti on the far side of the wrecker," he said.

Harris pulled up on the sidewalk and stopped the car. They got out.

"Don't even think of locking the damn thing," Payne said across the roof of the car.

Harris chuckled.

Detective Henry "Hank" Nasuti, whose grandparents had been born in Italy before moving to Philadelphia in the 1920s, was thirty-four, olive-skinned, black-haired, medium build. As he approached, Payne saw that Nasuti's dark eyes looked weary, and when he had spoken to him on the phone, the fatigue was evident in his voice.

Now Payne saw that Nasuti had a copy of the Wanted flyer that had been issued immediately after the murders. It had the images taken from the security cameras at Franklin Park and the description provided by the mother of the little girl who had been grabbed. He held it out to Payne.

"The miscreant's name is Jermaine Buress, black male, age twenty-six, just released after serving a year in Curran-Fromhold. And, I mean, not even a month ago."

Curran-Fromhold Correctional Facility, the largest in the Philadelphia prison system, each year processed upward of thirty thousand inmates. It was named in honor of the Holmesburg Prison warden and deputy warden murdered in 1973, the only staff from the PPS who had been killed in the line of duty. The prison had been built two decades earlier on twenty-five acres along State Road—seven miles from McPherson Square, just up the Delaware Expressway.

Nasuti went on: "Buress decided he wanted to streak across Needle Park in his birthday suit and then play in traffic. A co-ed from Bryn Mawr, Piper Ann Harrison, who said she volunteers for the free clinic near here, was bringing boxes of sandwiches to give out. Buress bounced off her bumper and wound up in the windshield."

"How'd you make the connection?" Harris said. "It's not like he was exactly carrying any ID on him."

"When we were questioning one of the crackheads," Nasuti said, "the guy was wearing a hoodie that was, like, three sizes too big. I asked where he got it and he said he found it on the ground. He showed me the spot up by the library. After he emptied his pockets, we found the crackhead had—along with a couple empty plastic capsules that look like they had held synthetic meth, maybe that alpha-PVP—Buress's ID and his EBT card."

The Electronic Benfits Transfer card, which looked like a credit card, was issued by the federal government's Supplemental Nutrition Assistance Program, previously called food stamps.

Harris and Payne exchanged glances.

Payne then looked at the Prius sitting on the flatbed wrecker.

"That alpha-PVP," he said, "would explain his choice of running clothes—or lack thereof—right before he lost his game of chicken with that glorified go-cart. His body was overheating."

"We ran his ID," Nasuti said. "Buress has got a long list of priors, most drug-related, but a few recent robberies and assaults, going back to when he was thirteen. One of the Twenty-fourth District guys—Manny Lopez, who had the Wanted flyer and called me after responding to the scene of this accident—said Buress had major anger issues. Was always flying off the handle. Which explains the assault raps, if not yesterday's random murders."

"Well, then, congrats, Hank," Payne said. "Another crazy off the streets. And you and Lucke get a couple cleared-case boxes to check off. Where is Lucke?"

Nasuti gestured to the other side of the white panel van.

"In the car. Doing paperwork. We were here for hours waiting for the techs from the medical examiner's office. Things are just now getting back to what passes for quote normal unquote after that Killadelphia Rally blew up. Anyway, we're going to finish up here, swing by the Roundhouse, then that should put us at around seven o'clock, and we can call the parents of Lauren Childs and Jimmy Sanchez, asking if we can stop by and speak to them briefly."

The Sanchez family lived in South Philly. The Childses were

from Bethlehem, up in northern Bucks County, and had checked into a hotel in Center City, whose skyline twinkled peacefully in the distance.

Payne nodded solemnly.

"That works," he said. "No reason to wake them at this ungodly hour. But telling them in person that you found the doer is best. After that, you guys go home. You've earned your rest. And it's not like there won't be plenty of work waiting."

"Thanks. Getting home early should be a nice surprise for Natalie. Although she might rather have the overtime than my presence."

Payne grunted.

With overtime pay, from working the gruesome scenes all night, then showing up during the day to testify in court cases, top detectives could double—or more—their base salary of $75,000. Payne could count on one hand those he knew who racked up close to a hundred grand in overtime.

But there was no question in his mind that they more than earned it, particularly those like Nasuti working Last Out—the busy midnight-to-eight shift, which got half of Homicide's jobs.

There was also no question that, while the money was good, the difficult toll the hours took on a detective—and particularly his family—was one helluva price to pay.

Payne knew that Hank had returned from his honeymoon only a month earlier, and he smiled and said, "Give your bride my best regards."

"Will do."

[FOUR]
Over Runway 33
Northeast Philadelphia Airport
Sunday, December 16, 9:10 A.M.

"Thanks for finally taking my call, Lenny!" H. Rapp Badde Jr. barked into his Go To Hell cellular telephone and then continued without pause: "What the hell are you doing? I thought that we had an understanding! You were going to tell Carlucci's guy that you were backing off from attacking the cops! Right?"

Finally, he paused, looked across the aircraft at Janelle Harper, rolled his eyes when there was no reply, and added, "Well . . . ?"

As soon as his cell phone had showed that he had service, Badde had been constantly redialing the two numbers he had for Skinny Lenny as the Gulfstream came in on final to the general aviation field.

Right before landing, as the aircraft had descended beneath the thick layer of gray clouds, Badde had glanced out the window. They were flying along the Delaware River, and just upstream from the casinos the property where his $300 million multitower project was going to be built came into sight.

In his mind's eye, he could see the architect's rendering.

There was the first phase, which would be a twenty-story, two-hundred-room five-star hotel covering two acres on the riverbank, with high-end retail shops and restaurants on the ground level. And then there was phase two, which would project out into the river itself, reclaiming another acre of land. It would feature a $120 million tower with one hundred fifty luxury condominiums, and have a boardwalk and docks.

I just can't screw this up, Badde thought.

Then, right before the beginning of the runway, he noticed that they were passing over the snow-covered Union League golf course.

And that's another thing. A small thing, compared to others, but another thing that's gonna go to hell if I don't play my cards carefully— my future Union League membership.

I don't think Mike Santos was happy that I said I had to get back to Philly to deal with some fires that were suddenly flaring up.

Real fires, it turns out.

What I do know is that Santos was pissed—he said he was, and that heads would roll in Washington—when he explained the problems he mentioned in that beach tent had to do with those EB-5 visas not getting approved yet.

I don't think that was my fault—HUD rubber-stamped them— but government types are always fast to shift blame, pointing their lazy fingers at someone—anyone—else.

Right now Lenny is my big problem.

What was that line that Willie Lane read to me?

"It's a crime to scheme to monitize one's official position."

Why would he bring that up? Everyone on the council does it in some way.

Then again, not everyone gets caught.

Willie said that Carlucci demanded I get "Skinny Lenny to re-

nounce that incredible notion that we allow illegal drug activity to flourish as a method of population control."

I don't know who the hell told him Lenny's real name. And about Lenny doing jail time.

But I'm pretty damn sure he didn't swallow the line Jan gave me about putting him on CPOC "because his time in the penal system gave him a unique perspective for the committee."

Willie said if Lenny doesn't take back what Carlucci called "outrageous nonsense and reprehensible," then the president of the city council should say that he was immediately transferring me from my seat on the Committee for Public Safety, "which of course would have an immediate effect on any and all of his appointments in such capacity."

I don't care one bit about being booted from Public Safety.

But if for some reason Willie does the same to me with HUD, then whoever takes over HUD can and will look into the details of the PEGI projects—and possibly cancel them.

And then if they make the connection that I am essentially the one behind Urban Ventures, Willie can get on his high horse and say that he warned me "it's a crime to monitize one's official position."

Rapp Badde felt an icy chill shoot through him.

Maybe that's why he did that!

He knows!

And if that's the case, kissing any chance at the mayor's office good-bye will be the least of my worries. And—Boom!—forget the new project.

I'll be busy just up the river serving time in Curran-Fromhold.

"Well, Lenny? What the hell do you want to stop this nonsense?" Badde barked into the phone.

The aircraft's tires began rumbling as they touched down on the 33 of the shorter of PNE's two perpendicular strips. Despite the runway having been plowed, it still was slick from the snow, and the pilot used up almost every inch of the five thousand feet of asphalt before stopping and being able to turn onto the taxi-way.

"You gonna calm down and listen?" Cross said. "Or just keep yelling that same thing over and over?"

You bastard, Badde thought.

He said: "I'm waiting."

"Okay, what I want is what you and your boy Willie's got."

You mean you want blackmailing assholes like you? Badde thought.

He said: "I thought you were all worried about stopping the killings in Philly."

"That, too," Lenny said, his tone sanctimonious.

After a long moment, Badde said: "Can you be more to the point?"

"I want a piece of the pie, Rapp."

He can't know about the hotel project.

The ink on those contracts isn't even dry yet.

"You're already getting a nice piece of pie, Lenny. You're getting eighty grand a year on CPOC."

"Yeah, and twenty of that finds its way back to someone's political action committee."

Badde grunted.

"Okay," he said, "then call it sixty. Sixty grand is better than no grand. Which, by the way, I know you're bluffing about walking away from."

"Funny you bring that up, 'cause I'm in my last year on CPOC.

That means it is about to be no grand. That's why I want in on something like you and Willie got going."

"You keep saying me and Willie. There is no me and Willie. Get that straight in your head."

"Maybe not, but you both got things going. I think it would look good to have Word of Brotherly Love Ministry listed as one of the investors."

"But you don't have that kind of money to invest."

"You're gonna take care of that for me. I let you use the name. You figure out how much that's worth."

There was a long silence before Badde said, his tone even, "How much, Lenny?"

"You tell me, Rapp."

"How much?"

Lenny was quiet a long moment, then he said, "What's a small slice of the new stadium pie?"

What? Even if I wanted, I can't let him in on the Diamond Development projects. Yuri will not go for it.

Unless it comes out of my share.

"I'll say it again, Lenny: how much?"

"I think something better than CPOC is good."

"Sixty grand?"

"CPOC was four years of sixty. I'm thinking round it off to two hundred and fifty."

"You want a quarter million?" Badde blurted.

He saw Janelle Harper raise her eyebrows.

"Yeah, but every year. I've got a mission to build."

A quarter mil a year! Badde thought.

You greedy bastard!

Badde rapidly went over his options—and just as rapidly kept coming back to the series of events he envisioned if Willie Lane followed Carlucci's lead and stripped him of his council committee seats.

Badde suddenly had a mental image of a fat brush dripping white paint being slapped across his name on all the Philadelphia Housing and Urban Development construction signs he had erected around the city.

And then one of an orange jumpsuit with CURRAN-FROMHOLD stenciled on the back.

"Look," Lenny said, breaking the long silence, "you think it over good, Rapp. Okay? I'll get back to you. I've gotta work on this next rally."

"What next rally, Lenny? The Turkey Day . . . ?" Badde began, but realized that he was talking to dead air.

"Damn it!" Badde then shouted, angrily closing his flip phone.

"You want to calm down, Rapp," Janelle Harper said, "and tell me what he said? A quarter million for what?"

Badde, his face furious, inhaled deeply, then exhaled audibly. Jan saw that he clearly was trying to control his temper.

"Once you give the bastards an inch," Badde said, "they want to be inside the tent."

"That's 'Give them an inch, they take a foot' and 'Once the camel's nose is under the tent, next his whole body is inside.' You're mixing metaphors."

"Same fucking difference!" he snapped.

"Good Lord, Rapp. Try to leave the street talk in the street," Janelle said, her tone icy. "Show some dignity."

"Oh," Badde said, thicky sarcastic. "So now you're better than that, better than me. An ol' Uncle Tom in designer clothes?"

Badde recognized the subtle angry look that suddenly swept

across Janelle's face—*Wanda always makes that same look—you've hurt my feelings but I'm not going to let you know it—when she's really pissed off*—and immediately knew he again had gone over the line.

Badde's flip phone vibrated and he saw that there was a new text from Lenny: "Forgot to say we're having Feed Philly Day as planned, so still need that check for the food. That will be the sign to my followers that we are moving forward despite being targeted by the police. Going to promote it at the new rally *MarchForRevCross*."

He showed that to Janelle, who used her phone to view it on the Internet.

"'Beat Down The Man'?" Jan said, making a face. "That sounds like a lot more of Lenny's population control conspiracy theory. That's not going to be helpful, Rapp. And by that I mean not helpful for you."

She stood, collected her bag, and walked to the front of the aircraft, where the main door was opening.

Watching as she deplaned, Badde thought: *Damn it! And I forgot to ask Lenny about that damn rapper who ripped off the jewelry store. That guy hunting him said, "Remember, Rapp, Urban Venture LLC has ownership in the casino, too. We need him so that we can get back the jewelry."*

Badde texted Lenny: "Okay, you'll like the next project. We need to start working out the details of your 'pie piece' so we can get this behind us. Name a time today and a place. And I'll bring the turkey check."

[FIVE]
Rittenhouse Square
Center City, Philadelphia
Sunday, December 16, 8:20 A.M.

Despite the fact that his apartment was in complete disarray, with half-packed moving boxes cluttering every corner, Matt Payne opted for Tony Harris to drop him off in Center City so that he could get his shower and change of clothes there.

While Payne had more or less already moved into Amanda Law's luxury penthouse condominum in Northern Liberties, going there would have meant him being very careful not to wake her—she had only a couple hours earlier texted him that she'd just returned from some emergency at the hospital.

To Payne, it simply did not seem possible that he could get in the one-bedroom condo, get past Luna without the dog greeting him with happy whines and her tail thumping on the wall, get in and out of the shower, then dig clean clothes out of the closet, and finally get back past Luna and out of the condo—all without making a sound, or sounds, that would disturb Amanda's rest.

And so it was off to Payne's tiny apartment, which was in the garret atop the hundred-fifty-year-old brownstone that presently housed the business offices of the Delaware Valley Cancer Society. The building, overlooking what was generally considered to be the most attractive of Philadelphia's public squares, and certainly was among the most expensive real estate in the city, had been in the Payne family since it was built.

When the brownstone's three lower main floors had been converted to modern office space, the existing apartment, its small rooms and slanted walls making it practically unleasable as office space, had been left alone. And Matt, because police department rules requiring its members, after a six-month grace period if necessary, to live within the City of Philadelphia, had made it his home.

Payne put the contents of his pockets next to his Colt .45 and cellular telephone on one of the glass shelves above the bathroom sink. He then tossed his dirty clothes into one of the cardboard boxes that sat just outside the door.

He poured a dab of face wash that Amanda had bought him into his palm and began scrubbing his stubble. He had immediately decided against shaving because, for one, he was exhausted and just didn't feel like it was a good idea to risk running a razor-sharp blade across his neck, and, two, because he felt that an unshaven look would be a better fit in the hood.

His cell phone made a *Ping!* and when he raised his head from the sink he saw an image of a Marine Unit vessel, its emergency lights flashing, holding its position maybe twenty feet off a brush-covered riverbank.

What the hell? Payne thought.

Most likely, the photograph had been taken from above, Payne decided, from a police helicopter.

The message read that it had been sent by Kerry Rapier.

There then came another *Ping!* and a new photograph from

Rapier, a close-up, appeared in place of the first. It was taken from the police boat itself. It showed a large male's body, clad only in a T-shirt and blue jeans and work boots, laying facedown at the water's edge along a strip of large rocks that protected the riverbank from erosion.

Payne's phone then began to ring, and he quickly wiped his face, then took the phone from the glass shelf.

"You got my attention, Corporal."

"Those images come through okay?" Kerry Rapier said.

"Yeah. What am I looking at?"

"The aerial shot of the scene I got from Tac Air. And the other—sent in from the Marine Unit—shows one of the doers in the O'Brien case. He was pronounced at the scene."

Payne always found it interesting that most people preferred the shorthand version of "pronounced dead." He thought it was almost like a superstition that no one liked to actually say the key word.

"No shit? That was fast . . ."

"At seven this morning," Rapier explained, "a maintenance crew—they were working on that train trestle that spans the Schuylkill River just upstream from the Bartram's Garden property—saw the body. It was below them, along the bank, caught up on that riprap."

"They get his fingerprints run?"

"In the process. But he had Kevin O'Brien's credit cards, an AmEx and a PNC Visa debit, in his jeans pocket."

"The Crime Scene guys confirmed that there were two distinct sets of bootprints," Payne said. "So, assuming this actually is one of the killers, at least one more is still out there."

"Maybe one guy whacked the other? Set him up with the credit cards?"

"That can't be ruled out. But, based on what we know about the killers of the reporter in San Antone, I'm betting that they both got whacked. And that's what I meant by 'one more still out there'—that other body will probably pop up next spring."

"Why next spring? That's four, five months."

"In winter, bodies tend to sink and stay down in the cold water."

"That's right. I knew that."

When the river water warmed in the spring, whatever bodies were in it also became warm, and, once warm, the process of decomposition accelerated. The gases that were created by that process then made the corpses buoyant, causing them to rise to the surface.

"That's always a lovely time of year," Rapier said. "Wouldn't want to be in the Marine Unit fishing them out."

"Yeah. Let me know when there's a positive ID, Kerry, and anything else," Payne said, then broke off the call.

Looking absently at the phone, Payne thought: *I wonder if there could be any connection with Cross and Hooks and O'Brien's story about the ring of Mexican nationals pushing black tar heroin in Kensington and Strawberry Mansion?*

Or is it simply a case of the streets being flooded with cheap smack?

They just took down a couple cartel guys in the Bronx with almost a hundred keys, all uncut, some of it headed for here.

It's everywhere . . .

Payne then texted Mickey O'Hara: "Just got word that the body of a Hispanic male was found on the shore of the Schuylkill. He had Tim O'Brien's credit cards in his pocket. More info when I know more. How are you doing?"

He hit SEND, looked a long moment at his phone to see if he would reply, and then put it back on the shelf and finally grabbed a shower.

Fifteen minutes later, Payne stepped around boxes in the apartment while pulling on a Temple University sweatshirt. He yawned deeply. He glanced at the couch.

I can get a coffee and be okay, he thought.

Then there came another yawn, this one deeper and long.

He looked at the couch again and realized that his eyes were so tired they felt rough as sandpaper.

Or . . . I can just lay down for five minutes, recharge—which will help me think more clearly—and then get the coffee.

He tossed a box that was on the couch to the floor, laid down, put his feet up on a pillow—and was almost instantly snoring.

Payne was startled awake by a banging sound.

What the hell?

He felt very groggy.

The banging came again. After a moment, he realized it was someone at his door.

Who the hell?

It was not common knowledge that there was an apartment in the garret. And of those who did know about it, only a select few knew the code to the door on the third floor that gave access to the steps that led up to the apartment door.

He checked his watch.

I slept . . . Jesus! . . . four hours?

From the other side of the door came Harris's voice: "Matt? You okay?"

"Coming!"

As he shuffled across the small room, he checked his phone. The screen was packed with a long list of voice and text messages. He scrolled through it quickly and saw the usual that he'd expect to see.

Then one caught his eye. It was from Kerry Rapier: "The blue shirt sitting on O'Hara's mother got a gut feeling and knocked on her front door. She didn't answer. He went to the back door. It was unlocked. He cleared the house. Said it looked like she had just cleaned it. But she was gone. And her car."

Jesus!

Then more knocking.

"I'm coming!"

Payne flipped the dead bolts and opened the door.

He greeted Harris: "Not dead yet, pal."

"McCrory said he was going to see Pookie," Harris explained once he was inside the apartment, "then tried to reach you. But when he could not get you, he called me."

"Sorry for the trouble. I just crashed. And hard."

"No trouble. I got a little sleep, too. You want to catch up with McCrory? He said the house is on Clementine, down the street from where Dante Holmes got whacked. Said to just let him know when you want to meet."

"Yeah. But hold on."

Payne scrolled through his messages.

"Nothing new here on Cross or Hooks. You hear anything?"

"Not a damn thing."

"Something needs to break," Payne said. "Let me grab a hat. You want to tell McCrory we're en route?"

"Sure."

As Payne was locking his apartment door, his phone vibrated.

Mickey. About time . . .

Payne thumbed the glass screen and the complete text of O'Hara's message came up: "Got it. Thanks. Sadly, that death doesn't bring back Tim and Emily. Remember me telling you about the EB-5 visas? There's more to that story. But, first, tomorrow I'm running O'Brien's next story—about the Cartel del Nuevo Acuña laundering its dirty money into gold. Erring on the side of caution, I'll be out of pocket for a few days after this story breaks. Be safe, Matty."

Gold? My God! Payne thought, then shook his head, recalling the conversation about the visas:

"Matty, you know that high-rise on Arch that you blew a gasket over?"

"The one the Poster Boy for Billionaires got the hundred million in tax breaks for? What about it?"

"You ever hear about EB-5 visas?"

"Yeah. And I remember hearing on a Philly News Now *broadcast that Rapp Badde's PEGI is using them for some of the funding of that new sports complex."*

"Well, ol' Willie Lane greased the skids for Fuller's company to get EB-5 funding to build his project."

"Why not Badde?"

"*Two reasons. One, Center City isn't suffering economically like the hard-hit areas and thus does not meet standards under the Philadelphia Economic Gentrification Initiative.*"

"*And two?*"

"*Two, Lane is council president and can yank Badde's chairmanship of HUD at any time—actually, officially 'reassign' his duties where he believes they best could be utilized—say, on the Parking Meter Coin Collecting Committee . . .*"

Payne chuckled.

"*. . . and thus Badde doesn't want to rock the boat.*"

"*But,*" Matt said, "*as damn disgusting as that 'fund a visa, get a fast green card' program is, it's legal.*"

"*The problem is where the money is coming from. That's a different story—a big one, according to O'Brien.*"

Payne then remembered how O'Hara had replied when he asked how O'Hara squared working for Francis Fuller—to wit, by quoting Sun Tzu's "Keep your friends close, and your enemies closer."

Now, Payne thought, *the lesson learned here is: Don't piss off an Irishman.*

O'Hara is not afraid of Five-Eff.

Or the cartels.

Tony Harris was behind the wheel of the unmarked Crown Victoria waiting at the curb. He had his cell phone to his ear.

Payne pulled open the front passenger door.

"Okay, Dick, we will see you in a few," Harris said as Payne settled in the seat.

Harris broke off the call and placed the phone in the dashboard mount.

"I'm starved, Matt. You hungry?"

"What the hell?" He pointed at Harris's phone. "Wasn't that just McCrory? What did he say about him—us—meeting Pookie?"

"There's no rush."

"Why?"

"Pookie's instead gone to meet his maker."

Payne slowly shook his head.

Harris went on: "Got whacked about a half hour ago. Dick's at the scene waiting for the M.E. to arrive. Happened right down the street from where Dante got whacked."

Payne stared out the windshield.

"Shit," he said, then sighed.

After a long moment, Payne then looked at Harris, raised his eyebrows, and said, "It's a bit out of the way, but I could really go for a Dalessandro's cheesesteak. I'll even let you buy."

Harris smirked, and dropped the gear selector into drive.

"You're the best, Marshal Earp."

XI

[ONE]
Clementine and F Streets
Kensington, Philadelphia
Sunday, December 16, 2:35 P.M.

Matt Payne shoved the last bite of his cheesesteak sandwich into his mouth as Tony Harris turned onto Clementine, wound his way around various vehicles belonging to the news media, and then parked the Crown Victoria with two right tires up on the sidewalk.

"Try not to rub your greasy fingers all over," Harris said, taking a drink of his coffee as he handed Payne a small stack of paper napkins, then put the gearshift in park. "You've already ruined one set of clothes this weekend. And you'll want to look your best for the media when you give them the silent treatment."

"What would I do without you, Detective Harris?"

As Payne wiped his hands, he looked out the windshield.

Just beyond the nose of the Police Interceptor was the perimeter of yellow police tape that was keeping the reporters and onlookers at a distance. Inside it, Dick McCrory and Hal Kennedy were standing at the foot of a row house's cracked concrete steps.

Payne chuckled.

"What?" Harris said.

"Even in plainclothes, those two look like cops."

Payne then pointed at the small group of five black teenagers, four males and a female, milling on the corner down at the other end of Clementine, near the intersection of E Street.

"And that crowd of knuckleheads doesn't seem happy to see The Man on their turf," Payne added. "Again."

The crowd, standing in front of Dante Holmes's grandmother's row house, were within feet of the faded bloodstain on the sidewalk that crudely marked where the nineteen-year-old had been gunned down thirty-nine hours earlier.

There was an irregular pattern of some twenty holes in the front of the house where the Crime Scene Unit techs had dug out bullets. And, in the house next door, a square of cardboard replaced the windowpane that had been shattered by the stray round that had struck and killed the young girl watching TV beside her brother.

As Payne and Harris walked up to the yellow tape in front of the row house, the group of five teenagers watched, their young faces cold and hard beyond their years.

Then suddenly the tallest male, a burly teenager wearing a heavy black North Face goose down parka, began moving in an aggressive manner toward them.

McCrory saw it and started taking steps to cut off the tall, burly teenager.

A news cameraman saw it, too, and turned his lens toward the action.

"Do not come any closer," McCrory said, using his command voice while holding out his left palm.

Once in front of the teenaged male, McCrory stood with his hands on his hips, his right hand close to his holstered pistol. Payne and Harris were just behind him.

The teenager stopped, then jabbed in Payne's direction with his right index finger as he practically spat, "*Fuck* the police! I know who you are!"

Payne's eyebrows rose.

"Look," he said evenly, "the last thing I want to do is hurt you. But with that attitude, that damn sure doesn't mean it's not on the list."

Payne flashed a big smile, said in a louder voice, "And you have a nice day, too," then turned and continued toward the row house.

"You wanna know what we think of the police?" the teenaged male went on loudly, glancing over his shoulder at his buddies, who were nodding their encouragement—the girl making it obvious with her cell phone that she was making a video recording—then looking back at Payne. "We say you're the enemy! You're the biggest gang out here." He then grinned. "And you know what? You're afraid of us. So *fuck you!*"

He's high, McCrory thought. *Punk reeks of pot.*

McCrory, crossing his arms, made a stern face as he cocked his head to one side.

"So, you about finished?" he said. "If not, I could probably see if you've got outstanding warrants or something else you might want to clear up. Pot's still illegal, you know."

The teenager puffed his chest.

"Fuck you," he said.

After a long moment, the teenager then marched triumphantly

back to his buddies. They greeted him with high fives and fist bumps.

McCrory turned and caught up to Payne and Harris and Kennedy.

"That bastard is all noise," McCrory said. "And stoned."

"Let him back-talk all he wants," Payne said. "He's just baiting, hoping he can push buttons and get me to respond. Then he can boast to his buddies that he was the one who pissed off the police and took down that Wyatt Earp Public Enemy Number One guy."

Payne glanced back at the group.

He smiled broadly, and, his right hand high over his head, waved, as he said: "Dick, a wise man named Anthony once cautioned me to be very wary of wrestling with a pig . . ."

"Because you can get very dirty," Harris finished. "And the pig likes it."

McCrory grunted.

"Hey, Killer Cop!" the tall teenager yelled, then leaned forward and with both hands gave Payne the bird.

"That's just his way of saying the police are Number One," Payne said, ignoring the teenager.

"But, for christsake, this is not a police problem," McCrory said. "It's a society problem. We're just sent in to clean up the messes. How the hell is it the fault of cops that there're no jobs for these delinquents? That they can't fucking read or write?"

"You're right, Dick," Payne said.

"It's like Jamal the Junkie. He got booted from Mansion. And that fine eighth-grade education of his? You can bet he stopped learning anything around maybe fourth, fifth grade. The schools—ones like those with teachers who get caught changing test answers—just kept bumping him to the next level. Until it all caught up with him in high school. Then he went to the streets." He nodded toward the row house. "And Pookie here. Another fine example. He's—what?—murder victim number 370."

"It's all way above our pay grade," Payne said. "They should be protesting at City Hall, blaming the crooked city council members they elected over the last forty years."

Payne looked at McCrory. He put his hand on McCrory's shoulder.

"Dick, you really think we have it bad being cops? Let me tell you, it could be worse."

McCrory was quiet a moment. Then he grunted again.

"Okay, I'll bite. How could it be worse, Sarge?"

"Could be Santa at an Eagles game."

"Not that one," Harris said.

Kennedy was shaking his head.

"What are you guys talking about?" McCrory said.

"You never heard that heartwarming Philly tale?" Payne said. "From back in, maybe, 1968? It's legend."

McCrory pointed to his New England Patriots knit cap. "I ain't from around here, you know."

Payne went on: "Made national news after the football game was televised. Anyway, it was halftime and the Eagles were losing—"

"Of course they were," McCrory said, smirking. "Tell me something I don't know."

"And the weather was miserable, bitter cold and snowing. And of course everyone's been sucking down the brandy and whatever else rotgut they'd snuck into the stadium. So, out comes Santa Claus—actually, the drunk who was supposed to do it was a no-show, so some poor schmuck actually volunteered at the last moment—and the minute he walks out onto the sidelines, waving to the crowd and doing his *Ho! Ho! Ho! Merry Christmas!* schtick— *Wham!*—he gets pelted by a snowball. Then the others in the stands, all in Eagles gear, join in. *Wham! Wham! Wham!* And Santa has to haul ass off the field."

"That's terrible," McCrory said, but he was grinning.

"Became one of those things that shored up Philly's tough reputation with the rest of the country," Harris said.

"Nice," Kennedy said. "Real point of pride right there."

"You know our motto," Payne added, "Philly, Kicking Ass Since 1776."

Payne saw that the group of teenagers had walked down the street.

"Notice they don't leave their sidewalk," Payne said, as he grandly waved again at them. "Tough guy's not so tough—he's a dead guy if he doesn't stay on his corner and out of someone else's turf."

A woman who looked to be in her late thirties stood at the police tape. Over her gray sweatshirt she wore a white T-shirt silk-screened with a photograph of a smiling, very young black male in a coat and bow tie and the words DANTE HOLMES, AT PEACE AT LAST.

She said, just loud enough for Payne and the others inside the yellow tape to hear, "I have to apologize for him. Rayvorris, he don't speak for all of us."

While watching the body bag that contained Antwan "Pookie" Parker get loaded in the back doors of the white panel van with medical examiner's office markings, Payne's phone vibrated and a text from Chuck Whaley read: "Got one! Can you talk?"

Payne glanced at Harris, hit the CALL key, and said, "Looks like Whaley has finally found his ass with both hands—or, at least, a doer's ass."

"That's right," Whaley reported, "it was a Transit Police officer, one Thelonious Clarke, who brought in Ruben Mora.

"The guy was unconscious and had no ID. Just a cell phone, which was dead, and a wad of cash and receipts in a pocket. The gas pump printout read Richard Moss on the credit card, and there was a Marion High School detention note with Dan Moss's name. Theo—that's what Thelonious goes by—he had seen the SEPTA alert about Moss getting nabbed for jumping the turnstile, then about Moss's buddy getting killed, and got ahold of me."

Whaley caught his breath, then went on: "When I told Mora that he was going to get charged for the murder, he rolled over on this Reggie Mabry character. He didn't seem to care about Mabry, something about bad blood between them—hard to understand with him rattling off in Spanish—and when I asked for a description and where he lived, it matched exactly what the Moss kid had said the shooter looked like. Undercover car wasn't in there looking for him two hours and he popped up."

"Good job, Chuck. I now need you to come help us work this murder scene. Looks like it's going to be another long night."

[TWO]
Seventeenth and Chancellor
Center City, Philadelphia
Monday, December 17, 8:05 A.M.

As Matt Payne went out the front door of Little Pete's while sipping a to-go cup of coffee, he suddenly felt a bit nostalgic realizing how many times, after a long night of drinking, he had walked the few blocks from his apartment at Rittenhouse Square to the diner.

And, thanks to Five-Eff tearing down the building for something shiny and new, Pete's is going away.

He glanced across the street at the Warwick Hotel.

I hope that place never disappears.

Payne snugged his cap down against the blowing snow. He turned and walked toward South Broad.

His mind flashed to the previous week, when he and Amanda had seen Melody Gardot perform in the Warwick's jazz bar. And thinking of Gardot made his mind flash to when he was driving Amanda in his 911 to drop her off at work at Temple Hospital and he had just vented about the crumbling of the city.

"This place is collapsing both physically and, even worse, morally," Payne said as Amanda had reached up to change the radio station.

"It is sad," she said as she tapped the radio's memory button labeled *1*, setting the tuner to the 88.5 frequency, the University of Pennsylvania's WXPN.

A sultry voice singing "La Vie en Rose" softly flowed from the Porsche's high-fidelity speakers.

"Ah," Amanda said, her tone brighter. "Our hometown girl Melody Gardot. She's an example of what makes this city great. I love her cover of this far better than Edith Piaf's original."

She turned up the volume and sang along, "*Quand il me prend dans ses bras / Il me parle tout bas, / Je vois la vie en rose.*'"

Matt glanced at her and smiled warmly.

"Very nice," he said.

After the song ended, she turned down the volume.

She looked at Matt and said: "'When he takes me in his arms / And speaks softly to me, / I see life in rosy hues.'"

Matt, braking as the traffic light cycled to yellow, then red, smiled and nodded, then said, "Gardot's version is beautiful, but I actually like Satchmo's take on it better than Piaf's."

"That's because you can understand Louis Armstrong singing the English lyrics," Amanda said, her tone playful.

"Exactly," Matt said, and then sang, not anywhere near on key, "'Give your heart and soul to me / And life will always be, / La vie en rose.'"

He leaned over, kissed her on the neck—then playfully squeezed her thigh.

"Life in pink," he said. "I think I like the sound of that."

"Mind out of the gutter, Matt! You are shameless!"

He grinned, clearly unrepentant.

Amanda went on: "It actually translates more to 'Life through rose-colored glasses,' you know. Don't be such a Neanderthal."

She was shaking her head but grinning.

He pointed at the radio.

"But look at that, getting back to my complaints about this place."

"Look at what?"

"I mean, look at her. There's a genuine success story. Gardot grew up here, raised in large part by her Polish grandmother while her mother traveled for work as a photographer. Their family had no money. Had to bounce from place to place. But they scraped together enough so that she could start taking music lessons when she was nine."

The light cycled to green, but Matt had to wait while what appeared to be a homeless male slowly pushed a battered grocery cart covered in a tarp out of the crosswalk.

He continued: "By the time she was sixteen, she was playing piano in Philly clubs on the weekend. She was working hard to get ahead—*and* studying fashion design at Community College on Spring Garden Street—when a hit-and-run driver turned her world upside down."

"She was riding a bicycle, if I remember," Amanda said, nodding gently as she looked out her window.

"Which offered zero protection," Matt picked up, "and she was left with broken bones and brain damage that made it difficult to even talk. Stuck on her back in a hospital bed for a year, she had to relearn everything. That was when?"

"Maybe ten years ago? When she was nineteen."

"Amazing. There she was, unable to sit at a piano, not to mention play. She began by humming, then later singing, and then taught herself to play guitar. When XPN heard recordings of the new music, the station aired them. And now? Now she's an international artist, with gold- and platinum-selling albums, even a Grammy nomination."

Matt paused, then grunted.

"There she'd been a year in bed," he finished, "recovering from broken bones, broken brain, broken everything. Except no broken spirit. You don't see her standing on the sidewalk corner, needle tracks on her arms, blaming The Man for holding her down."

Payne approached South Broad.

He heard his cell phone *Ping!* and saw the text from Daquan Williams: "I got real trouble. It's about Pookie. Can you come talk? I'm at work. Daily Grind diner. Broad/Erie."

Payne turned on Broad and saw City Hall ahead. He knew that when William Penn had put charcoal to paper in 1682 and mapped out what would become the City of Philadelphia, Penn had put City Hall at its exact center.

Payne looked up at the historic building—the country's largest municipal building, larger than the U.S. Capitol—his eyes going all the way to the bronze statue of Penn standing atop its dome, keeping vigil over his city.

Wonder what ol' Willie Penn would think of this place today? And all that's gone on in the chambers below his bronze boots?

Bet he'd shove a bronze boot up their collective corrupt asses if given the chance . . .

Payne glanced around at traffic.

Fat chance finding an empty taxi in this weather.

And my car is at Amanda's.

He looked back at City Hall.

Well, at least the place has one good thing going for it—the subway.

Hell, just take it.

Payne texted back: "Be there shortly."

Payne impatiently squeezed past the small groups of passengers that had just gotten off the subway train cars of the Broad Street Line, and moved with purpose down the tiled concourse toward the exit.

He then took the steps, two at a time, up to street level, then started across the deep gray slush of snow and melted ice that covered the sidewalk.

At the newsstand shack on the southeast corner of Erie and Broad, he quickly tugged a newspaper from a stack topped with a chunk of red brick, stuffing it beneath his left arm, then peeling from his money clip a pair of dollar bills. He handed the cash to the attendant—a heavily clothed elderly black man with leathery hands and a deeply wrinkled face and thin beard—and gestured for him to keep the change.

Payne turned and glanced around the busy intersection.

The storefronts were a blend of bars and fast-food chain restaurants, banks and pharmacies, barbershops and convenience stores. Payne thought that the facades of the aged buildings, as well as the streets and sidewalks, looked much like he felt—tired, worn-out.

On Erie, halfway down the block, Payne saw the coffee shop he was looking for—tall stenciled lettering in black and red on its front window read THE DAILY GRIND—then grunted.

As he pulled on the stainless steel handle of the diner's glass door, then started to step inside, he almost collided with a grim-faced heavy-set Latina in her twenties carrying three waxed paper to-go coffee cups. He made a thin smile, stepped backward, made a grand sweep with his free arm for her to pass through the doorway first, then went inside.

It was a small space, permeated by the smell of frying grease and coffee. The only seating was at a stainless steel countertop at the back that overlooked the open kitchen. Elsewhere, customers could stand at the nine round high-top tables and at the worn wooden counter that ran chest height along the side walls and the front windows.

There were just two customers now, both older men, who were seated at opposite ends of the back counter and busy with their meals. An enormous coal-black man in his forties, wearing a grease-stained white apron tied over jeans and a sweaty white T-shirt, stood stooped at the gas-fired grill, his large biceps bulging as he methodically worked a long-handled wire brush back and forth. Flames flared up with each pass.

The cook stopped, looked over his shoulder, saw Payne, called out, "Hey, man, he'll be right with you," then turned back to scrubbing the grill.

At the far right end of the counter, under a sign reading ORDER HERE/PAY HERE that hung from the ceiling tiles by dust-coated chains, was the cash register. And just beyond it was a faded emerald green wooden door with TOILET FOR PAYING CUST ONLY!! that appeared to have been handwritten in haste with a fat-tipped black ink permanent marker.

The bathroom door began to swing open and a brown-skinned male in his late teens stepped out, drying his hands on a paper towel.

Daquan Williams—in black jeans and a tan PHILLY—NOBODY

LIKES US & WE DON'T CARE *T-shirt—made eye contact with Payne, nodded just perceptively, then looked away as he went to the rack of coffeepots.*

He pulled a heavy china mug from a pyramid-shaped stack, filled it with coffee, then carried it to Payne, who now stood by a window in the front corner of the shop, opposite the door, watching the sidewalk traffic over the top edge of the newspaper as he casually flipped its pages.

The teenager placed the steaming mug on the wooden counter beside a wire rack containing packets of cream and sugar.

"Thanks, Daquan," Payne said, then yawned widely as he reached for the coffee. "I really need this."

He held out a five-dollar bill.

Daquan didn't take it. He nodded toward the enormous cook cleaning the grill.

"Boss man say you don't pay," he said, keeping his voice low so as not to be overheard.

"I appreciate that, but I like to pay my way."

Payne put the money on the counter, then sipped the coffee.

Daquan nodded. He took the bill.

Payne glanced at Daquan's left ear. What looked like a new diamond stud sparkled in the lobe. Payne considered mentioning it, but he instead gently rattled the newspaper's front page.

"So," Payne said quietly, "what do you know about this hit?"

Daquan's eyes shifted to the front page of the newspaper and his facial expression changed to one of frustration.

The photograph showed, behind yellow tape imprinted with PO-LICE LINE DO NOT CROSS, two members of the medical examiner's office standing at the rear of a white panel van. They were in the process of lifting through the van's back doors a gurney holding a full body bag. Splashed across the image was the headline: #360. AN-OTHER MURDER, ANOTHER RECORD.

The teenager, head down, quickly turned on his heel and marched to the cash register. He punched in the coffee, made change, then carefully closed the cash drawer as he scanned the front door and windows. Then, from beneath the register, he pulled out the busboy cart and rolled it to the front of the diner.

"Your change," he said in a normal voice, holding the money out to Payne.

"That's your tip. Keep it."

"Thanks."

Daquan stuffed it in the front pocket of his jeans as he immediately turned his back to Payne. He busied himself clearing the small plates and cups from the nearest high-top table.

"What about the drive-by?" Payne pursued, again speaking quietly as he flipped pages.

"I really can't say," Daquan replied, almost in a whisper, without turning around.

"Can't?" Payne said. "Or won't?"

Daquan shrugged.

"Peeps talk, they get capped. That's what happened to Pookie. Law of the street. That's why I texted you now, after they came . . ."

"Who did it?"

"Capped Pookie?"

"Yeah."

"That's just it—I don't know," he said, then looked over his shoulder at Payne. "Matt, I didn't even know the dude. They're threatening me over something I don't know."

"Any guess who did do it?"

Daquan turned back to busing the table, and shrugged again.

"I heard word that King Two-One-Five knows," he said.

Payne thought: Tyrone Hooks knows—or ordered it done?

He pulled his cell phone from the back pocket of his jeans, rapidly thumb-typed and sent a short text message, then tucked the phone back.

"When's the last time you saw your parole officer, Daquan?" he said, picking the newspaper back up.

"Few days ago."

"It go okay?"

"I guess."

"How's school coming?"

"Hard, man. Just real hard."

"One day at a time. You'll get that GED."

Daquan then pulled a hand towel and a spray bottle of cleaner from the cart and began wiping the tabletop.

Payne said, "Nice diamond stud. Is it real?"

Daquan stopped wiping.

"Uh-huh. S'posed to be, anyway," he said, made two more slow circles, and added, "Got my momma something nice for Christmas. And this earring, it was part of the deal."

"Really?"

Daquan grunted.

"Really," he said, then moved to the next table. "You know I'm trying to get my life straight, staying away from the street. You think I like busing tables? Only gig I could find."

"I know. Remember?"

Daquan sighed.

"Yeah, of course I remember. You know I appreciate the help, man."

"Keep your nose clean, make it through the probation period, and we'll work on getting your record cleared. Have the charge expunged. Then we'll find you something else. Right now, this is good, honest work."

"I know."

"You should be proud. Your mother told me she is. Especially now, after Dante's death . . ."

At the mention of his cousin, Daquan looked over his shoulder and at Payne.

Payne saw deep sadness in his eyes. They glistened, and it was obvious that he was fighting back the tears.

"I can't get past that, Matt. We were real close, you know, going way back. Now he's gone and I'm here." He looked down and rubbed his eyes. "But I'm really not here. I'm just a shell, walking around."

Daquan lifted his head, looked at Payne—then his eyes immediately looked past Payne, out the window.

Payne saw the sadness in Daquan's face suddenly replaced with fear.

"Shit!" Daquan said. "They're back!"

He grabbed the busboy cart and started pushing it quickly to the back of the diner.

Just then, as Payne turned and looked out the window, the glass front door swung open.

Two teenaged black males wearing thick dark parkas marched in, the first one, tall and burly, raising a black semiautomatic pistol in his right fist.

Payne dropped the newspaper and quickly reached behind his back to pull his .45 out from under his sweatshirt.

Daquan shoved the busboy cart at the pair and then jumped behind the back counter as the tall, burly teenager fired three shots.

The sound of gunfire in the small diner was deafening.

Payne leveled his pistol at the shooter as he shouted, "Stop! Police! Don't move!"

The ringing in Payne's ears caused his words to sound odd.

The tall, burly teenager turned and tried to aim at Payne.

Payne instinctively responded by squeezing off two rounds in rapid succession.

The copper-jacketed lead hollow points, as designed, on impact mushroomed and then fragmented, the pieces ripping through the teen's upper torso.

The shooter staggered backward to the wall, dropping the gun when he struck the wooden counter there.

The second teenager, who had frozen in place at the firing of the first shots, immediately turned and bolted back out the glass door.

The shooter slid to the floor.

As Payne rushed for the door, he kicked the shooter's gun toward the back counter. The two customers there were lying on the floor in front of it. The one to the left was curled up in the corner with his back to Payne and, almost comically, shielding his head by holding a white plate over it. The one on the right was facedown and still. Blood soaked the back of his shirt.

The enormous cook, who had ducked below the counter, now peered wide-eyed over its top.

Payne shouted, "Call nine-one-one!" then threw open the door and ran out.

Daquan, blood on his right hand as he gripped his left upper arm, crawled out from beneath the cash register.

He hesitated a moment before moving toward the shooter, who was motionless. He picked up the small-frame semiautomatic pistol from the floor.

The cook stood and shouted, "Daquan, don't!"

Daquan went out the door.

He turned right and took off down the sidewalk, following Payne.

The storefronts along Erie Avenue gave way to a decaying neighborhood of older row houses. Daquan Williams watched the teenager dart out into traffic and dodge vehicles as he ran across Erie, headed in the direction of a series of three or four overgrown vacant lots where houses had once stood.

He saw that Matt Payne, arms and legs pumping as he picked up speed, was beginning to close the distance between them.

"Police! Stop!" Payne yelled again.

The teenager made it to the first lot off Thirteenth Street, then disappeared into an overgrowth of bushes at the back of it.

Payne, moments later, reached the bushes, cautiously pushed aside limbs, swept the space with his pistol, and then entered.

Daquan started to cross Erie but heard a squeal of brakes and then a truck horn begin blaring. He slid to a stop, narrowly missing being hit by a delivery truck. It roared past, its huge tires splashing his pants and shoes with slush from a huge pothole. A car and a small pickup closely following the truck honked as they splashed past.

Daquan finally found a gap in traffic and made his way across.

He ran to the bushes, then went quickly into them, limbs wet with snow slapping at him. One knocked his cap off. The dim light made it hard to see. After a long moment, he came out the other side, to an-

other open lot. He saw Payne, who had run across another street, just as he disappeared into another clump of overgrowth at the back of another vacant lot between row houses.

While Daquan ran across that street to follow, a dirty-brown four-door Ford Taurus pulled to the curb in front of the house bordering the lot. Daquan dodged the sedan, running behind it, then started across the lot.

Ahead, from somewhere in the overgrowth, he heard Matt Payne once again shouting, "Stop! Police!"

This time, though, was different.

Almost immediately there came a rapid series of shots—the first three sounding not quite as loud as the final two.

Daquan heard nothing more as he reached the overgrowth and then, while trying to control his heavy breathing, entered it slowly. He raised the pistol and gripped it tightly with both hands.

More snow fell from limbs onto his soaked T-shirt and jeans. He shivered as he stepped carefully in the dim light, listening for sounds but hearing only his labored breath. He finally reached the far side.

He wiped snow from his eyes.

And then his stomach dropped.

Oh, shit!

Matt Payne was laying facedown in the snow.

The teenager, ten feet farther into the vacant lot, was making a blood-streaked path in the snow as he tried to crawl away.

Then he stopped moving.

"Matt!" Daquan called as he ran to him.

Payne turned his head and, clearly in pain, looked up at Daquan.

"Call nine-one-one," he said. "Say, 'Officer down . . . Police officer shot.'"

Daquan, now kneeling, saw the blood on the snow beneath Payne.
His mind raced. He looked at the street ahead.

There ain't time to wait for help.

I've gotta get him to it . . .

"Hang on, Matt."

Daquan then bolted back through the bushes. As he came out the
far side, he saw the driver of the Ford sedan, a heavyset black woman
in her late fifties, leaning over the open trunk, looking over her shoul-
der as she rushed to remove bulging white plastic grocery bags.

He ran toward her and loudly called, "Hey! I need your car . . ."

The woman, the heavy bags swinging from her hands, turned and
saw Daquan quickly approaching.

Then she saw that he held a pistol.

She dropped the bags, then went to her knees, quivering as she
covered her gray hair with her hands.

"Please . . . take whatever you want . . . take it all . . . just don't
hurt me . . ."

Daquan saw that a ring of keys had fallen to the ground with
the bags.

"It's an emergency!" he said, reaching down and grabbing the
keys.

Tires squealed as he made a hard right at the first corner, going over
the curb and onto the sidewalk, then squealed again making another
right at the next intersection. He sped along the block, braking hard to
look for Payne down the first vacant lot, then accelerating again until
braking at the next lot.

He finally found the one with Payne and the teenager—Payne was trying to sit upright; the teen had not moved—and skidded to a stop at the curb.

Daquan considered driving across the lot to reach Payne faster but was afraid the car would become stuck.

He threw the gearshift into park and left the car engine running and the driver's door open as he ran toward Payne.

He saw that Payne held his left hand over the large blood-soaked area of his gray sweatshirt. And, as Daquan approached closer, he saw Payne, with great effort, raise his head to look toward him—while pointing his .45 in Daquan's direction.

"Don't shoot, Matt! It's me!"

"Daquan," Payne said weakly, then after a moment lowered his pistol and moved to get up on one knee.

Daquan squatted beside him. Payne wrapped his right arm around Daquan's neck and slowly they stood.

"This way," Daquan said, leaning Payne into him and starting to walk.

The first couple steps were awkward, more stumbles than solid footing, but then suddenly, with a grunt, Payne found his legs.

They managed a rhythm and were almost back to the car when Daquan noticed a young black male in a wheelchair rolling out onto the porch of a row house across the street.

"Yo! What the fuck!" the male shouted, coming down a ramp to the sidewalk. "Why'd you shoot my man Ray-Ray for?"

Daquan said nothing but kept an eye on him as they reached the car and he opened the back door. He helped Payne slide onto the backseat, slammed the door shut, then ran and got behind the wheel.

"Yo!" the male shouted again.

As Daquan pulled on the gearshift, he could hear the male still shouting and then saw in the rearview mirror that he had started wheeling up the street toward the car.

And then he saw something else.

"Damn!" Daquan said aloud.

He ducked just before the windows on the left side of the car shattered in a hail of bullets.

And then he realized there was a sudden burning sensation in his back and shoulder.

He floored the accelerator pedal.

Daquan knew that Temple University Hospital was only blocks down Broad Street from Erie Avenue. Driving to the ER would take no time. But Daquan suddenly was getting light-headed. Just steering a straight line was quickly becoming a challenge.

He approached Erie Avenue, braked and laid on the horn as he glanced in both directions, then stepped heavily on the gas pedal again.

His vision was getting blurry and he fought to keep focused. He heard horns blaring as he crossed Erie and prayed whoever it was could avoid hitting them.

By the time the sedan approached Ontario, Daquan realized that things were beginning to happen in slow motion. He made the turn, carefully, but again ran up over the curb, then bumped a parked car, sideswiping it before yanking the steering wheel. The car moved to the center of the street.

Now he could make out the hospital ahead and, after a block, saw the sign for the emergency room, an arrow indicating it was straight ahead.

Then he saw an ambulance, lights flashing, that was parked in one of the bays beside a four-foot-high sign that read EMERGENCY ROOM DROP OFF ONLY.

Daquan reached the bays and began to turn into the first open one.

His head then became very light—and he felt himself slowly slumping over.

The car careened onto the sidewalk, struck a refuse container, and finally rammed a concrete pillar before coming to a stop.

Daquan struggled to raise his head.

Through blurry eyes, he saw beyond the shattered car window that the doors on the ambulance had swung open.

Two people in uniforms leaped out and began running to the car.

Daquan heard the ignition switch turn and the engine go quiet, then felt a warm hand on him and heard a female voice.

"Weak," she said, "but there's a pulse."

"No pulse on this guy," a male voice from the backseat said. "I'm taking him in . . ."

Then Daquan passed out.

TWO DAYS LATER . . .

[THREE]
Temple University Hospital, Room 401
1801 North Broad Street, North Philadelphia
Wednesday, December 19, 6:35 P.M.

"Oh, for Christ's sake!" Matt Payne said, pointing at the television screen while intravenous tubing dangled from the top of his hand. Then he exclaimed: "Shit, it hurts to move!"

Tony Harris looked to where he was pointing.

"What?" Harris said.

The image of Raychell Meadow, standing on the sidewalk in front of the hospital, cut away to surveillance footage from the emergency room entrance that showed the EMTs rushing to the crashed sedan with shot-out windows.

The ticker of text at the bottom of the screen read HOMICIDE SGT. PAINE HAS BEEN MOVED OUT OF THE INTENSIVE CARE UNIT AND IS EXPECTED TO FULLY RECOVER FROM HIS WOUNDS.

"I bet that was intentional!" Payne said. "Damn it!"

Payne then pointed to the wall of windows that overlooked Broad Street.

"If I could get one of those open, I bet I could hit her with my bedpan from here."

"What?" Harris repeated.

"That hack reporter bimbo spelled my name wrong!"

Harris looked, then chuckled.

"She probably would have left off the *e*, too," he said. "Glad to see you're feeling well enough to be concerned about the important things now."

Harris held up his right hand, fingers fanned out and thumb folded.

"Four what?"

"Four hours Daquan was in surgery. The ER works miracles here."

Payne nodded. "He got hit in both lungs and his liver. But he's gonna be fine."

Harris folded all but his index finger.

"What?" Payne said. "You're now asking permission to use the head?"

Harris ignored that: "And one deathbed confession. Daquan warned his mother to be careful of Hooks."

"Why? He told me 'word on the street' was Hooks knew who capped Pookie."

"That's because he had it done—Pookie was skimming from the drugs he sold in Needle Park and owed Hooks money. And Hooks took out Dante because he got cold feet being part of the casino heist and was afraid to talk. Hooks gave Daquan part of the diamonds from the robbery as a bribe—the message being 'Don't talk and I'll take care of you.'"

"He lied to me, or at least wasn't truthful about that damn ear stud," Payne said, shaking his head. "Sonofabitch! No good deed goes unpunished."

"Hard to blame him, Matt. Not sure he had a choice, considering he knew what happened to his cousin. Daquan, I think, was

trying to walk the straight and narrow. But Rayvorris Oliver—
your big fan Ray-Ray, homicide number 372—decided the diamond stud meant Daquan was going to get Pookie's turf in Needle
Park, which he thought he deserved, paid a visit to the diner,
and . . . Well, here you are, Marshal Earp."

Raychell Meadow came back onscreen.

"Why are we watching this channel?" Payne said, disgusted. "I
think I'd rather be back in my drug-induced fog."

Raychell Meadow, her tone highly dramatic, said: "In a horrific
twist of fate, the Reverend Josiah Cross, who was said to have
dodged death after gunfire erupted at his Stop Killadelphia Rally
on Saturday, was killed yesterday morning. Police report that a
forklift unloading a semitrailer full of frozen turkeys to be dis-
tributed for Feed Philly Day dropped a pallet carrying a hundred
turkeys estimated to weigh more than one ton. The Philadelphia
medical examiner's office said death from blunt force trauma was
instant."

The screen then showed a pudgy male's face.

"Ah, now there's one of our fair city's shining stars," Payne said,
"attempting to appear mournful."

Raychell Meadow's voice-over said: "Philadelphia City Councilman (At Large) H. Rapp Badde, who sponsors the annual event
at the Word of Brotherly Love Ministry in Strawberry Mansion,
issued a brief statement . . ."

Onscreen, Badde then said: "It's truly a tragic day for our city
to lose such a strong supporter of our citizens. He will be terribly
missed, but we take comfort in the fact that he passed as he was
performing yet another service to our people. Knowing him as
well as I do, I know he would want this ministry to continue. And

it will, including the Feed Philly Day, which will take place tomorrow, during which we will give thanks and prayers for all of Reverend Cross's blessings. I hope to see everyone there."

Raychell Meadow came back on: "In related news, police sources report that Tyrone Banks, known by his hip-hop artist name King Two-One-Five, who was to perform at Monday's canceled Feed Philly Day event, was found dead this morning. An unnamed confidential source said the twenty-five-year-old singer was found wearing a Lucky Stars Casino hat and holding a seven of clubs and two of diamonds from a deck of cards bearing the Philadelphia Police Department's shield on the back and two Homicide Cold Cases on their face."

Payne exchanged glances with Harris.

"Getting dealt a seven and a two," Payne said. "Arguably the worst beginning hand in poker. Can't do shit with it."

"Kind of like what he did with his life," Harris said.

Harris gestured at the television.

"There's more to the story about how they found Hooks dead."

"I guessing what Sully said—someone wanted to send a message about what happens to those who rob casinos."

Harris nodded.

Payne impatiently gestured *Give it to me* with his tube-covered hand, and said, "You're gonna tell me, I'm sure."

Harris grinned.

"That microphone he loved so much?"

"That one with the big chrome mesh ball at the top?"

"Yeah. You won't guess where they found it . . ." He paused, then said, "Wait. You're sick enough that you would guess."

Payne grinned as he shook his head.

"Well, don't let your guard down just because Cross and Hooks got their due," Harris said. "While the good news is you're out of ICU and going to survive the shooting—"

"The bad is?"

"Your fiancée is going to kill you, she's so pissed off at you."